M J GRE   OD

The Blue Hour

Dedicated to

'Vermouth'

1928–2021

Unforgettable

Chapter One

US Fighter Command,
St Eval Airbase,
Cornwall,
June 2nd, 1944

Darling Tilly,

The sight of us all going left a kind of tingling in my blood as we drive slowly to the harbour. The men are all cheerful and cracking jokes because the days to come are going to put an end to the long suspense.

I want you to know how much I love you. You mean everything to me and this gives me the courage to continue. When, if, I return we'll be married and head home to West Virginia with our baby.

My dreams for our future even outnumber yours and your plans are made of so many dreams! I think of every minor detail a hundred times. The money enclosed is for emergencies. I pray I live to make you happy my darling.

For always,

Jack

Somerway Rehabilitation Unit, Padstow, Cornwall, May 2015

A scent of tobacco lingered outside Tilly's door, on which an arresting black-and-white photograph was taped of her. Aged 19, tall, angular and poured into a skin-tight scarlet-tinted swimming costume. Lustrous blonde hair spilled over shoulders and framed a confident face with a direct, full-lipped smile. Arms loosely held behind her back highlighted the tiny waist and endless, slim legs. Beyond the grassy dunes she posed on were cloudless skies and white-tipped waves.

Morphine uncoiled in Tilly. It softened and dissolved the searing pain along each vertebra until her spine felt like a string of warmed pearls. She wanted to go home. Never to leave it again. Tilly closed her eyes, circled the rough nylon arms of the chair with the flat, creased pads of her fingertips and hummed along to Nat King Cole's *Unforgettable* playing on the radio.

She recalled the first time she'd kissed Jack Turner; 7th May 1943. He might have arrived from another planet. The warm sun was on her face and gulls wheeled like ribbons of light. Greedy gulls that nobody fed because there was so little food. She'd stood arm-in-arm with Rose Sinclair at Liverpool's Pier Head, facing the river, waiting for a ferry to take them dancing in New Brighton, when she heard a long, low whistle and deep American voice. Slow and sweet as hot treacle.

'If she looks as good from the front, she's mine,' he'd said. Brimming with confidence, just the kind of man Tilly wanted. There was the other American though. The one with a nasal, whiny voice, who never took to her.

'C'mon, Jack,' he'd drawled, 'this ain't time for blind flying.'

A pointed comment, an insult. Tilly hadn't turned; instead, she'd watched Rose's eyes widen, and reflected in her dark irises, two male figures.

'He's effing gorgeous,' whispered Rose, unlinking her arm,

straightening her green dress. Her thin-lipped mouth opened, revealing wonky teeth. 'A dreamboat.' Tilly focused on the turbulent expanse of river as clouds parted and sunlight flooded through. She'd checked her clean nails with their half-moon crescents and plucked a stray blonde hair off the grey pencil skirt Aunty Vi had made. It traced Tilly's hips along with a thin navy belt to highlight her waist. She'd pointed one navy shoe at forty-five degrees, because Aunty Vi stated it accentuated long legs. The ferry hooted; its metal sides ground harshly against dock walls. The Yank stepped closer to her left.

'First Lieutenant Jack Turner, ma'am. US 8th Air Force. Pleased to meet you.' Tilly saw his wide, white smile. Nothing like the mouths of native tombstone teeth she'd explored with curiosity and little pleasure. She'd smiled back, trying to hide her own sharp little canines. He introduced the other man, Second Lieutenant Danny Pierce. Short, blond and sturdy. He'd given a cursory nod, checked his watch and strode off with both hands jiggling in taut trouser pockets. He had a fleshy bottom.

'He's a busy guy,' Jack said. He smiled and blew a smoke ring over Tilly's head. The halo gusted away.

'She looks better from the front, doesn't she?' Rose said, smarmily.

'Truly.' He didn't return Rose's look.

'I'm Rose and she's Tilly,' stated Rose, trying to keep in with them. He smiled, but only at Tilly.

She remembered how like a movie star he'd appeared; a prescription for English womanhood, at six foot, broad-shouldered and slim-hipped. His fawn trousers were tucked into polished black, calf-length boots and beneath the olive cap his oiled, auburn hair shone. His speckled, pear-green eyes appraised and invited her blatantly and Tilly appraised him right back. There were his high cheekbones and a spill of freckles over the bridge of his tanned nose. Aunty Vi stated freckles were *Angels' kisses* and a face without them was *A sky without stars*. A leather bag hung across his shoulder; the same deep walnut colour of her mother's best church shoes.

Memories seeped into Tilly; the wash of tide, creaking ferry, shrill gulls, scent of tobacco and engine oil. Rose hadn't wanted to remain invisible but she'd been side-lined. Jack pulled a chunky, embossed lighter and pack of Lucky Strike from the pocket of his flying jacket and offered them cigarettes. He flicked the lighter and as Tilly leant forward the breeze nipped out the flame. He pulled open his jacket lapel; smiled an invitation. Tilly stepped into the shelter of his body like it was a bedroom. He smelt of Lifebuoy soap and the faint musk of fresh sweat. Shaving nicks scratched the paler skin beneath his chin. Tilly inhaled deeply to make sure the cigarette lit, and coughed. She wasn't an expert smoker then. Jack grinned and shifted back. Yards off, Danny kicked a stone as Rose took hold of Tilly's cigarette to light her own. Jack hadn't offered his body to her. A serpentine coil of smoke spilled from the American's curved lips. She blushed, and he grinned at the rising flush.

'Tilly's a lovely name,' said Jack, eyebrows raised a fraction.

'It's Matilda and means Battle Maid.' Snippy, challenging. Tilly couldn't help herself, then or now.

'I'd better watch out then. Do you waltz, Matilda? Could I persuade a Battle Maid to dance?' The way he looked. Full of it, she'd thought, and exactly the kind of man she'd longed for.

4

'What's yours mean?' she asked, as he'd taken a black diary from his trouser pocket, tore a sheet, licked the end of a pencil and scribbled.

'Turner? Supposed to be a carpenter but I make pictures.' He shrugged. 'Here's a number you can get me on at Burtonwood but only if you can't make it here next Saturday at 8pm.' He folded the paper and handed it over. Their fingers touched. She slipped the precious note deep into her navy handbag, closing the clasp with a snap. Danny sauntered off, his right hand performing a cutting motion over his head.

'Suit yourself, short-arsed Yank,' hissed Rose and turning, walked quickly to the ferry, expecting her best friend to follow.

Jack looked beyond Tilly and pointed out parallel shafts of light splitting clouds as dusk deepened to violet.

'The blue hour and they're God's fingers, crepuscular.'

'Sounds like something dug out of sand,' said Tilly, and Jack laughed. A deep, warm laugh. He asked to take her picture, telling her it might appear in the Force's magazine.

Like a shot, thought Tilly, and smoothed her hair as Jack opened the leather bag and pulled out a camera embossed with Leica. He removed the lens cover, blew on the glass and lifted it to his eyes, focusing entirely on her. Exactly what she wanted.

'There's best,' he said, thumbing at the Pier Head's sandstone wall. Tilly obeyed and leant against it. She glanced at Rose on the ferry, watching with eyes like slits.

'Turn a little to the right. Nope, that's left. Better. Look at me and don't smile.' An order. Another thrill. A gull landed beyond Tilly's outstretched arm and she caught a whiff of burning coal from the churning ferry. Her lips parted but she didn't smile as she looked directly at Jack. An old man in a greasy mackintosh walked past and spat in the gutter as the camera's flash popped and dazzled. Jack put it carefully away, walked to her and kissed her so deeply their teeth grated. She tasted a peppery tang of cigarettes, mint gum and whisky.

'Tilly!' yelped Rose from the ferry. Long seconds passed before Tilly pulled away. Jack pressed his lips together. The cat that got the cream, she thought.

'For Christ's sake!' Danny shouted, shaking his head.

Jack took out a bar of Hershey's milk chocolate from his jacket pocket and, pressed it in Tilly's palm.

'Payment?' asked Tilly, challenging.

'Not for all the tea in China. Good day, ma'am. Be seeing you Saturday.' He strode away with an easy lope and looked back three times before reaching Danny. They exchanged words with angry faces. Tilly hid the Hershey in her handbag and boarded the ferry. She wasn't going to share.

'I've never been kissed like that,' she told Rose brightly.

'It's not for the want of trying,' she'd answered, buttoning her coat fiercely. Tilly ignored the catty remark and tucked her arm through Rose's, who shook herself free. A bald ferryman in a washed-out uniform winked at Tilly from the quayside as the ferry cast off. Rain blanketed the boat and everyone but Tilly flocked inside. She sheltered by a wooden cover and snuck pieces of chocolate, enjoying the sweet melt of it. Darkness fell, with few stars. The blacked-out city disappeared and the ferry became a juddering, churning shadow. Behind the steaming funnel someone cleared

6

their throat. A fake sound, to draw her attention. Tilly turned and there was the man in the raincoat who'd spat in the gutter. He gripped his flaccid penis and jerked his hand.

'I've seen better cigarettes than that,' snapped Tilly, with more bravado than she felt. He'd scuttled away and Tilly's hands shook as she lit a cigarette. Only when the ferry docked did Rose come out, saying she didn't feel well and wanted to go home. It was a lie Tilly agreed to and they'd returned in silence and parted. In a newspaper shop near bomb-blasted Elliot Street, Tilly spotted a postcard. Drawn on its front was a voluptuous woman paddling in the sea, wearing a red swimming costume, posing to a photographer. It stated: *When there's something good about, the Press always spots it; Look out for my picture in the Sunday papers!* Tilly bought it from an old woman behind the counter, whose whiskery mouth turned down. She retraced her steps home through the derelict city centre, softly singing Dick Haymes' *You'll never know* until she reached sodden, deserted Watford Road and the door of her red-bricked terrace. In the blacked-out kitchen her mother knelt, scouring the oven. A cold, depressing home that smelt of mutton and cabbage. Elizabeth barely looked up as she asked why her daughter was back so early. Tilly told the same lie Rose had slipped her.

'Sulky girl, that Rose,' said Elizabeth, sighing and sitting on her haunches, cheeks flaming. Her mother had retained the harsh Northern Irish accent she'd mostly failed to remove from her daughters' Mersey-mouths with costly elocution lessons. 'And a shop-worn face. But Rose is a *Yes* girl who'll be married before the likes of you, who only ever says *No.*' Tilly ran upstairs, stamping the threadbare runner. She wouldn't mention Jack. Elizabeth stated

Yanks were, *For common sluts and couldn't be trusted as far as they'd like to throw you.* Tilly took out the postcard and crossed out *The Press* swapping it for, *A handsome GI*, and inserted *Hollywood* for *Sunday papers*. On the back, in her very best handwriting, she wrote:

Dear Jack, I can't wait to dance on Saturday and see my picture, with best wishes, a British Battle Maid.

She added one small x and addressed it to Flight Lieutenant Jack Turner, care of Burtonwood Airbase, Warrington, licked a gummy stamp and snuck past her mother to the post box at the bottom of Watford Road, kissing the address before she let it drop.

Nat King Cole's lyrics floated back to her, only now it was her mother singing. Elizabeth's creped skin looming close; dead-eyed, bitter-mouthed, hissing about secrets better left buried.

'Tilly, wake up.' Not her mother. Nurse Evangeline's almond eyes slid into focus as Tilly came to, pain-free, but not where she wanted to be.

'I hope you're not giving me those painkillers again because I can't shit without crying.' Tilly Barwise's bracing Liverpool accent sliced through the air.

'I'll give you something for that,' came a murmured response as the dark-haired nurse bent over her. Tilly had successfully avoided prescription drugs, until the brandy she'd smuggled into a lemonade bottle was discovered, confiscated, and poured away.

'And I don't want to go out there and see any of them,' she hissed. Tilly had remained resolutely self-confined from all other inmates, as she labelled patients, since the eighty-nine-year-old was admitted with three spinal fractures seven weeks before. She was now in the final three days allowed for her to shape up, or ship out to a nursing home.

'Tilly, your daughter's been on the phone,' said Evangeline. 'She'll call again after dinner. It seems she's found another carer. Now, it's nearly time to put some fat on those bones.' She patted the wheelchair.

'I'm not talking to her,' said Tilly, groggily. No point. Vicky had decided, and Tilly couldn't argue until she was steady on her feet again. Evangeline was silent.

'Can't you look after me?' asked Tilly, fractious, eyes shut.

'No, I'm happy working here but if there's an emergency I'll help.' She looked flustered.

'You mean I might die at any minute and you'd be jobless?'

'No. Anyway, let's go to the dining room and see how much sunshine you spread around today.'

'I'm not hungry, and I'm not having some stranger moving in and taking over,' snapped Tilly. She lit a cigarette, blowing smoke out of her nostrils. 'There's no way I'm doing what I'm told.'

Evangeline reached over, removed the cigarette from Tilly's hand, eased her bird-like body into a wheelchair, and paused.

Chapter Two

Diary entry: Burtonwood Airbase, April 2nd, 1943

At 12,000 feet in a B17 and even with a heat suit on it was cold enough to freeze my nuts off. The sun shone through clouds like sandbanks threaded with gold – until flak burst and jolted us all over the joint. The Lieutenant's voice came through our headsets:

'Guys, I think those Krauts want to kill us.'

'Who da' guessed it?' I said back.

We flew over forests, thick as the Blue Ridge Mountains and a railroad like a fallen ladder across a river's glittering bend. Visibility was 1,000 yards. I rolled my cameras as we dropped 3,000lb of bombs and 500 incendiaries to nail that target and the Jerry country club next door. Hit flak back at the coast and heard gurgling sounds over the radio. We dragged our tail gunner inside, covered in blood, his neck all cut up. I couldn't stomach the canteen's pink-gray sausages, gritty with bone. Drank whiskey and swallowed sleepers.

Newquay, Cornwall, May 2015

Ava felt the softening edges of Valium evaporate as the plane banked over the sheer salt-and-pepper cliffs at Newquay Airport. The aircraft rapidly descended. She glimpsed the shimmering green Atlantic, then clamped her eyes shut as she grasped the arm of the stonily silent man beside her. He flinched. In her heavy-duty haze of alcohol, sedatives and anti-depressants Ava hadn't so much as glanced at him since they'd take off from London.

'What do you do?' Ava's fingers rucked the sleeve of his suit.

'Accounting,' he stated, brusquely.

'Oh God,' Ava groaned, involuntarily. The engines laboured and, brakes roaring, the plane landed with three gentle jumps. With each one Ava yelped. When it stopped, she released her hold on the man. He pulled at his sleeve and stood without a word.

Ava waited until every passenger disembarked. She felt clammy and smelt strange; like pear drops, and sweat stained the armpits of her grey T-shirt. Fear, she thought, and gin. A cabin crew attendant patted Ava's arm at the top of the steps. That unexpected kindness brought tears to her eyes. She scuttled across the windswept tarmac and into a loo. The mirror reflected her ghost-like pallor, greasy hair pulled scraggily back into a scrappy pony tail, purple-black circles under her eyes, all framed by sallow skin and an angry red spot on her chin. She gulped tap water and splashed her face. By the time Ava reached passport control the queue had petered out. The inspecting officer did a double-take of her photograph before waving her through. A look of pity, thought Ava, as she skirted the barn-like concourse reeking of aviation fuel, coffee and pizzas. There, at the exit, was the sign she'd been told to look for. *Ava Westmorland*, it stated, scrawled in red pen on a large paper bag. It was strange to see her maiden name again, especially written above a smiling, cartoon image of a fish that lay battered and lifeless on a bowl of chunky chips. The small, stout woman holding the sign was in her mid-fifties and her tanned face glanced hopefully at each passing single woman, with not a flicker at Ava. Her blue fleece was emblazoned, *May and Jeff's Fish and Chip Emporium – A Cod above the Rest*.

May, thought Ava, had been well-described by Tilly's daughter, Vicky, as Trevone's best chip shop owner, Tilly's tolerant cleaner and carer, and someone who knows everyone like the back of her capable hands.

'Hi, I'm Ava,' she said, stopping before her. 'Thanks for picking me up.'

May's mouth opened slightly and if there was a look of someone's heart sinking, it was written all over this woman's lined face. 'Lovely to meet you, I'm May,' she replied, over-enthusiastically, in a soft Birmingham accent. She embraced Ava in a tangy fug of fish, chips, and vinegar, and crumpled the sign into a Sainsbury's bag-for-life. A centimetre of white roots grew at the parting in May's hair, like the striped pelt of a badger. 'Have you only got hand luggage?' Ava nodded. May frowned as she strode outside and Ava silently followed in her bustling wake. 'The car's this way and I haven't long on the ticket.'

May walked and talked at speed: about her arthritic knee, the weather, the price of houses, and her son in Australia. Ava imagined this was how she gossiped to chip shop customers while sorting orders. Her sturdy calves, in knee-length blue shorts, set a pace which showed no sign of arthritis.

'Oh, I better warn you there's not much of a phone signal there. Well, there is if you head to the Golden Lion and there's a glimmer at the lamppost by Cliff View's gate.'

'I haven't got one,' said Ava. She couldn't say she'd chucked it down the loo.

'That's a first. Tilly hasn't got Wi-Fi, even with those dongle things.'

Ava shook her head and stared as the salty-scented wind breezed in with billowing white clouds that tore themselves apart to reveal glimpses of sun.

'A good couple of days coming,' May said, checking her watch. 'Oh hell, we've got two minutes.' She rooted for keys and unlocked a red Smart car. Ava dropped her bag into the tiny boot and settled inside as May pressed a button and the sunroof peeled back.

'Hurray!' said May, chucking coins into the automatic barrier and roaring off. 'Tilly tries the patience of a saint and God himself. Three carers came and went before this latest hospital admission.' May put up three fingers, folding them as she explained: 'Doreen left after two days; Beryl, I liked her, lasted one; and Janine, just two hours. If Tilly went in a home full-time it would kill her faster than she's trying to top herself with cigarettes and brandy. Are you experienced?'

'No.' Ava could barely look after herself. Coming was a big mistake. She nibbled at the skin around her thumbnail and tasted blood.

'Look,' May said, pursing her lips as they passed a traffic warden. 'Wardens are the bedrock of Cornish high finance. Mind you, I get my own back when they buy chips.' May grinned and crunched gears. She suddenly slowed on a straight, empty stretch.

'Speed camera. We know where they all are,' said May, jabbing at one tucked behind a tree. She sped again. The undulating coastal road snaked twelve miles to Trevone Bay, with glimpses of sea on one side and opposite, clusters of towering wind turbines, fields of glittering solar panels, campsites, surf schools, pubs, and cottages. Ava let her eyes wander, only half taking in May's chatter.

13

Tilly, thought Ava, such a sweet sounding, powder-puff, old-lady name. This one sounded an exhausting old bag nobody would seek out in their right mind. Which said it all.

'Disagreements make Tilly feel better,' carried on May. 'She's more civil with men. Unlike me, but I've been married thirty years. Jeff's let me off the chippie to look after her Friday nights and Saturdays. Not the first weekend because there's an annual charity barn dance, so Evangeline's doing that one. You should come.'

Ava remained mute. She was done with dancing. May opened the glove compartment and scrabbled inside. She brought out a packet of cigarettes and a lighter. She extracted one and lit up while scooting in fourth gear down a winding lane of tall hedges and overhanging trees. Wild garlic and bluebells scented the air.

'Jeff thinks I've stopped,' said May, inhaling deeply. 'So, you won't let the cat out of the bag, will you?' She glanced over. Ava shook her head and May exhaled pleasurably. 'I haven't got time to show you around Cliff View. We have to make money now because it's a mausoleum in winter. We have a little apartment in Lanzarote. Never had nice chips there. I hope you're prepared for this isolation tank between November and February? If you stay. How old are you?'

'Thirty-three,' said Ava. Being isolated would be just fine and she gazed outside. White hawthorn hedges and verges of cow parsley and pink campions petered out into boggy moorland, with golden gorse and a carpet of purple heather. Raggedy-looking sheep dotted the ground, some with lambs tugging at udders, their tails waggling. Overhead, gulls screeched and swooped. The air smelt of sun lotion.

'Gorse has a lovely coconut scent,' said May, inhaling. 'There's an old Cornish saying, *When gorse is out of bloom, kissing's out of season*, but it's always in bloom!'

Ava willed every flower to scorch and wither. At a junction the car came to a grinding halt and with a flourish, May spread her hands, as if she'd personally unrolled the scene. There was the tang of sea under a forget-me-not blue sky above the wide curving sweep of Trevone Bay. Around it, a cluster of older properties were encroached by glitzy luxury homes with glass balconies and wall-to-ceiling windows. Building work spread in almost every direction.

'Place is a goldmine,' said May. 'Young'uns can't afford to buy, or rent, so they leave.' She shuddered. 'See those?' Ava followed May's finger jabbing at airy, spacious mansions with BMWs, sports cars and 4x4s on gravel drives. 'Sell for well over a million to owners who are here a few weeks of the year and rent them at astronomic rates.'

Ava could see why they'd pay for the spectacular view of the Atlantic as it poured into the horseshoe-shaped bay, dotted with surfers. The Cornish dream with cedar-boarded eco-homes next to acres of regimented caravans and tents.

'Look, Cliff View.' May tilted her chin.

There, clinging to the side of the headland and separate from all other properties, was a dilapidated bungalow. Unloved, thought Ava, and in that respect, it would suit her well. The lane petered out to a potholed track as they drew up on a stony parking bay. Close up, Cliff View was all peeling paint and scrappy, splintered wood. It stuck out like a sore thumb amongst its swish neighbours but it had the best view of the ocean. May yanked the handbrake and breathed heavily. Beads of sweat covered her face.

'No menopausal woman should work in a chippie, or in my case, far from a chaise longue and icy gin and tonic.' She swiped her forehead with her sleeve.

Unlike Cliff View's neglected exterior, Ava noted, its sand-engrained lawn had neat borders brimming with purple tulips, alliums, fading bluebells and delicate ferns. There was a peculiar echoing, breathy sound.

'What's that?' asked Ava.

'Round Hole – behind Cliff View. It's a collapsed cave the sea rushes through. Legend says it's where ocean gods talk to locals and when someone important dies, or there's a shipwreck, it shrieks like a banshee.'

'Does it ever stop?' Ava hated the ghostly winnowing.

'Quieter. You get used to it. A bit like Tilly though, there's always something brewing.'

'How long have you been here?' Ava asked, as they got out of the car.

'Parents came in the 70s when you could buy a place for a pittance. I'm an *Emmet* – an *ant* because us incomers crawl all over Cornwall – but I'm not a *blow-in*.'

'Which is?'

'Holidaymakers, who blow in and blow out. My lovely bread and butter.'

'What about Tilly?' asked Ava, lifting her bag. A gull dropped a mussel shell on the gravel path which smashed and the bird swooped down to gobble the fleshy contents.

'Outsider everywhere,' May replied, walking ahead as the gull soared up with its feast.

Cliff View's flinty stone walls were flecked with a salty residue and its slate roof wore a gritty sheen. A murder of crows balanced upon it, preening, as they cawed, rattled and clicked. The worn navy door was surrounded by rosemary and its blue flowers were alive with bees. May extracted keys from an old brick on the earth, unlocked the door and shouldered it open.

'You've got until noon Monday. Good luck.' May handed over the keys, ran a hand through a clump of rosemary, absently smelt her fingers and briefly touched Ava's hand.

'Thank you,' said Ava, feeling her throat constrict and eyes well.

'You're quieter than the others,' May said. Ava smiled thinly. She'd got a whole lot quieter in the last six months.

'There's food and wine in the fridge,' May added, walking off. 'My number's on the chalkboard if you need anything.' Ava watched a plume of blue smoke float above her disappearing head. She closed the door and leant heavily on it.

May tucked herself behind the lamppost and took out her mobile. She waved it until a one-bar signal appeared and called Sniffy Dave at the Golden Lion. The landlord answered.

'Are you still running a book on Tilly's new carer leaving by Wednesday?' May asked.

'Yep,' said Dave, sniffing. Bloody sniffing. He told everyone it was because his nose was allergic to beer but the rest of his body loved it.

'I think you better shorten the odds.'

'Right,' Dave sniffed, and the signal vanished.

Chapter Three

Morgantown,
Woodburn,
West Virginia,
April 5ᵗʰ, 1943

Darling Jack,

You haven't written me for ages and I'm wondering why? Is it because you're real busy on missions? I know you can't talk about them. I so worry about stories I hear of British girls wanting to snare our American boys. I know I can trust you. I can't wait for us to be married, darling, and have our own little family. I'm saving china, bed linen and cutlery in my bottom drawer. The congregation ask after you every week and I'm so proud of you. We all are.

I'm sitting in your Mom's garden and the sky is darkening so the trees turn black and velvety. The crickets make a racket but it's a sweet, spring sound. Do you remember swimming with me before you went away? The blue light was just like it is now. I long for you to be back in my arms again, darling. Please write soon.

All my love,

Jess

Somerway Rehabilitation Unit, May 2015

With a look of distaste, Nurse Evangeline ran Tilly's cigarette under the tap, dropped it in a pedal bin and scrubbed her hands with lemon soap. She pushed Tilly's wheelchair along the brightly lit corridor where a pungent aroma of urine, pine disinfectant and talc, combined with mince and onions, stole through the air. And sounds: televisions, groans, mutterings, trolleys, calls of *Nurse!* with many toilets flushing. Names like Enid, Lilly, Martha and Mabel floated around. There were the quick footsteps of staff and slower shuffles of patients on Zimmer frames.

Somerway's sage-green walls hosted prints of far-flung mountains and tropical vistas which most residents had never seen and certainly wouldn't now. Tilly looked straight ahead, ignoring open doors where patients snoozed as television channels seamlessly changed between gentle comedies, gardening, holiday programmes and news. Old men and women drooped in chairs, gripped commodes or lay, open-mouthed and snoring, in single beds with uniform green duvet covers.

'Where would you like to sit today?' asked Evangeline, as they entered the dining room. There were oval tables with high-backed chairs and walking aids, around which sat a gaggle of white-haired, whiskered women tucking into sloppy shepherd's pie. They silenced at Tilly's entrance.

'Not with them, for God's sake,' said Tilly, loudly. 'Where's Captain Birds Eye?'

'Arthur's over there, hiding.'

'Take me to him,' Tilly commanded. Arthur's baby blue eyes looked up and his white-bearded, ruddy face cracked a smile as Tilly headed towards him. Evangeline helped ease Tilly onto the padded leatherette chair opposite.

'Thank God you're here,' said Tilly. Arthur grinned,

19

displaying three brown teeth in his top gums. The 91-year-old former naval captain was recovering from a fall and stroke which had stolen his balance and speech. There was a gash across his forehead, fading to pink. His large, triangular nose exhibited a spidery web of dark blood vessels and crepe bags under his eyes appeared pinchable. As the only man, Tilly deemed Arthur worthy of her time, despite being – or possibly because – he was speechless. Other old women muttered but looked discernibly livelier. Tilly was the one inmate to be collectively criticised with complete impunity.

'Enjoy lunch,' said Evangeline and walked away with a straight back and majestic hip roll that transfixed Arthur.

'Captain,' said Tilly, 'I see beauty is not lost on an old sea dog. You're pleased with how Nurse Evangeline is coming on with her deportment, under my expert tuition?'

He winked.

'I like a man who winks,' she said. 'Not enough men do it now, or wolf-whistle. Too damn correct. I remember hitting 50 and if someone whistled, I bloody cheered.' Tilly warmed up. So did her tutting listeners.

'You look handsome today, Captain,' she said, raising her voice. 'What shall we chat about? I know – the last great lovers we had.' Other women stopped eating, some open-mouthed, and with loaded spoons suspended. The Captain flushed as Tilly launched into her one-sided conversation.

'We've talked about Jack. He was the best, so let's see… we'll miss out my dead husband; too complicated. For a bit of fun, I'll tell you about the police dog trainer. Fergus. The man, not his dog. He was Scottish, with black hair, legs like tree trunks and a chest like

Tarzan. He trained Major, my Boxer, who was a minor when it came to behaviour. Fergus got a good grip of him, and then me, in his capable Highland hands. Major eventually took a man down in ten paces. Not as fast as me though.' There was a dining-room-wide splutter as flossy female heads shook.

'I nicknamed Fergus *Ten Pence*,' Tilly explained, 'because that's the change I always had on me, so I could call him from a phone box and arrange assignations. We carried on our extracurricular training in the back of his Ford Cortina. It was the 70s and I was in my fantastic 40s. Don't you think that's a vintage decade for a woman?'

Captain Birds Eye nodded, and Tilly wondered if he'd ever had a vintage weekend.

'It was easy to have a lover then, not like today, with CCbloodyTV and mobile phones tracking your every move. You can't even have a crap without someone knowing. Like here.'

A woman with florid cheeks slapped her spoon down, heaved her stolid self upright and limped off. Other female diners hesitated, as if they ought to morally follow, but instead ate slowly, keeping eyes down and ears open. Tilly pushed the soupy shepherd's pie around her plate.

'Let's suck this and see, Captain,' she sighed, with every nuance available. 'How do people have a secret love life? Fergus lasted ten years until his wife ran off with a fireman. He was surprisingly upset, regardless of what he'd been up to with me.' She laughed. 'Captain, you look like a man susceptible to pleasure.' Arthur's eyes brightened. 'Not like anyone else here.' The rest of the chairs pushed back and their affronted occupants departed.

21

With the place finally to themselves, Arthur and Tilly settled into an easy silence. He chased peas around the plate with his good arm and once or twice Tilly nodded at his bib – the signal for Arthur to wipe his face.

'You know, Captain, I've cooked mince a million times. The *mince years* I called them when I was young. My daughter's too upmarket for mince. She prefers Cassoulet but that's just French Scouse with white beans and fatty bacon. She's too boring for lovers. My mother, Elizabeth, was the same. It's funny how generations skip isn't it? Mum cooked for England but boy, what a dull woman. I think back on my life and the food I've cooked and given little thought to, apart from the damn washing up. Dull. Now there's all these TV programmes about cooking. Like it's sex. I'm glad I was born when you ate to live and lived to love, not obsess about your alimentary canal. It all comes out the same doesn't it? Michelin Star or bloody beans.' Arthur laughed wheezily and Tilly wiped his chin.

'Captain,' whispered Tilly, 'do you remember how good it was to kiss, when you had real teeth?' Tilly closed her eyes and willed Jack Turner into her mind but recreating him was like netting an image cast in water. The Captain shut his eyes too but for different reasons. His mouth fell open as he cat-napped. Plates were removed and replaced with chocolate mousse. Arthur woke with a snuffle. He looked startled at the disappearance of dinner and appearance of pudding but took a mouthful.

'We've been here the same time, haven't we?' said Tilly. 'Are you going home?'

The Captain shook his head slowly. His eyes filled and Tilly dabbed them. She took hold of his good hand, kissed the knuckles and looked around at the remaining open-mouthed sleepers and empty-eyed TV-gazers.

Chapter Four

Burtonwood Airbase,
Lancashire
April 15ᵗʰ, 1943

Dear Mom,

Pa told me you haven't been well and Doc Reese says you might need a heart operation – but not if you rest and stop worrying about me here, and Joey joining up. I've been to church although not as often as back home. You'd like Father O'Dowd, he gives us a blessing before missions, no matter what time. The food's OK (nothing like yours!). I know I should write more but I never was a good letter writer. I'm thankful for Jess's kindness to you and especially to Marie with baby Dorothy.

I've got to go now, it's so much colder here; the rain and wind lash down. I'm heading out in it right now to mail this.

All my love,
Jack

Trevone Bay, Cornwall, May 2015

Inside Cliff View, soughing wind and waves vanished into a cool, shadowed silence, marked by the tick of a Grandfather clock. The house smelt of cigarettes, beeswax, fresh paint, and washing powder. Ava picked up a pile of mail, rifled through it and crumpled the lot. Advertising junk. She was glad to be alone. Cliff View might be vacant but it was noisy with crows, gulls, sea crashing against cliffs and Round Hole's creepy echo. A glass jar by the coat rack contained a set of teeth. Ava imagined crone Tilly, with dark, empty mouth and rank breath. She hung back in the dim light and as her eyes adjusted, noticed a photograph of a dazzling blonde in a scarlet-tinted halter-neck swimming costume. The woman was beautiful but not in any conventional way, with her too-wide mouth and slanting, light eyes. Next appeared a sepia shot of her seated on an outcrop of rock, wearing a clinging calf-length dark skirt and white blouse. Like a mermaid, thought Ava; a siren. She walked slowly through the hallway, past five closed doors, into a rectangular kitchen with French windows leading to the walled back garden. Speckled yellow floor tiles swelled and dipped beneath mismatched navy cupboards, with a scrubbed granite work surface and dresser crammed with colourful mismatched plates and cups. Gleaming copper pans hung above a Rayburn. One wall was scattered with black and white aerial photographs. There were grainy patchworks of fields, expanses of wave-flecked ocean and shots of cities. A misty harbour appeared like a lozenge of black water with a cigar-shaped submarine tucked inside. A grey flotilla of boats hung next to a photograph of train tracks that lay like zips across the land and a squiggle of river which skirted a forest resembled a dirty, upturned brush. Ava made a black coffee with half a sugar in a mug that stated, *The bitch lives here*. A list on the fridge blackboard read: *Salted butter, spuds, brandy, cigs,* Hello *and* Grazia. She carried her drink to the hallway and carefully pushed at the first door. Sun poured through a window overlooking the sea; opposite was another, viewing the hill where Round Hole echoed. Recently whitewashed, it was furnished with a wrought-iron double bed, small mahogany wardrobe and matching chest of drawers. This, Ava presumed, was hers, with its fresh towels, ceramic pink bowl filled with apples and oranges on the bedside cupboard and vase of purple tulips.

The bathroom next door was compact and made more so with a bath hoist, along with sink railings and a sturdy frame surrounding a high-rise toilet. There was a small handwritten note on the wall telling Ava to take care with the shower control because it could get stuck. It felt claustrophobic. This was where Ava would deal intimately with Tilly. She grimaced and retreated. The next room, also recently painted, was bland, beige, and chintzy. Guest room, she guessed. Ava entered what appeared to be the living room. Nicotine-stained, with apricot-coloured walls and an amber glass ceiling light that might once have been clear. There was a real fire surrounded by green tiles and, Ava noted, bird crap in the grate. A cherry-coloured sofa sat opposite a hulking old TV and a winged-backed recliner with a greasy impression where possibly Tilly's head rested. Above the fireplace hung an oil painting of a diving Spitfire between polished silver candlesticks at either end of the mantlepiece. Ava recognised a small photograph of Vicky from the brief interview she'd had. She was younger in this, with fine brown hair, cradling an infant, tucked in a shawl with star-like splayed fingers. Ava moved to Tilly's vinyl record collection: James Last, Latin Jazz, The Beatles, and Tijuana Brass. She picked up Nat King Cole, placed the record on the turntable and gently lowered the stylus. His liquid tones sang, *When I fall in love.* After a minute, Ava lifted the needle from the too-painful lyrics. She opened another door to a small dining room with an ancient gas fire and dark table with six matching chairs. It felt unused. The last room must be Tilly's. Ava let it be; she'd gird herself later. Everywhere was worn and stained but dusted and polished. The phone rang. Ava hesitated, and picked it up.

'You've got there OK?' came the cool enquiry in clipped tones.

'Yes, Vicky,' she replied hesitantly. She'd know those orotund vowels anywhere.

'I've spoken to Mummy and she's accepted you're going to look after her.' Ava winced at how anyone over the age of ten said Mummy. 'May called to say you've settled in.' Vicky paused, waiting for a response.

'Yes, thank you,' said Ava, unsure how to play the part of efficient housekeeper, twiddling with the wire on the phone, wondering what exactly May had said. 'May was very helpful and I'll do my best for your mother.' Desperate Doormat that I am, she thought.

'Good, I'll call when Mummy gets back.' Vicky breathed heavily. 'I've made it clear that if you leave, Mummy moves into a home. My son and I have tried numerous carers.' No pressure then, Ava thought. Vicky said a swift goodbye. Ava pulled the band of her ponytail, raked a hand through her lank hair, then dialled her mother's Spanish villa in Alicante.

'What's the matter?' Josie said, before Ava had opened her mouth.

'I'm fine. How do you know it's me?'

'It's the way you breathe. You've arrived then? Eddie, you've missed a bit! Sorry, Ava, I'm directing him with DIY. The Brits are selling up and we'll have to hold tight or lose a fortune. How's your

27

rich OAP?'

'Back on Monday. The place is beautiful, perched on a cliff over the Atlantic and it's nearly as sunny as Spain.' Ava's tone breezed over its shabbiness and old woman's vile reputation. Or that she felt like throwing herself off the cliff. Josie swallowed and ice tinkled in her glass. There was a weighty silence. Ava knew what was coming.

'And have you heard from Him?' her mother asked, swallowing. 'Is He still with that…' She couldn't bear to say Josh or Sadie's names.

'No, I haven't heard, and yes.' She was loathe to reveal how Sadie's parents had bought them a two-bedroom Victorian semi in Blackheath. Once Josh would have said that was, *Utterly dull suburbia*, but not now he was going to be a mortgage-free father.

'Good riddance,' her mum muttered. There was a rattle of ice.

'Thanks, Mum. He still dumped me.'

'I didn't like to interfere. A mother's place is to put up and shut up, but not now. He was a limp lettuce, Ava. You should have taken his wallet out through his gonads. Sadie was nice as pie to me at your wedding but she has a backbone of pure sulphuric acid.'

'Well, Sadie's due in November, her parents are loaded and they've bought them a house worth nearly a million pounds.' It was impossible to hide things from her mother.

'Damn and blast. I was never a great picker of men, either. Sorry Eddie, not you, I saved the best till last, love.'

'Mum, the worst thing, before we split – Sadie asked me about sex with Josh.'

'And what did you tell her?'

'I'd had a few drinks. That it wasn't good. She must have been sleeping with him then. Why did she want to know?'

'Checking he wasn't still laying you. Well, that's that,' said her mother, brighter. 'If sex isn't on the boil at your age, forget it, because by the time you're mine, it'll be dead in the water. Isn't that right, Eddie?'

'Ever thought of working for Relate, Mum?'

'Look at us,' she said brightly, 'been together five years and I still adore him. Carry on tiger, you've got too much to do. If it doesn't work out with the OAP, come here. It'll do you good; a bit of sun and romance. There's lots of lovely waiters with time on their hands.'

'Thanks, but no.' Ava had once spent a week with the legion of semi-pissed expats, tucking into steak and chips while slating Britain, Europe and the rest of the world. 'I've got to go, Mum. Talk soon.'

'Don't be sad, lovely. Life's too short. Josh will be bald and ugly by the time he's 40, and you'll grow more beautiful. Trust me. Have I got your address?'

'No, I'll send it soon.'

'Love you lots.' Josie was gone.

Ava imagined her predicament was talk of the enclave. That alone was reason enough to steer clear. She poured a large white wine for her empty stomach and unlocked Cliff View's French windows, stepping onto a mossy patio and brick path into the garden. Ivy, pink clematis and scented wisteria clung to six-foot-high stone walls. Ferns and foxgloves crowded neat, weed-free borders with sharply cut edges. An apple tree, bright with pink blossom, provided shade near the patio. On the roof of a shed two crows fluttered and strutted, as if Ava was the interloper. She slumped on a rickety wooden chair under the tree; its arms covered in lacy lichen on which a glossy beetle ambled. For an hour, she observed the sea turn from green, to grey to navy. With the courage of a second wine, she rose, curious to explore Tilly's bedroom.

The opposing windows offered glimpses of ocean on both sides, leaving the room feeling unmoored and floating. Shadows flickered across the ceiling, strobing the walls light and dark. Despite May's plentiful use of polish and a lick of paint, the walls and furniture testified to the fact that Tilly smoked in bed. Ava thought she'd better check with Vicky, who'd told her to control Tilly's alcohol intake but hadn't mentioned cigarettes. To Ava, the chances of a possibly inebriated, drugged-up 89-year-old setting fire to the place, with her in it, were sky high.

Tilly's bed had a safety rail and was of a moveable height to make it easy for Ava to help. A box of mattress pads lay on the cover. Ava pulled one out; it was bulky, absorbent and grim. There wasn't much surface clutter: a few photographs of Tilly and Vicky, with enforced smiles. One seemed to be of Tilly's grandson as a boy, half hidden behind a surfboard. He had blondish-brown hair and a wary look, without the trace of a smile. There was a calendar next to Tilly's bed with shorthand writing. Ava deciphered the swirling hieroglyphic curves, dots and dashes. *Lonely, in terrible pain*, and *Vicky's not going to…* Ava put it down with a sudden chill. She remembered a TV programme about relatives who'd installed secret cameras to check on carers. Vicky might be watching right now. She smoothed the bed and pulled back the curtains, so she wouldn't appear a snooper.

After unpacking her few things, she showered without touching the dodgy temperature control. Cliff View creaked, window panes rattled, crows cawed and Round Hole hissed. Her hands shook with exhaustion. She ate Cheddar cheese on crackers and, gazing at Tilly's photographs, thought of her own wedding album, which she'd burnt in the yard of their rented flat, watching the expensive prints brown, curl, blacken, and melt. In numerous shots there was the vision of blonde, beautiful Sadie, smiling at Josh. All her hopes and dreams had turned to ash and the unpleasant paperwork and painful division of divorce. Ava swallowed a Valium and lay flat on the soft mattress with its body-shaped hollows and hint of Febreze. Round Hole sighed and waves shushed. Her eyes closed.

Chapter Five

Burtonwood Airbase,
Lancashire
April 20th, 1943

Hi Joey,

I'm sure looking forward to you coming over but I know Mom isn't! I hear she's on bed rest and Pa's making himself real busy in his shed and vegetable patch. There's long stretches of nothing here, followed by short, intense action. We were on a Flying Fortress hunting U-boats for weeks; nine hours at a time, in grey skies over a grey Atlantic. Then, North of Cape Finisterre, chowing on steak and potatoes (a miracle up there) and the radio operator yells U-boat contact. Plates spun off knees and hit the deck. We spotted it gliding on the surface. There was a hunter's moon so we didn't need the Leigh Light. We dived fast, attacking at fifty feet. While gunners strafed the deck, we let off four shallow-set 300lb Torpex depth charges. The U-boat lifted out the water like steam from a suddenly opened valve. I filmed the bow rise vertically and slide into the depths. Krauts flung themselves into a sea thick with wreckage as we circled and picked our cold food from the deck. Don't tell Mom. Take care (not so little) brother,

Jack

Somerway Rehabilitation Unit, May 2015

Inside Tilly's room Glenn Miller's *In the Mood* lilted on the radio. Her high-backed chair had been dragged out through the French windows and placed on the lawn, allowing Tilly to smoke. A breeze blew; catching a corner of net curtain on a red rose bush, where her cotton pants hung to dry. Tilly hummed and shakily painted a last fingernail purple, wafting the perfume of varnish. She waved her hands and the loose skin under her arms flapped. Her bare, tanned legs were elegantly crossed from knee to ankle and dusted with powder-dry skin flakes. A faded bruise extended from left shin to ankle.

'I'm not waiting to shuffle off this mortal coil. I know what Vicky wants, *Mummy* safely deposited, drugged up and in some home. Over my dead body,' she muttered, frowning at a varnish smudge on her thumb. She wiped it off, then smeared pink lipstick on her toothless mouth, tucked straggly white hair behind both ears, straightened her back and winced as she lit another cigarette. She directed its exhalation towards the open window of the nurses' station next door.

There, thin-lipped sandbag-breasted Sister Lynch glared at a computer. She pushed back as smoke drifted in, rubbing her nose so hard it wiggle-danced, stood, slammed the window and pulled down the blind. Tilly grinned and put up two fingers.

'Is the coast clear?' whispered Robbie from behind a six-foot high laurel hedge, where Somerway's part-time gardener was lopping.

'It is now misery isn't watching,' said Tilly, without caring to lower her voice or smooth the tone. Antagonism made Tilly feel instantly younger. Robbie slipped to a recess in the wall next to Tilly. His fleshy broad back slid until he was crouched level with her. The gardener was almost as wide as he was tall, with ginger hair, pale-blue eyes and sunburned jug ears. He laid the hedge-clippers by his side and took the proffered cigarette. Tilly winked and squinted as smoke drifted in her eyes.

'I hope you're looking after my garden better than this place?' said Tilly, knowing Robbie was not to be goaded but nevertheless enjoying the attempt.

'Course. You pay me more but make Sister Lynch look like a saint.'

'Ha bloody ha,' said Tilly, wiping biscuit crumbs off her jogging pants. Sparrows fluttered down to peck. 'Well?' said Tilly, extinguishing her cigarette by rolling it under her slipper. 'What was I saying? I remember. Looks mean that little after the age of forty.' She snapped her fingers. 'It's personality that counts, and money, which sadly you don't have. Plus, your hair's a state and that beer gut makes you look six months' pregnant.'

He'd heard it all before. He puffed out his cheeks and patted his springy hair down with blackened, bitten fingernails. He let his belly out as he picked up Tilly's discarded stub, with its smudge of lipstick and dropped it in his boiler suit pocket.

'I wanted no hassle after my missus left.' He tipped his sweaty head back and blew out a stream of smoke from the side of his mouth, away from the nurses' window. Tilly pulled out another cigarette for herself and, well-trained, Robbie picked up her lighter and lit it. Tilly liked him. She liked any man who talked about his love life, or lack of it. At least Robbie didn't rattle on about cooking, children and grandchildren – or, in here, great-grandchildren.

'Your looks narrow choice but you've a nice arse and you're kind, which compensates for being skint. Slightly.'

Robbie laughed, revealing a dark gap on the right side of his top teeth. There was a knock. He quickly picked up his clippers and repositioned himself at the hedge, chopping leaves and setting sparrows in flight. Nurse Evangeline. She spotted Robbie and hesitated. He looked lingeringly at her glossy skin, generous breasts and hips which nearly blocked the doorframe. Evangeline smoothed her blue-gingham top and stepped in.

'How are you now?' asked Evangeline, shaking a thermometer and popping it under Tilly's arm, ignoring Robbie.

'Bored and fed up.'

'But it's a lovely day. All that sun and I'm not in it!' Evangeline put her shoulders back like a soldier on parade. Tilly looked her up and down and smiled.

'You've come on well, thanks to me,' she said.

Evangeline flashed a glance at Robbie. He smiled, keeping his lips closed to hide the missing tooth and chin lifted to negate the excess flesh. Because he wasn't concentrating, he snipped off a stem of roses and winced. Evangeline rolled her eyes, rattled drugs out of jars and poured a glass of water.

'Robbie, put those in a vase before Sister Lynch sees.' He did as he was told, holding in his stomach and letting it expand only when he returned behind the hedge. Tilly eased slowly on to the Zimmer frame and towards her bed. Evangeline followed, picking Tilly's knickers off the bush and placing them on a radiator.

'This is the place to dry them,' she said, wearily. 'OK, you've had morphine for pain, plus something to help your bowels.' She tipped her head to Robbie. 'You shouldn't encourage him.'

'He fancies you and that's why he's hanging around me,' said Tilly. Evangeline stole a look in the mirror, touching her intricately braided hair. Tilly swallowed the last tablet and gagged. 'I wish this was brandy. Anyway, you've got a fine figure now.'

'I've lost a stone but Ghanaian women are gloriously curvaceous,' Evangeline smiled.

'The ogler agrees. Hourglass is fine, and your posture is perfect.'

'Don't lose another ounce and you've a lovely walk,' Robbie butted in. He held her look for a long second.

'You shouldn't be listening,' said Evangeline, as she glided out.

'It's good to have a flirt,' said Tilly, as Robbie returned to attack the hedge. This was nearly her last day at Somerway.

Chapter Six

Diary: Burtonwood Airbase, April 29th, 1943

We'd flown through an exploding steel curtain of night tracers and cannon. Towering flames danced over buildings – dark orange, acid yellow, blood red. Then Buck's plane got hit and spewed a sheet of raw gasoline over his left wing and the waist gunner's capsule. Buck stuck right alongside. It would've taken one hit for him to burn up. Poor Buck, 26, a joker, with a pretty young wife and baby boy in Wyoming. He'd showed their pictures so often, we'd teased him. Our gunner fired machine guns, swearing every time tracers dug in the ground. We dropped our bombs, clearing factory roofs by feet. Buck jettisoned his payload and held steady as fire lapped the fuselage. He turned sharply towards open fields but was too low to bail. He fought to control his Lib and we willed him to do it. For a moment, it looked like he'd make a crash landing, when the left wing sheared off like a piece of burning paper, sparking as it twisted into darkness. Buck's Lib smashed into the ground; somersaulted, bounced and cartwheeled twice in a starry shower that span in all directions. I thought of his blissfully ignorant wife and baby.

Somerway Rehabilitation Unit, May 2015

Tilly, sedated, stared at the ceiling. A nurse called out *Violet*, exasperated, like a reprimand. The name echoed down more than 70 years to the day that had changed Tilly's life.

'Vi's a filthy, slutty sister,' her mother had wept, slapping her

37

upper chest. Aunty Violet who taught Tilly how to walk, dress, sit, smoke elegantly, and wink seductively. Violet, unlike Elizabeth, had been bestowed all the good-fairy wishes when it came to looks, figure, and a low sweet voice. When she moved, her hips swayed like a pendulum in figure-hugging, brightly-coloured dresses while her older sister plodded, feet splayed like a duck, in shapeless shirts and sagging dark skirts. Vi, the aspiring actress who'd followed Elizabeth from Londonderry to Liverpool and quickly married smitten George, an English engineer, who'd promptly marched off to war. Vi didn't seem in the least heartbroken, unlike other wives lining up to wave tearful goodbyes on Lime Street Station.

The morning after meeting Jack, Tilly had longed to lie in bed and daydream about possible bright foreign futures that had nothing to do with murky Liverpool but her mother insisted she go church with 12-year-old sister, Mabel. Their father, William, as usual nursed his hangover. During the service, Mabel threw up in the aisle just as Reverend Davidson intoned the importance of eating up leftovers. The Reverend paled at Mabel's regurgitated porridge. They'd returned home, abandoning the usual post-service two hours of watery tea and dreary Christian chit-chat. Their kitchen smelt of slow-roasting pork cheeks. Forever after, that pungent aroma turned Tilly's bowels to jelly. Her mother had stood stock still at the sound of rhythmic, bouncing bed springs above. She'd looked up, mouth gaping, then with eyes like chargers and roaring like a bull, stormed towards the sounds. Tilly and Mabel listened to footsteps stampeding this way and that; to Elizabeth screaming over and over *You dirty bastards!* so loudly the whole neighbourhood must have been spellbound. There was shoving, banging and yelps. Dad bellowing *No! No!* A woman's voice desperately whimpering and apologising. Tilly saw a doll-like figure stumble downstairs, halting at the front door. A black handbag hung open on her arm and tangled, dark hair spilling down her back. For a split second she'd turned and her mouth twisted at the sight of her nieces. Her white face had red splotches on each cheek. Dad wrestled with his struggling wife, as Vi tucked blouse into skirt, fastened buttons and yanked open the door. Elizabeth broke free of William and clattered down. Her mother was stopped on the brink of utter shamelessness by a passing old couple staring at the spectacle. She slammed the door. *My sister!* she'd screamed. *Get out! Get out, you dirty bastard!* William fled. He didn't return that night. The next day their crying mother dished out his portion of fatty mince between her daughters and knitted, clacking needles like weapons and working up a blazing temper.

Vi's a disgrace to the church and decent women. Oh God, what am I to do? How will I survive? I hate him, hate, hate him. It's disgusting and she's married. Poor George when he hears.

Reverend Davidson called that evening, no doubt alerted by neighbours, and sipped tea from Elizabeth's best china cups in the polished front room. He dropped into the stilted conversation the sanctity of marriage and deep testing of vows. Tilly wanted to point out that it was while her mum was on her knees, listening to him drone on, that Aunty Vi had dropped on hers, in her sister's marital bed. After he left, Elizabeth turned Jesus' bleeding-heart picture to the wall. Her rage simmered to a rolling boil. She ironed, spitting on the hot metal surface and slammed it down. William's key turned in the door at 6pm. He slunk to his chair, face flushed, thanks to Dutch courage at his working man's club. He picked up the *Liverpool Echo*, shook it out and hid behind the pages, casting hopeful, furtive glances at the kitchen, where nothing was cooking. Mum thumped the iron. William sneezed and fished out a grubby handkerchief, blew loudly and inspected what came out.

You're disgusting, Elizabeth snapped and launched into all his many filthy physical habits. William took it for two minutes before storming off, slamming the front door so hard the glass rattled.

It was all ancient history, like that first time in Jack's arms, with his marrow-melting voice, his warm fingers unbuttoning her dress, strong hands slipping around the curve of her buttocks, unclipping her stockings.

'Tilly, wake up, time for a bath,' called Evangeline brightly.

'Fuck off.'

Chapter Seven

Diary Entry: St Eval Airbase, Cornwall, April 30th, 1943

I saw a dead hare today; its bleached bones exposed under a matted, dark pelt; eyes gone and wind fluffing its tail. I imagined being dead in a woodland with nothing to mark where I fell but snuffling creatures. It's what I want. War has shown me how to live, even if I haven't long. I can't share this with Jess.

Trevone Bay, June 2015

Ava woke groggily. Sunlight slipped through chinks of the room's slightly-too-short curtains. For a moment she wondered where she was and why Josh wasn't with her, then it flooded her veins all over again; a sour and dirty sickness. Him and Sadie arriving hand-in-hand unfolding their meticulous plans and a baby on the way. The nauseous, molten rage and grief which had marooned her in this shabby house. She was bathed in a cold sweat, as if her body leaked toxins. It was 6.30am; the longest she'd slept in months. Peeking out to sea, Ava watched surfers seeking waves under the rippling skin of water where long swells appeared muscular. Sugar-spun pink-tinged clouds, all fluffy on top, as if sliced by a knife beneath. The glinting sun dissipated a thin mist even as she watched. A bracing swim was just what she needed to immerse herself in this new life. The last time Ava swam in England she'd been thirteen. Her newly single mother flirted with a deckchair man on Weymouth sands and Ava was sent packing with a Mr Whippy ice cream and strict instructions to stay in her depth. She'd licked the vanilla cone, tentatively wading into shallow water, inch by freezing inch, while boys and men flailed past and dove straight in. She'd so wanted to emulate them. The deckchair man got busy and her mother called her back. The water had only just lapped Ava's thighs. Since then, it had been heated pools and warmer, foreign seas.

Now, she pulled on a black stomach-control costume, bought at vast expense for her Grecian honeymoon, wrapped a long threadbare towel around herself, locked the front door and tucked the keys under a stone. First, she climbed to moaning Round Hole's concealed, grassy rim. It was an enormous crater. Ava knelt and stared into its dank and mossy mouth. Crows flapped around the edge, blown like scraps of silk. Waves flooded and drained nearly 100 feet below, muttering and gurgling across rocks. How easy it would be to slip and stop everything, she thought, as she forced herself up and retraced her steps to the bay. Chest-high waves pounded onto iron-flat sand where a group of male surfers chatted on the shoreline with the top-half of wet suits pulled down, revealing taut, tanned bodies. Ava shot away from them, towards deserted, iron-hard, ridged banks beneath cliffs. Here, the water appeared calmer. The beach was pockmarked with worm casts and studded with a chain of rock pools. Inspecting one, Ava observed an amber-shelled crab scuttle and a speckled starfish manoeuvre along, tentatively feeling the slack water with pincers and suckered limbs. Invisible ventricles in the rocks pumped a seemingly syrupy liquid through seaweed that spread like hair, while blistery barnacles fanned the bubbling broth which abruptly silenced. Ava inspected a leathery Mermaid's Purse, holding its translucent body against the sky. Inside, something wriggled. She placed it carefully back into pinkish, sour-smelling seaweed, from which banks of flies rose and settled. A cormorant on a boulder fanned out jet feathers like some gorgeous, drenched gown. Ava halted between two corridors of surging waves, separated by a flat section of sea, which smoothed out enticingly. Here, the ocean appeared inviting and safe. Ava dropped the towel and kicked off her flip-flops. Her goose-pimpled, milk-white office skin was almost blue and her bikini line required the kind of attention only sun-drenched holidays and new lovers warranted. She'd need a wet suit. Determined to execute a speedy entrance, Ava strode in. Waves frilled over feet, ankles and calves like icy gauze. Pressing her lips together, she balled her hands into fists and waded on, stepping on shells so sharp she staggered and flopped ungracefully forward. The sea rose to circle her thighs, then, in one swell, stomach and chest.

'Shit,' she yelled, bringing legs up like pistons. A wave hit her face like a slap and filled her mouth with salty water. Spitting, Ava could only just stand on tiptoe, despite being so close to shore. It shocked her how deep she was so quickly. She breathed deeply and rapidly, her heart pumping in response to cold and fear. She struck out in breaststroke towards the shore and heard a distant bellow. A surfer belted towards her; board tucked under his arm. She waved him off to show she was perfectly fine. He yelled again, more fiercely, just as Ava felt herself inexorably drawn out. Her strokes shoreward wrapped her further into a steely, dragging current. Ava flipped on her back and flung beachward but was tugged relentlessly away. She was now thirty feet from land and moving further and faster into deeper, darker swells. The water felt denser and bitingly cold, turning her limbs numb. *Oh God no*, came into her head as waves stung her eyes so she could barely see. She thrashed upwards, pressing her hands on the water as if the ocean might turn solid as a table, while her lead-heavy legs climbed fruitlessly on swells like they would transform into rungs of a ladder. Gasping, choking and coughing, the coast was a black blur. The sinews of her neck stretched to keep her mouth out of water as icy threads crept into Ava's core. Between waves sweeping over her head, she breathed quickly, swallowed water and vomited. She couldn't believe she'd drown, even as the sea took possession of her.

Like an apparition, the man appeared but out of reach. His face, a pearly blot in darkness. Ava wanted to fasten herself to him. Something sharp thumped into her belly. She threw up. The man bellowed. Angry, garbled, senseless words. He rammed something into her chest now, scraping across it. She tried to clasp its rough edge but her hands trailed off and head slipped underwater. She heard her own gurgling. Her costume was roughly grabbed from behind and an object slid forcibly beneath her. Her body pinned to it. Ava tasted blood. Her skin felt on fire and vision darkened while flashes of luminescence sparked the periphery. She was propelled forward. Flashing lights and an orange inflatable bobbed beside her. Men in fluorescent helmets and waterproofs hauled Ava up while the man behind shoved her exposed arse over.

'Christ,' she heard him say, coughing, as she slithered to the deck to be swiftly wrapped in foil and blankets.

'You're safe,' a voice said kindly, as Ava retched.

Chapter Eight

Diary Entry: Burtonwood Airbase, May 2ⁿᵈ, 1943

Woke in the early hours, hungover and drugged. For an instant, horrors forgotten but they crowd back in. I'm not afraid of dying quickly, it's a slow death that terrifies me. I talked to the priest and he hears my confession with his hand upon my head. A warm, forgiving hand. There are so many things I've left unsaid to friends who have died, to my family. Today, the rising sun shimmers on the runways. The cool air is pungent with aviation fuel, on clothes and skin. The sky beyond the coast black and lead-heavy. Just how I feel.

Trevone Bay, June 2015

Shivering, teeth chattering, Ava was acutely aware of a gathering crowd around the dinghy as it beached. She covered her face with her hands, fearing someone would take a photograph that would spread to the local Press and beyond. Specifically, to Josh and Sadie. Paramedics lifted her onto a stretcher and into the waiting ambulance. She glimpsed mobiles trained on her until the doors shut. There was a strong smell of antiseptic and a fainter one of greasy pastry. A paramedic with cool fingers and a local accent discreetly eased off Ava's swimming costume, slipped on a green gown, foil and extra blankets.

'I'm Eve. You're OK now. So lucky,' she said, gently turning Ava's face from side-to-side. 'Where does it hurt? Can you breathe OK?' She attacked a black clip to Ava's finger, a machine bleeped.

'It's some blow-in idiot caught in a riptide,' a man outside the ambulance said tersely.

'Take no notice,' the paramedic murmured with a tight smile. 'Let's start with your name?' She clicked a pen.

'Sylvia Weston,' lied Ava, hoarsely, amazed how her brain could function. 'I feel OK honestly, just cold. I'd like to go home please, thank you.'

'Date of birth, Sylvia?'

'27/12/82.' Not a lie. Her skin crawled with what felt like fiery ants. She took a deep breath trying to control the shivering, coughed and coughed.

'Next of kin?' the paramedic asked, turning up the heating.

'Mum's in Spain and I'd rather she didn't know. There's nobody else.' Not a lie, not now.

'And address?'

'Near Padstow.' The paramedic put the pen down.

'You're on holiday then?' she asked, popping the thermometer in Ava's ear checking another screen with flashing red lights.

'Sort of.'

'Right. OK, allergic to anything?' Her voice impatient now. Ava shook her head. 'You'll have a thorough once-over in hospital. Trevone's dangerous unless you know it. How long have you been here?'

'A day,' whispered Ava, her throat burned.

'Ahh.'

'I don't want to go to hospital.'

The paramedic shrugged and Ava returned to Newquay less than 24 hours after arriving. She was rolled into a green-curtained cubicle and left alone. Ava padded the scrapes on her face and realised she would meet Tilly in a mess.

'Tea's here. Do you take sugar?' came a voice behind the curtain.

'No, I mean yes, two please,' said Ava. She needed them. There was a sound of brisk stirring and a mug was pushed through, held by a weathered hand with gold rings on four fingers. 'Thank you.' It hurt her lips but Ava forced herself to drink. She was warmer. It came back to her why the man had used only his surfboard to rescue her: drowners grab saviours in a death-clinch and take them down too. Shoes squeaked past, stopped, and went on. Ava's right eye was swelling and finger-print bruises bloomed around her upper-arms. She stood, shuddered, and the room swayed. Wrapping the flimsy gown tightly around herself, Ava saw another folded on a chair and pulled that on top, so there was no longer a great gap at the back. She picked up the plastic bag her costume was in and drained the tea. Through a gap in the curtains Ava spotted an Exit sign above a swing door. Staff huddled around a cubicle at the far end. Holding her breath, she walked out barefoot. It was 8am and A&E was busy. A woman rested a bandaged foot on a chair. A boy leant against his father's chest and a teenager, pressing bloody tissues on his forehead, gabbled to the receptionist. Nobody took the least notice of her. Ava headed through automatic doors and to the first of three waiting taxis. She tapped on the half-open window and a grey-haired driver frowned up. He resembled an old owl with bushy beard and tawny eyes, that didn't quite look at her.

'Should you be out?' he asked.

'Yes,' said Ava, hoarsely but authoritatively and opening the rear door, slid into the furthest corner, as if it was normal to depart hospital battered, bloody and barely dressed.

'As long as you aren't on the run?' said the man.

'Hardly,' snapped Ava. He shrugged, released the handbrake and waited for instructions. 'Trevone Bay, please.' She stared out of the window. 'Please put the heater on.' Reg switched it to full-blast.

'Are you the one who near-drowned?' asked Reg after a mile, with a self-satisfied smile. Ava's mouth opened. If she'd been dressed, she'd have stopped the taxi and got out.

'Recognised your face. There's a video on Facebook. You were lucky,' Reg said. Ava frowned and rubbed her still-numb arms; what a complete mess. She should never have taken this job. 'Where in Trevone Bay?' Reg asked, and when Ava told him, the smile widened, like the penny had dropped.

'Tilly Barwise's new guard. I'm Reg. I've delivered brandy, fags, fish, papers, and vitals to her for years. She's had a few of you carers. I took them all back to the train station. One only lasted an afternoon. Have you met Tilly yet?'

'No,' said Ava sharply but couldn't help asking, 'Why did they leave?'

'She's intolerant, spiteful, selfish,' said Reg, tapping his finger on the steering wheel and thinking he'd have to call Sniffy Dave and up his bet. 'Drink-dependent and all that comes with it,' Reg added, 'like my dad, who's dead, thank God. Tilly was a beauty and hates being old and decrepit, and anyone who isn't or is.' Reg glanced at Ava in the driving mirror. She looked away. Working at a computer for a decade had given her a bumble bee-shaped body. Ava decided if she left Trevone, this man would not have the satisfaction of depositing her at the railway station or, God forbid, the airport. Reg pressed down his window and sniffed the air.

'Fishing tomorrow, should be cod out there now. Do you want me to bring some? Cash only?'

'To check if I'm still there?' Ava said. He was silent as they drew up outside Cliff View. Ava retrieved the keys and finding her purse, handed Reg two £20 notes. She took back the £6 in change. He was not getting a penny tip.

'Here's my card if you need anything,' said Reg, cheerily. He ground the gears and roared off. Ava tore up his card. She imagined Reg embroidering a graphic account of Tilly's new carer, who'd nearly drowned and legged it, barefoot and practically naked from hospital. Ava took an anti-inflammatory with her tea and topped it off with a Valium. She threw the hospital gowns in the washing machine and ran a steaming bath, scented with lavender salts, in which she drank instant hot chocolate. Afterwards, curled up in bed with a hot water bottle Ava watched a sea mist seep and thicken as it dropped over Round Hole, enveloping and obliterating Cliff View. A rainstorm blew in on the back of it, howling over the headland, rattling window panes and making Round Hole wail. Ava dreamt of Josh and Sadie laughing as they pushed her out to sea on a pink, blow-up dolphin.

Chapter Nine

Watford Road, Anfield, 14th May 1943

William's adultery became a pleasurable diversion from the horrors of war along Watford Road and well beyond. While William was allowed home and ate, separately, he slept downstairs. It was time for Elizabeth's usual Saturday church coffee morning but she couldn't bear the flickering eyes, fake smiles and ceaseless sharp tongues of the gossipy congregation. Instead, she organised a bike ride with her daughters and behind their backs, bristled with plans to travel to her sister's in Ireland, away from domestic shame and global war. She'd demanded money from William which he'd handed over painfully and unquestioningly. Tilly would only be told at the last minute.

'I don't want to go cycling,' Tilly stated firmly to her mother, filing her nails. She had set aside eight leisurely hours to get ready for Jack. The thrilling thought made her heart flutter and she felt the thread of it rise to her throat. She couldn't eat breakfast's refried potatoes and green beans.

'Are you ill, Matilda?' her mother asked, coldly, picking up the untouched plate.

'I've a headache,' Tilly replied wanly, knowing she looked pale without a scrap of make-up. There was a little bowl of salt in the bedroom ready for her to exfoliate her skin in the inch of bath water allowed.

'That's what your father says whenever we do something. It never seems to affect visits to the pub. Or elsewhere.' She said this loudly enough for William to lift his paper in front of his frowning face. 'If you don't come cycling, you won't go dancing later, it's as simple as that,' said Elizabeth, tipping left-over food into a bucket of slops for community pigs and hens.

Tilly acquiesced; she had to see Jack, so while Elizabeth hummed some hymnal dirge, Tilly slipped on a bright yellow dress; one created by Aunty Vi, and was completely inappropriate for cycling.

'You can't wear that,' Elizabeth said, as if it was sackcloth stitched by the devil. 'You'll catch your death.'

'It's sunny out, and this is clean.' Superior and polite as she swept into the yard, pigeons cooing on the wall. She took hold of her black bike with its narrow leather seat and jangled the bell, so the birds flapped up. Sensible Mabel joined her, wearing a calf-length brown skirt and matching jacket. Elizabeth hesitated at the mirror by the kitchen sink, patting on peach-coloured powder that only highlighted her lines, and struggling to fasten pearly wrist buttons on her worn kid gloves. Elizabeth's cheeks flamed as they walked through the alleyway, into Watford Road. Housewives, brought out by the sun, were a line of bobbing bottoms as they proudly donkey-stoned their front steps, painting them creamy white with a pungent mix of ground dust, cement water and bleach. The gossip stopped as one spied Elizabeth, and in seconds bottoms stilled, spines straightened, heads turned and silence fell. The tick, tick, tick of bike wheels filled the air. Tilly flashed back the neighbours' curious looks with daggers. Nobody liked the Irish, even if they were half-English.

Only old Mr Jackson, bespectacled and tweed-suited, limping along with his newspaper and cane, doffed his flat cap and remarked about the weather. His rheumy eyes glimmered over Tilly and she wrinkled her nose.

They pedalled beyond the city's back-to-back terraces, along the East Lancashire Road, and slowly lush countryside took over, with green fields of young wheat and potatoes. There seemed to be a million birds flitting through hedges and pecking at soil. Banks of scarlet valerian, buttercups and cow parsley lit up lanes. Elizabeth cycled as if she was late for church and Mabel's little legs kept pace. Tilly dawdled, allowing distance to spool between them. Sweat trickled down her back, sticking the dress to her skin as she weaved dreamily along, quivering as she recalled Jack's kiss.

'Matilda, hurry up,' her mother called, a steely edge to the tone. 'Don't swerve all over the road.' Tilly put a spurt on, and then slowed, waiting for the next demand. It wasn't long coming.

'Look at your dress. Pull it down. Can't you have a bit more ladylike decorum?' A fox ran in front of Tilly, dragging a half-dead blackbird in its mouth, its wings still flapping. She stopped, forcing a car behind to brake. The pudgy-faced driver thumped the horn as his black car skimmed close. The man stared at Tilly in the mirror and slowed, until he saw Elizabeth and Mabel and put his foot down. Tilly recognised his silky look; like the one that shot across William's face when he eyed Aunty Vi. Her mother never got a glance like that. Tilly lost sight of Elizabeth and Mabel at the top of a hill but reaching the crest, she saw the pair of them waiting, half-hidden by silver birch, outside a high barbed-wire fence. Elizabeth waved urgently and it was then Tilly heard the slow, sweet notes of an accordion. Scores of dark-haired men dressed in dark boiler-suits with yellow circles on their backs and right legs. Italian POWs. She decided to give them a treat.

Tilly let go of the brakes, swung out her legs and flew downhill. Her dress rose, fluttering like a silk flag. Guards in a tall tower stopped smoking. The accordion player hesitated and there rose a murmur *Bellissimo, bella, bella*. Tilly's smile widened as her speed increased, wind blowing her hair back. The accordionist launched into a fast tune and tapped his shoe, so the loose sole flapped. Prisoners blew kisses, whistled and called her over. A sullen guard jerked his gun to signal her on. Tilly responded by pulling her dress to the top of her thighs. The Italians roared and clapped and she felt like a movie star.

'Matilda! Have you no shame? Those are the enemy,' screeched her mother as Tilly sailed towards her, gravel grinding on brakes. Elizabeth grabbed Tilly's arm and belted her cheek. 'You're like Her!' she bellowed as Tilly sprawled on the ground. The accordionist stopped and the prisoners fell quiet. Tilly wiped her mouth, tasted blood, scrabbled up and brushing her dress, placed the bike between herself and her mother.

'I'll never marry a man who prefers whisky and other women to me,' she spat out. Elizabeth raised her right hand but Tilly was off, waving at the prisoners.

'I'll ride here every bloody day, Mum,' she shouted, 'and dance with every American going. See if I don't!'

The accordionist struck a sad, operatic tune and for miles Tilly heard the prisoners' beautiful singing linger. Her father opened the door, ready for another blast of marital fury but seeing only his daughter's blotched face, stood aside. Tilly dragged her bike through the house and into the yard and locked herself in the outside toilet. Twenty minutes later, Elizabeth blazed in, unbuttoned her gloves, throwing them on the kitchen table. Ignoring her husband, who'd taken refuge behind his paper, she rolled up her sleeves, splashed water on her face, tied on an apron, and peeled potatoes without a word. William tapped the skirting board with his shoe in the certain knowledge it would infuriate Elizabeth. When she turned on him, knife in hand, it was William's cue to pick up his tin hat and head for the calm all-male oasis of the Pall Mall Working Man's Club. After that he'd do a cursory check on World War II's air safety, followed by a more comprehensive investigation of Aunty Vi's personal security. Elizabeth took this opportunity to inform her daughters they'd been booked onto the ferry to Ireland the next day, with a one-way ticket.

Chapter Ten

Burtonwood Airbase,
Lancashire
May 14th, 1943

Hi Joey,

Your mail means so much. I'm real busy, training and filming. Last week, we tracked down a Jerry destroyer and our gunners were braced into harnesses shooting hundreds of rounds at a Focke-Wulf on our tail. Empty shell cases bounced all over the deck. Here was death heading for us and those guys threw it right back. The enemy plane spiralled down and we dropped a 550-pounder astern of the Kraut destroyer. The water exploded and the ship rose and fell, shaking itself like a wet dog. Another bomb hit it mid-ships. She looked like an egg cracking open. It's horrible to watch even as we punched the air. When we got back the Doc hands out pills like candy, I can't remember the last time I slept without drugs or booze.

Your loving brother,
Jack

Trevone Bay, June 2015

Ava stirred to hear the sea pounding on the beach so it roared like a busy motorway. A whole day and night had passed. The sky was a washing machine of churning grey clouds and Round Hole emitted an ear-piercing whistle. She'd woken once, taken another sleeping tablet and now it was 7am. Tilly's D-Day. Overnight, sand had shifted, resculpting the smile-shaped bay into a grimace. The choppy ocean looked like mixed cement and was entirely void of surfers. Far beyond the shallows, where the riptide had swept her out, the sea slid in dimpled circles, like huge snaring nets. Strands of bloody-looking seaweed embroidered the shoreline and a silver-winged heron struggled against the headwind. Ava ached all over. Looking in the mirror, she flinched at the red scrapes on her forehead and swollen, blackening right eye, which no make-up would disguise. She showered, put cream on cuts and made porridge with water, raisins, grated apple, cinnamon, and drizzle of honey, along with a mug of sugarless black coffee, repeating, *Alive, alive, alive.* Her split lip burnt. She fretted what to tell Tilly, or that Vicky would find out. To calm herself, Ava prepared Tilly's first and possibly last dinner if she proved to be as awkward as everyone said. The braised beef would be cooked long and slow to accommodate toothless gums, with onions, diced carrots, stock and red wine. She peeled potatoes for buttery mash. Ava twiddled every knob of the Rayburn, aiming for the lowest heat and hoping for the best, popped the casserole dish in. She put together a lemon sponge pudding, with zest and cardamom seeds. Cooking relaxed her. It riled her to think how Josh had joked Sadie couldn't make a meal if her life depended on it. Culinary arts obviously weren't what had attracted him, Ava fumed as she cracked eggs, separated and whisked whites. Looking up, the weather had transformed. Puffy, lighter clouds streamed offshore, revealing strips of violet sky and the promise of better weather. The phone rang. Wiping her hands on a tea towel, Ava answered.

'It's me, May. I heard what happened. Are you OK to pick up Tilly?'

'Yes. How on earth did you hear? Was that taxi driver in the chip shop?' asked Ava.

'No, someone on the beach showed us a video of the rescue in the chippie. Sorry. I recognised you but didn't tell anyone. Reg came in and told me about picking you up at the hospital.'

'Bloody hell. Is this the sort of place where nothing goes on without everyone finding out?' She could hardly breathe; malicious talk was what she'd left London to escape from.

'There's been centuries of practice in the finer arts of gossip. The church and pub used to be the hub, now it's the chippie, hairdressers, Co-op, WI, Facebook, tweeting and all that social malarkey. Not that I use a computer. The main thing is, are you OK?'

'Battered, like your fish. I don't know who rescued me but he must be livid. I was so stupid. I risked his life.'

'Finn Blake.'

'Oh.' Of course, May would know.

'Blacksmith. Been away a few years, messy divorce, returned a while back with a young son and keeps himself to himself. He's not a gossip, so whatever he thinks he won't be saying.'

'I'll have to thank him.' Ava's skin crawled at the thought.

'Soon but let's see how Tilly is when she gets home.' Ava thought, *Let's see how long she lasts.*

'There's directions to Somerway in the car and I'll pop by tomorrow,' said May. Later, she told her husband that Ava was the most unlikely carer ever at Cliff View. Jeff retorted May wasn't a born chip shop owner by any means and there ensued a frosty silence.

Ava dolloped make-up over the worst of her bruises but rather than conceal, the damage was highlighted. She dreaded her rescue ending up in the paper with link to a video. Sweat seeped under her arms, staining the grey T-shirt. She changed into a black one and sprayed on more deodorant, donned sunglasses and tied a green silk scarf from the coat stand around her neck to cover her rescuer's fingerprints. As she locked Cliff View, Ava counted crows on the roof, eyeing, preening, clicking and shifting from leg-to-scaly-leg. One for sorrow, two for mirth, three for a funeral, four for birth, five for heaven, six for hell and seven for the devil, his own self. A chill ran up her spine.

Chapter Eleven

Diary Entry: May 14th, 1943

Jess can tell I don't feel the same. She writes me about buying china and linen, cutlery and place mats. I can't see the damn point. If I live, I won't be that kind of man. Hemmed in like Pa. Surrounded by family. I can't be, not after what I've seen.

Somerway Rehabilitation Unit, June 2015

Clover House was fronted by triple-locked, sturdy glass doors strengthened with steel wires. Ava stood inside, facing another reinforced door and a CCTV camera. She adjusted her glasses in its reflection. Not good. Several orders were pasted on panes and the largest stated to disinfect hands with the supplied gel. Ava splurged it on and bit her split lip as it stung the chewed skin around her fingernails. Another notice outlined strict visiting times which Ava had not adhered to. A small one in red ink ordered: *Please be patient when you ring the bell. Staff are busy with patients who might be your relative. It also frightens them.* Ava pressed it for a fraction of a second. Nobody came. Women in blue gingham tops and navy trousers loomed into view, moving swiftly from room to room. A short, blonde nurse cast Ava a glance and trotted away. Five minutes later she returned and punched a code on the electronic keypad. The door opened a fraction. Heat and the scent of body odours, disinfectant and food seeped out.

'Visiting's not for another hour,' she stated, blankly. A name tag stated Barbara Adams. Her brown eyes skimmed Ava's bruises and cuts.

'I'm sorry I'm early,' Ava said politely. She flashed her driving licence and Nurse Barbara blinked. 'I'm Tilly Barwise's carer; Ava Westmorland.'

The nurse swung open the door like Ava had pronounced *Abracadabra and Open Sesame.*

'So, you're taking her? Best of British. Follow me please. Have you been in an accident?'

'Sort of,' said Ava, uneasy with the sudden, effusive warmth. Nurse Barbara steamed ahead and Ava kept pace as her surprisingly bouncing posterior passed rooms of dozing patients. A toothless, near-bald woman with no eyebrows and copious facial hair hovered in a doorway. She smiled at Ava and held out her hand, like an ancient toddler.

'Not now, Nancy,' said Barbara brightly, 'your daughter's in later.'

This place, thought Ava, feels like a human battery farm. Barbara paused at the doorway of a spacious lounge. A talk show, watched by nobody, filled a sixty-inch screen. The brash TV presenter blasted the husband of a two-timed wife. He talked earnestly to the camera, asking anyone watching with an unfaithful partner to get in touch. Ava imagined Josh and Sadie appearing as calm, professional, parents-to-be and she, the dumped, demented loser. A male patient shuffled towards them with a catheter bag of cloudy urine looped on his walking frame. Barbara said hello to him but he drifted by with no acknowledgment. A nurse outside a toilet asked a crinkled, crooked woman with a beaky nose about her bowel movements. Barbara halted outside a closed door, pinned onto which was an enlarged copy of the photograph in Cliff View. Siren Tilly in her scarlet bathing costume.

'Thank God I won't have to eat mince again because I'm not going to that graveyard of a nursing home,' a guttural accent stated within. 'This carer can get her arse straight back to where she came from as soon as I'm able.' There was an indiscernible reply.

Barbara clasped her hands as if about to pray.

'Voice of a harridan,' she said. 'But look what she was like when she was in love with the GI. She pinned it up to remind us who she was and to eat less. She calls it her *Gut Buster Diet*. Most of us are on it. Lots of fruit and veg, no treats. More walking. Simple. Don't you love those white sandals and endless legs?' Barbara sighed. 'She told me I've got wonderful eyes and face structure, now I've found them. We don't bring chocolates or cakes to work anymore and I've joined the gym; it's a killer.' The nurse's gaze flashed to Ava's hips, who automatically sucked in her stomach. The hairs on the back of her neck rose at facing this nemesis.

'Evangeline, look what I've done for you; now walk for me. That's it. Beautiful. Roll those hips. Make sure your feet don't splay out. Toes at midnight – not quarter-to-three. Don't slouch, and straighten your back! It's like you've got a book balanced on your head and a rod up your rear. Smile. Flash those peepers and remember when you look at someone don't turn your head, let your eyes rove; like a cat seeking its prey.'

'More like I've got a stigmatism,' came the reply.

The door opened. Nurse Barbara stepped aside as Evangeline slid between her and Ava, swivelling eyes and smelling of violets.

'Mouth shut,' Tilly commanded from inside. 'Nobody wants to see teeth when you smile. Concentrate on your body.' The smile promptly vanished when Evangeline saw Ava's face but she sashayed on.

Barbara, straightened, breathed in and stepped forward. 'I see you're raring to go, Tilly, no more bossing us. The ambulance is ready in 15 minutes, so while I sort out paperwork, I'll leave you to say hello to Ava Westmorland.' She moved aside and Ava froze.

'No way,' snapped Tilly petulantly, her voice rising behind a wing-backed chair on the lawn.

'Good luck,' Barbara said, retreating. A pall of smoke floated above Tilly. Beside her a meaty-looking man with red hair plucked dandelions.

'Robbie,' said Tilly, 'someone's about to annoy me but not for long. Take a photograph of me and I want to stand up.'

Robbie pulled at the neck of his sweatshirt with its bright yellow logo: *Sunshine Care is Age Aware*. It was far too tight. Robbie crouched, and Tilly leaned on his outstretched arm, shakily rising. Ava recoiled at the sight of her cobweb-like white and yellow hair clinging to rounded shoulders. The pink rims of Tilly's ears poked through, attached to a skull the size of a child's. She was almost bent double, tiny, skeletal, wizened. Robbie shuffled as she tottered forward, slowly revealing her body. Tiny Tilly was less than five foot, bent almost double, with spindly-thighs and calves like two flat bread rolls. Ava noted the faces of a huddle of wheelchair-bound female patients register disgust and curiosity. Tilly ignored them.

'I've only got my mobile,' said Robbie, holding out his phone which was the size of a matchbox in his shovel-like hands. 'And you haven't got one.'

'That doesn't matter. Wait, let me get in the right position.' Tilly pointed her foot in its blue slipper. She tried to straighten. Only her piercing blue eyes lifted and neck extended, tortoise-like. Her mouth stretched. Without teeth to shape her face she appeared cadaverous.

'I'm ready,' she commanded. Robbie hesitantly removed his hand. He took one step back and clicked.

'Got it,' he said, and took quickly hold of Tilly again. There was rapping on a window. 'Sorry Sister,' Robbie said, putting the phone in his pocket. 'Now I'm for it.'

'I don't want to see Lynch when I go. She's not the sort of National Health employee I want to die in front of.' Robbie supported Tilly to her chair. She rocked from side to side and her bra-free breasts swung at waist-height. She did not look at Ava. 'Where did Evangeline put those presents from the world supermarket?'

'Amazon. Under your bed.'

'Good,' she said. He eased Tilly into the chair turned it to face the room. He lit a cigarette for her.

'We're telling – you're smoking nearly inside,' announced one of the patio tea drinkers.

'Well, I won't be getting detention,' Tilly snarled. She shoved the packet of Benson and Hedges into Robbie's right trouser pocket. He tried to stop her and there was a tussle in and out. 'For God's sake keep them, Robbie, or those horrors will wonder what I'm wrestling with!'

Robbie accepted in a flash, his cheeks flaming. It was then Tilly glared at Ava with the bluest eyes she'd ever seen. Robbie took in Ava's battered face and scarpered.

'Come nearer, so I can look at you,' said Tilly, her crooked finger beckoning. Like a witch, thought Ava, and stayed put. 'Where did they drag you from? And that's my scarf.' Ava touched it. Tilly inhaled and exhaled slowly through her nose. The long, curved purple nails on her gnarled and mottled left hand played with a silver locket. The smallest finger stuck out at a peculiar straight angle.

'Your daughter appointed me,' replied Ava, with the same kind of tone she'd used as a copywriter dealing with a demanding client. Tilly's eyes widened and her dark mouth slackened. I must look after my teeth, thought Ava. A couple of long white hairs on Tilly's chin shone in the sunlight.

'Appointed. By Her Majesty Queen Victoria.' Tilly waved her hand regally. 'I don't want you. Vicky's after one thing. My money. I'm capable of looking after myself. Aren't I, Robbie?' Robbie was long gone. 'I'll pay you to go back to wherever you were from and make it worth your while.' Tilly opened her handbag and rooted inside. From that position her head looked like a plucked chicken's. She took out a cheque book, hands shaking so much, the pages flapped.

'Vicky insists, Mrs Barwise,' said Ava resolutely. She wasn't ready for Spain. 'Your doctor won't allow you home without me.' There was silence.

Tilly vacuumed her cigarette and pulled a face like she'd trodden in crap. Outside, there was the clink of cups on saucers as patients listened, giving the unfolding scene their undivided attention.

'Hear that?' said Tilly, jerking her head. 'Nothing better than nose at me. Wait until my daughter and you face your end surrounded by zombies. I'm calling Dr Singh.' Tilly picked through her bag, brought out a large piece of paper and handed it to Ava. She pointed to a mobile on the window ledge. 'I can't read numbers.' Tilly's icy eyes swept over her. Under such scrutiny, Ava fumbled and twice pressed the wrong numbers. Finally, the surgery answerphone connected and went through its options. She listened and pressed each number, scanning the few get-well cards. One featured a naked half-man, half-beast in a forest, complete with stag horns, animal legs and stallion-like erection.

'Handsome, isn't he?' said Tilly, following Ava's eyes and open mouth. 'Apollo Vindonnus – the healing God. My lover sent it.'

Her lover? thought Ava, barely hearing the surgery's instructions. She was number three in the queue, then two and finally, a weary-sounding receptionist answered. Ava explained she was calling on behalf of Mrs Barwise who was set to be discharged into her care but the patient wanted to discuss this with Dr Singh. The receptionist asked to talk to Tilly. Ava passed over the phone and Tilly clamped it to her ear.

'Angie,' said Tilly, with syrupy, fake warmth, 'Vicky's sent another one. Would you credit it? Dr Singh can sort this out.' She played with the locket. Whatever was said made Tilly frown, press every button on the phone and chuck it on the bed. 'Well, you won but not for long.'

Chapter Twelve

Diary entry May 14th, 1943

Visited Bud after the crash. I thought he was lucky to be alive but not when I saw him. His head was three times the size and his eyes, like dirty raisins, peered at me through raw, melted scabs. He was in a long hut with 20 beds. In each, lay men with terrible injuries. One was missing most of his lower jaw, another no eyelids. Others had charred stumps for hands, a melted nose, liquified ears. Bud, covered in bandages, stretched his lips. It was a crusted gap. On his chest lay a long trunk-like flap of grafted skin. He called it a pedicle. It was anchored to a fresh blood supply, like a miniature elephant trunk. I slipped him whiskey and cigs. He told me he was going to finish with his girl. I said she'd still love him. He swore and tears rolled down his face.

Somerway Rehabilitation Unit, June 2015

'What's your name again?' asked Tilly, bringing Ava into focus. The blue of her eyes was distinctly black-ringed, the whites threaded with pink veins and loose, lower lids, inflamed and watery.

'Ava,' she repeated to that ancient, scowling face.

'Hardly the Hollywood waif.'

Ava fidgeted, loathing Tilly's scrutiny. Tilly grimaced, tucking her cigarette pack down the elastic waist of her pants. She hoisted her handbag on her left shoulder and eased slowly from chair to Zimmer frame. Her body curved over it. She lifted the right side of the frame forward and, turning, let it drop, and her body followed. She repeated the action to the left. Each time, her bag slid and dangled awkwardly from shoulder to wrist. Tilly stopped to shove it up and in this painstaking fashion headed to the corridor, where her handbag promptly opened and spilt. Ava scooped its contents: an ancient brown purse, three packs of full-strength cigarettes, two lighters, a frosted-pink lipstick, smeared mirror, four packets of medication, matted blue comb, tissues (mostly used), a wad of £20 notes, a handful of change and bits of scrawled-on paper. Ava dropped everything in the bag. A scattering of dusty detritus was left on the tiled floor.

'Would you like me to carry it?' Ava asked quietly, reminding herself that Tilly was in pain, most likely had dementia and adversely affected by a toxic mixture of drugs. Tilly nodded her ashen face. Slowly, they proceeded to the entrance hall where a line of female staff, fronted by Robbie, awaited. A wheelchair rolled up and Tilly eased into it. The women were poised, beauty-parade-style, with left legs pointing to forty-five degrees, heads forward-looking and eyes swivelling. It appeared totally disconcerting to Ava. Robbie's wetted hair was brushed flat but reasserting itself upwards. He stepped forward, holding out the roses he'd lopped off and tied with red ribbon. Tilly looked at Ava who guessed she was meant to take them, like a lady-in-waiting. She felt a curtsey would not have been amiss.

'Fetch the box from under the bed,' Tilly commanded.

'Please,' said Ava, standing her ground. Seconds passed and many eyes swivelled.

'Please,' hissed Tilly, with a sullen twist of her lips, moving her jaw from side to side. Ava fetched the hefty box.

'Open it,' said Tilly, imperiously. Ava waited. 'Please, for goodness sake. The pink ones are for the women and blue for Robbie.' Ava handed them out. She noticed Evangeline didn't open hers. There were three spare blue packages.

'Evangeline,' announced Tilly. 'I'm glad you ditched that miserable man because you are a whole lot happier.' The women nodded and Robbie smiled. Tilly rolled along. 'Maisie, don't drag your feet again. No clippity-clop. Pick them up.' Maisie beamed. 'Hannah, you've made a sterling effort over the last seven weeks.' Hannah looked around, blushing. 'Remember, let your hands swing at your sides and stand a little way back from people. You're a giantess, so you mustn't stoop. Keep your distance. You could be a model and earn more in a day than here in a month of Sundays.' Hannah looked like she'd won the lottery. 'You all need to think elegant, confident and upmarket. Dress like you are about to meet your worst enemy, or me. There's been a marked improvement in your figures and deportment. Especially you, Barbara.' Barbara looked down. 'Another couple of months and you could get that dream job with EasyJet!' Barbara did a shimmy with a hand on her hip and everyone but Ava clapped.

'Robbie,' Tilly said, 'last but not least. You've got the longest way to go. But you're a man and that's only to be expected.' There was laughter. 'Thank God I've never seen you in that stretchy black stuff middle-aged men wear.'

'Proper English men don't wear that, or dance,' he stated.

'Fine with the first but you should learn to dance, women love it. Now open your presents.'

The women took the pink boxes, unpeeled bubble wrap and pulled out mugs. They had an image of a clean-shaven, muscle-bound man with a slippery smile. He had a naked, bronzed torso and wore skin-tight, shiny red shorts. Robbie's version was a buxom blonde in a red bikini and white stilettos, wielding a drooping hosepipe.

'Make tea,' commanded Tilly, clapping her hands. 'Barbara, there's two blue boxes for the ambulance men and can someone bring that one to Captain Birds Eye? I want to say goodbye to him.' Barbara waited. 'Please,' added Tilly, irritated. Barbara winked at Ava as she wheeled Tilly to the lounge. Ava noted how other female residents ignored Tilly and greedily listened.

'Captain Birds Eye,' said Tilly, kissing the white-bearded man's hand. 'I ordered this from that Amazonian market, so you can think of me with every sip.' A nurse placed the Captain's mug on the table and poured in tea. There were gales of laughter from the kitchen. The hot water melted away the woman's bikini, leaving a pneumatic-nude holding a now upright hosepipe.

'The effect only lasts a minute if it's cold,' said Tilly, watching Captain Birds Eye's lopsided grin. 'So, it'll stay for hours in this furnace.' The Captain nodded, wiped a tear away and put his good thumb up as Tilly waved and was rolled out.

'What an eyeful,' a nurse said, at the front door, holding her male mug. 'Tilly, you're a terror. This guy would shame a cucumber.' She silenced as a frowning nurse bustled over, carrying two large plastic bags which she held out to Ava. Tilly blanked her.

'I'm Sister Lynch,' she said. 'Here's Tilly's washing and her medication. I've written down her drug regime. Mrs Barwise hasn't drunk brandy for nearly eight weeks.' Tilly made a growly sound and shut her eyes. 'You'll have to be vigilant.' Tilly puffed out her lips. Nurse Lynch's face softened. 'I'll put Tilly's suitcase in the ambulance and hope you feel better soon; those cuts and bruises look nasty. You'll have your hands full.'

'Thank you,' said Ava. Another nurse squeezed Ava's arm, 'Good luck,' she whispered and handed Tilly the poster-sized swimsuit photograph.

'No, it stays, so you don't guzzle and slouch,' said Tilly, with a hard stare at Nurse Lynch. Ava noted Tilly's eyes filled and her bottom lip trembled as she was rolled outside.

Chapter Thirteen

May 14th, 1943

Woodburn

USA

Dear Son,

I'm on my knees morning and night praying for you to come back to your loving family and fiancée. Jess is pining for you. She's so helpful looking after your sister and baby Dorothy – whom I have to say looks a lot like you and is as noisy as you were at the same age. She also seems to need very little sleep and your sister's exhausted. I've been very poorly – my heart and all the worry about you going and your brother joining up. Thank God for Church. The congregation is so good to me. Your father doesn't talk about anything much. He listens to the radio in his shed for hours and hours on end. I've knitted you more thick socks. I'm counting the days until you're home. Do you remember the Sudbury's over the road? The father was run over by his own car when he was changing the wheel. There you are, in harm's way and yet, he was simply changing a tyre. It's God's will and that's why I pray night and day.

All my love,

Mom

Trevone Bay, June 2015

Ava followed the ambulance through winding lanes. Thoughts of

Josh and Sadie flooded her and memories of former colleagues and friends – the 349 of them on Facebook and Instagram. For Ava, there were no more snaps of cheery nights out, cosy nights in, drinks drunk, restaurants enjoyed, holidays experienced, weddings attended and babies born. Being dumped and divorced was to be a social media pariah. Once, Ava would have uploaded photographs of the bright gorse blossom as it blew across moorland like confetti. She'd have Instagrammed delicate, unfolding ferns, velvety mosses and lichens that crept over ancient stone walls. She might have printed a shot of the fairy tale, wind-stunted trees. Now, her life was undocumented; disconnected. The matted sheep that cropped the carpet of cowslips to an impressionist furzy yellow and jewel-like heather crammed in granite outcrops where terns flipped in gusts, were just hers to remember. Halting at a crossroads, Ava heard a curlew's mournful cry. She had never felt so alone.

At Cliff View, paramedics trundled Tilly up the bumpy path. Her head jerked at each step, as if her neck would break. Ava ran forward and put the key in the door. From behind, there was a scrabbling noise. A rat? She hesitantly shouldered it apart a fraction, hoping it would skedaddle. Silence. She eased it open and a flapping bird with taffeta-stiff feathers flashed past. Ava stared into a yellow-rimmed eye. A paramedic shielded Tilly as the bird batted over, trailing a pervasive oily smell.

'Crow,' said Tilly. 'Means big changes and death coming. A fine welcome.'

'No, you need a chimney pot cover,' said the driver, pointing at the roof where crows bobbed and fluttered. Ava stepped into the front room to knocked over photographs, vase and candlesticks.

Gooey brown and green crap smeared furniture and blue-black feathers blew about the floor.

'I'll clean up,' said Ava, efficiently, as the men lifted Tilly through and gently placed her into the high-backed chair by the TV. It seemed to enfold her. She closed her eyes and winced, as her face drained to grey. Tilly lit a cigarette, inhaled. Ava grabbed a spray, cloth and paper towels to mop the mess, then dumped Tilly's bags in the kitchen and tipped out the medication. There was a pile of liquids, tablets and creams fit to stock a pharmacy.

'Thank you, gentlemen. I've left your gifts in the ambulance,' Tilly announced. 'They're the same as Robbie's, so enjoy.'

'I prefer the male version,' said the bald, muscular one.

'What a waste for us women,' said Tilly.

'Guys don't think that,' he answered cheerily.

Ava came and said goodbye, shutting the front door. It felt like sealing herself inside a sarcophagus.

'Thank God I'm home, if not alone,' said Tilly, loudly. Ava waited. 'I want to watch TV and have a brandy.'

'I'll be with you in a minute,' she replied, heading back to the kitchen, biding her time, biting her nails. Ava made tea in a spare Ann Summers mug, watching the man's shorts turn translucent and disappear. He must have had surgery, Ava thought, holding a spoon in the air.

'Do you take sugar?' asked Ava. She didn't have a clue of even the basics.

'Not in brandy,' replied Tilly.

'In tea,' answered Ava, firmly.

'Bloody tea, I've been swimming in it. No sugar, a splash of milk and brandy on the side. It's been two months for God's sake.'

Ava sympathised, having survived on gin for the last six. She put tea on a tray with a cream cheese sandwich, minus crusts and cut in quarters. The mug man's shorts re-formed as she handed the tray over.

'I've seen men come and go a lot quicker,' said Tilly, eyes roving the tray. 'Where's my brandy?'

'Not yet,' said Ava. It was tucked under the kitchen sink; cheap stuff, bright orange. Tilly screwed up her face, smoking. She's like a vacuum, thought Ava, imagining the tarry, popcorn surface of her lungs.

'There's no point you being here if I can't enjoy what I would alone, is there?' Tilly waved the TV controller at Ava, as if she were a channel she could zap off. Ava commiserated silently; she'd be mad as hell if someone treated her like a child at nearly 90.

'Vicky told me I wasn't to allow alcohol until after 6pm,' Ava said, 'and then a little one. Nurse Lynch didn't think you should have it at all. I understand it's difficult but I have my orders.'

'Vicky, Nurse Lynch and orders. You'd have done well on the other side in the war. We'll see.' Her face flushed and fingers tapped the chair.

'I can leave,' replied Ava, icily. 'But you'll be in a home.' Tilly inhaled and flicked her cigarette in the ashtray. A corrosive silence bloomed.

'What time is it?' asked Tilly, her eyes sliding to the folded *Daily World* next to her.

'1.15pm,' said Ava. The newspaper was picked up. Ava weighed up calling Vicky and booking a train but didn't feel up to travel. The grandfather clock ticked. Tilly switched on the TV and it crackled into life. A woman on screen ate a mouthful of food which she spat straight out. It drew Tilly's attention like a magnet.

'OK, here's the deal. Morphine now and brandy at 6pm. Only because I can't manage but the minute I can, I will.' Tilly pulled her lips into her empty mouth. 'What happened to your face?'

'Swimming,' said Ava. Bitch, she thought. It was a relief when the phone rang.

'Hello lovely, is Madam back?' May's breezy voice asked.

'Yes, like a hurricane,' whispered Ava, although the TV was loud enough to speak normally.

'Mmm. Asked for brandy? Threatened you?'

'Both.'

'Did you give in?'

'Negotiated a weak brandy at 6pm which Vicky said was acceptable. Tilly's only agreed because she can't find it herself.'

'Good, stick to your guns from the start. Jeff said you must be a tough cookie after what you've gone through.' Ava winced at being the subject of continued gossip.

'There was a card of a well-endowed faun in her room which she says was from a lover?' Now, here she was, gossiping.

'Oh that,' said May, dismissively. 'It's from Padstow's upmarket estate agent, Peter Hogwood. He's buttering her up to sell Cliff View if she goes into a home. Or dies.'

'Who's that?' Tilly shouted.

'May,' said Ava.

'It should be me she's talking to.' Tilly increased the TV volume to ear-splitting proportions.

75

'I'd better go,' said Ava.

'Don't try to be Tilly's friend, Ava. I'm coming in to clean tomorrow morning. You'll need a break after 24 hours. Oh, there's arnica gel for bruises in the first aid box in the bathroom.'

She said goodbye and stood listening to Tilly rant at the TV. Ava had no intention of being Tilly's friend. Not ever. May called Sniffy Dave at the Golden Lion to check how betting was going. Sniffing, Dave informed her there was £300 in the kitty since news of Ava's near-drowning and Tilly's return. He'd closed the book but not before someone came forward at the last minute to bet Ava stayed. He wouldn't divulge who, no matter how May pried.

Ava gathered Tilly's medication and signed it off in a little black book.

'Here you go,' said Ava, handing it over with water. Tilly put out her shaky hand, glued to the TV programme of Z-list celebrities competing to cook.

'Eating's the new religion,' said Tilly, swallowing the tablet. Ava noticed she'd torn her sandwich into small bite-sized pieces. Tilly's jaw clicked and the stringy sinews of her neck moved up and down like an ancient tortoise. Her face was ghastly white.

'Are you OK?' asked Ava, hoping she was not going to die within half-an-hour of being solely in her care.

'I have to wait until the morphine works. Don't look at me. I want you, as far as possible, to keep away.' And she promptly fell asleep, letting the TV control slip from her grasp. Her mouth opened, revealing a furry, white tongue. A crumb of moist bread clung to her lower lip. Ava plucked the cigarette from her hand and stubbed it out. She'd like to be a million miles away. She'd have to watch this crone like a hawk. She observed Tilly's sleeping face; the gouged frown lines and a deep lattice work encircling her mouth. Crepe-like wrinkles hung on cheeks and neck. Sun damage had created swirls of splotches and merged freckles. The skin on Tilly's upper chest was so creased it resembled a puddle of congealed gravy with its own delta-system. Ava tucked a blanket over Tilly's legs, then stepped into the sheltered garden and breathed: a cool, clear draught. The grey sky near Cliff View was rinsed of rain which stippled the darkening ocean. Swallows darted into eaves with liquid, high-pitched chirping and lilac blossom perfumed the air. A ladybird landed on her hand. For twenty minutes thoughts of what she'd lost raced through her mind.

'I want to go to bed and watch the dance programme at 8pm,' Tilly called croakily. Ava eased her onto the Zimmer frame and they moved, as if underwater, to her bedroom.

'I can tell you're a Catholic by your eyebrows,' stated Tilly. 'Bushy. And your nose; the way it spreads.'

Ava recalled school bullies who'd picked on her; the quiet, shy girl with NHS glasses and a pink patch over one lazy eye. But Tilly was right. Her mother was a lapsed Catholic who'd kept Ava well away from church.

'Right,' Ava said stopping. 'Say every nasty thing you want and then maybe you can be civil or at least quiet. I don't need to talk to you. Or listen to how mean you are. I know I'm not beautiful and you have been but I'll never grieve for my looks. You can choose to get on with me and make our lives easier, or I can leave right now.'

Tilly pursed her lips until they touched her nose and blew over them. Her fungal breath was a noxious mix of cigarettes, age and medication.

'I'll be on my feet in two weeks and then you can go,' Tilly snapped.

'Good. My face will be healed and I'll be happy to leave.'

'As long as you know I'd rather be on my own,' sniffed Tilly.

'And I'd rather you were on your own.' They shuffled on together.

Tilly sighed. 'Finally, I need a crap.'

The toilet's extra-high plastic seat resembled a giant potty with handrails. Tilly backed on and perched. Ava eased her jogging bottoms and pants down, exposing thin, flabby shanks. She took a breath and averted her face. There was the body noise, fetid reek and groan. It turned Ava's stomach. Without looking Ava tore paper and handed it to Tilly who tried to clean herself but couldn't. Ava took many more sheets and eyes closed, wiped the fleshless, cold bottom. She gagged, bile flooding her mouth and Tilly froze. Ava flushed the loo, turned to the sink, spat in it and scrubbed her hands with lemon soap under scalding water.

'Sorry,' she said. Tilly was mute. Ava felt shame sting her cheeks as she helped Tilly forward, catching sight of a straggle of white pubic hair. Wrinkled skin wrapped the drooping envelope of her pale striated belly, etched with silvery stretch marks as if scaly talons had raked it long ago. For a moment their faces almost touched until Tilly leant on the walking frame. It must be vile to have someone wipe your arse; thought Ava and she'd rather die than be in that position.

'What's for dinner? I hope it's not pasta or rice rubbish.'

'Braised beef with carrots and potatoes,' said Ava, relieved to cover up the awkwardness. Tilly's eyes widened. 'Then steamed lemon pudding and custard.'

'Meat's hard without these,' said Tilly, pointing to her mouth.

'It'll melt,' Ava hoped, as she eased Tilly into bed and drew the thick curtains. The room darkened, Round Hole soughed and a blackbird languidly trilled. Tilly's eyes closed and she slept as if a light was extinguished. She appeared wizened and something else, thought Ava, as she washed her hands again, goblin-like after all her incandescent beauty. Looking in the mirror, she touched her own face; her young, elastic skin, despite the injuries. Ava needed a spark of life in it. Accompanied by Tilly's robust snoring, she put on Nat King Cole singing *Stardust*.

The poisoned meadows of my heart, thought Ava, as she mashed potatoes with melted butter in warm milk, adding chopped spring onions and a pinch of sweet and peppery nutmeg. Needle-sharp rain pattered in. She put the heating on low and Cliff View felt cosy. The telephone rang and Ava answered quickly so Tilly wasn't disturbed.

'How's Mummy?' asked Vicky in her unmistakeable clipped tones.

'She's fine, asleep and not had a drink. I've sorted her medication and made beef casserole.'

'Good,' said Vicky. 'Anything else?' She sounded suspicious.

'No,' said Ava, touching her bruises. She wasn't going to complain; she'd manage.

'Ava,' said Vicky, 'Mummy will not show the slightest appreciation for what you do.' Vicky sounded vastly experienced.

Chapter Fourteen

Watford Road, Anfield, Liverpool, May 14th, 1943

'Anaemia,' Elizabeth diagnosed, with one hand pulling down the lower eyelid of her daughter's pale and truculent face, while the other rested on dusted suitcases, ready for Ireland. Tilly twisted her head away. 'At least I hope it's that.' The air crackled with her mother's bad temper and innate accusations. Tilly slammed her bedroom door, dressed and soaped the faint bruise on her left cheek where Elizabeth had struck her. Nothing that couldn't be disguised by a dab of foundation and stolen puff of her mother's powder. Tilly hid the last scrapings of Helena Rubenstein's Regimental Red lipstick, black mascara and stub of eyeliner that doubled as eyebrow pencil into her handbag. These would be applied on the top deck of the bus. She buttoned a close-fitting cream dress, well hidden under her navy coat. No stockings; her pale legs would be smeared in a light coating of gravy browning. She prayed it wouldn't rain.

Elizabeth waylaid her in the hallway, arms full of pressed clothes and eyes narrowed.

'I'm telling you now, if you ever get in the family way,' she hissed, 'you'll leave home and never come back.'

'I'm not stupid, Mum,' she snapped.

'There's many a girl who said that and lived to regret it,' Elizabeth replied. Of course, her mother hadn't got pregnant before marriage but regretted everything anyway. Tilly's heels clipped down deserted Watford Road, butterflies in her stomach. She hummed Glenn Miller's *Moonlight Cocktail*.

Oh, how she longed to dance with Jack! She waltzed, holding out her hands as if they were on the small of his back and shoulder. Her Dad turned the corner and stopped at the sight of his daughter.

'And where are you going?' he asked, amused, taking out his cigarettes.

'To the flicks. With Rose.' She felt the prickling heat of a blush. William raised an eyebrow, tapped a cigarette on the back of his wrist and handed it to her.

'Well, enjoy yourself because your mother never has.' He pressed a sovereign in Tilly's hand. 'For emergencies; don't pay for a damn thing.' William adjusted his hat and walked on, whistling *Waltzing Matilda*. It was the last time she'd see him alive. On the bus, Tilly applied make-up, spitting on the cake mascara to moisten it. She lit a Pall Mall, staining the end with scarlet lipstick, knots snaking in her stomach.

From the top deck, Tilly spied Jack at the dock wall. Hands shoved casually in trouser pockets and cigarette dangling out of the left side of his lips. Lips she wanted on hers. He scanned the milling Saturday crowds. Tilly got off the bus a little way ahead, so he'd get a good look at her arrival. She walked like Aunty Vi had drummed into her: shoulders back, rolling hips, chin tipped slightly up and looking dead ahead. When Jack's eyes locked on to hers, he flung his cigarette down, opened his arms and Tilly poured herself into them. He kissed her like she was the best meal in the world and instantly undid all the knots in her.

'Do you need to be home by midnight, Cinderella?' he asked.

'No,' she said, firmly.

'Mmm that's good... You look a million dollars, ma'am,' he murmured, and she felt he'd said it inside her head with his deep, gorgeous accent. Jack walked with his arm circling her waist, keeping himself nearest the road; a gentleman. He stopped at an open-top jeep and as if she was a princess, pulled open the passenger door for her. She remembered what Aunty Vi had taught her. Turn to the side and sit, slide across the seat, pick up your pointed feet and keeping them close together, from ankle to thigh, twist into the car, elegantly. Bingo.

Jack jumped over his driver's door, tugged his cap on, jammed in the keys, yanked out the choke and kissed her until the engine kicked in. She didn't care who saw. Tyres squealed as he reversed. He raced along the dock road and Tilly, laughing, held her hair down until he gave her his cap. It smelt of citrus oil. Tilly's dress flared up and Jack pulled the hem down, leaving his hand on her thigh, like an anchor, unless he changed gear. Someone threw a bottle at the jeep and it smashed off the side.

'Jealous,' said Jack, 'and who wouldn't be with you next to me? I got your postcard, although a lot of other guys wanted to claim it. And here's your picture, it'll be in our *Stars and Stripes* newspaper.' Tilly thrilled as he rummaged under the dashboard and handed her an envelope. Tilly opened it and there she was, against the harbour wall, seagull to one side, light pouring through clouds over the Mersey and her stealing the scene: reed-slim, full-lipped, looking straight into the camera, intent in her eyes. She thanked him and slipped it into her handbag. Guards saluted as they swept through the gates of sprawling Burtonwood where scores of jeeps rocked along deep muddy ruts. Despite the black-out Tilly noted the decent-looking men checking her out. She'd finally found heaven.

'Welcome to USAAF Station 590, Battle Maid,' Jack said. He jumped out of the jeep and opened her door. Tilly slid out, legs first, bottom last, and into his arms like mercury. He lifted her across mud and pulled her into a doorway where he kissed her deeply and she kissed him back. He pushed the door open. They were inside a hangar as big as a cathedral, filled with Liberators, Wellingtons, Beauforts and Spitfires. The planes had paintings near the cockpits of well-endowed women, wearing French knickers, or swimsuits, with names like Heavenly Body, Briefing Time, Stripped for Action, and Honey Bunny. The fuselage nearest them was criss-crossed with gashes and holes.

'This is where the fixable get fixed,' he said, smoothing a section of damaged wing with his palm.

'Well, I've come to the right place,' she said, and as they kissed, an ear-splitting rumbling erupted. Tilly's body vibrated. Jack shouted it was engine test beds and they could be felt in Warrington.

'I know where I feel them,' Tilly yelled back and he laughed. Jack led her to the blacked-out Officers' Mess, bright with lights and buzzing with music, talk and laughter, mixed with the scents of smoke, hair oil, perfume and fresh sweat. Couples danced and drank in candlelight and tasselled red standard lamps. Jack told her that 18,000 servicemen were stationed there: English, American, Czech, Canadian, New Zealand, Australian and Polish. It was as if the uniformed male world was decanted in this ramshackle space. The main room had numerous Allied flags draped on walls, along with a dartboard, juke box and football games. A long bar was laden with beer barrels, whisky, gin and drinks Tilly had never seen. Even an icebox. Cash passed over the wooden counter like confetti. Jack offered her a rum and Coke. She'd never tasted one and nodded. A barman smiled and winked as he crammed ice into a tumbler half-full of golden rum. He topped it with Coca-Cola and a fat squeeze of lime. Another thing she'd not seen or tasted. The short blond guy who'd been with Jack that first time gave Tilly a slimy look and strutted out. She was mystified but didn't ask. The rum tasted sweet, sour, cold and delicious. Jack drank and passed an ice cube from his mouth into hers. She took it out and went to put it down his collar but he grabbed her hand, shook the ice free and led her to the dance floor as the band struck up a jitterbug, *Nat Bookbinder and His Chapter*. Tilly followed his steps, slowly at first but she was a good mover and quick learner. He danced, Tilly thought, like a devil on hot bricks. She loved it. After two more drinks and an hour of dancing she asked for the lavatory.

'Restroom,' said Jack, 'is through the door and turn right.' He traced his hand down her spine, resting it on the small of her back, his thumb moving in a slow circle.

The shadowy bathroom had scrawl over the walls: hearts, kisses, lewd swear words and crude drawings. In the gloom Tilly held her face an inch from the mirror to reapply lipstick. A short woman with dark hair emerged from a toilet and loomed close enough for her breath to steam over Tilly's reflection. She stank of drink.

'Hello,' Tilly said, putting her lipstick away and shutting her handbag. The woman was too close for comfort.

'Keep to your own kind,' the woman slurred, in an American

accent. 'Our men are lonesome enough to fuck a woman who hasn't had stockings or chocolate for a while.'

'Some of us are just plain lucky, as opposed to just plain,' retorted Tilly smoothly, and swept out. The band played *Bounce me Brother with a Solid Four*, and Jack bounced her over a wooden floor, sticky with drinks, and air fogged with smoke. He controlled her and for Tilly it was the perfect vertical expression of horizontal desire. He held her wrists tightly, flung her out and pulled her close in a second, tipped her to one side, bringing her up and in for a kiss.

'You move swell,' he said, his left hand sliding around her waist, gripping it.

'So, do you,' she said, breathless. They were a team. The admiring crowd made space around them, cheering and whistling. Sweat trickled down her back. When the song ended, they were clapped off the dancefloor.

'A surprise to drink?' he asked, and caught the bartender's eye, waving notes in the air. He bought frothy beer for himself and a whisky sour – bourbon dashed with lemon and sugar – for her, another new, explosive taste. It made her eyes water and chest burn.

'Tell me Jack, where are you from and what you do when you aren't saving our country?' He watched her mouth as she spoke. She pressed her lips together hoping they were still a little red and that her face wasn't the same colour.

'Ma'am, I'm from Woodburn, near West Virginia's Blue Ridge Mountains and it's the prettiest place in the world but not as pretty as what I'm looking at right now.' She nodded, practically purring. 'Woodburn has hot summers, big rivers and huge forests as far as the eye can see. I'm a geologist hunting oil from the air, and because

I fly and take photographs I was posted to reconnaissance. We're the eyes of the army, ma'am.'

'Oh, that's quite something,' said Tilly. It was quite something impossibly glamorous to be drinking whisky sours with a geologist, pilot and photographer from the Blue Ridge Mountains. It sounded like paradise on earth compared with what she did for a living in sodden, terraced Watford Road at the arse-end of Liverpool docks.

'What do you do, Battle Maid?' he asked.

'Look after records for convoy ships, making sure, if they arrive, to record what has been delivered.' To Tilly it sounded every bit as uninteresting as it was. 'Why don't we play darts?' she asked, to divert him from her dull occupation and prevent him from asking about her even duller family. Jack looked surprised and even more so as Tilly gathered a bevy of male admirers as she hit the board with expertise, easily beating Jack. Thanks Dad, she thought, taking a winning curtsey.

A bell rang out and there was a great cheer. Jack led Tilly through double doors into a side room. There was a long table covered in crisp white linen and laden with silver cutlery. Upon it lay food fit for kings and queens: chicken, salmon, proper white bread, ham, eggs, and crispy chips.

'I'm starving,' Tilly said, and like a rat out of the trap for food she hadn't clapped eyes on, ever, let alone during rationing, fell upon the feast. You could spot the British women because decorum flew out of the window. Tilly ate like a wolf, with her hands, licking fingers. Jack smiled. She finished everything on her plate plus two more chicken thighs and a heap of salted *fries* as he called them.

'Little Gannet,' Jack teased. The woman from the toilet strolled by, flashing Tilly a dirty look. Tilly smiled and kissed Jack with her salty lips.

'Let's go,' he said, taking hold of her hand and they left the party. Rain drummed on the mess tin roof, like a thousand rolling marbles. The muddy ground was now a squelching quagmire and wooden boards crossing it almost floated. Jack bent and with cigarette dangling, jerked his head for Tilly to jump on his back. She took five steps back, ran and leapt, clasping her long legs round him. He gingerly trod on the planks, slithered but didn't fall. Tilly squealed and grasped his shoulders. The rain drenched them. When his cigarette dropped, Jack stopped to ensure it was out. At a building not much bigger than a stable, he unlocked the door and slid Tilly inside. She was dripping but didn't have a speck of mud on her. Her gravy-dyed legs however, were streaked and she quickly wiped them with her handkerchief. Jack put a finger to his lips, closed the door, locked it and switched on a bare light bulb. It swung so their faces flared and disappeared, illuminating a single bed, chest of drawers, taped and blacked-out window. Jack opened a drawer and drew out a stub of candle. He lit it, with his back to her.

'Do you want me to take you home now?' he asked in a low, warm voice.

'No,' she answered, hearing her unsteady breathing. There was only the guttering candle as he drew her close, kissing and unzipping her damp dress, dropping it on a chair. She thrilled at the touch of his hands confidently curving around her buttocks. He unclipped her stockings and slipped off her underwear giving a low whistle at her nakedness in the flickering darkness as he stripped off his clothes, strewing them on the floor. He pulled her on the squeaking bed and she felt the heat of his skin and beat of his heart. He smelt of fresh sweat and she loved the dark chest hair that became a single line over his flat stomach to his cock. He took out a Johnny from under the pillow, put it on and pulled Tilly on top of him; like she was weightless. He steadied her there, moving slowly inside her. It was worlds away from the all-too rapid thrusts of the farmer's son she'd jettisoned her virginity with.

'Steady,' he said, holding her waist. 'Slowly,' he commanded. Tilly felt as if she was building up to sneeze with her entire body, and the more deeply she breathed, the more intense that feeling became. Jack waited, kissing her until she cried so loudly, he put his hand over her mouth.

'Good,' he said, and let himself go too. That was her first orgasm. She didn't even know what it was; only that he lit a fire in her that would last a lifetime. He tucked her beside him and they shared a cigarette, the glowing ends illuminating their mouths.

'I'm heading for Cornwall tomorrow,' he said, softly. She replied she was being forced to Ireland. And that was that.

'Do you like children?' he asked, inhaling, lacing her fingers with his.

'I find them generally irritating but not as much as a lot of adults I know.' Jack laughed.

'Very well Battle Maid, what do you think of this? A British Major is heading to Trevone Bay, near the airbase I'll be stationed at. His ill wife and two young sons are there already. She isn't coping. The nanny sent to help them has been struck down with Scarlet Fever. You'd have to come tomorrow.'

Tilly hesitated for all of three seconds. 'Yes.' Her heart

hammered. What else was there? Her mother, sister, and Ireland.

'Good. Then there's a letter to write.' He got up, pulled open a drawer, took out a pen and paper and stood there. Tilly thought he looked like a stunning Greek statue.

Snap decisions were easy in the war. You could disappear like frost in May. If something needed to be done there were no questions asked. Tilly concocted a letter from her mother giving herself permission to leave home and work as a nanny with her exemplary child-rearing abilities. Jack dressed and went to track down the Major, who'd taken to whisky and rubber-stamped his approval. Tilly washed at the room's sink and when Jack came back, mission accomplished, they returned to Anfield; laughing and chatting; thrilled at their plans. When Jack pulled up, Tilly wrote a note to her parents, explaining about the job but not where it was or who it was with. Her hands shook. At 1am she stole into her home for the final time. It smelt of ashes and cabbage. Heart thudding, she crept in and up, knowing every creaking stair to avoid, listening to double parental snoring and took a last look at her younger sister, sucking her thumb. Tilly picked up the suitcase her mum had packed for Ireland, her ID and papers. She propped the letter on the kitchen table, took a final look around and slipped out to Jack.

Chapter Fifteen

Diary entry: Burtonwood Airbase, May 15th, 1943

On the move and I've sent a dame to where I'm headed. Danny picked a fight but I punched him right back and laid him out. I don't know why I've been so reckless, only that I met Tilly and never felt like that before. She slept with me and that should make me feel bad about her. I know I don't want to marry Jess. Or hurt her. I probably won't live to sort out the mess.

Trevone Bay, June 2015

The grandfather clock chimed 7pm as daylight turned a translucent green that foretold rain. Ava made tea in the naked-man mug and tapped on Tilly's bedroom door. There was no answer and she gingerly opened it. Tilly was on her back; her puckered mouth a slack, dark O shape. Her breath puffed out and saliva tracked to a damp patch on the pillow. The smell of her; sour-milk and fish. Ava stepped back out of the room, closed the door, breathed deeply and rapped.

'Vicky?'

'No, Ava.' She counted five seconds and entered. Tilly regarded her blankly.

'Your carer,' said Ava, placing the mug on a coaster which stated, *When Irish eyes are smiling, they're up to something.*

'I know who you are. I'm not bloody senile. Help me sit up.'

Fair enough, thought Ava, as her hands wrapped around

Tilly's rib bones, which felt light and fragile as a bird's. Tilly wouldn't look at her. Ava returned to the kitchen, ladling stew onto a wide plate, heaping on carrots and mash. The tang of steaming lemon sponge almost covered the stink of cigarettes. Ava opened the French windows and decided this and her bedroom would be fag-free zones. She carried in the tray.

Tilly was engrossed in TV and without looking, leant back as Ava placed the tray before her. On screen, a bottle-blonde called Chelsea, with waist-length hair extensions, wiggled along a city street in knee-length white boots. Her clingy cream dress only just contained pneumatic breasts. Trotting alongside Chelsea, a chatty presenter halted random, unremarkable men, asking if they'd *Snog, Marry or Avoid* the blonde bombshell? Tilly was transfixed. She picked up her knife and fork but made no move to eat.

'Thank you,' said Ava to herself, and waited.

Tilly peered at the food, sniffed it, forked a piece of meat but let it hover by her lips, as man after man rejected Chelsea. Ava thought Chelsea's drone would be a turn-off as much as the caked orange foundation, navy eye shadow and tarantula lashes. Ninety per cent of the nondescript manhood swore they'd avoid her like the plague. Ten per cent admitted they'd kiss her after several pints, and not one wanted to marry her. Despite the poor quality of testosterone on offer, crestfallen Chelsea acquiesced to a make-under. Her clothes, shoes, hair, and nail extensions were dumped. It took half a pack of cleansing wipes to denude her face. Post-transformation, Chelsea's hair became a sleek, auburn bob and she emerged in a figure-skimming navy suit, teamed with crisp, white shirt and black Cuban heels. She now kept pace with the presenter.

'Will you look at her?' declared Tilly, fork finally entering her mouth. 'Walks like a duck, croaks like one and dressed like a boring bank clerk.' Tilly gummed the stew. 'She's so bloody Marks and Spencer now,' she muttered, as gravy dribbled. She frowned, forking another mouthful. Ava thought Tilly must have gums of steel the way she clamped them up and down.

'Not bad. What's your name again?' she said.

'Ava.' She wondered about a name tag.

'Perhaps you're too good a cook,' said Tilly, her rheumy eyes skimming Ava's hips as she shovelled in creamy mash. 'You've put spring onions and butter in, like I used to eat in Buncrana in the War.' She swirled her fork and stabbed buttery carrots. Onscreen, Chelsea prepared to repeat the street walk of fame or shame.

'The only memorable things about that windswept spot of rural Donegal,' mused Tilly, 'was zero food rationing and the Lough Swilly Hotel. That's where I got shot of my virginity in May 1941 before I met the love of my life.' It was Ava's turn to be transfixed. 'I always dressed glamorously, even there; no drab bank style for me. When the war started, I was 16. Mum sent me to live with her older sister in the hope of keeping me out of trouble. I sneaked out of my Aunt's via the bedroom window and into Swilly's bar. It was easy to drink underage if you were decent-looking. A farmer's son chatted me up and we ended up out on a balcony overlooking the Lough. The kissing was sloppy and the sex, fast and forgettable but watching a U-boat rise in the water wasn't. The Germans opened the hatch and clambered on deck. Their accents floated across the moonlit lough. God, what was that lad called? He had red, beefy hands and no idea what to do with them. He zipped himself back up and told me U-boats visited because Ireland was neutral, and he didn't mind the Jerries. I slapped him and left him standing. He didn't have to cower in a Liverpool cellar waiting to be blown to bits.'

Ava saw Tilly's younger self rise up in her like smoke, as she savoured the stew and Chelsea was triumphantly proclaimed a man-magnet.

'She's dull,' sneered Tilly. 'I'd like brandy now. You said I could and I've waited long enough. Please.' Her tongue was practically hanging out.

'Of course.' Ava retrieved the bottle and poured a shot. It smelt as if it could strip stomach lining. Tilly's hands shook as she clamped her lips on the rim so not to spill a drop and knocked it back. A minute later her face flushed. She looked the best Ava had seen her.

'Do you want to get up now?' asked Ava.

'Not tonight. It's been a long day. Only for the loo later and I'd like another,' said Tilly, pleading.

'I'm not allowed.' She felt cruel.

'I'm not allowed,' Tilly repeated in a whiny voice, wobbling her head. Ava wanted to dump the bottle on her lap. She saw how miniscule Tilly's world was. She took away the plate and brought in lemon pudding. There was no thank you as Tilly tucked in and polished it off. Ava retreated to her smoke-free zone and wrote down Tilly's Donegal story, for something to do. Writing, rather than typing, felt strange and her fingers throbbed. It was terrible scrawl. All the while, Tilly talked at the TV like it was a real person.

'She's got a face like the back of a cow in action,' Tilly ranted. 'I'd rather have Dracula crawl over me than him.' Ava ate her dinner on the patio, watching the sun bleed into the sea. Bats swooped through the garden; tiny scraps of velvety darkness. A dance programme blared next and elicited Tilly's happiest responses, although she slated the panel's judgements and condemned one female contestant for flirting, 'With every single bloody man.' Jealous, decided Ava, and poured herself a cold, grassy Sauvignon Blanc. She wrapped the clean hospital gowns in brown paper, with an apologetic, anonymous note to A&E. Cigarette smoke seeped into the kitchen, so Ava double-checked the fire alarm batteries. At midnight she took a sleeping tablet for herself and made Horlicks for Tilly, who looked deliriously happy and rosy-cheeked as she slipped a shot glass under her duvet. There was the sweet tell-tale smell.

'Where did you get that from?' Ava panicked, and Tilly triumphantly pulled out an empty quarter-bottle.

'That's the last of it.'

'If you're ill, I'll be blamed,' Ava said, with visions of headlines in newspapers as the killer carer. 'It's time for bed.'

'Boring bloody bed,' she scowled. 'I've had to go to bed early for eight weeks.' Ava picked up the ashtray. Six stubs floated in cold milky tea. Ava presumed it was Tilly's fire precaution. 'I don't need to get up early and I've had my Ativan.'

'I wasn't told about Ativan,' said Ava, bewildered. It wasn't on Sister Lynch's drugs list.

'A sleeping tablet I've taken for twenty-nine years. Out like a light, every night. I need the loo now.' Ava eased Tilly out of bed and into the bathroom. The light turned Tilly's skin parchment yellow. 'I need one of those pads for my pants. They're in the cupboard.'

Ava took one out. 'I can tell you don't like being here, so you know how I feel.' Ava silently handed her the pad and Tilly pressed it down. 'You'll be in my position one day. Why are you really here?' she asked, easing off the toilet.

'Because I love looking after a grumpy old woman who hates the sight of me. It's a perfect way to earn a living.'

'Then go.'

'I can't wait.' Her temper flared. 'But for the record my husband, now ex, had an affair with a woman we worked with. She was our friend.' Rage surged like vomit through her veins. 'She's pregnant while I lost my job, husband and home. So, until you're better and I find an alternative we're stuck together.'

Tilly leaned on the Zimmer frame. 'My father had an affair with mum's sister, Aunty Vi. It ruined their marriage and I never went back home.' They were both quiet. Ava pulled up Tilly's padded pants and helped her to bed. Tilly's gnarled cold feet twisted across one another and the papery skin was blue-tinged and flaky. There were socks on the radiator.

'Do you want these on?' asked Ava. Tilly nodded. She eased socks over toenails that were thick, split, ridged and yellow-brown.

'Aunty Vi was gorgeous inside and out,' said Tilly, her eyes focussing on Ava. 'You could be striking if you lost weight and walked better. That could be a project while you're here.'

'I don't want to be your project.' Ava folded her arms.

'Don't fold your arms like that.' Ava kept them crossed. 'What did you do for a living?' Tilly asked, lying back, a playful smile on her lips.

'Wrote advertorials for a newspaper,' Ava said, unfolding her arms and plucking at the skin around her thumb.

'Oh, a writer?' said Tilly, her gummy smile widening. She folded her hands on the duvet. 'Don't disturb me until 9am, unless I call,' she commanded.

Happily, thought Ava, switching off Tilly's bedside light and transporting the filthy ashtray to the sink, scooping out butts with a spoon and into the pedal bin.

'Striking,' muttered Ava, scrubbing her hands. She thought of Sadie's all-encompassing glamour. Sadie would have had every high street man offering to marry and snog her, without retouching a hair on her wealthy head. Ava checked on Tilly. Half-dead looking but noisily alive with rasping breaths.

Ava cleaned her face, put cream on cuts and lay down with the curtains open. A gibbous moon, swathed in gauzy clouds was surrounded by twinkling stars. Waves clattered stones and Round Hole's breathing was easily surpassed by Tilly's snores. Somewhere a dog barked and a car clumsily changed gear along the coast.

Chapter Sixteen

USAF Station,
VIII Bomber Command,
RAF Daws Hill,
High Wycombe
May 15th, 1943

Jack,

You shouldn't have given in to cupid's itch with that bitch. Jessica's my cousin and you've left her in the lurch. If you don't get rid of that one, I'll tell Jess everything and never see or speak to you again.

Danny

Trevone Bay, June 2015

Ava dreamt she'd tumbled down Round Hole, plunged under the ocean and this time there was no rescue. She woke suffocating and scrabbled out of bed. Her legs and ribs ached and the green and purple fingerprint bruises of the man who saved her were well-defined. It was 6am. Ava peeked in on snoring Tilly. The airless room smelt sour. She went and sat on Tilly's high loo and peed. From the window the ocean was a mass of ruffled waves, like a shaken-out bedsheet. One lone woman ran on the beach. Ava decided a short run for five minutes, if she could manage, would be her new body-enhancing routine with no risk to life. As long as the beach was empty and Tilly stayed asleep. She rechecked and slipped on jog pants, an old black T-shirt and bare feet because her flip flops had been abandoned in the rescue. The fleet-footed woman ran way ahead with easy liquid movements. Ava jogged for two minutes; she would need a better bra, then walked until she could breathe, and repeated. Her legs fought every step of the gritty, wet sand. Swirls of slack water slid towards her and flowed slowly back. Pockets of white foam blew across the sand in sudden gusts from bubbling craters where worm-casts clumped like miniature dog turds. A flock of gulls strutted and clustered around a sea-smoothed tree trunk, the colour of over-brewed tea. The runner came near, barely rosy-cheeked compared to Ava's scarlet, dripping face. She smiled and stopped, bouncing on her toes.

'Hi, I'm Charlie. I rarely see anyone so early,' she said, eyeing Ava's injuries.

'Ava, and I don't normally run. I only started today and it's so hard.'

'Good for you, and don't worry, it takes a while. I loathe the first fifteen minutes.' Ava balked; she could not imagine overcoming that hurdle. 'I sit down all day and work with people who are reluctant to move so running feels good. Your face looks very sore.'

'Getting better. I got caught in a riptide,' Ava said, touching her neck. Shame and embarrassment prickled her skin. 'I'm lucky to be alive.'

'Oh, it was you. We heard about it. There should be more signs. You were really lucky.'

'How did you hear?' Ava asked, heart plummeting.

'Facebook. A clip with the dinghy coming in.' Charlie loosened her hair from its band; corkscrew red curls tumbled and blew wildly. Irritated, she put it straight back in a bun that resembled a rosy apple. 'You were very lucky. Are you on holiday?'

'No, I'm looking after an elderly woman in that bungalow,' Ava pointed at drab Cliff View amongst its shiny neighbours.

'Odd one out but best view. Not an easy job, I imagine,' she said, checking her watch, still bouncing.

'What do you do?' asked Ava

'NHS dietician. I came from Nottingham two years ago to be with my partner. I thought it was going to be heaven working with fit surfers, yummy mummies and walkers but Midlands deprivation is nothing compared to here. Ten miles inland and there's unemployed families in rented homes whose staple diet is takeaways and frozen food. Their kids have never seen the sea. Tourists don't glimpse that.'

A flock of Arctic Sanderlings fluttered along, all soft-grey wings and fluffed up white bodies. Their twiggy black legs blurred as they chased waves back and forth, jabbing and probing beaks in to the shoreline.

'There are families who don't eat fruit and vegetables, or fish that doesn't come in batter. My job's to persuade them to cook from scratch and exercise. It's like asking them to eat iron filings and climb Everest. I run to stop going mad.' She hesitated. 'Sorry, I'm ranting.' Ava thought about Tilly's weight obsession and how she'd grown up with strict rations, walked everywhere and didn't watch TV – regardless of her current obsession with screen, brandy and cigarettes.

Charlie checked her watch again. 'I've got to dash. Lovely to meet you and hopefully see you again? I'm out most mornings.'

'That'd be great,' called Ava, as Charlie ran off. She'd been out six minutes. Gulls flooded inland, pushed by incoming clouds and deepening sea swells. Back at Cliff View, Tilly was still fast asleep. At 9.20am there was a piercing scream.

'Morphine.'

Ava grabbed the liquid and found Tilly shaking and pale. A fishy-smelling tang hit Ava and she saw a soaked patch through the duvet. Ava dribbled the drug through her lips and waited. Five minutes later her face relaxed.

'Leave me alone,' she hissed.

'I'm going to have to change you and the bed,' Ava replied, calmly.

'Not yet. Get out.'

In the kitchen Ava watched clouds sag and split over Round Hole, cutting Cliff View adrift. Fifteen minutes passed before Tilly demanded a cigarette and tea. Ava gave her both and ran a bath, pouring in rose-scented oil and salts. She helped Tilly into the bathroom and averting her eyes, peeled off the wet nightdress and dropped it in the sink. Tilly stood on her frame, naked and bent double, like a crumpled, shell-less sea creature. The alabaster-smooth skin on her buttocks was ghostly white where the sun hadn't touched it. Her pale, flat, pendulous breasts drooped, and dark, pigmented areolas stood out. Ava gently guided Tilly into the hoist, buckled her in and pressed the button. Tilly slowly lifted and swung, inch-by-inch, up and across like a raddled Cleopatra over steaming, perfumed water.

'I'm Peter-bloody-Pan,' laughed Tilly, waving an arm, every

part of her skin loose and floppy. She was lowered into the water up to her ribs.

'Put music on, will you? And give me a cigarette.' Ava hesitated. She would probably inhale about ten of Tilly's 40-a-day. 'Please, and wait in the hall. I don't have to be watched like a baby.' Ava placed the ashtray at the side of the bath and said she'd be just outside. Tilly swished and hummed along to *Here Comes the Sun* and *Always on My Mind*, which would be men, brandy and fags. Ava donned rubber gloves, changed the bed, squished sheets and nightdress into the washing machine and wondered how her life had been reduced to this. Half-an-hour later Tilly was installed in front of the TV, mouthing buttery toast spread with honey.

'What a foggy morning!' came May's disembodied voice, through the hall. 'Then it'll be mizzle that'll turn to drizzle and a good job I know my way like the back of my hand.' She swept into the kitchen, taking off her rustling waterproof. 'Ava, your face, what a crap introduction to Cornwall.' She patted Ava's hand. Ava withdrew it. 'Give yourself a break. I'll keep an eye on her.' Relieved, Ava brushed her hair and slathered on make-up, as May sweet-talked Tilly.

'Did you hear about Dave's grandson, Alf?'

'Tell me all,' said Tilly, gleeful.

'He got completely rat-arsed in the pub, stole a tractor and careered home, writing off six cars before he tipped into a ditch. Not a scratch on him. His dad's chucked him out.'

'I'm not surprised,' replied Tilly. 'His grandson's like clotted cream; too thick and rich for his own good. Dave was the one with all the brains and looks. Well, he was in the 1970s. He once took me on a tractor ride. We enjoyed a different kind of ploughing match.'

'It's too early for that Tilly. You'll give me a hot flush. Did you watch that holiday programme last night?' She stopped as she caught sight of Ava walking down the path.

'Well? What's she like?' May asked Tilly.

*

A foghorn boomed as Ava traced her way along lanes she didn't recognise. The hissing waves, gulls and Round Hole were muted. Homes were shrouded, fields blanketed and high hedges appeared like rough, white walls. Ava shivered. She passed a half-built mansion where builders drank tea, chatted and laughed. Their radio played and the glowing tips of their cigarettes moved up and down. Ava opened the door of Beach Stores, setting off its jangly bell. Towering shelves were crammed from floor to ceiling with everything from loo rolls to cheese rolls, safety pins, frozen meals, surfboards and sunscreen. A little cafe was squeezed in at the back, all pine tables and mismatched chairs padded with green gingham cushions. There, impatient surfers bided their time with bacon butties and hot drinks, checking phones, talking surfing and reading. With coffee and the local paper, Ava sat in the far corner. The family nearby was unnaturally quiet. The bored-looking father stared into his mobile as his frowning wife spooned baked beans into their baby boy's mouth, who wriggled in a high chair. His lips and cheeks were smeared orange. The mum stopped to cut-up a pancake for their toddler daughter.

'Oh Harry!' she gasped, as her son upended the bowl on his head. Beans and sauce stuck to his hair and slid down his face, dripping onto the high chair and plastering his clothes. His sister laughed as mum picked up the bowl and dabbed at the mess with napkins. Dad's face set as he shoved his phone in his pocket and stood.

'John,' his wife spat, 'if you could just keep an eye on them instead of that bloody thing 24/7. Why do I have to do it all?'

'Calm down,' he hissed, which had precisely the opposite effect.

'Don't bloody tell me to bloody calm down.' Her voice quavered. 'I didn't want to camp in the first place. I can't sleep, neither can the kids. I'm cold, wet and I've absolutely had it.' She used a serviette to wipe her tears, transferring sauce to her face. The husband gave her a clean one. She snatched it and rubbing fiercely, spread the stain.

'Mummy, you swore,' their daughter whispered. The husband paid while his wife strapped the baby on herself, his sister in the buggy and left. It was a few minutes before conversations started. Ava opened *The Cornish Mercury* and saw the story about a rogue young tractor driver and on the next page a photograph of Evangeline and Robbie leading a line-up of smiling Somerway staff. They held the stripper mugs, carefully turned from the camera, and presented an outsize cheque for £1,000 to a veteran's charity after an unnamed female patient inspired them with her World War II Gut Buster diet and beauty tips. There was the photograph of Tilly in her scarlet costume. Nurse Evangeline Johnson was quoted:

She's still so beautiful with a stunning figure and gorgeous bone structure. Thanks to her example and dietary advice we've lost more than ten stone between us. This lady even coached us how to walk elegantly, sit down, and step out of a car, or in my case off a pedal bike. We feel healthy and raised money for a great charity.

Ava knew a potential national story when she saw one. She flicked through the paper and found her rescue on page eight. *Riptide Heroics*, three paragraphs, no name mentioned and praise for the anonymous rescuer and heroic RNLI. There was, however, a link to the video which made Ava feel sick. She turned over quickly and browsed the job pages. There was little on offer – waitressing, chefs, shop work and plant nurseries. All minimum wage, zero-hour, seasonal contracts. She glanced at properties for sale and winced. Absolutely unaffordable, even studio flats.

The fog cleared, rain fell but five minutes later, the blue sky was trailed with puffy steam-engine clouds. Chairs scraped, surfers left and Ava followed.

*

'Have you seen this?' she said, back at Cliff View, smoothing out the newspaper for May and Tilly. They pored over the story and May read it out.

'Where's my name?' she demanded, smoothing her cobweb hair. 'May, call and tell them it's me. Not my age though.'

'They aren't allowed to name you,' said Ava. 'You have to give permission because you were a patient.'

'How do you know that?' asked May, turning to her.

'She's a writer,' said Tilly.

'No, I'm not, I put together adverts.'

'That's unusual,' she said, weighing her up. 'Those girls look lovely in that photo. I need your advice Tilly, even if my catwalk's between deep fat fryers and the till. There's no chance of hip swinging there. I'd have Jeff in a health and safety spin.'

'It's a story that could take off,' warned Ava. 'It's heart-warming, plus it deals with obesity and it's nearly seventy years since World War II ended.'

'I'd better get my hair done then,' said Tilly, patting the nest. 'Trouble is, I made the diet up. Could you make it sound better, Ava? Please.'

'It's not my job,' Ava said. There was no point enlightening Tilly that cosying-up to the Press was like leaping in bed with the devil, because she'd love that.

'I could do with a bit of fun,' said Tilly. 'That disappeared long ago.'

May winked at Ava. The doorbell rang and Ava left May chatting about struggling with rationing versus a gastric band. It was Taxi Reg. Ava felt a wave of pure irritation at the sight of his great hairy face.

'Morning,' he said. 'I've brought fish.' He avoided her eyes.

'Checking I'm here?'

Reg shifted from foot to foot. His belly bulged over tatty black shorts. Clearing his throat, he said: 'It's all fresh, caught earlier and you can have the pick – before May.'

'I heard that, Reg,' May snapped.

He grinned and placed the box down, lifting its polystyrene lid. It released a sharp, fresh tang of sea. 'I've got cod, ling, whiting and pollock.' He hovered his hand over each species, like a blessing. 'That lemon sole is beautiful and mackerel's best eaten today.'

'What's that?' asked Ava, pointing to an eel-like creature with a sharp beak, green-blue back and silver-scaled belly.

'Garfish – caught it with the mackerel. They like to swim

together. Tasty but its bones stay green, like veins in leaves and a lot of people don't like that.' Ava thought it looked muscular and delicate; part bird, snake and fish. She imagined Reg hauling up each creature, twisting out hooks, bashing heads, skinning and gutting. Sometimes, Ava never wanted to eat a once-living thing again but fresh fish was still irresistible, as long as she, hypocritically, had no hand in its demise. Reg rubbed his raspy palms together; capable, working hands, thought Ava, with stubby fingers and, like hers, bitten-to-the-quick nails.

'Nice weather now the mist's lifted,' said Reg. 'Your face has gone and healed. I hardly recognised you in clothes. Sorry, you know what I mean. Are you coming to the barn dance on Friday?'

'Not even if I'm still around. I'll have smoked cod and something to make fish pie, please.'

'Nice bit of pollock and brown shrimps.' Reg wrapped each bundle in greaseproof paper and handed them over.

'How much?' queried Ava. Reg nibbled his grey beard with stained top teeth. He looked over her shoulder so intently Ava turned. Nobody was there. He simply couldn't look her in the eye.

'£15,' he said, rubbing the lobe of his right ear. 'It's good pollock.'

'No,' said Ava, '£12 and I'll consider.' Reg nodded once, without enthusiasm. Ava grabbed her bag from the coat stand and handed over the cash. 'I need a receipt.'

'I got no pen or paper,' Reg said, startled. Receipts were the last thing he wanted as they could lead to unhappy entanglements with the taxman.

Ava got both. Reg sighed, leant on his box and wrote a receipt, his hand hovering.

'It's £12.'

'I know,' said Reg, with a weak smile.

'I want the correct amount. This is for Tilly.' Reg did as he was told and trudged down the path, letting the gate slam. Ava wasn't going to give him the chance to tell anyone she'd pocketed cash and fiddled Tilly.

Chapter Seventeen

Liverpool to Cornwall, 15th May 1943

'I got this for you,' said Jack, handing Tilly a brown paper parcel, tied securely with string. 'Lunch, prepared by one Chef Brady. He remembered you dancing last night.'

'You shouldn't have told him I'm still here!' Tilly flared even as she took the package.

'I didn't, honest,' said Jack. 'It was probably some guy who let us back onto the base that spread the happy news.' Servicemen saluted them out of Burtonwood. Tilly shrank in her seat, exhausted and anxious. There was no going back. Not now, not ever, after what she'd done. Jack took hold of her hand, held it all the way to Lime Street train station, apart from changing gear. That felt better. He parked near the gothic North Western Hotel and carrying her case, they dodged trams to climb the station's steep steps and walked through arched pillars supporting a vast Victorian iron arcade and curved glass canopy. It smelt of coal, iron and dust. There were announcements, metallic clanking, hoots and whistles (of trains and men), belching smoke, along with calls of *All aboard*, slamming doors, running feet and slow-turning wheels.

Posters were plastered on every wall and designed to make Tilly feel guilty. One asked, *Is your journey really necessary?* It most certainly is, she thought, looking at Jack striding along in his gorgeous, tight-fitting uniform. Another stated, *The time has come for every person to search his conscience before making a railway journey.* My conscience is clearer by the second, she mused. One informed her: *Food, shells and fuel must come first. Do you mind if your train is crowded or late?* Definitely not, decided Tilly.

She slung her gas mask across her shoulder and while Jack bought a ticket, double-checked her National Registration Identification Card, food and clothes rationing books. She felt light as air, repeating to herself that she'd done the right thing, she really had. Anyway, it was too late. Jack strolled up, kissed her, and arm-in-arm like a newly married couple, they headed towards a chocolate-and-cream coloured train billowing steam. Her heart beat so quickly she thought Jack would feel the pulse of it in her fingertips.

Tilly stopped at the door of a second-class carriage. It was packed to the gunnels with passengers, mainly servicemen, who were like sardines on seats and even up on roof racks with legs dangling. Many more crammed into corridors. Jack shook his head and walked on a few yards to open the door to a first-class compartment. He stepped in and put out his hand to her.

'Howdy,' he said brightly, to a couple inside, who replied, 'Good morning,' barely smiling. He was an older, tired-looking man, with his left arm in a sling. His wife cradled an infant. Jack, loading Tilly's suitcase on the rack, turned to her and said quietly, 'Take care, and the Major will meet you at Newquay. If you don't like it you can always come home.' Tilly, eyes widened as she tried to stop her face showing disbelief and horror. He had no idea of the magnitude of what she'd done. Her mother would disown her. She'd also lied to Jack that she was 21, the age of independence, not

18. Vice-like fear liquefied her insides. The whistle blew on the platform and calls of *All Aboard* echoed. He kissed her again, squeezed her arm and stepped outside. Steam clouded around him as the train pulled away. She realised, coldly, that Jack thought this was all a casual plan and he'd done her a favour; got her a job and put himself in a major's good books. She sat quickly, stomach clenched, eyes down. The baby cried. Tilly glanced at its face, screwed up and scarlet. The man pulled down the corridor's blind. His wife undid the neck of her dress, covered her shoulder with a shawl and fed her son. He gulped noisily and his little hand kneaded his mother's breast like a kitten.

The heated compartment had red cushioned seats, with fold-up armrests, individual ashtrays and reading lamps. Tilly had never travelled in anything so luxurious. She stared out of the window, jittery and exhausted. The train, huffing and hissing, clattered beyond the sleepy city and into the countryside, through stations with no names and blacked-out lamps. She was due in Newquay at 2.30pm give or take an hour or two depending on trains that had right of way.

Tilly needed the toilet and taking her gas mask and handbag, slid the compartment door aside. The narrow corridor was crammed with uniformed men, American, Canadian, Polish and English, standing, sitting, sleeping, playing cards and chatting. They quietened when she stepped out and, squeezing carefully forward, was forced to make a treacle-slow way to the cubicle. It was a walk of 10 yards that felt like 100. The men tried to engage her; smiling, joking, whistling. One stated loudly that she must be a *Lady* to be in first class.

'No, she's definitely an officer,' quipped another, 'because she makes my privates stand to attention.' They roared at that. Finally, at the lavatory door, a man opened it, bowed, then smoothed his hand from Tilly's waist to hip until she stamped on his foot and everyone laughed. She was relieved to lock herself inside, barring the filthy pan. There was not one piece of Bronco paper. In desperation, she used her cotton handkerchief and flushed it away. There was no soap or towels, so she ran her hands in cold water, shook and wiped them on her skirt. She braced for the same catcalls, smiling serenely. They were interrupted by an old man in a white jacket, trundling a trolley towards them along the corridor, serving tea in jam jars because there was no crockery, or sugar, and only a drop of sour-smelling milk. But it was warm and welcome. A soldier winked as Tilly took her jar and dreamily crooned Vera Lynn's *We'll Meet Again.*

It was bliss to get back inside her plush little compartment. At a bend there was the plaintive screech of the train's whistle as it headed for a level crossing and a stationmaster swung a flag as the nameless town flashed by. Villages and farms disappeared and Tilly imagined the many different lives spent in them. Steep embankments rose, choked with nettles and brambles, ablaze with red campions. Tall grasses skirted cuttings and flared silver in sunlight as the train swept by. Horses and cows barely lifted their heads. Tilly felt each turn of the wheels hurtling her into this new life with a man who might not want her and if he did, could so easily die. It was too ghastly to dwell on.

There were fewer stations now, amid longer stretches of countryside with ancient long stone walls, framing and carving up land, old farms, low barns and fields dotted with sheep or blooming with clover and crops. A dark river rushed alongside, with bobbing ducks, fluttering up as the train rumbled alongside.

Tilly untied Jack's lunch, carefully folding the brown paper and string to reuse. There was a bar of Hershey's and two fried spam sandwiches, with real butter on soft white bread, not the awful brown stuff she was used to. Tilly offered the couple half a sandwich to share. The woman shook her head and the man said: 'No thank you.' Their eyes said something different. Tilly replied she couldn't possibly eat both. The wife thanked her and took one round, tearing it to share. There was sweet silence as they ate and Tilly looked out of the window. She gave them half her chocolate too and the mother's eyes closed as her baby slept.

Finally, Tilly drifted off; her exhausted body rocked with the swaying, jolting carriage. She awoke to grinding brakes and commotion as people gathered their belongings, pulling into Newquay. The couple got slowly on their feet. Tilly reached to get her case but the woman's husband, even with one arm in a sling, grabbed the handle, lifted it down and smiled in a way that made his wife's lips pinch as they departed.

Tilly took her time, checking herself in her hand mirror, brushing and smoothing her hair, pinching her cheeks and slicking on Victory Red lipstick. She would start the way she meant to go on. Stepping onto the platform, it was deserted but for a porter, helping a woman with three small children. The whistle blew and train departed. Tilly struggled with suitcase, handbag and gas mask to the station office, where an elderly lady with silver hair looked up.

'How may I help?' she asked, her country accent dipping down and up.

'I'm meeting Major Douglas Fairwood. I'm his sons' nanny.' She thought she sounded important.

'Ah,' she said and stood, hands on her ample hips. She was barely five foot and rocked from side-to side as she beetled to the station entrance where an impressive black car was parked. Inside, a man in uniform remonstrated with two young boys. He was red-faced and wagging a finger. Tilly gently tapped on the car's window.

Douglas Fairwood startled as if he'd been clipped around the ear. So did the boys. He got out. Slight, straight-backed Major Fairwood had what seemed a near-constant frown and bristly moustache, like a baby squirrel's tail. He shook her hand; a proper grip. The boys now hit each other and appeared to enjoy every second.

'How do you do,' the Major said, in the poshest accent Tilly had heard.

'Very well, and yourself?' She answered in the un-poshest accent he'd probably ever heard.

'I've been better,' he said, matter-of-factly. 'I'm sorry I wasn't there to meet you. But they were just too naughty.' Tilly tried not to smile.

'My wife, Martha, will be very pleased to see you. Pleased and relieved.' The boys sang 'Row, row, row your boat gently down the stream, if you see a crocodile don't forget to scream.' They both let rip ear-piercing screams. The Major shouted at them to be quiet. 'They're not nearly as easy to deal with as my men,' he added wistfully.

The Major put Tilly's case in the boot and unlocked the

passenger door. Tilly slid in elegantly and turned to the boys. Douglas introduced Alex and Jamie, aged six and five. Auburn-haired, green-eyed and freckled, they looked like twins. After shaking her hand, they were temporarily quiet, weighing up the opposition. Douglas drove out of town and along the coast. It was a bright and breezy day, with hundreds of gulls circling.

'Martha's not like she was,' he said carefully, blinking rapidly and rubbing his moustache between thumb and finger. 'Jamie was born only 11 months after Alex, and Martha's been treated twice in a sanatorium. I thought leaving London would help.' He shrugged.

'It'll be fine,' Tilly said, sounding confident but not feeling it.

The Major didn't look optimistic either. A while later, he pointed out some of the grand hotels surrounded by soldiers and airmen which had been taken over as hospitals. Ambulant patients wore bright blue uniforms with white shirts and red ties. Smaller hotels were used as barracks for the army and air force training carried out all around Newquay. Even better than Liverpool, thought Tilly, although there was only one GI for her. According to the Major, the acres of beach she longed to wander barefoot upon were out of bounds; protected by multiple strands of barbed wire surrounding mine fields, and even tennis courts were now parade grounds. She didn't mind the latter. Tennis was not a game that city girls played.

'Daddy, I want a wee,' piped up Alex.

'Can you please wait until we get home?'

'No,' piped both boys, giggling. Douglas pulled over at the side of the road.

'Hold on,' said Tilly, 'leave this to me. She stepped down, heels sinking into the gravelly roadside. Opening the back door, Tilly offered her hand to Alex first.

'I want daddy, not you,' said Alex, huffily, folding his arms and immediately copied by scowling Jamie.

'No, it's me or you have to wait until you get home.'

'We'll wait,' snapped Alex, and they were silent the rest of the way. Tilly caught the beginnings of a smile flicker across the Major's face.

Chapter Eighteen

Woodburn,

USA

May 15th, 1943

Well Son,

How are you doing? It's sweltering here and I'm planting more vegetables than ever because we finally have rationing! Your Mom's not happy because it's shoes first, and a bad Government choice given how much women favour footwear. It's nothing like shortages in England but we're cutting back on canned food, meat, cheese, butter and cooking oils. Mom and all the other housewives are like locusts in the shops. It's your Mom and sister's birthday next month and they've ganged up and asked me to buy tickets for the new musical Oklahoma. Marie keeps singing Oh What a Beautiful Morning. I'll buy a ticket for Jess as well because it means I won't have to go. I'm sure you'd agree, Son.

With love,

Pa

Trevone Bay, June 2015

Friday, and Ava's first free night was hours away. The long, hectic days of looking after another's needs completely had taken on a pattern, set around managing debilitating pain, doling out drugs, making palatable food, washing, toilet, sniping, endless TV, smoking and battles with booze. But she'd made it longer than anyone else.

It was alien to be so intimate with such a fragile fractious woman, who didn't want Ava yet couldn't be without her. For the time being, Ava was in the same strange position. Before she came to Cliff View, a friend had asked if it was all about wiping bottoms and giving baths, Ava had shuddered. Now, that was the easiest aspect. Tilly was changeable as the weather, swearing she'd be better off dead than *stuck in this prison*. There were times when Tilly revealed a chink in her critical armour, regaling Ava about her life as a young woman; a teenager in love with a man who died and left her pregnant. Often, when Tilly had hooked Ava into a tale about him, tears rolled down her cheeks and to Ava, it seemed cruel to uncover these memories, dust them off, make them shine and long to be young once more. It was a terrifying glimpse into her own future.

First thing, for her sanity, Ava checked Tilly was asleep and jogged slowly on the beach before surfers arrived. It was painful but she persevered and the first ten minutes were a real battle. Charlie would join her, running twice as far and fast before looping back to almost walk at Ava's pace. She chatted because Ava couldn't. About the weather, food, pubs. Later, when Tilly woke, she required drugs, washing, dressing, feeding, had peed the bed, or worse. Dealing with that became less stomach-churning. Ava surprised herself with how matter-of-fact she'd become, barring the earthiest smells. She was curious about Tilly's body; how some skin, untouched by sun, looked young and soft. There was no muscle tone (apart from her tongue), and her flesh felt like cotton wool. When Tilly snoozed after lunch, Ava popped into the village stores and enjoyed the warm hello she got with her coffee while she scanned the *Western Morning News* for work. There was little suitable and all required a computer to apply. Ava's face healed, helped by gardening or reading outside while Tilly watched TV. Despite wearing sun screen, freckles appeared for the first time in years. A sprinkle of them over the bridge of her nose, a scattering on shoulders and a spill between her breasts.

Vicky phoned daily and seemed surprised, disappointed even, that Ava didn't sound desperate. Ava was polite and professional. Tilly barely spoke to her daughter and appeared to want to get off the phone quickly. Afterwards, Tilly was quarrelsome. At night, when Tilly was knocked out, snoring and peaceful, Ava wrote down her stories and insults which took the heat and sting out of them and being told she looked, *faintly like Aunty Vi, only faintly.*

Emptying rubbish into the bin outside, Ava picked an envelope off the mat. It was handwritten in beautiful, cursive writing. She handed it to Tilly.

'Read it,' she commanded. 'Please.'

'Don't you want to read it yourself?'

'I can't.' She was wrapped up in a TV programme about celebrities doing up cheap homes. They didn't look cheap to Ava. 'What's it say?' Ava unfolded the creamy watermarked paper. It was astonishing.

'Someone called Nigel Fitzpatrick wants to give you £800,000 for Cliff View.'

Tilly tore herself from the screen. 'I've had other offers but that's the most. Carry on.'

Dear Sir/Madam

*I apologise about contacting you in this way and that you
do not consider my enquiry or the offer rude or
impertinent.*

'Jesus,' said Tilly, 'he sounds like Charles bloody Dickens!' Ava
continued.

*We have fallen in love with your home and wish to make
it ours. I work in the city but we could imagine nowhere
better to spend weekends in the UK.*

*We hope a price of £800,000 is of interest and please do
not hesitate to contact us if you are tempted by another
more lucrative offer.*

Yours faithfully

Nigel and Rosalind Fitzpatrick

'There are contact details,' said Ava. She estimated Cliff View was
worth £300,000 tops, for the view alone. The man must have
surmised the shabby property was owned by someone elderly and
hoped to buy it before it was put on the market. Undoubtedly, Cliff
View would be rebuilt on a grand twenty-first century scale. It was
beyond Ava's wildest dreams to own a home and here was someone
with bags of money to spend on a weekend property.

'Well, I never,' Tilly said, taking the letter. She held it a foot
away but even squinting was unable to make out the words. 'If I had
control of my body, I'd be on a first-class ticket to somewhere
exotic.' She put the letter back in the envelope, tucked it under the
cushion behind her and requested cheese on toast – minus crusts,
with plenty of Worcestershire sauce. After Tilly slept, Ava sat on a
deckchair, thinking about the impossibility of her buying

somewhere but then, one day selling it to pay for care.

There was a loud knock – not the kind to ignore. She headed for the door thinking of the numerous visitors to Cliff View, more than ever there'd been in London, where Amazon deliveries were the main contenders. Friends always prearranged to see her and Josh. He'd loathed spontaneity, asking that guests take off their shoes and slip on shapeless grey mules to ensure their cream carpet remained spotless. For a moment. Ava imagined Sadie with frumpy slippers and a puking baby crawling over velvet sofas.

'May I help?' asked Ava, to a scruffy middle-aged man in a worn suit, teamed with checked blue shirt and shiny grey tie. Unlikely to be a potential house buyer, Ava thought as he beadily regarded her. In that look Ava recognised something.

'I'm Ollie,' the man said, all friendly smarm, and fake chumminess, offering his hand. Ava didn't take it.

'Journalist?'

'Yeah,' said Ollie, hand suspended, dropping his smile and diffidence like a dead weight. 'Who are you?' He revealed his estuary accent.

'What do you want?' Ava too bypassed pleasantries.

'Does Ms Barwise live here?' he asked, looking over her shoulder as if Tilly might materialise.

'Why?' Although she knew. The man looked irritated, got out a notebook, opened it, clicked his biro and scribbled.

'Staff at Somerway,' he said, without looking up, 'lost loads of weight and raised £1,000 for charity because of Ms Barwise. My editor thought it'd make a great feature. If I could chat to her?' Dead pan and dead bored dealing with Ava.

'Who do you write for?' Ava asked, persistent. Ollie tapped his right foot. His scuffed suede lace-ups had seen better days.

'UK Media Gold.' Ava's blood ran cold. It was a huge company with a cut-throat, tabloid reputation.

'Give me your card and I'll get back to you.' Ava wouldn't budge.

'But,' he said, clicking the biro rapidly, 'it'd be a lovely story.'

'And it'll stay one.'

'She's nearly 90.'

'Correct, and not about to cope with Press harassment. I'm Tilly's carer and I'll talk to her. Write down your questions and if she chooses to answer, I'll send them back.'

Ollie blew out his cheeks. He wrote for a few minutes, then reluctantly put his hand in his top pocket, handing Ava notes and a dog-eared business card. 'What's your name again?'

'I didn't say. By the way, we don't have email so I'll get back to you via the library or snail-mail.'

Ollie set his jaw and shook his head as he shoved notepad and pen in his jacket pocket.

'Goodbye,' said Ava.

'Give my best wishes to Ms Barwise,' Ollie said loudly, hoping to lure her. 'And here's a contract. He fished a creased sheet from his trouser pocket. 'If she signs this Ms Barwise will get paid but she can't talk to any other Press.' He sloped off and Ava saw him scrutinise her in the cracked wing mirror of his rusty BMW.

Ava digested the contract and smiled, thinking the hard-bitten world of the Press would have its work cut out against the wildest woman in the South West. Ollie's initial questions included Tilly's age (over her dead body), phone number (she never answered) and why she'd come up with the diet (love, boredom at being old and superiority at being slim).

'Ava, I need the loo,' called Tilly sleepily, and they slowly, shakily walked together. By the time she'd got Tilly perched, the doorbell rang.

'Did he not get the damn message?' Ava muttered to herself and looked out of the window ready to let rip. There was beaming Nurse Evangeline. With Tilly safely settled, Ava ran to let her in.

'Your face looks heaps better,' Evangeline said, picking up her black holdall.

Ava smiled; her heart lifted. 'I'll get Tilly off the loo and make you a cuppa.'

'No need; you're off-duty as of now. May showed me around already.' With that, Evangeline cruised into the bathroom, practising the Tilly-taught wiggle. 'Hello, you look wonderful, maybe not on the loo,' she announced. 'Did you see our story in the paper?' They moved to the front room and Tilly was installed on her TV chair.

'Barring the fact, I wasn't in the picture,' said Tilly, huffily. 'Oh, and will you look who's in the garden! Yoo hoo!' Tilly waved. 'Robbie, like a cat on a hot tin roof.' And there he was, striding along borders, with a new haircut, clean cream T-shirt and dark jeans. He ignored his audience while fully aware of them.

'He's never done gardening dressed like that or come on this day!' said Tilly, 'He's smitten, Evangeline.'

'He gave me a lift,' she said, coyly. 'Robbie's on a diet too but he's not giving up cider or joining the gym. He says some things are beyond the pale. Somerway is aiming to lose 400lbs for charity. Oh, and a journalist called yesterday asking who the patient was and if he could talk to her. We didn't give out your name.'

'Someone did because he arrived today,' said Ava.

'I hope they didn't say how old I was,' said Tilly.

'Too late,' said Ava. Evangeline blinked. 'He's been here and knew it.'

'Damn. I'll talk but if they want a photograph, I'd require a face-lift or something like those jet-cleaners that scour centuries off old cathedrals.'

'I'd kill for your gorgeous bone structure,' said Evangeline. 'Anyway, I've got some hot gossip about Sister Lynch.'

'Why on earth would anyone gossip about her?' asked Tilly, all ears.

'She's on a diet, waxed her top lip and eyebrows and had her teeth whitened. Someone spotted her on a dating website. The write-up mentioned: *Caring nurse, good sense of humour, thoughtful.*'

'Well,' said Tilly, 'she'd need white teeth to dazzle because it's not her personality.'

'Oh Tilly, she's lonely. You understand that.' There was no reply.

Later, Ava showed Evangeline the guest room and warned her about the journalist. Finally, it was time to think about herself. She changed into the navy dress bought from a Brighton vintage shop. It was vaguely body-shaped but forgiving and, pleasingly, a good deal looser than when she'd last worn it. She teamed it with her only ankle-strap red shoes, small silver hooped earrings and simple silver bracelet. Ava twisted from side to side. She didn't look bad but *avoid* was written through her like a stick of rock. Still, there were 24 hours to fill and she wasn't going to waste them.

Ava drove to Padstow, feeling she'd sprouted wings as she wandered the narrow, cobbled streets, threading her way past chatty families and couples holding hands. She pushed open the library door and entered a hushed space filled with the heavenly scent of well-thumbed books. A friendly librarian with smooth dark hair and violet eyes behind steel-rimmed glasses took her to three public computers tucked between crime and poetry. A giant of a man seated there briefly acknowledged Ava. She perched on a metal chair leaving a space between them. In the far corner story time was in full flow. Small children enthusiastically chanted, *I'll huff and I'll puff and I'll blow your house down!* Ava's fingers automatically assumed their usual positions above the keyboard. The tips of them lightly traced the worn keys, which had a slight tackiness. She felt an urge to unarchive her Facebook account, dismissed it, imagining *Memories you have to look back on* with photographs of her, Josh and Sadie. Soon, it would be awash with their baby pictures. She let out a sigh which made the man glance. Ava switched briefly to news, Tilly usually turned it off, saying *the future is of no concern to me now*, compared to the likes of *Snog, Marry and Avoid*.

It was for Ava though, and she focused on regional jobs. There were adverts for gardeners, call centre workers, cleaners, shop assistants and waitresses. Living-in, if she was lucky. There was nothing for editorial assistants and copywriters. Worried, she allowed herself to be waylaid, investigating Cornwall in World War II with faded photographs of the airbases used by the thousands of Americans who breathed new life into towns (and their women).

She discovered the US army's slang for prunes was *strawberries*, an *armoured cow* was tinned milk, *asparagus stalks* were submarine periscopes, *blind flying* was a dubious date with a girl you didn't know and *a broad with a load of lettuce* was a wealthy woman. She read how antique railings had been torn up and turned into Spitfires, bullets and bombs, locals collected old pans and scrap metal to help in any way. There was a piece about pregnancy during the War: *Illegitimate births in England and Wales jumped from 24,540 in 1939 to 35,164 in 1942. Venereal disease soared by 70 per cent. The blackout and dark underground shelters offered anonymity and excitement because if bombs fell, why not die happy? One air raid warden asked a sheltering crowd:* Are there any expectant mothers here? *A woman replied:* Give us a chance! We've only been down ten minutes!

Every so often, her neighbour accidentally clicked an advert and a noisy jingle about cat food, house insurance or second-hand cars blared. He apologised, hammering the keyboard into submission. In the local online paper, Ava caught sight of a three-paragraph council story outlining a planning application on land abutting Tilly's. This drew her attention. It was for six luxury five-bedroom homes and four little back-to-back properties. It was exactly the sort of snippet that once would have deserved a decent half page but without the clickbait that attracted advertising, this local news was barely visible. The main picture story featured a man complaining about a bag of chips someone had emptied on top of his car, turning it into a mobile takeaway for a flock of scavenging, crapping seagulls. It garnered thousands of shares. Ava navigated the district council's user-unfriendly website and discovered the land was owned by Daylight Developments based in Guernsey's tax haven. She wondered if Tilly knew. As she left, the librarian smiled asking if she'd found what she needed.

Outside, the sun slipped down the horizon as Ava headed for the harbour. Being alone was something she'd hated after Josh left, now it was to be relished. She bought fish and chips from a family-run shop on the corner. Salted and vinegary, they were boiling and she held them close like a hot water bottle, sauntering by little shops whose owners pulled down shutters. She sat on a bench by the harbour and opened a gap in the packet to let the chips cool and stop greedy birds pinching any as they flocked around her feet, begging. There was the lapping of water and ticking of boat masts in the light breeze. Laughter spilled from pubs as drinkers replaced shoppers.

'Oi dreamer,' a friendly voice said behind. Ava turned to see Charlie, the runner, accompanied by the librarian, now in matching strappy, gold dresses. 'This is my partner, Becky.' The smaller woman smiled, said hello and shook Ava's hand.

'We met at the library already.'

'Where's your pensioner? asked Charlie.

'Being looked after, and I'm free until tomorrow.'

'Good, then come and join us, we're heading for something to eat and a charity barn dance,' said Charlie.

'Absolutely not the barn dance,' said Ava. 'What are you going as?'

Charlie pulled two long string of carrots out of her bag and golden masks: 'Darling, we are 24-carat gold.'

Ava laughed. I'll have one drink and then…' She hesitated; it would be back to Cliff View.

126

Chapter Nineteen

Cliff View, Trevone Bay, 15th May 1943

At 10pm on her first day at Cliff View, Tilly perched on her single bed, drinking weak tea and warm toast with a scrape of butter and lumpy blackcurrant jam. She laid out her clothes. Sensible garments her mother had joylessly packed for wet, boggy Ireland. A green cardigan, brown, boiled woollen skirt that thankfully did not show stains while she tackled the boys and at least hugged her figure. She felt unmoored from all that had happened in 24 hours, how thoughtlessly she'd behaved and what she'd recklessly committed herself to.

The Major's wife was really unwell. Her bedroom curtains had been drawn when Tilly arrived and by the look and smell of it, she'd been in that high-necked, fawn nightdress for far too long. The boys fidgeted next to her and Alex, the older one, chattered about catching a fish as big as a plane, and jellyfish he'd poked with sticks, (Tilly had grabbed the stick off him). He showed shells they'd collected and poured a handful on the bed, encased with wet sand which stippled the coverlet. Martha grimaced. She tucked her unwashed, frizzy, mousey hair behind her ears and her grey eyes filled. She's only young, thought Tilly, but like a middle-aged fogey.

'That's enough boys, time for a bath,' the Major had said, hands on their backs, propelling them out. 'Martha, this is Tilly Barwise, she's here to help.' The boys were herded into the bathroom where their father ordered them undressed. Martha touched her book, as if she wanted that, not conversation. She had a delicate, slightly featureless face that was not unattractive but easily missed in a crowd, thought Tilly, sunless, with thin eyebrows and bloodless lips.

'I can't stand the noise. It's constant. Douglas is away so often.' Martha put her hand to her mouth, squeezing her eyes shut. Tilly took three quick steps to her bed, sat on the edge of it and held Martha's other hand gently.

'That's why I'm here, so you don't need to worry about a thing. And tomorrow I'll take them out all day.'

Martha nodded and squeezed Tilly's hand back. Tilly was not so selfless. Being out meant more chance of seeing Jack. The boys squealed their bath was too cold. There was splashing and chatter about boats and crocodiles and Jerries. Tilly stood, rolled up her sleeves and went into action, politely asking the Major to make his wife a cup of tea and then read his paper in peace. He looked like he'd won The Derby and St Leger cups. Tilly washed the boys' hair in bright red carbolic soap, noticing the tell-tale signs of nits and clusters of eggs attached to hairs. She'd douse them in paraffin and ensure they didn't go near a naked flame. With the boys dried, wrapped in padded dressing gowns and eating Bovril on toast with warm Horlicks, she read stories from *Peter Rabbit*. After their bedtime, the Major pointed out early nights were important for his wife's recovery and that he would be away for the next few days. Then he bid her goodnight.

Tilly's room was small and situated next to the boys' room who were deeply asleep. The Major's wife had only got up for the toilet.

Tilly ruminated on Jack's flippant remark about being able to go home if she didn't like her new job. It was terrifying but what else could he say to someone he'd only just met? And so easily slept with, she scolded herself. She thought through the alternative, being marooned in Ireland with her bitter mother and wittering Aunt Tricia plus her five scrapping children. She had at least escaped that, and it was up to her to sort out her future, with or without Jack. Restless, she'd undressed, washed in cool water, slipped on her old blue nightdress and wrote to Jack, saying how wonderful everything was (even if it wasn't) and that she couldn't wait to see him. She didn't say go to bed with him because she felt a measure of decorum was necessary. For the time being.

Tilly opened the window and leant out into the salty, sea-perfumed air. There was Round Hole, like a snoring troll under the hill. The stars glittered and a full moon enamelled the rippling ocean. Fairyland compared to Liverpool. Tilly shivered. Martha's window was firmly shut. Clouds piled in from the sea, dark wisps dramatically whisked across the moon. The wind flapped the letterbox and the grandfather clock ticked in the hall. Cliff View had a lonely, sad feel but she had never seen a sea so blue-green, green-blue, navy-grey all at once, and skies that transformed in minutes from pale to robin's egg blue and warm rose-blue. Nothing like Blackpool and Southport with their murky waters and bustling, tacky promenade and beach upon which her father sunbathed; a knotted handkerchief on his head, much to her mother's mortification. Trevone felt pristine; the very air medicinal.

'Tilly,' her name hissed through the darkness. And there was Jack, coalescing out of shadows, under the trees by the gate. Tilly laced up her shoes and slipping over the window ledge, raced to him. All worries allayed. He placed a package on the ground and pulled her into his arms, took off his coat and wrapped it over her shoulders. Kissing and kissing. An owl hooted. He drew back and brushed hair from her face. She had never looked into someone's eyes like this before.

'Is it all OK?' he asked. Tilly nodded. 'I brought you this,' and lifted the damp parcel from the grass, tightly wrapped in newspaper. 'Fresh cod; a Jerry plane was shot down and these washed up on the tide.'

'Oh, thank you,' she said, kissing him. He was a good man doing this for her, for this family.

'I'll try and be at the bay by 3pm tomorrow,' he said. 'If I don't get back, I'll get someone to phone you.'

Just like that, he talked about the possibility of his death. She placed her palm on his beautiful cheek. She didn't want to hear about dying when he made her feel so thrillingly alive. He held her hand and wordlessly slipped between the trees, and leaning against one, he quickly entered her. She felt like an animal and it was a good natural feeling; breathless and hot, though not satisfying for her like it had been in bed.

'Go on now, back in,' he said as she clung to him. 'I don't want you to catch cold. Take the cod.'

'I'm glad to be here,' she whispered. He turned her around and patted her buttocks, waiting until she'd climbed back over the window sill. He melted into the darkness but all night burned brightly in her dreams.

Chapter Twenty

18th May, 1943
Cornwall

Dear Aunty Vi,

You're the only person in the whole world I can write to about this. No doubt you've heard I didn't go to Ireland. I can't imagine how cross and upset mum is. But I had to leave, you'd understand. I'm working as a nanny for a couple far from Liverpool. I'm in love, Aunty Vi. He's an American reconnaissance pilot and so handsome and romantic and everything I want in a man. There's no going back. I can't live like mum and dad. I can't say where I am because I don't want them tracking me down and causing a terrible fuss. I'm so happy, I find myself humming all the time! The sea is beautiful and I'm busy with two young boys. The woman I work for is suffering from nerves and I'd so like to see her smile. I hope you're OK Aunty Vi? I only miss you.

All my love,
Tilly

Padstow, June 2015

'Have you been to Padstow before?' asked Charlie, tucking wayward curls behind her ear. Becky listened. The quieter one, thought Ava.

'Nope,' said Ava. 'Not sure why.' But she knew. Josh preferred cultural European breaks in far-flung cities, or long-haul holidays, ticking off sites to see and carefully curated on social media. When Ava put forward vacation ideas Josh dismissed them with *too done*, *too hot*, and *too suburban*. She'd always followed his lead.

'I'm glad to be here,' she said, 'even if I'm a tourist.'

'Tourists are fine, barring hen and stag parties but they're needed,' said Charlie. 'Parties stick around Newquay leaving Padstow for families and foodies. You don't linger here for ten expensive pints of lager, minus karaoke and kebabs.' Three tanned old ladies ambled past licking cones of melting ice-cream. One limped, another rocked from side to side and the last used a stick.

'Not easy being old but they look happy,' said Charlie. 'How's it going with your pensioner?'

'She'd love to walk – with a man on each arm. She longs to be young and flirting. I've lasted longer than any other carer, which is apparently a record.' The evening cooled as the sun slid into the sea, leaving a rim of scarlet at the navy horizon. Stars twinkled and white lights flickered along the harbour. They headed to The Shipwrights. The pub's slate roof stopped halfway down the red brick building and baskets of colourful flowers hung outside every window. Customers drank and chatted alongside the water, filling the air with laughter and familiar scent of cigarettes.

'I must reek of smoke,' said Ava. 'Tilly's on 40-a-day. Her lungs are a miracle of self-preservation. Apparently, she hasn't had a cold for a decade. I doubt germs survive the toxic wasteland.'

'A faint odour,' said Charlie, 'and overladen with vinegary chips. Still, that's a traditional Friday scent. There's a band on before the barn dance, not sure who but as long as it's not Death Metal.'

'I'll be gone before the barn dance,' said Ava, decisively stuffing chip papers into a bin, on top of which two scrounging seagulls padded.

The pub had low beamed ceilings and candles glimmering on the long wooden bar. On every rough-hewn table sat jam jars of fragrant sweet peas. Carved pews and sagging sofas rested on wide-planked floors. Dogs of all shapes and sizes sat, begged or slept at owners' feet. A constant clatter and calls for service erupted as the kitchen doors swung back and forth with white-aproned staff bearing plates.

'Lovely food here but right now, eating's cheating,' said Charlie, 'So drinks and then order? Are you OK with proper Cornish cider?'

'I've cheated already. I don't like cider but as it's traditional, just the one, thank you', said Ava. She did not want to let her guard down.

'Rattler it is then,' said Charlie. Becky frowned.

'It's very strong, Ava, I'm warning you,' Becky said.

The amber-coloured pint smelt sweet and tasted of sharp cooking apples with a sour after-bite. Within five minutes there followed a warm, flowing sensation as Ava's arteries fizzed and her entire body relaxed like she'd been put through a warm wringer. Charlie asked Ava how it felt living with Tilly. Ava became expansive.

'I'm an observant servant. She isn't easy and I've never been up so close and personal to old age. It's brutal. Tilly's body's packed in but her brain is sharp as a tack with no trace of dementia, despite the booze. She doesn't like me or being looked after. I get that.'

'Some of my patients, sorry, *clients*' – she raised her pint – 'aren't going to make it to fifty let alone ninety but since Tilly's story appeared in the paper, I've had questions about rationing. In the war the government sold it to the public with a sense of humour, like, *The fish we get in this country is the finest in the world and makes brains. It must do – look at the brains you need to open a tin of sardines.* A family of four were allowed a pound of meat, half a pound of fat and sugar, each, per week. Plus wheatmeal bread, home-grown vegetables and salad. If my patients ate that and walked, they'd have a fighting chance. No wonder Tilly's lasted.'

'Rationing?' asked Becky, one eyebrow arched, as a waiter bore three more pints of Rattler placing them on the table. 'I thought you were only having one, Ava?' Ava shrugged and smiled, picking up her second drink. Froth glided down the sides of glasses, soaking into sodden beer mats. 'Saint Charlie, is it to be your usual sinful large battered cod, twice-fried chips, mayonnaise mountain and mushy peas, set to float upon this golden cider sea?'

'Guilty as charged, gorgeous woman, but it's once a week, not every night and I run every day. Cheers everyone.' They clinked glasses.

The pub was rammed and noisy now, with a gaggle of barn dancers – all in fancy dress. There was a man with a horse's head, accompanied by a plump chicken. Two seals waddled through followed by Bart and Marge Simpson, Donald Trump (with hay for hair) linked arms with Tinky-Winky and a Brad Pitt caressed a curvy Angelina Jolie's bottom, while a witch cuddled a vicar.

'They're impressive,' said Ava. 'Glad I haven't got anything to wear.'

'Yes, you have,' Becky pulled out a pretty gold mask with silky partridge feathers pluming on one side and tied with gold ribbon. 'A barmaid asked me to bring this but she's off ill. There's a spare Godzilla outfit too but I think this one suits you more.'

'That's very thoughtful,' said Ava, 'but I'll get a taxi, thank you.'

'You'll be lucky before 1am,' said Charlie. Ava's cider-swilled brain acquiesced and, halfway through her second pint, she told Charlie and Becky it was a godsend to meet them, then revealed why she'd escaped to Cornwall.

'I don't think you should drink any more,' said Becky, gently placing her hand over the top of the glass. Ava, firmly removing Becky's hand, gulped and launched into a brief history of Josh and Sadie.

'That's tough but the best thing,' said Charlie, patting Ava's arm, 'is your shit-radar's on high alert. Nobody's going to hassle you. If you can't get a taxi you can stay with us tonight.'

'And slow down on that stuff,' added Becky. 'I was married once. To a man, and it was never going to work. He moved to Glastonbury, selling pottery with a Pagan celebrant. Much cheaper property there.'

The food arrived in a flurry of trays, serviettes and sauces in little white jars. Charlie tucked into a battered cod that stretched across her entire plate and Becky dipped skinny chips into a bowl of wine-soaked mussels. Ava remembered how Sadie loved mussels and oysters, prizing them open, tipping her head back theatrically, and exposing her long, elegant throat. Ava drank half her cider. Becky winced and a man in a Harris Tweed suit with a fox's mask excused his way by with a guitar, apologising as he bumped into Ava.

'We got together online,' Charlie carried on. 'You'd think women would be less hassle to each other; a sisterhood. But it's just as tricky. I'm glad I'm not out there anymore. Becky, get off!' She prodded Becky's hand with a fork as she pinched a piece of battered fish. 'Within five minutes of meeting Becky I felt we were right and my shit-detector was on full-beam. We appreciate what we have.'

Becky nodded. 'You'll be happy again, Ava, but that's not much solace now. It took me two years to feel human, so you're doing brilliantly, isn't she Charlie?' Charlie nodded, swirling mayonnaise on her chips. The jukebox was turned off and tables dragged to walls to make room for dancing. Ava rang for a taxi and was told it would be midnight at least. The barn dance caller, dressed as a badger, wore sunglasses, even in candlelight, and placed his iPad on the music stand. He stood with legs apart and mouth virtually on the microphone, repeating, 'One two, one two.' After a minute a customer responded, 'Three, four, five, once I caught a fish alive.'

Rattler had loosened her bladder as well as her tongue. She'd had one pee already and was ready for another. At the loo, there was a queue for the ladies and nobody in the gents, so Ava slipped in there, locked the door and seemed to pee an entire pint. A man entered, whistling, and used the latrine. Brazen with booze, Ava stepped out and saw the back of the tweedy fox. He looked around, silenced, zipped himself up and shook his head.

'I'm sorry, there's never enough loos for women,' she babbled, and shot into the ladies to wash her hands. Glancing up at the mirror she saw her cider-flushed face with mascara smudged under her eyes but she looked healthier and at least five years younger than when she'd arrived in Cornwall.

Charlie and Becky put on their strings of carrots, adding cardboard golden masks and crowns. 'Stray Surfboards,' said Charlie, as Ava settled back in the pew. She glanced out of the window. It was pitch black, apart from white lights flapping between lamp posts.

'No, not stray surfboards outside,' laughed Becky. 'It's the name of the band.' Ava looked at the stage and saw it in double-mode. She pressed a forefinger to her right eye and the band swam into focus. The guitarist fox she'd seen in the loo was now on stage. He was tall with auburn hair, and oddly, a pair of glasses over his mask. The most intellectual fox she'd ever seen. His hands, she noticed, were scarred; old white marks, new livid ones and some paler pink. There was a large plaster on his left hand. Rattler coursed through Ava. She felt a tap on her shoulder. It was a giant cod with glittery eyelashes, accompanied by an overblown pink shark. The cod removed its head. May.

'It's me. I didn't think you'd come.'

'I didn't mean to.' She introduced Charlie and Becky and the shark next to May lifted his jaw.

'My husband, Jeff,' said May, as the bald, bearded man pumped each of their hands. He looked like someone who'd spent a lifetime hefting potato sacks. His body was packed into the fluorescent pink shark costume which was so tight around the middle, the zip twisted to the right.

'Glad you're still here,' he said to Ava. Her anxious heart was sufficiently buoyed by Rattler to smile. May gave him a dig in his protruding belly.

'It's good Evangeline could look after Tilly. I never miss this dance. Do you like my outfit?' asked May, smoothing her nylon silver scales and batting fake eyelashes. 'I'm a *Cod above the Rest*. Jeff's *The One That Didn't Get Away*! What are you?'

'Call centre worker. It's the only dress I've got.'

'Well, it's lovely and you look great in it.' Charlie handed Ava the partridge mask. May cooed over it.

'You'll be the centre of attention,' said Jeff. 'I don't mean because of the rescue,' Ava closed her eyes. 'Just someone new here and under fifty. There's not much fresh blood unless you count blow-ins.' Ava felt her stomach turn.

'Bloody hell, Mr Diplomat. Sorry Ava, he's clueless. You know, when he met me, he said, *You've a lovely shape; like a rugby ball.*' Charlie and Becky groaned.

'It's my favourite sport and we're still together twenty-five years later,' said Jeff, shrugging.

'Don't dig yourself in deeper. What he meant to say, Ava, was you'll have to be light on your feet. Fellas here only dance between being drunk and still able to stand, while clinging on to whoever is brave enough to step out with them. I don't suppose you're used to that in London?'

'You'd be surprised,' said Ava, tying on her mask. She immediately felt better. This was just the ticket to conceal her.

'Lovely,' said May, 'isn't she, Jeff?'

'Yes,' he said, obediently. Becky and Charlie agreed.

'Why's the shark pink?' asked Ava.

'It starred in a Gay Pride parade until it got too ropey,'

explained May. 'It was the princely sum of a fiver on eBay. I had to sew part of the jaw back so it looks a bit like Frankenstein around the throat.' Jeff stretched his head up to reveal May's obvious repair. His tie featured eels, fish and seahorses. He offered to buy a round.

'None for me,' said Ava. She was losing focus. Nevertheless, another half arrived. A glitter ball switched on and spun brightly illuminated circles across ceiling and walls. The band's singer belted out Shania Twain's *That don't impress me much* while an old man in checked shirt and jeans hoarsely directed dancers. Every adult not drinking shuffled in long muddled lines through puddles of booze as they mostly failed to follow complex instructions. Vague circles knotted and span out again. Around the periphery children played and ran from side to side. Ava was glad the almighty din and chaos allowed her to watch and not join in, especially after the caller thanked the RNLI for all the amazing work they did. Charlie and Becky plunged into the surging crowd to *Cotton-Eye Joe* and May chatted to just about everyone. Dance-averse men clutched their pints like they were new-born babies, to be lovingly tended. It was then a man, dressed as a bear, with an RNLI badge taped to his furry chest, grabbed her hand and pulled Ava to the dance floor. May swiped Ava's handbag as she passed. Ava couldn't distinguish what the caller said but it was irrelevant as she was propelled haphazardly along to *Mustang Sally*. Ava got no sense of what to do. Nearby, Tinky-Winky held a giggling toddler and they were clapped down the dance line. For twenty minutes, Ava perspired as strangers' hands slipped around her waist and squeezed in a friendly manner as she was pushed, pulled and prodded forward, back, round and sidewards. Finally, Ava stood sweating at the head of a line, opposite the fox, who'd broken free from the stage. She felt surprise in the way he caught her eye. Lifelike fur trimmed his intricately painted mask. He reminded Ava of a short-sighted, fairy-tale beast.

He held out his hand and Ava took it. Firmly, he led her between the rows of raised arms at a pace that neither lingered nor sped.

'Eh Foxy,' a man slurred as they reached the end, 'that's the riptide woman you saved and won you all that money! And she's a partridge – just right for a fox!' The rowdy group roared and fox held tightly on to Ava's hand.

'What do you mean, won money?' she demanded of the tousle-haired drunk. His smile slid to one side. She tore free from the fox's hand. The blabbermouth stilled.

'After her other carers left,' the man mumbled, 'there was a bet on you not lasting three days with Tilly Barwise. Only Foxy here, bet on you staying.'

Ava fled to the toilets and locked herself in the only empty one. She closed the lid and slumped, feeling a rush of blood to her pounding head. She wanted to crawl out of the pub. Ava battled the impulse to flee. She couldn't drive or walk far. Mutterings grew outside the door.

Ava pinned back her shoulders, exited, scrubbed her hands and got angry. Even in their inebriated state people gave her a wide berth as she strode across the dance floor. Ava lifted her handbag from May's outstretched hand.

'Did you know about a bet?' Ava asked snippily. May looked sheepish.

Reg, dressed as a pirate, raised his glass to Ava.

'He was in on it too?'

'He'd bet on his last breath,' said May, palms up.

'Right, well, I'm glad I won.'

Mr Fox watched her, handing a cupcake to a small red-haired boy in a fox cub outfit, complete with scarlet bushy tail. She owed this man her life and he deserved thanks, even if he'd bet on her. Ava paused at her table and threw back the last of her Rattler, then cut through a circle of dancers.

'Thank you for saving my life,' said Ava, hiccupping. Fox looked very serious. 'The bet I don't understand, and it's horrible.' Ava remembered how he'd yelled in the ocean and the force he'd used. 'I'm very sorry you took that risk. I had no idea swimming there was so dangerous.' She smelt charcoal, smoke and soap.

'It's not something I'd do again,' the Fox said, a gentle, local accent. 'If I'd thought of my son, I wouldn't have gone in. I'm glad you're alright.' It was a deep, measured voice. 'I'm sorry I hurt you.' He took in the faint bruises on her neck and around her arms; like tiny bites. Ava nodded and hiccupped loudly. Her anger fading fast.

'What I don't understand is why you gave me the vote of confidence to stay when nobody else did?'

'You didn't run off after nearly drowning. I thought you could tackle anyone, even Tilly.'

The cub's small hand reached from under a table, tugged the hem of her dress, leaving a distinct white handprint. 'My Daddy's Fantastic Mr Fox and he's very clever. He's cleverer than Boggis, Bunce and Bean, the nasty farmers who sell their land.' Father Fox bent and said something. It resulted in the boy with gappy front teeth and beautiful almond-shaped eyes, beaming. 'Daddy won money and got me my first big bike, without stabilisers. I like your pheasant feathers. Is it because you like *Danny, Champion of the World*?'

'Yes.' Ava smiled, catching sight of grazed knuckles and scabbed knees as he bobbed back under the paper tablecloth. Foxfather smiled. That was all Ava could see of his face. A good smile: white teeth, one slightly crooked canine on the left.

'I'm Finn and my cub's Joe. Good to meet you on dry land.'

He held out his hand and Ava shook it, a strong hand, covered in bumps, sticking plaster and cuts. Finn removed his mask. He had a carroty nose, cheekbones you could cut glass with and the same dark eyes as his son. His smile was relaxing and warm.

'Pleased to meet you properly too,' said Ava. She took off her mask. He didn't seem displeased at what he saw but gave nothing away.

'How much money did I make you?' She asked, feeling she should be more irked than she was.

'Nearly £300. I bought Joe the bike and the rest is for something interesting. I hope.'

'No one but you expected me to stay?' Finn shook his head. Joe ran off. Ava felt pleased with herself. 'What interesting something?' Ava noticed how he kept track of his son while he spoke to her.

'I thought you'd like surfing lessons?'

'No way,' said Ava, hiccupping and laughing.

'Failing that, lunch at a pub with a good view? Not near riptides.'

She noticed May nudge Jeff who'd tipped his shark mask back

to eat pizza. They smiled over and May did a tiny wave.

'I might have to check my diary,' said Ava, looking up at the ceiling and, after a second, 'Well, that would be yes, then.'

'May said you're off Saturdays, so next week?'

'She's in on this too?' Ava laughed. A whole week to wait. 'I haven't got a phone.'

He pulled a crumpled card out of his pocket. 'I haven't got a pen, so call me if you can't make it, otherwise, I'll come by Cliff View at 10am.'

Cool and calm, thought Ava. She looked at his card, a silhouette of a man hammering an anvil. *Finn Blake: Blacksmith*, it stated with number and website.

'I'm back on stage now,' said Finn, as the singing badger began his one two, one two sound check. 'And then home with Joe.' He left her and the music began. A sturdy man in a jester suit appeared and took Ava by the hand.

'You won't remember me,' he said, 'I'm Archie. I was on the lifeboat and wrapped you up. That's what makes my job worthwhile.' Ava fought the desire to put her hands over her face by hugging him and putting her mask back on. The badger belted out Johnny Cash's *We got married in a fever*. It was one of Ava's all-time favourites. She was passed from person to person, often the wrong person but carried on regardless. An hour later she saw Finn button his son's coat and leave without glancing back. May danced on, sweating like a boil-in-the-bag fish, mask abandoned and glittery eyelashes long gone. Jeff's shark head was lying on its side by a chair being petted by a child.

'I'm sorry about the bet,' said May, sidling up. 'I couldn't bring it up and I thought you might not find out – if you left. I'm glad you're still here. What do you think of Finn?' Her eyes rounded and she wiped her face with the sleeve of her costume.

'He saved my life. Nice guy.'

'I wouldn't call him nice.'

'Why?'

'Gorgeous and red hot,' May laughed. Ava felt the novel sensation of smiling; the corners of her mouth actually lifting without force. It was months since she'd felt those muscles flicker. Becky and Charlie whooped and an old guy took hold of Ava's hand, leading her in a large circle that involved men lifting up women (or doing their best) and she flew round and round. Her head spun.

Chapter Twenty-One

Cliff View, 1st June 1943

'Jack, did you have a sweetheart back home?' Tilly asked lightly, brushing sand off his shoulder as they sat watching the blood-red sun set on Trevone Bay. Jack clenched a pebble in his hand.

'Well?' Tilly asked, her hand stilled, wanting the right answer – a fast and hard *No*. 'Do you have a sweetheart back home? Were you courting? Are you?' She repeated with an edge to her voice, her hopes fraying. It had frequently crossed her mind that someone as handsome and clever as him would be admired but she hadn't summoned up the courage to ask.

'Fiancée. I had a fiancée. Not anymore,' he said looking at her, his pupils small and lips set. She doubled with the stabbing pain in her stomach, pressed her hands on the beach, leapt up and ran. He chased her and as he grasped Tilly, she thumped his chest to tear herself free.

'Wait. You're not going anywhere. Hear me out.' He gripped her shoulders.

'A fiancée. Not just courting. You were going to marry!' She faced his furious face with her own. 'When were you going to tell me? You took me to bed and brought me to live here on a whim while someone else is waiting for you at home.' Tilly shut her eyes. 'You've used me. I'm nothing but a cheap comfort while you're far from her.' She hit his arms. He didn't release her.

'You didn't take much persuasion to come here. Or to bed. Listen to me. Her name was, is, Jessica – Jess. I've known her forever; since we were babies. Our Moms always planned for us to get married. I took it for granted, then I met you. I was always the obedient son; dutiful. Joining the army was the first fight I had with my family. I asked Jess to marry me because I was going away and didn't know whether I'd be back. I thought it would help her, and her Mom and mine. When I proposed, I knew it wasn't right. I can't unmake what's happened. I didn't know how to tell you. I thought if I died, I wouldn't have to hurt either of you.'

'That's cowardly to both of us. Me and her.' He let her go and she stood rigidly apart from him.

'You have to believe what I say. I wrote to Jess and my family after you arrived here,' he took the fabric of her dress in his hand. 'All hell broke loose but I want an honest life with the woman I love. However long I've got.'

She drank in the word *love*, let it fizz through her body like champagne. Tilly imagined his heartbroken fiancée. He murmured sorry; his hands slipped around her waist. He kissed her and she reciprocated because she loved him and she'd burnt all her bridges.

'Forgive me.' He bunched her skirt in his fist, tugged on it. In the darkness they found a private place in the dunes and made love, him promising she was the only woman for him and Tilly, longing to believe him.

She asked to see a photograph of Jess. The next day he showed a wallet-sized shot of a woman with a sweet round face, dark-haired and dark-eyed. Solid. Tilly felt better. The day after Tilly asked to see Jess's letters. Jack had thrown them all out. A clean slate, he said.

Tilly decided to let it be. She could only go by the way he looked at her, touched her, talked to her. She did not want to be far from him while he lived on this earth.

Chapter Twenty-Two

Diary Entry: Medmenham, Danesfield House,
Central Intelligence Unit, June 3rd, 1943

I'm working alongside the model-making section in a damp old wine cellar that smells of yeast, wood and glue. It's got its own weather system depending on how much people smoke. I like the team a lot and while they wear RAF uniforms, it's like a costume on a bunch of sculptors, artists, illustrators, engravers, and a silversmith. Guys stick rubber over a wooden base and glue on a mosaic of recon photographs. They add miniature tanks, ships, harbours, sand on beaches, miniature buildings, and railroads with toy engines and trucks. Hedges are painted as lines. The set-up makes me feel five years old. We study them under a lighting rig that replicates moonlight, so when we're flying in the dark, we know what to look for. At 6pm we head for The White Hart, where one pint leads to seven and singing. I've grown to love warm Brit beer. The dregs are kept to kill slugs on vegetable patches. They sure die happy. Tilly would love that.

Padstow, June 2015

Ava looked around a compact bedroom containing a computer desk covered with messy files, books in higgledy-piggledy piles and four floral mugs. Her head throbbed, mouth tasted vile and she felt nauseous. Photographs of Becky and Charlie holding surfboards took up half a wall opposite. She reached out to the bedside table and touched a cool glass. Leaning carefully on her elbow, Ava drained it. She remembered then – Finn, the date, the bet, the Rattler – but not getting back here – and groaned. Cars bumped over cobbled streets outside. There was an aroma of smoked bacon.

'Are you awake? It's 10am,' said Charlie, tapping the door. 'Breakfast's in 20 minutes.'

'I'd kill for just tea and a painkiller.'

'In the kitchen. I'm making a fry up guaranteed to cure any known hangover. There's a clean towel on the bed and shower's to the right. OK? Oh, and a new toothbrush in a packet on the sink.'

'Thank you.' A fluffy dressing gown lay on the bed. Ava took off the clothes she'd slept in, slipped on the dressing gown and into the bathroom which had two slatted doors opening into a caravan-sized interior. The shower was hot and blissful. Dressed, she went into the narrow, light-filled kitchen, half covered by a glass roof through which a seagull peered; its pink, webby feet parading back and forth. The soothing tones of acoustic guitar played. A suspended wooden dryer was festooned with T-shirts, bras, knickers and shirts, scenting the air along with the fry up. A vase of pastel sweet peas was on the pine table. Becky looked up, smiled and set aside the newspaper.

'I told you not to drink any more, it's so strong,' said Becky, shaking her head, 'and you look in need of your own bodyweight in carbohydrates. Sorry about sitting in our launderette, it's not often you have breakfast under multiple gussets.'

'Hi, it's lovely,' said Ava, shyly. Her stomach gurgled as she sat opposite Becky who slid across *The Guardian* Saturday magazine. Charlie amassed eggs, sausages, bacon, hash browns, tomatoes, mushrooms and toasted soda bread. Becky passed plates and buttered toast.

'It's like coordinating NATO. Baked beans, Ava?'

'Yes please, it's really kind.' She was suddenly ravenous.

'It's good to have a proper blow-out,' said Charlie, mopping splashes of oil off the work surface. 'Apologies about our tiny space. We're lucky to have it though, aren't we?' Becky nodded, setting out knives and forks. 'Padstow's landlords can make £900 a week from tourists instead of £900 a month from us.'

'It's perfect,' said Ava, and it was; light, warm and inviting.

'Padstow's got potential for turning into one big holiday home,' said Charlie, shrugging. 'Like Amsterdam without the special cafes.'

'OK Foodie Queen,' said Becky. 'Here we go, forks to the ready.'

'Painkillers next to you.' Charlie said, sitting.

'Maybe one to ease me into the day,' said Ava, creating a bacon and egg butty.

'That Foxy guy's dishy, lovely kid too, and like my mum says,' said Charlie with a smile, *The man who takes the child by the hand takes a woman by the heart.*'

'Mr Fox saved my life but also laid a bet on me. Loads of people wagered I wouldn't last three days with Tilly. He was the only one who believed I'd stay. He made £300. And I saw him in the men's loo having a pee before I found all that out.'

'Oh yes,' said Charlie, 'and what did you notice?'

'Nothing! I didn't look.'

'Pity, you could have saved yourself time,' laughed Charlie, spearing a sausage.

'Hush. He's a talented blacksmith,' said Becky, 'not a player. He keeps himself to himself with his son.'

After breakfast they moved to sofas in the small living room and Ava told them about the planning application near Tilly's land.

'Go see Gillian Jones, she's District Head of Planning but a real jobsworth.' They chatted and read and Ava felt her eyes close. She was woken by Charlie with hot chocolate and carrot cake. 'Courtesy of the WI. My cakes rise as much as a Frisbee.'

At 1pm Ava set out for Trevone Bay, thinking she had her first friends, and then of Finn and she should make the most of it, given she wasn't going to be here long. At Cliff View, Tilly sunbathed; her face gleaming with oil like wet, cracked leather. Evangeline sat in the shade and Robbie, next to her, fiddled with a length of wire and pliers. Round Hole breathed easy.

'Hi,' said Evangeline, brushing her dress. 'Hope you've had a good rest? We've had a relaxing time, haven't we, Tilly?'

'I'm relaxing myself to death,' said Tilly, one lizard-slow eye opening. 'You two go now.'

Evangeline could not contain herself. 'That journalist, the one you said called the other day, came back.' She sounded nervous. 'I tried to say no but Tilly invited him in. A photographer was there too and we had our pictures taken.' Tilly kept her eyes closed and mouth shut.

'Ollie?' said Ava, annoyed. 'Did you sign anything?'

'That was him. Tilly signed a contract,' said Evangeline. Robbie stood. Tilly pursed her lips. 'He said it means Tilly will get money for herself and some will go to charity.'

'Does Vicky know?' asked Ava. She knew a boozy, feisty, smoking pensioner making a care home lose a ton of weight was quality clickbait and mother-daughter relations were fragile enough.

'It's nothing to do with Vicky and I didn't mention her or my grandson,' snapped Tilly, eyes narrow and flinty. 'This is about me and the war; how to eat better, and be beautiful.' She looked positively impish. 'He said the *Daily World*'s interested and everyone reads that.'

'Really,' said Ava. 'Did you talk about Jack?'

'Did I hell. I don't want the world and his relations checking him over. His mother never liked me.'

'Well, that hardly matters now,' said Ava.

'She'd revolve in her grave,' said Tilly, patting the arms of her chair, smiling. 'You'll have to stay until the story comes out Ava.'

Ava said nothing. Robbie tugged on an ear, fluorescent with sunscreen.

'It's going to be a lovely evening,' he announced. 'How about we go for a walk and pop into The Golden Lion? I think there's a quiz and meat raffle.' He ate Evangeline up with his eyes, like she was fillet steak.

'I'm veggie and no good at quizzes,' said Evangeline, smiling. 'Also, I get competitive and liable to cheat but I'd love a gin and tonic.'

'I won't share the meat if I win then,' said Robbie.

'And make it slimline tonic, Evangeline,' said Tilly.

'Nothing else passes my lips,' she replied, as Robbie waited at the garden gate, where overhanging honeysuckle flowers attracted feeding bees. Tilly lit a cigarette and asked for a brandy.

Chapter Twenty-Three

St Eval

June 6ᵗʰ, 1943

Darling Tilly,

We'll go to Constantine Island again but this time with fishing tackle. I was mad to see that mackerel shoal and not have a feast on the beach but I have developed pictures of this beautiful mermaid in the dunes. I'll see you at the Golden Lion on Friday. I still don't know what the Hokey-Cokey is all about, only that I love doing it with you.

All my love darling,

Jack

Trevone Bay, June 2015

The afternoon slipped into evening and banks of soft grey clouds flowed across cliffs, falling and spreading so that sea and coast became indistinguishable. Round Hole hissed like static and the TV blared its usual background chatter.

'I'm so bloody bored,' grizzled Tilly, flicking ash off her jogging pants. There were burn marks of varying degrees scattered from thighs to knees. They were her favourite pants and it was the devil of a job to get her out of them and into anything else. 'But I was never in Mum's miserable position. Let that be a lesson. Jack taught me life should be one long party. Not like living with me.'

Tilly flicked TV channels.

'You're being mean,' said Ava. Tilly managed to easily unsettle her.

'I forgot,' said Tilly, with a sly smile.

After dinner, Ava strolled to Stepper Point at the mouth of the River Camel where it slid against Doom Bar, avoiding stepping on the many black slugs that slimed the narrow, precipitous coastal path. She gazed across the water to where, long ago, Tom Yeo was said to have mistaken a mermaid for a seal, then shot and killed her. In revenge, a boat-wrecking storm threw the sand bar across the river to teach sailors a lesson not to mistake mermaids for seals. In the fading light, two grey seals dipped in an out of the milky-looking ocean. Ava felt the shackles of her old life loosening and floating away.

Chapter Twenty-Four

May 24th, 1943
Morgantown
USA

Dear Brother,

I miss you. I know you made the right decision about Jess. It must have been so hard. I will take care of her, don't worry. I love you both.

Baby Dorothy is cutting her back teeth and is up a lot in the night, every night. I could do with my big brother to take her out in the day and exhaust her but I know you have far more important things to work on, like saving the world from the Nazis! Pa is treating us all to tickets for Oklahoma! and looking after Dorothy while we do! Your letters have been a lot about the weather which I'm sure is very interesting and changeable in Britain! I know you can't tell us what you're doing – or wouldn't, as Mom can't hear anything worrying. How are you really and do you think you'll be able to settle again!?

All my love,
Marie

Cliff View, June 2015

The doctor's surgery rang at 9am with a message for Ava to pass to Tilly. Doctor Singh would visit at noon to see his longest-standing patient. When Ava informed Tilly, who was glued to an auctioneering programme, she pursed her lips until they touched her nose and zapped off the TV. She even agreed to change her jogging pants. Royalty was arriving.

'I need a bath, and everywhere must be clean.' Ava set to work.

Dr Singh strolled up the path and entered with a youthful step that belied his startling silver hair. They shook hands, and Ava offered him a drink. He asked for black tea with a slice of lemon, following her into the kitchen, observing.

'How are you finding the redoubtable Mrs Barwise?' he asked, sipping the bitter brew.

'Challenging, rude; an enigma,' said Ava, mixing a spoon of honey with a squeeze of lemon in hot water for herself. 'Pitiful,' she added quietly.

'How polite. That's not what her other carers informed me before departing. What's made you stay?'

'Curiosity and circumstances,' replied Ava. He smiled and patted his pocket.

'Being curious is good, and circumstances always change, for better, or worse. Have you got a pen? I don't know where mine all go. No matter how many I buy they disappear like pairs of socks and combs.' Ava found one. 'Tilly reminds me of my grandmother in Mumbai,' he continued, putting her pen in his pocket. 'She drove herself and everyone else to distraction but when she died, there were so many stories about her, we laughed for days. Sometimes, people have too much character for their own good and create a kind of slipstream which you have to be careful not to get swept up in.'

He sipped his tea and listened to the blare of Tilly's TV.

'Tilly's fiery temperament was wrought by a world war. I admire her but it's a wonder anyone can live with her.' He cocked his head and smiled. 'I hope you don't mind me saying, I heard about your incident.' A moment of calm quietness unfolded. Ava thought she might cry and pinched her thigh under the table to stop herself.

'I'm fine, I was lucky.'

Dr Singh touched her other hand; light as a feather. 'Good. Thanks for the tea and chat. I'm always happy to listen. Now, I have to deal with the Battle Maid.' He cleared his throat as he entered the living room. 'Tilly, I do not wish to fight for your attention with dancing and singing. And no smoking while I'm here.' The TV was instantly off. Ava was amazed how this gentle man was obeyed in an instant.

Fifteen minutes later Dr Singh returned to Ava. 'Tilly looks better although I think there's a deterioration in her eyes, and while her blood pressure is higher than I'd like, her pulse is strong – but never a match for her language.'

He warned Ava about careful supervision of medication and alcohol and he would book an eye test. 'I believe you are a tonic, Ms Westmorland. She tells me you're a writer.'

'No, I'm not at all,' said Ava, mortified. 'I put together copy for adverts but it seems to make her happy to talk about the past, and me to write notes while she does.'

'Ah, that would be because she's talking about herself, and the light in which she wants her past presented. I asked how she was getting on with you and she nodded. Great praise indeed. Call me if you need anything.'

Ava wondered about another Valium prescription but bit her lip. She'd run out and was finally sleeping better than in the last six months. She walked Dr Singh to the door and watched as he pedalled off, wobbling, on a rickety black bike.

Chapter Twenty-Five

Woodburn
Morgantown
West Virginia
USA
May 24th, 1943

Dear Jack,

 Doctor Reese had to be called when I found out about that British woman. Everybody will know soon; all the neighbours. Poor Jess. Do you realise what you've done? I'm worried sick, night and day, about you being killed or injured but I never thought you'd do this! Jack, you were happy with Jess before you went away and will be when you return. She's been so good to me and Marie, helping her with little Dorothy. Son, this woman is stopping you thinking about the risks you take with your life and being lonesome so far from home. Go to confession and pray for forgiveness. Jess will forgive you and so will we. I cross every day off the calendar – the one in the kitchen above the oak chest where Jess is saving linen and crockery. Don't break her heart, and mine. The doctor says I've had a major shock and not to go out at all.

 All my love,
Mom

Trevone Bay, June 2015

After Ava got Tilly into bed she thought of Ollie, about whom she could do nothing, and the council planning application, which she could. It would take courage to face but Tilly should know what was going on.

Ava booked to meet Gillian Jones. The *Daily World* was delivered and she flicked through to check for Tilly's story. Nothing yet. A newly-divorced stick-thin celebrity teetered across the front page in a pair of $3,300 heels. A four-paragraph sidebar mentioned poverty-stricken pensioners forced to choose between food or fuel and the main story featured a £400million financial injection to allow cash-strapped and time-hungry GPs to speed up diagnosis. The *Daily World* branded it, *A waste of time and tax payers' money.* It ramped up anxiety in Ava. Tilly blanked negative news and hoovered up gossip like nicotine.

'Am I in there?' were her first eager words as Ava handed it over.

'No, it'll be ages but I read in the local paper about new homes that might be built nearby. Do you know anything?' Sounding her out.

'I had a letter but it won't be happening while I live here.' She shook her head and picked up the paper and her magnifying glass, ballooning and illuminating her eyes. Tracking the words slowly, she was absorbed by the actress's shoes, clothes and lucrative divorce.

'I should've been an actress,' she mused. 'I loathed the miserable 50s when wives were meant to be pregnant, barefoot and tethered to a twin-tub bouncing across the kitchen lino. I had to pin that bloody machine against the wall, while Terry nappies thumped inside. No dryers then. It was rooms full of damp washing, dripping in front of a coal fire and windows misted with condensation. In winter, I scraped ice off them.' Ava shuddered. 'Women were supposed to breed, wash, knit, and cook. And go quietly mental. Or not so quietly. They shouldn't go to the pub because that was only for loose women; like me. Housewives met for Tupperware parties and Camp coffee where they clacked on about kids over cake and tea. Nothing worse. Men don't do that. Well, there's the equivalent dullard who plays golf and rattles on about how to drive from A to Z via B-roads.'

'It's only me!' May interrupted, letting herself into Cliff View like a warm breeze, carrying a bag spacious enough to take her on holiday for a fortnight. A waft of smoke and vinegar arrived with her, as she swapped Crocs for fluffy slippers. She'd dyed her hair, smothering the grey parting with a helmet-like walnut-colour.

'Nice hair,' said Ava, and May smiled, patting it like a pet.

'£3.99 special offer. It was near its sell-by-date. Like me. You look a little bit tired,' May said to Ava, smiling as she lugged the vacuum out of its cupboard. 'Good dance wasn't it?' She winked. Ava felt her cheeks flush.

'I'll make you a cuppa,' said Ava, and disappeared. She heard May telling Tilly about one of the men at the barn dance.

'He was done up as that handsome TV actor Poldark – that one who gallops around cutting wheat, bare chested, swinging a scythe with a six pack you could play like a drum. Only this one was called himself *PullintheDark* and shaped like a barrel. In all my years, I've never seen a handsome man riding a horse around here. You'd run a mile if one of our local farmers cantered towards you.'

'What about Jimmy Valentine?' said Tilly, mouthing toast. 'The one with dark hair that curled over his collar? He was worth riding.'

'What are you like?' May said. 'He was handsome. Pity he emigrated to Australia.'

'Plenty of bush there,' screeched Tilly, and they roared. May bustled into the kitchen, plugged in the vacuum and slurped tea.

'Well,' said May, quietly. 'I want to apologise again. The bet was a mean thing to do and I'm happy you stayed. I'm glad Finn won it although he's doesn't know Tilly like the rest of us.' May swiped her red face with kitchen roll and went off to spray Tilly's TV screen with lemon-scented polish, as contestants on a dating programme camped in the bitterly cold wilds of Scotland.

'Get out of the way, May,' ordered Tilly.

'Guess who's pregnant and it's not her husband's?' said May, polishing the campers' faces. Tilly instantly focused.

'I'll run your bath,' said Ava, timing it for a dull gardening programme which Tilly disliked and before *Loose Women* which she loved, despite stating they *weren't nearly loose enough*.

'Your bath smells like a rich man,' said May, sniffing.

'How do you know?' asked Tilly, easing on to her frame.

'I clean for one.'

'Well, I'd better get in up to my ears,' said Tilly. Ava had a lot to learn from May, she thought, as she lowered Tilly in. Extracting her later, droplets streamed off Tilly's folded wet skin, like some dredged-up bog-body. Suspended above the bath mat, Ava used the position to carefully separate and dry each contorted toe.

'Heels did that to me,' said Tilly, 'but I looked like a goddess in them. Who cares now? I won't be dancing again.' Her legs were marked with deep blotches under tissue-thin skin. Vertical creases appeared like scores of bloodless paper cuts and her hips had a waxy, vellum-like texture. Ava proffered Tilly a hand-towel to dry between her thighs and handed over Yardley's English Lavender Talc which she sprinkled over herself like icing sugar.

'You look like a ghost,' said Ava and could have kicked herself.

'I'll be one soon enough,' said Tilly, smoothing the powder.

'What was life like here in the war?' asked Ava, moving swiftly on. 'My grandmother talked about the Americans' gorgeous accents.' Tilly shook her flossy hair, putting up her arms so Ava could slip on a white cotton vest. She never wore a bra.

'And the rest,' said Tilly, as Ava eased on pants and joggers. 'Everything about them was to die for. Great hair, skin, teeth, wads of cash they were generous with, and tight-fitting uniforms. Jack was everything to me. All I wanted was a life with him in America.' Tilly clasped her fingers, unclasped them. She looked excited. 'I want to show you something I haven't looked at for years.' She hesitated, 'It's in an envelope, under the magazines in my bedside drawer and we've got fifteen minutes before *Loose Women*.' Tilly sat on her bed and Ava pulled the drawer open. Beneath used tissues and old magazines lay a small, padded envelope.

'Give it me. Please.' Tilly picked it open, her hands shook. She emptied two framed, palm-sized black and white photographs into her hand. She smiled, kissed one and passed it to Ava. 'Jack.'

Here he lay in the palm of her hand, tanned and muscular, with the kind of sculpted torso surfers worked long and hard for. The

164

shot captured him on a sunny beach in loose shorts, swinging a baseball bat in his right hand at shoulder-height. His dark hair was parted on the left and a wavy forelock escaped. He looked at the camera with a brazen smile and a lit cigarette clamped in the right side of his mouth. Because of sun or smoke, Jack squinted, deepening creases across his eyes and forehead.

'Handsome,' said Ava, 'and talented.'

'Talented and courageous. He wouldn't talk about what he saw but, in his dreams, he'd shout and struggle.'

'I can't see Vicky in him or you.'

'Jumped a generation. Vicky looks like my mother but she's got my brains.' Ava raised her eyebrows and Tilly cackled. 'Well, not the interesting parts of it.' Tilly shrugged, handed over the other photograph. In this, she wore a tight, belted white dress with a soft bow at the neckline. Her curled blonde hair fell loose and spread across her shoulders. She looked doll-like beside Jack who was in full uniform with Tilly tucked under his left shoulder; her hand laced with his. Tilly smiled with small, white teeth. It was strange seeing real ones in her mouth.

'No wonder you fell for him,' said Ava. 'Any woman would.'

'He fell for me too. Jack never made me feel anything less than completely loved and desired. What more could a woman want? Open that next.' Tilly pointed to the oak chest at the end of the bed; the one embossed with vines and leaves.

Ava gave it a tug but it wouldn't budge. 'It's locked.'

'Where did I put the damn key?' said Tilly, screwing up her face. 'Somewhere safe, which means I can't remember. Check the wardrobe floor.' Ava rummaged through a pile of petticoats in assorted colours. It was an archaeological rummage through multi-layered shades of nylon.

'Nothing,' said Ava, sneezing as dust rose and swirled with cigarette smoke. 'Have you ever thought of patches?'

'What for?'

'To stop smoking,' Ava sneezed twice more and her eyes watered.

'Only if they were stuck over my mouth,' she laughed. 'What's the point of giving up?'

'I'm thinking about my health,' said Ava. With a sigh, Tilly stubbed it out.

'Thank you.' She was surprised and pleased.

'I remember!' said Tilly, clapping. 'It's in a pink potty, in the hat box on top of the wardrobe.'

'Potty?'

'I used it on long drives for emergencies. And no burglar's going to look in a potty, are they?'

'Great,' said Ava, taking down a dusty octagonal box. A plastic bag inside it contained the pastel-pink potty. It didn't look big enough even for Tilly's tiny bottom. Ava gingerly picked up the key between two fingers and with a sharp tug the chest opened, releasing a scent of cinnamon, and revealing yellowing tissue-paper. Underneath the first layer was a pair of ankle-strapped white sandals. They were soft kid-leather with cracks across the toes.

'Beautiful,' said Ava, holding them up, turning them over.

'I had gorgeous fairy toes and ankles like a deer,' said Tilly, as she bent her swollen, twisted feet with bunions the size of boiled eggs. Ava traced her fingers along the leather, feeling the subtle indentations of Tilly's soles. Next, Ava brought out a faded swimming costume. She lay it on Tilly's lap. She estimated it was a size eight at most.

'It was big on me,' said Tilly proudly. Pinkness suffused her cheeks. 'It's the same one I wore in the photograph.'

'And fit for a sea goddess,' said Ava, placing it on Tilly's lap. Ava lifted a musky-smelling, brown herringbone suit. It had padded shoulders, cinched pencil skirt with a kick-pleat which was cut to flare. 'Gorgeous, wasn't it itchy?'

'Extremely,' said Tilly, 'but the wolf whistles were worth the irritation.' Ava took up a red beret and baby's lace shawl wrapped around a blue box delicately patterned with pink roses. She handed them over and Tilly set the beret jauntily on her head, then opened the box. Inside, was a pile of blue envelopes tied with red ribbon. The top one was addressed to Tilly at Cliff View, dated July, 1942. 'L.O.W.E.S.T.O.F.T' in capital letters was written down the left-hand side.

'Love letters,' she said, kissing and rubbing them against her face like a cat.

'I thought Jack was based here,' Ava said. 'Isn't Lowestoft in Suffolk?'

'Those capital letters have a secret meaning,' said Tilly, with a sly smile. She touched each capital. Legs Open Wide Enter Slowly To Obtain Full Treatment.'

Ava gasped. Tilly pulled out another with E.N.G.L.A.N.D written diagonally across the back.

'Guess,' said Tilly, delighted Ava couldn't.

'Something patriotic?' Ava wracked her brains.

'Ha! Every Naked Girl Loves A Naked Dick.'

'Oh my God. I only know S.W.A.L.K is Sealed With A Loving Kiss. Did other people understand?'

'Everyone. It was a laugh for the posties and us. Here's one of my favourites. C.A.P.S.T.A.N?'

'No idea!'

'Can A Prick Stand Twice A Night?' Tilly beamed. She held the letters to her nose, breathed them in. 'Write it all down. I once knew a journalist in London. He wrote for *The Telegraph* and invited me to lunch when I'd written to him about being a successful businesswoman. We met at a swanky hotel, and after I was wined, dined and bedded, my business got a five-star review.

'I bet it did,' said Ava. 'Could I read Jack's letters, please?'

'Not yet, but one day.'

In the yellowing envelopes lay Tilly's younger self, in shadowy rooms, beaches and lanes. Here was the thrill of the man who'd held her heart; his longed-for voice, the lines of passion he'd written to her, which Tilly had never relinquished but tucked away like half-remembered dreams. There was, thought Ava, a breath of smugness at the grand passion but she did not pine or feel reverential about this disrupted, enduring love. Jack was safe in these folded letters; safe from change, from further loss.

Ava repacked everything in the same order, locked the chest and replaced the key in the pink potty and hat box on top of the wardrobe.

'I'm glad you're here, Ava.'

It was the first time Tilly had used her name kindly and May, who had come to say goodbye, beamed.

Chapter Twenty-Six

Cliff View, Trevone Bay, 20th July 1943

Major Fairwood briefly kissed Martha and departed on a mission he couldn't discuss. Tilly noted that while Martha's face fell, the Major's, just like her own father's, brightened with his bags packed. Reserved Major Fairwood practically ran out the door when his driver honked the horn. He whistled along the garden path. Martha's eyes welled. Tilly's only concern was that seeing Jack might prove trickier. *Where's there's a will there's a way*, she decided, as she cleaned cupboards under the sink. Her mother would have been astounded at Tilly's domestication.

Alex and Jamie had spent the morning at the beach acting out war games with blood-curdling screams and play-fighting. She'd had to prise them apart every five minutes. Tilly swore she could locate them from a hundred yards and their yelling was capable of stripping leaves off trees. She was forever wrestling them into washing, dragging a comb through their nit-riddled flossy hair or scouring muddy faces with flannels. She'd banned meals until the filth under their nails was scoured out. The only time they quietened was when they were with Martha until a squabble would invariably arise which saw them packed off sharpish. Tilly realised she sounded scarily like her own mother: cleaning and complaining.

Tilly had acclimatised to Martha Fairwood's nervous nature and extreme inclination to remain in bed. If she'd had her sons, she'd have done the same. Tilly focused on cooking the kind of plain food her mother was an expert at making taste good but sadly, she wasn't. The carefully followed government instructions for Potato Floddies, Woolton Pie, Carrot Roll, Kidneys with Mustard Gravy, Syrup Loaf, and Bread Pudding, ended up burnt, under-cooked, sloppy, or tasteless as cardboard. Nutritious cheap meals were her mother's forte but given how unhappy Elizabeth's marriage had been Tilly wasn't too concerned about her own culinary failings. Not when she had Jack and America's land of absolute plenty to fantasise about. The main issue was getting the boys in hand and in a routine. This she was better at. Tilly made sure they got to their tiny village school on time and when they were at home, created dens with them under the kitchen table, played hide and seek in the garden and took them fishing at rock pools where they caught starfish and slimy, slithering creatures; Tilly had no clue what they were. Alex and Jamie were naturally feral, reeking of mud, sand, grass and sea. Tilly marched them to the beach daily to monitor the sky for returning planes, praying Jack was safe. If he was grounded, he chased the boys until they pleaded with him to stop and begged him to build elaborate sandcastles. Tilly knew Jack would make a wonderful father and husband. Her husband and their own children. While the boys created, Jack took Tilly to the nearest sand dune to be thoroughly, privately kissed. Once he asked if she'd written to her parents and if they were OK with her in Cornwall? Tilly lied and said yes, in a way that closed down the conversation. She had no intention of elaborating to him or informing them where she was. Jack lit fires and they'd cook potatoes she'd dug up from the garden and fish he'd caught. He told tales about horses, cowboys and Red Indians because, of course, he was American. The boys, licking their sticky fishy fingers, wanted to hear about bows and arrows, smoke signals and riding bareback. Tilly listened to his ingenious fabrications and loved him more by the minute. The gloom in Cliff View gradually shifted and lightened. Barring Martha's own personal black cloud.

Lipstick finally persuaded Martha out of bed. During the boys' afternoon nap, while cleaning, Tilly discovered a box on top of Martha's wardrobe and inside, a treasure trove: brand new Elizabeth Arden's Victory Red lipstick, face powder, foundation and untouched mascara.

'Look at this beauty,' Tilly announced, lipstick in hand as she pulled open the bedroom curtains and daylight flooded into the musty bedroom. The space perfectly matched Martha's pale skin and fawn hair, so she all but disappeared in the stale, rumpled sheets.

Tilly opened the window. Burbling Round Hole was accompanied by a groan from Martha; a noise Tilly heard numerous times at night and had nothing to do with making love. It was usually followed by Major Douglas getting up and sleeping in the sitting room. Tilly had crept around Cliff View and closely observed the miserable couple. She had witnessed the blueprint of an unhappy marriage at home. After lunch one day, when the boys were occupied sticking pictures with flour-based glue, Tilly tidied Martha's room, babbling about films she'd seen – and magazines she hadn't a hope of getting her hands on. Martha stared mutely at the ceiling, until the lipstick was waved back and forth like Tilly was hypnotising this morose mother.

'You can have two inches of my bathwater. I can manage with

less this week, so that means you can have five inches and I've put pans on to boil,' announced Tilly.

'For God's sake, OK,' Martha said sulkily, but there was a trace of a smile, something that had to be extracted with force. Tilly laid Martha's beige cotton dressing gown on the bed and she eased it on, like an old woman rather than the 28-year-old she was. Martha smelt of mouse breath and mouse sweat. She needs a rocket under her, thought Tilly, looking at the blank face, framed by lank, greasy hair.

It was one of those warm, clear afternoons which felt as if the world was bathed in greenness. The blue-green ocean spooling into the curved bay thrilled her. The bright and dark green of trees and pale, spikey greens of growing potatoes and silky, carrot fronds. It may as well have not been there as far as Martha was concerned. While Martha washed, Tilly put on the radio and Glenn Miller's *Moonlight Becomes You* saw her glide and shimmy down the hallway and into the kitchen, dancing with one hand on the doorknob pretending it was Jack. Martha finally emerged out of the bathroom in a beige dress which made Tilly's heart sink but she smelt soapy and her clean hair was pinned into a pretty chignon. Over twice-stewed tea and a slice of Tilly's soggy syrup cake, Martha opened up. It turned out she was a vicar's daughter whose mother died when she was 13, her father followed five years later from TB. Tilly held Martha's hand. They ate and drank in silence for a while, listening to the radio, Tilly slid over the make-up and told a terrible joke.

'A man walks into the records office and asks to change his name. The clerk asks the man's name and he replied: "Adolf

Stinkfoot". Well, who wants to be called that? "What do you want to change it to?" asks the clerk and the man says "Maurice Stinkfoot".'

Martha didn't laugh but an actual proper smile appeared and she allowed Tilly to dab foundation on her and finally, lipstick. For the next two days Martha got up, dressed, washed, combed her hair and put on make-up. She even read a good night story to the boys and allowed Tilly to put her hair in curlers. On the third day, Martha stepped foot on the beach. Jack was waiting and was charm itself. He played baseball with the boys and so delighted Martha that she talked about the weather. Her first tongue-tied conversation with someone else since Tilly had arrived.

When Major Fairwood returned home he looked astounded at the sight of his wife in the garden, wearing a white dress of Tilly's, lipstick on, clean hair in soft waves and throwing a cricket ball to the boys.

'Welcome home, sir,' Tilly said, handing him a whisky, and winked. The Major nodded at Tilly and slowly took in his glamorous wife as she smiled shyly at her husband. He raised his glass to them both as the boys hurtled to him and climbed all over their laughing father.

Chapter Twenty-Seven

Woodburn,
West Virginia,
USA
June 4th, 1943

Dear Son,

Mom asked me to write as she's too under the weather. Nerves and her heart again. Doc Reece's prescribed pills and bed-rest. She can't be still for a minute, (especially her tongue, but keep that to yourself). I've made her go to bed and she's actually stayed there. I'm in the shed with the radio, listening to what's happening in the world. I'm making a long oak table, with a pattern of oak leaves for us all to eat off in the orchard. I'm making no comment about Jess or the woman. I want you alive and happy.

I heard the US Fifth's captured Naples and liberated Corsica. People feel victory in the air; like cattle let out at spring after a long, cold winter. Your sister and Jess saw the new Betty Grable movie, Sweet Rosie O'Grady, while Mom looked after baby Dorothy. I don't think she's up to toddlers, who don't do what they're told, can't talk, and run like the wind.

I'm looking forward to seeing you, Son. The sugar maples and dogwood are so tall and green now. I love this time of year. It's quiet (apart from chaffinches and your mother). It's a good season for fruit and vegetables and we're lucky to eat so well. It'll be great to go

*for family walks together again. We went to Dolly Sods meadow and
I showed baby Dorothy the lion-face rock – just like we did when
you were a baby. The spruce hemlock and black cherry turned inky
when the sun went down. I aim to go fishing this week for the peace
and quiet or as soon as your Mom is moving (slowly) and talking
(quickly). It's what you learn to do when you're married for a long
time.*

    Love Pa

    *P.S. There's a development of new houses with white picket
fences, five minutes' walk from us. Marie saw one that would be
perfect for you, with four bedrooms and sizeable garden – it even
has space for vegetables and I could help you build a shed.*

Trevone Bay, July 2015

'Jack kept a diary, although I never read it,' said Tilly, talking over a
TV advert about air freshener. 'He said it was to remember the war
when it was over. I told him he wouldn't need to because he'd have
me. I have a photographic memory – as you can tell. I suppose his
mother has them. I'd love to know what he wrote about me. I bet
she needed smelling salts.'

    'Hospitalisation, I expect. I'm surprised she didn't contact you
though,' said Ava, passing Tilly a quartered soft cheese sandwich. 'I
wonder if his family knew you were pregnant?' Tilly shrugged.

    'It doesn't matter now. Let's go sit in the sun and I'll watch TV
from the patio.'

    'It might be too hot for you.'

    'I'll decide on that.' Snippy Tilly surfaced. Ava promised
herself she wouldn't watch TV like she used to; glued to box-sets

and watching other peoples' lives go by. She dragged Tilly's chair, foot rest and side table under the shade of the apple tree but in sight of her programmes. The air was alive with insects, birds, sea and breathy Round Hole. The sun was gorgeously warm.

'I need olive oil.' Ava found the oil which Tilly poured and rubbed on her skin until she glistened and smelt like salad dressing.

'You should have sun screen,' warned Ava. Tilly puffed out her lips.

'No, and this chair's still too much in the shade,' said Tilly, frowning. The dappled light transformed her into a spotted, shadowy creature with skin the texture of ancient bark. She leant on her walking frame and directed Ava until her chair was in the blazing sun.

'Good. There's no point worrying about skin cancer in ten years' time.' She watched a wedding programme in which a bride's friends and family chose the dress. Tilly said the lacy gown was too restrained and needed shortening, cinching-in, with more cleavage action. TV was Tilly's best friend and distraction. There was a lull in conversation. The day turned hazy, pressing down on them like a heavy blanket. Sunlight dazzled over the ocean and clouds breezed across yachts, filling their colourful sails as they tacked and criss-crossed the rippling surface.

'You'll really burn,' said Ava, offering her Factor 30.

'Good!' she said, rubbing more olive oil in. 'At least it's not extra virgin – that'd be wasted on me!' Drops of oily perspiration slid from Tilly's face to sweaty décolletage. Her eyes closed and breath quietened, then became loud snoring as her mouth gaped. Ava recalled how she looked before the ravages of drink, nicotine, age and pain took their toll. She mustn't waste a moment. It was four days until the date with Finn, if he didn't change his mind. She crossed her fingers. The sun slid over Cliff View's slate roof and crows flapped off in search of shade. Tilly's face finally slipped out of the sun. She was the colour of cooked Alaskan salmon. Ava turned down the television as the bride, in a gown as wide as the aisle, swished towards a gloomy-looking groom. Ava turned the TV off. For ten blissful minutes silence reigned.

'I'm parched,' were Tilly's first words. 'What happened to the bride?'

'She did a bunk with the best man,' said Ava, turning it back on and going to make tea. 'Your skin's bright pink.'

'I would have liked to see that,' she shrugged, lighting up.

'I love those photographs of you,' said Ava, buttering Tilly up. 'You must have been a model.'

'Of course,' she said, warming to the subject closest to her own heart. 'You should have seen the way I walked then. I wish I could show you but I'll give you a proper lesson. Well, try to.' She didn't sound confident.

'OK, let's do it,' said Ava gamely, and stood before Tilly. She could do with learning how to move confidently.

'Up straighter. That's better. Your shoulders need to be right back, as if there's a cord from spine to sky. That's it.' Ava felt muscles elongate and head balance oddly. 'Try not to seem in pain. Smile. Mouth shut; it's not the dentist. Right hand on right hip. And don't look so embarrassed Ava; you're not undergoing a gynaecological examination. Put your left leg out at forty-five degrees and point that foot but not as if you're about to kick a ball.

OK, better. Now, head high – don't look at the floor, tilt your chin slightly and look down with eyes only. Roll your hips. Don't allow your feet to stick out at 10 to 2; they must point to midnight. When you arrived, you had thigh chub rub, now it's gone. I read that in *Heat* magazine. Hold your arms loosely by your sides and move with a relaxed swing that matches hips. Don't turn your head, use your eyes, it's far more elegant.'

Ava set off like a badly-strung marionette.

'Oh God. No, no, no, no, no. Come back. Your feet stick out like a waddling duck's. Imagine there's a line on the grass and you're like a magnet on it. One in front of the other, easy-peasy. It's as if you're crushing a woodlouse with each step, that'll give your hips the correct swing.' Ava over-balanced, tottering off the make-believe line. 'Again!' commanded Tilly. 'Shoulders back, head high. That's more like it.'

For the next half hour Ava paraded up and down the garden at a snail's pace until she glided faster and smoother. She heard a car toot-toot its horn.

'You've got it, just about. And we're going to practice every day until it's second nature. Didn't your mother teach you?'

'No.' Her mum had to focus on earning a living after her dad left. Ava didn't ask why Vicky hadn't succeeded with style and posture.

'Gran, can't you leave women alone?' Ava, her back to the speaker, wobbled as she turned. The man by Tilly kissed her cheek and placed his hand on her shoulder. He was in his mid-30s and resembled Vicky but taller, slim and with the same slanting blue eyes as his grandmother.

'Oh, she's got a long way to go, Edward.' Ava froze. 'Come and sit, while Ava makes tea,' said Tilly, patting the deckchair Ava had vacated. Ava made for the kitchen like the good servant but as she passed Edward, he thrust out his hand. Ava shook it. A limp, soft touch. He let go, frowning.

'I thought I recognised you.'

'I don't think we've met,' Ava said, firmly. She was as good with faces and voices as she was bad at maps and maths.

'I sat next to you on the plane coming into Cornwall. You grabbed my sleeve and asked me to talk about what I did. When I said finances, you groaned.'

'Oh God, I'm sorry.' Ava wanted the ground to swallow her up. Edward held Ava's eyes with a satisfied look.

'Are you afraid of flying, Ava?' asked Tilly, curious.

'I've no idea why I'm terrified of sitting in a metal tube thousands of feet up,' Ava mumbled, scuttling inside, shoulders hunched, with Tilly's walk forgotten and face scarlet. The kitchen window was open and she heard every word as she arranged mugs, sugar, milk and bourbon biscuits on a tray.

Edward cleared his throat. 'Gran, sorry I've not been around. I had urgent business but I've seen Mum and she'll be here soon. Mackenzie's confirmed she's coming to your ninetieth although I hear you don't want any fuss.'

'Who said that?' Tilly's mouth pulled down like a five-year-old. 'I like fuss. I'm not interested in a tea party though, or anything that states my age while I can knock off twenty years.' Edward laughed and with it, snorted. As Ava carried out the tray, he looked her slowly up and down. Not pleasant, she thought.

'You're a typical man,' said Tilly, with great satisfaction. 'Always on the go.' Ava squirmed. He smiled briefly and dunked the biscuit into his tea but left it too long and only half came out. He looked at the cup as if it was its fault.

'Mackenzie's looking forward to meeting you, Gran, having heard so much from Mum,' he said, fishing out bits of soggy biscuit. Tilly pursed her lips together. Ava could only imagine.

'It'll be good to hear an American accent, like the old days,' Tilly said, breezily. 'I wish I could still dance, though.' Ava went to her room and left them to it. Edward departed an hour later, calling goodbye at her bedroom door.

Chapter Twenty-Eight

Woodburn,
Morgantown,
West Virginia,
USA,
June 18th, 1943

Dearest Jack,

You've broken my heart into a thousand pieces. I think of all the promises you made and solemn vows we were going to take. I can't believe you didn't mean them when you looked into my eyes and said you loved me. I think it's because death is all around you. I don't care about this English woman. I love you and you'll come back to me. She is nothing and will be forgotten with our history together as a family. Do you remember our first kiss when we were 14, at the river after the rope swing broke and you helped me out? You told me you loved me then. I'm heartbroken now but you are the dearest man and I'm going to keep your ring until we meet again. You'll have to say you don't love me to my face for me to believe you.

Still with my love,
Jessica

Trevone Bay, July 2015

Tilly roared at an old TV comedy about an Irish priest living on a small island, with a mad drunk, a dopey apprentice, and a tea-loving housekeeper. Ava sympathised with the housekeeper as she made kedgeree and mulled over what she'd say to District Councillor Gillian Jones about the proposed housing plans.

'What's that?' asked Tilly, prodding the rice.

'Smoked haddock with boiled eggs and rice and it's really good for you,' said Ava, matter-of-factly.

'Disgusting,' said Tilly, sifting through it. She separated out the fish, plucked out parsley and placed them on the side of the plate.

'Taste it,' said Ava, keeping her tone neutral. 'When May arrives, I'm popping out.'

'Fine,' she said, cautiously chewing a mouthful. She swallowed and slowly smiled. 'It's OK, and I don't like rice.' She polished off the lot. Ava scraped plates and washed the dishes looking out of the kitchen window. The sea churned the shoreline into a muddy-brown smudge. The colour reminded her of the Thames. At this hour she'd have battled her way through the daily commute. In eight years, she'd come to recognise regular passengers; the glamorous blonde 30-something in a yellow wool coat, who vanished, returning six months later with an infant strapped to her. Ava had felt a stab of envy as the woman kissed her baby's hidden face. That would be Sadie soon. Ava shuddered as she emptied bins, wishing it was as easy to empty her heart and mind. She changed into her multitasking corporate dress again.

'Cheekbones,' she said to herself, looking in the bathroom mirror and putting blusher on. 'Welcome back, you've been gone a long time.' Her dress was looser, and body leaner. She thought of seeing Finn imminently. It was strange, minus technology, not being able to scope him out beforehand. When May arrived, she asked about Gillian Jones.

'Absolute busybody whose husband dumped her for their Polish cleaner. Very friendly with Vicky, and equally as dull,' May said, spooning up left over kedgeree in the pan. 'This is delicious,' she mouthed.

Ava parked at the drab brick offices of the District Council and forked out three pounds for the privilege of parking. She signed in, hung a lanyard around her neck and travelled to the fourth floor in a lift that reeked of sausages. She turned right along a strip-lit narrow corridor to the scuffed door of Gillian Jones. Her title was written on a scratched, dull metal plaque. Ava rapped three times. 'Enter,' said a steely-sounding voice Just like school, thought Ava, and her armpits prickled.

Gillian Jones was ensconced on a black padded chair. She was a bird-like woman in her late fifties with a helmet of frizzy grey hair which last looked like it had been combed, styled and set forever in place in the early 80s. Judging by the look on her face, it was also the last time she'd smiled. Ms Jones wore a plaid, black and grey skirt with steel-coloured jumper, rife with wool bobbles. There wasn't, Ava thought, much to choose between her and the carpet. On her feet, flat pewter shoes with tarnished gold chains across the toes which jiggled as she crossed one foot over the other. They didn't quite touch the floor.

'How may I help?' said Ms Jones, without a trace of warmth. Ava didn't answer as her eyes swept the beige room with its fluorescent lighting and low, suspended ceiling. Stuffily hot, it drained all hope. There was a hint of garlic combined with a spicy, sickly perfume. One wall had a water stain, half-hidden by a triptych poster. The first was a photograph of Cornwall's coastline: *Our Vision*, it stated. Next, was one of a smiling family licking ice creams: *Our Mission*, while the third featured a countryside composition: *Our Core Values Going Forward*. It included a signpost pointing to three directions, stating: *Integrity, Reliability and Unity*. It was just the sort of pointless crap, thought Ava, which had crept into her office before she got the boot. The worn carpet tiles highlighted a dingy, grey track between door and MDF desk. Councillor Jones' eyes were expressionless as she grasped a thick wad of papers in both ringless hands, tapping them on the scuffed desk. She placed the documents to her right, laid her palm on them and tweaked her beak-like nose.

'Ava Westmorland. I booked to see you about some plans I saw on the council website.'

'How are you involved?' Ms Jones asked sniffly. She didn't offer Ava to sit on the small, hard chair opposite. Ava sat anyway and took out her notepad and biro. That always put the wind up people if they thought notes were being taken.

'Well,' said Ava, doodling. 'I'm enquiring about the new homes proposed by Daylight Developments around Cliff View.' In her former life she'd enjoyed asking questions – even if they were about selling products and services. Gillian Jones almost said something but stopped and gathered her thoughts. Ava drew a scarecrow and ravens.

'Why are you taking notes?' demanded Gillian, splitting her lips into a crocodile smile.

'Mrs Barwise lives at Cliff View and she wants me to relay what you said. I hope that's OK?' lied Ava, dating and timing the page. The councillor gave a curt nod, took off her glasses and shoved them in the nest of her hair.

'Mrs Barwise's carer, I believe?' said Gillian, checking her watch. 'You were the one dragged out to sea when you first arrived?' Ava flinched. Her idiocy had spread like an oil slick. 'I've got ten minutes before my next appointment and a day of back-to-back meetings.' Oh, how often had Ava heard that tedious statement in her previous working life.

'Of course,' replied Ava. 'Thank you for agreeing to see me.' Politeness was her best weapon with jobsworths. Gillian's mouth twitched. 'Cliff View would be encroached and surrounded.'

'I assure you,' said Ms Jones, stroking her throat with thumb and forefinger, 'That is to be taken care of.' As if no further explanation to the likes of Ava were required, she put her glasses back on. A tuft of frizzy hair stood up on her head, like a cockerel's, wafting about. Ava felt like Tilly now, needling and getting pleasure from it. Josh used to say some councillors preferred their general public not to have a clue about plans, until a decision was taken behind closed doors, whether voters wanted it or not.

'People need to live somewhere,' said Ms Jones, tapping the sheaf of papers with each word. 'There's a shortage of housing in Cornwall. There is social housing on this site.' She leant back.

'Tiny, and back-to-back. The other properties are luxury builds. So, none for locals on an average wage?' Ava scribbled. 'And isn't the social housing outside the gated part of the development?' She'd learned useful tactics from Josh. Ruffled, agitated, Gillian breathed heavily. Ava doodled Gillian's face into the scarecrow.

'That may well be,' said Ms Jones, trying to smooth the kinks of irritation out of her voice, 'but people who buy here inject vital money into our cash-strapped economy. Daylight Developments has given generously towards a new community centre, doctors' surgery and retail business. For locals.' She looked pleased with herself now.

'I'm glad you mentioned that. I nearly forgot,' said Ava. 'I believe those will be five miles away where the other much larger development is planned. That's a long trek for anyone without a car, plus the bus service has been cut to the bone hasn't it?'

Ms Jones' mouth pursed, highlighting creases fanning around it and the pupils of her lustreless eyes contracted.

'You seem to know an inordinate amount, given your position at Cliff View?'

My lowly position, thought Ava, who felt like a tiger in mouse's clothes. She might have no business being here but a little of Tilly's backbone had transplanted itself in her.

'Mrs Barwise wouldn't want houses surrounding her.'

'You're not an architect, I believe, and she's going into a home soon,' retorted Ms Jones and clamped her lips. 'Have you always been a carer?'

'No,' Ava said coolly, without further explanation. Gillian looked at her watch. Perspiration beaded her upper lip. She picked up the papers with both hands and shoved them in an old leather briefcase.

'I have a meeting,' she said curtly, standing. 'You can wait for the planning committee's decision.'

'Thank you so much for your time,' said Ava. 'The meeting's

next Wednesday isn't it?'

'Good day,' said Gillian and strode to the door, shoe chains rattling. She wrenched it open and waited until Ava went through and shut it sharply behind her. Ava hummed to herself. It felt good to cause righteous trouble. Gillian Jones had been rattled from her jangling shoes up. First, Ava needed to alert the local Press and headed to Padstow library. Becky was surrounded by a crowd of pensioners but gave a little wave. Settling at a computer, Ava dropped an anonymous email to *The Cornish Mercury*, mentioning Gillian Jones's advocacy of properties well beyond the price tag of ordinary locals.

Chapter Twenty-Nine

Cliff View, 26th August 1943

Tilly hummed to herself under a bright and cloudless sky. She darted around the garden picking a handful of violet periwinkles and a few blowsy, blood-orange flowers she didn't recognise. A patch of them had survived when the garden was dug up for root vegetables and greens. They were a joy to see. She put the flowers in a vase on the kitchen table. The Major was at home for two days, and with the boys at school she'd been given the day off; thrillingly, it coincided with Jack being free. She chose her favourite white cotton dress, belted around her waist, with a high collar (designed by Aunty Vi) and rolled up her swimming costume in a towel.

Tilly baked a dozen honey biscuits for a picnic lunch, spiced with cinnamon and for once they hadn't burnt. They could eat Martha's rosemary-flavoured cold roast potatoes with lots of salt. Tilly could pretend she'd made them with her own not-so-fair hands (but still manicured, despite harsh domestic duties). She'd baked brown bread that was dry but OK with a sliver of butter and a dollop of Martha's home-made, if a little sharp, Humpsie Dumpsie Dearie jam with apples, pears and plums. Jack brought a bar of Hershey's, a hip flask of whisky and the all-important rug. It was the thought of lying on that which put Tilly in such a joyous mood that she hummed tunelessly as they walked. He put his fingers in his ears and she pinched his arm.

Jack had hold of a pre-war map and while there were no road signs now, he read the contours of the earth as well as he read hers. Tilly took the map from him and turned it around in a circle. He raised an eyebrow and she handed it back. Her father was the same; a map man. The beaches had varying amounts of mines, barbed wire entanglements and pillboxes. But there were still secret, war-free spaces you could slip through. Strolling arm-in-arm along the headland Jack revealed it was his 25th birthday.

'Well, let's not waste this sun and find somewhere good to celebrate in the best way,' said Tilly, kissing his lips.

'For a beautiful woman such behaviour utterly becomes you.' That was exactly what Tilly wanted, unlike her mother: the good God-fearing woman, in love with suffering and not a lewd word from her prim lips.

'Do you think your mother will like me?' Tilly asked, hesitant. Jack mainly talked about his brother and sister. And never about Jess. She still felt anxious about his ex-fiancée.

'Of course, Mom will, and my sister will be your best friend,' he said, as they climbed. 'Look.' Jack pulled her to the top of the ridge and below lay Treyarnon Bay, wide, white-sanded and backed by dunes and cliffs. The limpid green water appeared slack and shallow for miles. To one side, there stretched a chain of rock pools and in front, Trethias Island.

'It's a rocky, tidal outcrop,' he informed her, lacing his hand with hers. 'This makes me miss my old job.' He shared his knowledge about tides and the layered cliffs which revealed their molten, glacial histories. As a geologist he'd taken aerial photographs of the creases and folds of earth's crust in America's frenzied hunt for oil. Tilly was entranced and mouthed *geologist's wife* to herself. She liked to think of him digging out earth's secrets. He talked about the fossilised creatures he'd found that stopped him believing in God.

'We return to the earth,' he said, throwing a pebble into a rock pool, watching the spreading circles on the water's surface. 'After what I've seen people choose to do to each other I can't wait to go back to photographing the earth.'

'I can't wait either,' she said, wistfully.

'As long as you don't map read.' And she threw a pebble at him. 'That's quartz,' he said, catching and inspecting it. He pointed out slices of angular greenish slate in the cliffs, thick yellow clay and a grey-white glitter of quartz veins, created in miraculous, godless aeons.

They found the perfect rock pool with sand at the bottom and they were all alone. The water was like green glass. Jack stripped and had to cajole her to do the same; swimming wasn't something Liverpool children were taught. Certainly not naked. Tilly shrieked as she edged in, so he hauled her to him. She could just about doggy paddle, which made him laugh so she splashed him. Afterwards, shivering beneath cliffs where noisy razorbills and guillemots nested, they made love in a cave that stretched on into darkness.

'Smugglers came here,' he said. 'Come on, let's explore.' He grasped her hand and using his flickering lighter, they entered, deeper and deeper. Just as Tilly became disorientated and afraid, there was a pinprick of expanding light and minutes later, they found themselves through the other side of cliff, in a sheltered deserted bay. They made love again on the beach without a condom.

He felt so much better naked inside her, even though he came on her belly. An hour later, Jack insisted on returning when Tilly was all for staying and sleeping. It was sheltered and warm and felt like their own private paradise. But he propelled her on. Half-way through the cave, they felt seawater trickle along the floor, rising quickly to ankles, then knees. By the time they emerged it was up to their thighs and had swallowed the beach. He quickly pulled Tilly up the rocks.

Their clothes and rug were soaked but his camera was safe. Jack found a sand dune, where they lay their sodden things on the grass.

'Let me take some photographs, here like this with the light falling on you.'

Tilly lay, hands behind her head and looking up, with the faintest glimmer of a smile.

Chapter Thirty

Diary Entry: St Eval, June 22nd, 1943

> *Gritty-eyed but can't sleep, even with the Doc's tablets. Letters from Mom about Jess but there's no going back. Spent hours in the dark room, with its vinegary taint, spools of film in rows, metallic solutions, swilling and waiting. Everything's quiet and bathed in soft red light as destruction surfaces: a falling plane, running people, ruined buildings.*
>
> *I keep Tilly for last, tint her bathing costume red. Sky and sand frame her; body angled to me, better legs than Betty Grable. Another, lying on her stomach, hands cupping her face and eyes so blue they appear pale gray. I pin her up and blow the surface. She sways and dazzles.*

Trevone Bay, July 2015

Tomorrow Ava would see Finn. Her stomach flipped and it was a thrilling feeling she'd not had for a decade. School holidays had arrived in Cornwall and so did the *ants*; thousands upon thousands of holidaymakers flooding in to camp, surf, drink, party, and gorge their way through the next six hectic weeks. The crowded beaches smelt of sun screen and barbecues. Jammed roads drove Ava and May to distraction as Trevone's high-hedged, narrow lanes became clogged. Nosy parkers sauntered past Cliff View, staring in to what appeared a shanty home amongst its plush neighbours. Ava hung net curtains so Tilly had privacy. If a passer-by spent too long prying, Tilly put up two fingers and swore outrageously. Ava dreaded queues at the local shops and May fumed at being asked directions by *The posh and rude* so she'd send them the opposite way or pretend she couldn't speak English. Tilly loved that.

On Friday, Ava's shoreline jog with Charlie was the best yet, despite dodging numerous surfers and dog walkers. Lacy waves crumbled over themselves, dribbling green to white, as if too exhausted to froth. Surfers floated like basking seals in a long, straggly line, thirty feet out. She discussed Daylight Developments with Charlie.

'Do I tell Tilly?'

'She's *compos mentis*. Just because she's old doesn't mean her views don't count on the future of her property.'

'Mmm. Maybe I should tell Vicky first?'

'She wants Tilly out of Cliff View.'

'It's nothing to do with me but I feel caught up in it. I don't like knowing something that has such an impact.'

Ava found Tilly tapping her cigarette, painfully folding one leg over the other with ankles joined. She looked elegant but agitated as she waved Ava to sit down.

'I miss having a body that works. Don't waste yours, Ava. For many years, I ached for Jack too. But you can only mourn so much when you're young, so I married and had lovers, who liked me because I didn't want to get involved. I wasn't concerned about what was going on in their heads or their lives. Uncomplicated pleasure was what I wanted. Nobody was better than Jack. You should look out for a love like that and taste it once in your life.' A couple danced across the TV screen. The woman, dressed like a bird of paradise and the man, black-suited and not very able, waltzed after her. Tilly sighed.

'That's what I'd give my right arm to do now. Don't become the sort of woman obsessed with cakes and cats.'

'Why are you telling me this?' asked Ava. She'd loved cooking programmes and quite fancied a kitten.

'Because you're wasting time. Look at her on the dance floor. She's like quicksilver,' said Tilly. 'When do you think the story will go in the *Daily World*?'

'Nearer the 70th anniversary celebrations. The Press is a nest of vipers you know,' said Ava, about to bite a fingernail but stopped when she saw how they'd grown and looked startling white against her tanned hands.

'But it's not boring is it? It's not staring at the four walls and TV.'

'No, you're right, it's not boring.'

'There's something I need to tell you, Tilly.' The old woman inhaled her cigarette and turned her blue eyes on Ava.

'You can say anything to me.'

Ava told her about Gillian Jones, Daylight Developments and future plans around Cliff View. Tilly closed her eyes and inhaled deeply.

'Should be called Daylight Robbery. Vicky's in the thick of this. Like a vulture circling, set to pick over my bones. It's to be expected but I have my own plans.' An advert for toilet paper appeared and they watched a labrador puppy chase an unravelling roll. 'God knows what that's got to do with crapping. Did you buy loo rolls, Ava?'

'We have enough to last a pandemic, or Armageddon.'

Tilly smiled. A dating programme began and absorbed Tilly as a line of heavily made-up women, in tight revealing dresses and complex hairstyles, vied for one timid man who asked dull questions in order to choose his perfect match. Ava squirmed as combatant females, with scripted, innuendo-laden lines attempted to entice the computer programmer.

'He looks like he prefers a mouse in his hand rather than a real woman,' said Tilly, flicking through a gossip magazine with her huge magnifying glass.

'Look at that Kim Cardigan,' she said, peering at the reality star's ballooning bottom.

'Kardashian,' said Ava laughing.

'Whatever, you've got a better rear than Cardigan.'

'Thanks, I think.'

After preparing Tilly's lamb casserole with potatoes roasted with rosemary and buttery carrots, Ava got ready for her first date in a decade. She shaved with a blunt razor that left her legs bright red, plucked her Catholic eyebrows and slathered herself in moisturiser. If Finn turned up, she fretted about what would she talk about, other than Tilly and why she'd ended up here? She absolutely mustn't mention Josh and Sadie…

Chapter Thirty-One

Trevone Bay, 30th March 1944

Tilly bundled Jamie and Alex out before 9am. While Martha was much better, the sleeping tablets she took rarely saw her stir before mid-morning. It had stopped raining inland but out to sea it trailed like gauze. The cold air was fresh and hundreds of worms wriggled on the ground. The boys squealed at them as they tore down the hill to Trevone Bay, to excavate like terriers in wet soft sand, exploring for fossils. Jack had told them how dead animals gradually turned to stone, to be sealed and preserved for millennia. After five minutes digging, Alex hit Jamie on the head with his spade. He screamed and retaliated, so Tilly took both implements away, until they promised to behave. It took three sulky seconds to agree and resume their tunnelling. They were soaked, filthy and perfectly happy.

The sky turned a downy blue as if the icing-sugar clouds had been thoroughly whisked until dissolved above a navy sea with deep swells. Tilly built a sandcastle and they all collected shells for tiny windows and doors, with a tangled seaweed garden. At long last she heard the noise she longed for, and filled her with dread.

The steady humming sound of four-engine Lancaster bombers returning after their mission filled the air. Unwaveringly, the great whirring increased until it roared, scattering flocks of gulls. The vibrations triggered a palpable sense of distress in Tilly. The boys gazed up, shading their eyes. Jamie grabbed hold of Tilly's hand and sucked his other thumb. Tilly counted them, 17, including one that wobbled and smoked as it dropped out of formation to land first at St Eval. She sank to her knees. Jamie eased himself onto her lap and Alex looped his arm around her shoulder, playing with a lock of her hair. The last plane tipped its wings, once, twice. That was Jack, it's what he did if he saw her. She waved frantically, until they'd dropped away. The world was the same once more; clattering waves, shrieking boys and gulls. At 1pm she took them home, scrubbed and fed them, put them to bed for a nap and gave a jellied vegetable salad with brown buttered bread to Martha, who promised to get up once she'd eaten. Excusing herself, Tilly freshened up and ran back to the bay. There he was, hands in his pockets, one leg crossed over the other, leaning on a rock, smoking. Alive and divine, she thought, counting her blessings.

On good days, he asked her to tell him what she'd been doing. Tilly chirped away like a sparrow about the boys, lethargic Martha, bookworm Major, digging vegetables, any old tripe. She embroidered it all, like a tapestry, making herself the dazzling queen of unglamorous domesticity. She hoped he could see her as his wife in the Blue Mountains of Virginia, even if she wasn't the bride his mother wanted. She loved it best when Jack teased her. He asked her to repeat a word because it was *cute*, or fetch something that wasn't necessary because he loved the way she walked. She liked watching him skim stones into the sea, counting how many times they bounced. And loved it when he chased her on the beach, picked her up and lay her down in the dunes where the whispering grass concealed them. She could not make him forget what he'd seen in the air but she could make him happy because he made her world perfect.

At times he was deathly quiet and Tilly would instinctively know to hold her tongue. After a difficult mission his hands shook. He took tablets for that and tablets to sleep and more tablets to stay awake for missions. She wondered he didn't rattle.

When the Major was away, she'd sneak Jack in at night through the bedroom window. Martha wouldn't notice with her sleeping tablets and Tilly ensured the boys were busy to the point of exhaustion and never woke. In deep sleep, Jack muttered and she whispered *Hush, hush.* When he came to, not quite conscious and disorientated, he'd whisper about dying and about his friends' deaths. She cried then.

Occasionally, Jack picked her up in a jeep. They'd race to the Pavilion cinema above Towan beach and watch movies with 750 others, wrapped in a warm pall of mauve smoke. *The Gentle Sex* and *Women Aren't Angels* were her favourites. Jack was content holding hands in the fuggy darkness. They'd have tea at a little café rammed with servicemen and their girls. He'd take her dancing at the Blue Lagoon on Cliff Road and drinking at the RAF Officers' Club in the Grantham Hotel. There, weary air crews from St Mawgan and St Eval gathered to sink themselves into a stupor.

There was a chip shop which opened once the pub next door closed. They entered via a long, dark curtain, to ensure the blackout was maintained and such was the queue that some drunken GIs who needed a pee staggered to the harbour wall. One or two toppled in, to a mixture of laughter and panic as a life-ring was thrown down and they were hauled up. Jack was always careful driving her back because intoxicated GIs belted around narrow lanes like race-tracks and there were a few *smack-ups* as he called them. And every day now, thousands more Americans arrived by plane and train. Something big was coming.

'Please don't die,' she whispered. It was a mantra she repeated last thing at night and first thing in the morning, 'Please don't die.'

Chapter Thirty-Two

Morgantown,
August 11th, 1943

Hi Jack,

I'm heading to Blighty but not been told where and doubt I'll see you. Marie's doing swell, although Dorothy is a bit put out by baby Donald. She wants to bake him in a hot pie! Donald's doing a sterling job diverting Mom's attention from me and you. Her palpitations are daily and she blames two sons in the war. Pa's retreated to woodwork. We visited Cheat Canyon yesterday. A month ago its river banks were stacked up until a storm washed them away, exposing sandstone, shale and fossils. Mom dismisses fossils because they don't fit in with God's making of the world. I hiked on up to the plateaus. The forest seemed folded in heavy, dark drapes rising out of quartz beds. It's real beautiful and I fear not seeing it again.

Your brother,
Joey

Trevone Bay, July 2015

Torrential rain woke Ava at 6am. A squall barrelled in over the Atlantic and gutters flushed roads with streams of muddy water. Ava dressed in jeans, white T-shirt, blue jumper and minimal make-up. Her stomach felt like jelly and she couldn't eat a thing. May arrived, all bright eyed and excited for Ava, as she rustled up Tilly's scrambled egg and chopped bacon. By 10am the storm had blown itself out and steam rose from damp, warm, and sweet-smelling earth. Birds sang and Round Hole murmured. Ava forced down tea. What to talk about? Divorce, redundancy, taking on this job through sheer desperation? All vetoed, she vowed. Tilly said women generally talked about bloody boring subjects and looking after an OAP was number one.

'Ava, practise your walk,' called Tilly, while May ran her bath.

'Hopefully, we'll drive!'

'But you have to walk at some point. Go on.'

'Leave her alone,' said May, and the pair undressed Tilly and hoisted her up. The phone rang and May answered.

'We didn't know. I'm sorry. Your mother's in the bath.' May returned, handing Tilly the phone mid-air.

'I don't give a damn, Vicky,' said Tilly. 'It's about me. You aren't mentioned, so why should you care?' Vicky must have put the phone down this time. Tilly looked smug as they lowered her into the water.

'It's in the *Daily World*,' said May, offering a squeeze of lemon shower gel to Tilly.

*

The doorbell rang and Ava, heart pounding, answered. It was Finn, holding the newspaper he'd picked up off the doormat. She swiped it off him. May was behind and whisked it to Tilly, who, rapidly washed and dressed, demanded to see it.

'I didn't think anyone was still so enthusiastic about print,' said Finn. 'How are you?'

201

'Fine,' she said, but not really, she thought. 'Come in.' He followed her. Ava's mouth was dry, stomach in knots and mind electric. He wore a long-sleeved indigo T-shirt, black jeans, and desert boots. Nice grassy smell. Perched on his head was a pair of glasses and directly over them, sunglasses with a crack across one lens. They looked stupid but he obviously didn't care. Ava admired that.

'There you are!' said May triumphantly to Finn, and flicking open the paper until she came to the page. 'Tilly, you look amazing.' Ava picked up her coat and bag.

'Did they airbrush me like I asked? Pass the magnifier. Damn it, I can't read a thing.'

Finn looked at her carefully. She might need to sit down if he carried on like that.

'Tilly's in the *Daily World*, about dieting and beauty,' she blurted to him, as May showed them the photograph. There was Tilly beaming out of the double-page spread. Her false teeth made her lips protrude like a duck's. Robbie stood behind Tilly with his arm around Evangeline and their hands lightly on Tilly's shoulders; like a freaky family photograph. Tilly looked preening and imperious, holding a cigarette in one hand and brandy glass in the other. The photograph of young Tilly on the beach in her scarlet-tinted costume leaned against her chest.

May read out the headline: *Wartime Beauty launches charity-funding retro-diet across Cornwall.* She described how Evangeline and Robbie were just two of her numerous slimming successes set to transform the region's clotted-cream lovers into ration-conscious gym bunnies – the diet, it extolled, allowed the odd drink and smoking.

'It's only an odd drink because you lot hide it,' snapped Tilly, smiling.

May revealed how Tilly's criticisms of the weighty staff had led them to shed half a ton between them. Nurses quoted Tilly as, *Being cruel to be kind* because she'd told them, *Their bottoms looked marshmallow ginormous*. It went on to state that while Tilly smoked 40-a-day and drank, what she called, *A reasonable amount*, she believed her longevity was due to *Diet, good genes and romance*. A doctor, drafted in to comment, stated Tilly was *A freak of nature and a one-in-a-million smoker and drinker*, warning her lifestyle *Was a recipe for early death that nobody should copy*. There was no mention of Vicky, Edward or Jack. Ava was glad of the latter, as one mention of a long-lost American lover would have journalists slavering to find out what happened to him and track down his family.

'*Freak of nature*,' said Tilly, delighted. 'Well, I don't mind and they didn't reveal my age but they did mention I was 20 when the war ended, so it's not difficult.' Tilly lit up and finally squinted at Finn, like a specimen under a microscope.

'So, you're the date?' said Tilly, arching non-existent eyebrows. Finn remained silent at the threshold of the room. Tilly went back to the paper. Rude, thought Ava, utterly bloody rude, glancing at Finn. She assumed his broad shoulders were down to blacksmithing rather than the gym and unlike Josh he'd not checked himself out in the mirror, even once.

'What's your name?' she asked, handing the paper to May.

'Finn Blake.'

'And what do you do?' asked Tilly. Ava, prickly with embarrassment, wanted out.

'Blacksmith,' came the calm reply. He wasn't going to expand, flatter or wheedle.

'All those sweaty horses. You must be strong then; like that Pull Dark,' said Tilly, glinty-eyed. Ava edged for the door.

'Not horses, metalwork.'

'That's not as interesting.' Finn didn't respond.

'It's good to meet you Finn,' May butted in, glaring at Tilly.

'Men and women can't be friends,' announced Tilly. 'Maybe after sex but not before.'

'Well, fortunately we've dealt with that,' said Ava brazen, without looking at Finn. Ava decided it would be the first and last time she'd see him so it didn't matter. Tilly cackled.

'I thought so!' said Tilly. 'She's been living with me, lost weight, walks better and finally gets laid.'

'Right, see you later,' said Ava, preparing to say goodbye to Finn and take herself for a long singular walk. 'Don't talk to anyone who rings or calls,' she warned Tilly. 'May, if someone does, please just take their contact details, OK?'

Finn waited at the gate, while Ava tied a red waterproof around her waist.

'Tilly's jealous and he's gorgeous,' whispered May behind her. Ava walked self-consciously towards him as Round Hole hissed and water gurgled downhill. The grass verge squelched underfoot, soaking her canvas shoes.

'I didn't know we'd slept together. I think I'd have remembered,' he said, a mere trace of a smile.

'Sorry, it was to shut her up. Look, we don't have to go out.'

'No wonder nobody bet on you staying. It's a lovely day and I don't have many without Joe, and you don't without Tilly, so let's not waste it. You deserve a medal.'

'You're right,' said Ava, looking for the car. Finn headed to the trees where a tandem bike leant against a trunk.

'I've never ridden one,' said Ava, laughing.

'If you get bored you could stop pedalling and do a crossword, make a call. I wouldn't notice, except going uphill.'

'I don't have a mobile and can't do crosswords. Not even simple ones, or map read.'

'I know the way,' said Finn, handing her a tatty black cycle helmet. The inside of which was torn and sweat-stained. 'Sorry it's knackered. I hate them but Joe made me promise to wear one and if I do, you do.' Finn held the bike steady for her and she clambered on. As they set off, wobbling, she bumped her nose on his back.

'Ouch. Sorry,' she said, tears welling.

'It reminds me of when we first met.' He pedalled downhill at a rate that alarmed Ava so much she lifted her feet. Finn whistled and they cycled in silence, accompanied by the tyres' rhythmical splashes in puddles. A flock of swans slow-flapped overhead, webbed feet trailing, their wings making a humming whistling sound. A huge four-by-four zoomed past, splattering water and soaking their legs. He cursed, turning into a narrow lane lined with cowslips, red clover and swaying cow parsley, alive with birds. Through gaps Ava saw crops, plastic tunnels, horses, sheep and cows. Poppies blazed in a field of moon daisies. A branch cracked and Ava spotted the russet pelt of a fleeting deer melt through a mushroom-scented canopy. Finn halted at a junction signposting St Eval.

'I'd love to see that place. Tilly danced there in the war.' She didn't mention the long-lost love. He turned towards it.

The periphery of the base was all towering twenty-first century listening equipment tuned to other countries' top secrets. Dilapidated sea-worn buildings clustered around the entrance, leading to ivy-covered hangars and half-fallen-down ruins. A crumbling tower loomed at the intersection of grassy runways where swift-moving clouds cast shadows across the dereliction. Sweat trickled down Finn's back. The smell of him now; rich and sweet.

'I'll leave the bike at the gate.' Finn held the frame while Ava performed a one-legged stagger off.

'Don't you lock it?'

'Not here,' he said.

That wouldn't last five seconds in London, thought Ava. They strolled, feet apart, as Ava imagined Tilly in high heels and dresses, partying, dancing, and making love to Jack. The cracked concrete runways were bordered by knee-high grass, laced with buttercups and daisies. Petals shivered in the wind like thousands of lights. They sat near the cliff's edge watching seals slip around a couple of paddle boarders. Loops of fragmented light danced on the underside of an anchored yacht. Trailing behind its rudder, a layer of oil formed slick lines that turned patches of clear green sea glassy calm.

Finn offered Ava a bottle of water. She felt observed as she tipped her head back and swallowed. When he drank, she watched his tanned throat moved slowly. Ava leant back on her hands and he copied. Gulls gathered in front of clouds that were bright with coppery threads. The silence was palpable.

'Are you always so quiet?' said Ava, unable to help herself filling the void.

'No. Tilly doesn't strike me as one for silence. I thought your ears might like a rest.' Finn picked a long blade of grass, pressed its feathery seeds and scattered them. He chewed the end and squinted out to sea.

'When she sleeps the talking stops, but there's snoring,' said Ava. 'Mostly she chats to herself and the TV. I switch off unless she says my name, or some other name. She gets a bit muddled.' Ava felt the light brush of a ladybird land on the back of her hand.

'How did you end up here; you don't look the domesticated type?' Finn asked, twisting the grass stem between his fingers, so it flattened and turned deeper green. There was no getting away from that question.

'OK. Briefly, because it's boring,' Ava said. 'My husband of a year left me for our friend and colleague. They were journalists and got promoted. I wrote adverts and was made redundant and homeless. She's expecting his baby. Tilly's daughter was desperate for a carer which is why she took me on with zero qualifications.'

'I see,' he said, his face unrevealing. Across the horizon two huge tankers, like slow moving cities, glided in opposite directions.

'Your turn,' said Ava.

Finn chucked the grass away. 'I met Cassie when I was a sewage engineer for Oxfam in Kenya. I was Mr Sanitation of Mukaru. Cassie was thirty-six, from Texas. We had Joe but she had postnatal depression and didn't bond with him. Depression's a greedy illness.

She was in and out of hospital. We tried living in Texas but Cassie's family was part of her problem. We came back here and mum helped with Joe. Cassie headed for Somalia and being without Joe in war zones banished her depression.' Finn looked out to sea. 'She met someone whose kids have left home and sees Joe two or three times a year. It works.'

'That's tough.'

'No, manageable.' He smiled. 'Joe's my absolute priority. I'm glad I've just got him, he's enough.'

Ava understood how having one would be enough. She'd be happy with one.

'I thought you were a blacksmith?'

'Retrained. I couldn't go all over the world and leave my lad,' he said, picking another blade of grass.

'Does Joe miss his mum?'

Finn rubbed the side of his face, and pressed a hand to the back of his neck.

'He's OK; happy as far as I can tell. Mum, Dad and my sister dote on him. You're the first woman I've told. And the first and last I've bet on.' He looked at her in such a way she held her breath.

'Glad on both counts,' said Ava. Finn reached out his hand and Ava took it to stand up. 'I've got a surprise,' he said. Ava felt something peculiar and fizzy. Happy, she thought, a very novel sensation.

'Where are we going?' asked Ava, as they cycled uphill. It was tempting to let him do the work and she slowed a little. Tomorrow her thighs would throb.

'Somewhere to take your breath away, I hope,' said Finn. 'By the way, I can tell if you don't pedal.' Ava laughed. He paused at signs for Carenwas and Bedruthan Steps.

'The first means rock pile of summer dwelling and the other is red-one's dwelling. A red-haired giant is supposed to use the sea stacks as stepping stones. In reality it was a ship-wreckers' and smugglers' haven.'

The razor-edged triangular stones thrust out of the sand like the sharp fins of a prehistoric sea monster. Sheer steps poured down the cliff face like a stone waterfall.

'Stunning.'

'And deadly with riptides,' said Finn. Ava saw through the deceptive tranquillity. 'There are swimming pools at low tide and the sand is better than the Bahamas. You can reach Constantine Island as long as you know what you're doing.'

Tilly had mentioned that island; it was where Jack rowed her, and where Tilly liked to think she got pregnant.

'Lunch is my treat,' Finn said, approaching the snug, low walls of the New Inn. The cosy bar had checked orange sofas, wood-burning stove and spectacular views of the rippling ocean sweeping around the stacks. A waiter seated them at a reserved table-for-two by the window. A bunch of moon daisies and cow parsley spilled out of a white vase. Silver cutlery and crisp linen napkins lay on the table.

'Your champagne, sir,' said the waiter. He poured a glass for Finn and waited for him to sample it, but he slid it to Ava. She tasted and nodded; all champagne was good to her.

'A toast to the RNLI, winning a bet, and jobs we take when least expecting them,' said Finn, grinning.

'And a fantastic fox, barn dances, and tandem riding.' Their glasses clinked.

Ava ordered goat's cheese and red pepper brochette, home-made crab-cakes with chips, coleslaw and green salad, followed by meringue and strawberries. Finn had pate, steak, coleslaw, salad, chips, and a platter of local cheeses.

'Thank you for my life and today,' said Ava. Finn leant back, putting his hands behind his head. It showed off the breadth of his chest. They chatted about music, parents, favourite food, books and festivals. The conversations were easy and Ava warmed to him. No, completely, joyfully relaxed, as if she'd known him years. She asked about his damaged hands. He admitted his skills as a blacksmith did not include avoiding frequent burns and cuts. Ava caught herself wanting to press her lips to the wounds but instead took another sip of champagne.

'What time is it?' asked Ava, as the sun's reflection broadened into a shimmering pillar on the water.

'Nearly 4pm.'

'I have to get back. I can't be late.'

'OK, Cinderella, we'll take a shortcut. And I've got some cash over for another outing, if you'd like?'

Ava smiled. *Yes please*, she thought and nodded. Finn whistled as they cycled through towering pines, spruce and beech woods. The trees tangled roots lay in deep shadows. Ava thought they resembled Tilly's twisted feet and hands. Moss-cushioned undulating earth buzzed with insects and soft rustlings of birds and animals. An old car, left to rot, had transformed into a strange furnishing. There was a hiss and gurgle of fast-running water trickling over stones. The tapering smokestack of a ruined tin mine came into view, overlooking the ocean and surrounded by shoulder-high nettles, thistles and knotted brambles, as if sleeping beauty might be there. Some of its blackened bricks were missing, allowing sunlight to spill through arched, lichen-covered windows. Bright ferns sprouted from ruined walls and doorways.

'We've got five minutes and this is the best view,' said Finn. He led the way through a barely-visible path, banked by tumbling ivy. Ava touched the tower's warm stones. Water oozed underfoot and a cormorant preened on a bed of lady's mantle, whose silver leaves held droplets of water like beads of mercury. Finn stood close as waves shivered across the ocean's surface.

'Look,' he said, picking three tiny red berries. 'Wild strawberries.' He handed them to Ava, she gave one back. They were the sweetest, most perfumed fruit she'd tasted. She smiled at him. Surely, he'd kiss her now?

'I better get you back,' said Finn, already turning. Ava felt a stab of disappointment as they pedalled past dripping caverns half hidden by dense pockets of undergrowth. She asked to walk up the steep meandering lane to Cliff View.

'But for you I would not have had this day,' she said.

He stopped. 'It's been good. Give me your number so I can see you again,' he said, quietly.

'I've only a landline,' replied Ava. Finn wrote Tilly's number on his blacksmith's card. And then, without a kiss, he was gone, wearing his two pairs of glasses. Ava noticed an elegant vintage open-topped sports car parked outside Cliff View. Definitely not a journalist, she decided.

Chapter Thirty-Three

Morgantown
August 20ᵗʰ, 1943

Dear Son,

I hope you're well. I've heard on the grapevine that a big push is coming and know from the last war what that feels like. My heart is with you every step of the way.

Jess is here often and asks about you. I don't know what to say; so I keep quiet. It's what long-married men do. Increasingly, I find silence the best option. Besides, you can imagine your Mom doesn't need any encouragement to converse on the subject.

I'm expert at vegetable planting and wood-turning and both are best done in tranquillity. Don't tell your Mom but when you come home with this other woman, I'll deal with your Mom. That's all now, Son. I'll be thinking of you every minute.

Love,

Pa

Trevone Bay, July 2015

'I hope you had a good time?' asked May, welcoming Ava back. She slipped on her coat and stepped out the door. 'Mr Hogwood, the estate agent's here. And you were right; there were calls from journalists. Very pushy. I told them to ring back but Tilly insisted on speaking. I couldn't stop her.' May hesitated as she buttoned her coat.

'How many and do you remember who?' Ava asked, her stomach churning. Vicky would hold her to account.

'Five. I wrote down their numbers by the phone. A TV station asked to visit but Tilly vetoed that. She told them she needed more time – about a year – to get screen-ready. All the conversations were pretty much one-sided. Tilly's side.'

Vicky would be incandescent, thought Ava, as Tilly erupted into a cackle in the front room. In response there was a light, inaudible voice.

'I'm off to the cinema. Jeff wants to see *Terminator* but I'd prefer *Amy*. Tilly says I'll win because, as she delicately put it, Jeff wants to, *Feel me up in the back row*. There's a diehard romantic.' And off May stalked. Ava sloped to the kitchen but Tilly called.

'Come in, Ava, and tell us all about your new lover.' Ava prickled. She loathed the way Tilly could be fine with her alone but with company transformed into a diva. Ensconced on the sofa perched a tiny man in his late 50s, who flashed a smile that didn't reach his eyes. He reeked of expensive floral aftershave. His luxurious black thick thatch of hair was most definitely a wig and the wispy salt and pepper goatee his own.

'Pleased to meet you,' he announced, in a tinny voice, rising and gingerly shaking Ava's hand. He was barely up to Ava's shoulders. His skin was cool and clammy as a frog's.

'Peter Hogwood, of Hogwood Estate Agency.' He released her hand and eased himself back in position. Hogwood oozed car salesman's charm in his perfectly-fitted pale grey suit and pastel pink shirt. He gave his rapt attention to Tilly. Ava had been measured up and found wanting in a second. She was neither a home owner nor future buyer and therefore, of no interest. He reminded Ava of an elf as he drank tea with his little pinkie finger extended; an affectation.

'Ava's my carer, Peter,' said Tilly. 'She looks a lot better now than when she arrived. Where did you go with the new man?' Mr Hogwood took his china teacup and smiled thinly. Ava was not in doormat-mode.

'I need to know about the journalists.'

'We'll talk about that later,' Tilly said, holding up one hand. 'Mr Hogwood's building some lovely new homes nearby.'

Mr Hogwood's smile stretched like a Cheshire cat. 'If you're considering buying, my dear,' he turned to Ava, 'it's cheaper off-plan. As a friend of Tilly's, I could stretch things.'

'Not far enough, Peter,' said Tilly.

'You're rude,' said Ava, abruptly and marched out. Perhaps Tilly deserved what was coming as she gave her strong views about a house renovation programme, saying the architect was, *A man who'd need a decade to design a shed.* Mr Hogwood concurred and moved the conversation on.

'Remember the Smyths?' Mr Hogwood, said. 'Well, they just got planning permission for a chunk of their garden and without a stroke of work I sold it for £400,000. But you have the best views of Trevose Headland, Gulland and Round Hole.'

'I know how much this place is worth, Peter, and I'm not selling. How's Margaret?' Asking about his wife was enough to see Mr Hogwood wrap up their conversation and say a swift goodbye. He stepped in to the kitchen, handing Ava a bouquet of handtied red roses.

'If you could pop them in a vase,' he said, dismissively. Ava wanted to throw the odourless bunch in the bin. She plucked out the white card which stated, *To a beautiful woman*. Creep, she thought, shoving them in a jug as Mr Hogwood roared off in a cloud of black exhaust smoke from his beautiful car. She carried them in and turned on Tilly.

'I felt embarrassed by the way you spoke to me in front of him. You have no right, and don't do it again.' Her hands shook. Tilly at least looked shamefaced.

'I'm sorry, I can't help it,' said Tilly. 'I don't plan what I say.' As if to prove a point, she added, 'That car of his once belonged to a film star. It never gets out of third-gear and cost so much to buy and keep on the road it ruined what little hope he had of marital sex. And there's not much chance of extra-marital because while his bank balance is big, nothing else is.'

'I don't care, I don't want you talking about me to other people. OK?'

'OK.'

'Right. Journalists,' said Ava, not bearing to think about the sex-starved elf in his classy car.

'I got fed up with their questions so I spiced things up and made them laugh. At least I'm not boring.'

'Vicky won't like it.'

'She loves righteous anger, and treating me like an imbecile. She's coming tomorrow by the way. At 11am, but she's always late.' Tilly's eyes flickered and her face drained. 'I'm tired.'

She turned on the TV to dismiss Ava as she tuned into

celebrities training to high-dive into a swimming pool. 'You could have played guitar on my ribs when I was their age.'

'A lot of people take offence at what you say.' She sounded prim and proper. Tilly, the child without boundaries and Ava, the restrictive parent.

'Let them,' she said. Later, Tilly tuned in to *Coronation Street*. She was so firmly entrenched in this soap's characters after more than 50 years of watching that she spoke as if she were their virtual life-coach. She pointed out the (many) errors of their ways and not to cross that road, just then, because they'd be pushed under a car by a jealous lover, which she knew from the previous week anyway. She groaned when her warnings went unheeded, as if the script would magically change with her voiceover. Ava took her usual position in the smoke-free kitchen to try and recapture her blissful afternoon. But Vicky was coming and there were Gillian Jones' plans. It was then the beaming faces of Becky and Charlie pressed against the back window, gently tilting a bottle of fizz.

Chapter Thirty-Four

Cliff View,
4th September, 1943

Darling Jack,

The boys ask for you every day. I think they're pining (but not as much as me). I know you're busy and I try to keep myself going to make time go faster. I've sown late salad, spinach and Brussel sprouts (I know how you love them!) My fingers are black and nails so ruined I'm ashamed to look at them. We have so many apples and come October, I'll pick and wrap them in newspaper and then lay them in the loft to last through winter. Someone in the village has a cider press so I guess there'll be some going to that! My potatoes are doing us proud, with home-grown mint and the extra butter you gave us. We may even have enough to make potato wine, or if the Major has his way, home-made brandy, as long as I can get demerara sugar, raisins and pearl barley. So probably not. Please darling, when we live in America, I don't want to grow vegetables and the only potatoes I want are fries. I can't wait to be on that boat with all the other brides and meet your family. I hope they like me. I think of the bathrooms and kitchens over there and clothes I long to wear. Or not wear when I'm alone with you.

A hundred kisses,
Tilly

Trevone Bay, July 2015

Ava greeted Charlie and Becky with a kiss, putting a finger to her lips. Not even George Clooney could disturb *Coronation Street*.

'Hi,' she whispered, rolling her eyes towards the living room where the familiar tune played out. Becky and Charlie stole in with a bulging hessian bag and Ava closed the kitchen door.

'Bloody hell,' hissed Charlie, 'it's like sneaking past my parents when I was a teenager, only I'd be escaping, not breaking in. We've brought gifts and maybe we'll say hello to the *Coronation Street* queen after it's finished.' She hefted the bag onto the table.

'She won't endear herself,' Ava warned.

Charlie popped the cork, saying they'd better preload and Tilly would be none the wiser, because it would be mean to drink in front of her. She poured three large glasses.

'I'm not worried about Tilly,' said Charlie, sipping. 'I've dealt with every tricky client you can imagine. Often been sworn at and doors slammed in my face.'

'That's sometimes me,' said Becky, smiling and reaching in the bag, brought out crisps, a chilli dip, dark chocolates (with brandy – for Tilly), massage oil (she'd started a course), a wad of paper, pens and sticky tape for a game. Ava didn't think Tilly would play. There were also three gossip magazines, DVDs, and half-a-dozen audio books which thoughtful Becky sourced from charity shops. All were about love affairs but with gritty stories starring heroines whom Becky said, 'Could walk further than five yards without needing a man to carry them or their handbag.' They drank, ate crisps and waited, listening to Tilly telling someone on *Coronation Street, Not to lie on your back waiting for a kicking.* The programme finished, which meant time for tea. Ava made it, along with her nightly draught of brandy. Tilly sat contented in a swirl of nicotine as she downed the shot.

'Ava, that drove me mad,' she said, on her highest horse. 'Why is it some women accept a man having adultery but if a woman does the same, there's dire consequences?'

'Double standards,' said Ava. Men having affairs was a touchy subject. 'Becky and Charlie are here. They'd love to meet you and there's not much on TV until 8.30pm.'

'Really,' Tilly said, smiling, 'just until 8.30pm, if they aren't dull. May told me Becky's a lesbian.' Ava said nothing. Her face felt so hot she thought steam might come out of her ears. There was shuffling behind the door. 'At least they aren't WI types.'

The pair entered and Becky leant down and kissed Tilly. Ava thought Tilly might be frosty but no, she accepted the kiss and Charlie's. Without hesitating the pair made themselves comfortable on the sofa. Charlie admired Tilly (vital), complimented the room and best of all seriously discussed *Coronation Street* characters. Becky snapped a piece of dark brandy chocolate, highlighting its content. Tilly popped it in her mouth, took a sip of tea, closed her eyes and smiled. Ava strangely felt like the newbie.

'I'm taking up massage, so would it be OK to practise on your hands?' Becky asked. 'They're so complicated.' Without waiting for her answer, Becky poured lavender-scented oil into her palm, warmed it between her hands, and sitting on a cushion by Tilly, took hold of her right hand.

'That's lovely,' Tilly practically purred, her lips stained with chocolate. Becky circled the ancient skin, smoothed knobbly fingers and rubbed the creased palm. 'Someone will have to light my next ciggie,' she added. Ava acted as handmaid and the dreamy scent of lavender was obliterated. Charlie winked at Ava.

'I love that picture of you in the swimming costume, Tilly,' Charlie said. 'and your diet's working wonders on my patients.'

'You're welcome,' said Tilly, nodding. She appeared to ruffle virtual feathers like a contented hen. She wasn't even watching TV. Ava surreptitiously turned the volume down. Becky worked her gentle way up Tilly's arm and Ava realised how little touch Tilly received for a woman who had thrived on it. Charlie talked Tilly through the DVDs. Tilly approved, especially the one featuring Angeline Jolie as a spy set against her husband.

'She was a lesbian once,' said Tilly. 'Maybe still is or should go back to being. I wasn't keen on Brad Pitt; too blond. I like dark men, dark chocolate and dark brandy. This is lovely; I'm glad you're Ava's friends because I was worried she'd end up as a woman who preferred cooking to fucking but she's proved me wrong.'

Charlie and Becky shot Ava a protective look that made her feel they were real friends. Tilly agreed to have her feet massaged next and Becky didn't flinch when she removed a sock to reveal the gnarled, purple-tinged foot. Ava turned the TV to silent and looked through Tilly's music. She put on Dusty Springfield (*The Look of Love* and *You Don't Own Me*) and lined up Tom Jones (Tilly's favourites: *Sex Bomb* and *Delilah*). Then Becky said they should play a game. Ava winced.

'Boring,' moaned Tilly. 'That's why they're called *bored* games.'

'Not this one,' said Becky. 'It's stupid. I stick a piece of paper on your head with someone famous written on it and you have to guess who it is by asking questions.' She got out the wad of paper and tape.

'I can't read,' said Tilly, happy at her solid excuse but Ava waved her magnifying glass. Tilly took it reluctantly and said she'd watch.

Becky wrote Tom Jones and stuck it on Charlie's head, Ava scrawled Mickey Mouse for Becky and Charlie wrote Ava Gardner for Ava. They each had to show Tilly so she'd know.

'Am I an actor?' began Becky.

'No, you're an animal cartoon,' said Tilly, and they all shouted 'No!' Suddenly competitive, Tilly agreed to join in. Charlie wrote Marilyn Monroe for her. Perfect, thought Ava. Becky massaged Tilly's other foot. Ava realised it was 8.30pm and Tilly's dating programme was about to start. She would have to say.

'Who cares?' sighed Tilly. 'If this is how lesbians treat each other I've been missing out for nearly a century.' The game continued and they were all helplessly laughing.

'Am I Marilyn Monroe?' asked Tilly eventually. And it was like she'd won the lottery. Tilly needs more of this, decided Ava. And so did she; more pleasure all round. She wanted to see Finn again. Soon. It was a very long time since she'd felt healthy, happy and giggly. At midnight Charlie and Becky left with big hugs and kisses for Tilly and Ava. When Tilly was tucked up in bed her face had a rosier glow than she'd seen since she'd returned home.

'Thank you, Ava,' she said. 'I've had a lovely, lovely evening.' And she kissed her hand. Ava squeezed her oil-scented fingers back. For a moment Tilly looked beautiful and half her age.

'You're too young to do this but don't find another job just yet, I need you. Don't waste a single second. And take no notice of Vicky.'

Chapter Thirty-Five

RAF Medmenham,
Danesfield House,
Central Intelligence Unit
December 12th, 1943

Darling Tilly,

It feels like I've been here months not ten days. I hope the driftwood I chopped is keeping you warm? It's freezing, grey and wet here, like Cornwall but without you darling. It's so damp in this mansion my clothes steam in front of fires. The heating's on for an hour, morning and evening – so people can eat without their teeth chattering. We move fast and wear lots. A little Christmas tree with paper decorations is up and branches of holly, ivy and mistletoe decorate the dining room (don't worry, I avoid the latter – only your lips for me). We get extra rations and I'm saving my chocolate for you.

Two of my pictures got included in the RAF officers' Evidence in Camera magazine. When you see the shots together it's a god's eye view of what we do. We've also had camouflage training – the Krauts paint their plane runways green like farmland, cover factories under nets painted with houses and anchor battleships in the shadow of cliffs, draped in tree-patterned nets. I fly over too fast to distinguish tricks like that so it's down to interpreters to spot. Got to go to my (freezing) bed now darling. I miss you with me. Keep your Christmas kisses for me.

All my love,
Jack

Trevone Bay, August 2015

Tilly was kinder, or was it, thought Ava, that she knew better how to handle her? How would Vicky deal with her mother and her? Ava hoped she would see a change in Tilly for the better. The only time Ava had met Vicky was at the interview, when she'd mentioned working at the *Evening Mercury* and her lack of experience in care. Vicky said she didn't like journalists; that they were snoops, until Ava explained she wasn't. But here was Tilly at the centre of a double page spread in the *Daily World*, and the digital globe beyond. At least Jack wasn't mentioned. In readiness for Vicky's visit, Ava cleaned windows and it occurred as the grime washed away that she hadn't thought of Josh and Sadie for days. Happy thoughts of Finn had taken up that bitter, seething headspace. Cliff View had become a healing, breathing haven, despite its angry occupant or perhaps because of her. Ava picked up a bundle of letters delivered with the post, to *Tilly, World War II Gut Busters Diet, Cornwall*. She read one out, written by an elderly lady in Oxford, who said she was still slim and elegant and had shown Tilly's story to her granddaughters. Now they were both trying to, *Eat less and move more, like in 44*. Another, from a veteran, stated his charity had put Tilly's story on their website, calling her a health heroine (regardless of drinking and smoking, which was somewhat admired by wily veterans) and people had made generous donations because Tilly was one of an ever-diminishing generation. Tilly revelled in her fan mail. The local paper launched a WWII region-wide weekly rationing (allowing weekend blow-outs) with readers sponsored to lose weight for the charity backed by Tilly. Tilly was on a high. Ava doubted Vicky would be up there with her.

Another handwritten envelope had Ava's name. She opened it.

Dear Ava,

I hope you enjoyed the other day as much as me. I have to go to London with Joe. Don't go swimming while I'm away and come to the forge when I'm back tomorrow, I've something for you.

Take care.

Finn

Ava looked for hidden meanings and found none. She'd venture to the foundry. Tilly had taught her that time truly was the coin of her life and it was up to her how she spent it.

Chapter Thirty-Six

Diary Entry: St Eval Airbase, December 20th, 1943

It was like the sermon about God raining brimstone and fire on Sodom and Gomorrah. We flew to the city, jettisoning anti-radar chaff but after three days of heavy bombing, it was a free run. Flames spiked to 1,500 feet and smoke reached 20,000. The buildings melted and roads oozed; even the harbour flamed water. I thought of the women, kids and old folks burned to death. The pictures turn my stomach. I'm sick of it. The doc's given me tablets to sleep and tablets to fly.

Trevone Bay, August 2015

Vicky was now two hours late. Cliff View had been polished, scoured and vacuumed into scented perfection, aside from its permanent nicotine haze. Even that had been wafted out of opened windows. Ava made Tilly's favourite lunch; soft white crustless bread soaked in whisked egg, fried golden brown and cut into manageable squares. Nat King Cole sang *Route 66*, *Autumn Leaves* and Tilly's favourite, *Unforgettable*. The air was filled with the heightened air of an impending state visit.

'Late, as usual,' announced Tilly, nodding and upping her smoking because it would be vetoed when Vicky arrived. It felt like a storm-front brewing. 'I love this fried bread. We used to have it in the war, if we got eggs. Jack wolfed it down.' She looked Ava up and down in her leggings and baggy T-shirt. 'Vicky will notice everything.'

'OK, I'm changing,' Ava said, picking up Tilly's plate but hovering as Tilly stubbed a cigarette on an uneaten square of fried bread.

'Bloody hell, what about the ashtray?'

'You forgot to bring it in,' Tilly said innocently.

Ava put on the corporate dress, now pleasingly loose, cleared the kitchen, checking with a hyper-critical eye, and sprayed bleach on the spotless sink. Tilly was perfumed and prepared in navy jogging pants and white cotton jumper. 'Nautical and nice,' she called it. She asked Ava to twist her hair into a chignon, clip on silver earrings and matching necklace. She dabbed on mascara, eyebrow pencil and lipstick. The make-up and jewellery sat strangely, as if it didn't belong. Tilly asked for her teeth. The Queen's really coming, thought Ava, gingerly pouring them out of their glass jar and swilling them. They felt cold and peculiar with their plastic pink palate. Tilly inserted them and her face ballooned.

'It feelssss like shhhtones in my mouth,' she said, hissing her words. 'I'll take them out, for later.' She placed them by the ashtray. Ava moved the dentures to one side in case she tapped ash into them. Every time the wind blew the letterbox, Tilly started.

'My back hurts,' she said. 'I need morphine.' Ava looked at the clock. It was 1pm. She measured the dose carefully, signed for it and poured a little liquid calm into Tilly.

'Look, it's that holiday programme you love,' said Ava, trying to divert her. It usually allowed Tilly to imagine being stretched out on a sun-drenched lounger, served by attractive waiters at her beck and call. But she groaned at the prize offering a Spanish home with hot tub and sea views all for the paltry cost of answering an obvious question.

'Pointless, I couldn't get in a car, let alone a plane. Vicky's arrived. I can feel her.' Ava neither saw nor heard anyone. Tilly bit her lip. Outside heavy dark clouds built up, mirrored by a turbulent grey sea. The tops of trees wavered. Five minutes later a car rolled into the lay-by, a door slammed, feet crunched up the gravel path and keys rattled. Excitement and anxiety flashed across Tilly's face as she shoved in her teeth and chewed them around to bed them down.

'What a dreadful journey of road works!' came forth the confident, home-counties tone before she'd stepped a foot inside. Ava watched Tilly paste on a toothy smile as Vicky hauled in an expensive-looking black suitcase. 'Hello Mummy,' sighed Vicky, breathlessly, kissing Tilly's powdery cheeks. 'Afternoon Ava,' she added, the smile pinched on peach-painted lips. Vicky wore a shapeless grey linen shift and pewter-coloured linen coat. Posh but dour, thought Ava. Her shiny black sandals fastened with Velcro across ankle and toes. An up-market black handbag was placed on the sofa. Vicky surveyed the room like a landlord checking her property.

'I'm livid about the Press,' she said, mouth pulled down, raking a hand through her short, grey hair. The gloves were off.

Chapter Thirty-Seven

Morgantown,
West Virginia
May 20ᵗʰ, 1944

Darling Jack,

I know you face the greatest danger. Everyone's so frightened for their men. In my heart you are still my man. The only one I'll ever love. In the early hours I feel you'll come back to me and all that has happened will be forgotten in our happy every after. I pray to God to keep you safe and bring you back to my arms and your loving family.

Still my love,

Jess

Trevone Bay, August 2015

'You shouldn't have spoken to a single journalist, Mummy, and Ava, you shouldn't have allowed it,' Vicky began. 'It's a piffling story that's gone mad because it's August and there's nothing else.' She carried on in that vein. Ava noticed how her mouth opened and shut like a trapdoor, the furrowed frown and that feeling of being told off in the head teacher's office. Tilly looked contrite for a few minutes and then disinterested, at which point Vicky switched focus entirely to Ava. She was questioned about her role and why she hadn't informed her? Ava offered to resign. Vicky pursed her lips and Tilly raised her right hand like the naughty kid in a classroom.

'You've only just arrived, Vicky,' she said. 'Stop it now. Ava had nothing to do with this. In fact, she tried to prevent me. It's done, I've had fun and all these letters,' she pointed to the pile, 'are from people who want to lose weight but find it difficult without rules to follow and someone to impose them.' She eyed her daughter beadily. Vicky was only a little plump.

Vicky blinked and swallowed: 'I'm assuming there'll be no more articles, Ava?'

'It's nothing to do with her,' yelled Tilly, eyes wide. 'Don't treat me like an imbecile. Are you here to see Gillian Jones, your trusted friend?'

Vicky looked flustered. Ava shivered.

'I'm simply worried about you, Mummy. This is the twenty-first century and news goes global. It's not just the local rag, or even the nationals,' she said, scratching her right foot. Ava eyes were drawn to Vicky's fleshy ankles and pale skin bulging between sandal straps.

'Have you quite finished, Vicky?' said Tilly. 'The local paper is going to raise money for charity with a sponsored diet across Cornwall. Would you like to sign up?'

Vicky pulled up her top lip as she breathed in. Silence prickled. Ava thought there was something majestic about the solidity of Vicky combined with her all-pervasive self-righteousness. The bungalow seemed to shrink and Tilly became smaller and older by the second. Ava couldn't believe Vicky was handsome Jack's love-child.

'You must realise,' said Vicky, breathing out heavily and

smoothing her creased dress. 'You simply can't manage Cliff View much longer. Even with paid help.' She looked at Ava coolly. 'It's costing a considerable amount and we really need to talk about me having Power of Attorney over your finances.'

'Not on your life or mine. It's thoughtful of you to worry about costs but I'm well cared for now. You finally found the right person in Ava.'

Vicky jutted her chin forward and stepped to the mantelpiece. She ran her finger pointedly across a photograph frame, inspected it, found nothing.

'Would you like tea or coffee?' asked Ava, desperate to leave.

'Tea with a little splash of milk – added afterwards. And half a sugar,' Vicky said. Behind her back, Tilly pulled a face.

'Please,' said Tilly pointedly, to her daughter, glancing at Ava and winking.

'Please,' snipped Vicky. 'I'm seriously concerned about you, Mummy and it's playing with fire with the Press.'

Tilly drummed her fingers on the chair. She picked up her cigarette packet, puckered her mouth and placed it down. Ava left them to it. The tea Vicky demanded was dark and unappealing. Ava added a teaspoon of brandy to Tilly's milky affair and piled a plate with thick slices of delicious lemon drizzle cake.

'Edward's coming later,' Vicky said, taking her cup from the tray. Ava dreaded seeing Mr Finance. Vicky sipped, then shovelled in a large bite of cake, wiping crumbs from lip to lap. Tilly smiled thinly, poured tea into her saucer, blew on it and slurped. Ava had never seen her do that. Her blue eyes glinted at the taste of alcohol. She beamed.

'Please, that's disgusting, Mummy. You're like a dog. May told me you've cut down on drinking but not smoking.' Vicky had polished off her slice of cake in three bites.

'Thanks to Ava for the first,' said Tilly. 'Cigarettes no, barring while you're here. How long will that be?'

Ouch, thought Ava. Vicky looked at her watch and brushed crumbs from lap into hand and back on the plate. With her forefinger she dabbed up pieces and popped them into her open mouth. Her eyes were flinty.

Chapter Thirty-Eight

Diary entry: Falmouth, June 6th, 1944

> *Tilly's pregnant, very thin and sick. She told me in a lot of tears, her body shaking in my arms. I'm afraid for her and me. I want to take care of Tilly, make her happy and live to see us all back in the Blue Mountains. It's all out of my control now.*
>
> *Every road, lane and field are jammed with stinking vehicles. Falmouth harbour's packed with Mulberry Harbours and Rhino Pontoons. Our planes are painted black and white – invasion stripes to protect us from our own artillery. Blue Boy called us together.*
>
> *'This is it guys,' he yelled, in his New Jersey accent. 'Operation Overlord. The invasion of Europe and history in the making. Not all of us will come back but those who do will tell their grandchildren, and they'll tell their grandchildren. I want all of you to play your part so you'll look back with honour. May God be with you all.' He turned to the ocean.*
>
> *'Right, you Nazi bastards,' he yelled. 'We're ready. You're gonna shit your pants when we land.'*
>
> *Then it appeared; a white rainbow, tinged blue and arching through mist. We took off, aiming to fly at 15 feet over Normandy beaches and shooting up to 500 exposures.*
>
> *Eleven thousand planes stretched from one horizon to the other as far as the eye could see; blackening the sky. Halifaxes to Horsa gliders, packed with troops. Libs and Fortresses drop bombs on Nazi fortifications. The French shoreline's covered with craft-wrecking*

*mines and further up, huge triangles of concrete nick-named
Dragon's Teeth. We give our men cover along six miles of coast, with
shingle beaches and sheer cliffs to fight up. Seven thousand landing
craft converge on beaches. We saw dozens half-sunk and flaming.
Guys zig-zag on beaches like rabbits across a devil's fairground of
smoke, flames and explosions. Slept badly, even with tablets, dreamt
about Tilly being alone with our baby. Tomorrow we press on and
the weather's closing in.*

Trevone Bay, August 2015

From the kitchen sink Ava watched Vicky stomp to the lamppost
where she waved her mobile around and, catching a signal, talked
loudly, albeit sped up in case the signal vanished.

'It's tourist madness but Mummy's better than expected.' Ava
thought she sounded disappointed. Vicky shook her watch. 'I've
optioned £250,000. Remember it's not a black hole you're seeing but
an opportunity to be grasped.' Ava was reminded of the bland
redundancy team shipped into her newspaper office. Managers had
also spoken about, *Grasping opportunities, drilling down and going
forward.* They'd concocted indecipherable matrixes with bright felt
pens on huge sheets of brown paper – for no apparent reason Ava
could see – other than to highlight that the writing was on the wall.
They'd criss-crossed the office and stood behind anxious employees
like human swords of Damocles.

Vicky listened for a minute before carrying on. 'They'll make
a decision soon.' There was a longer pause. 'It's all about money,'
stated Vicky, digging out dirt from a fingernail. 'We have to keep
these people sweet.' Vicky paused from nail cleaning to scratch her

right ear vigorously, inspecting what she'd extracted. 'It's tricky receiving emails here so I'll work with what I have.' Vicky kicked off a sandal, tipped out a stone and tried to shove her foot back in. Her heel crushed the back. 'I have some ankle-biting bureaucrat to deal with.' She twisted her foot back and forth and stamped it down but it refused to go in. 'These lot can actually get blood out of a stone. Bye for now.' Vicky tucked the phone in her pocket, leant over, yanked on her shoe and marched up the path. Ava saw she was more than a match for Tilly. Mother and daughter buzzed at, rather than talked to, each other. Two queen bees, thought Ava – and she, the little worker.

'Ava,' said Vicky, at the doorway, hugging a sheaf of papers in a plastic folder and puffing out her cheeks. 'I've got urgent work and Mummy needs the toilet.' She strode to the dining room.

'Of course,' said Ava. In the toilet Tilly emitted a growl which had no connection to her bowel movement.

'Thanks for the tipple. Vicky's efficient, isn't she?' sniped Tilly. They were on the same side.

'You must be proud of her capabilities,' said Ava, diplomatically. Tilly stuck out her tongue.

'Vicky thinks I'm common and thick. Edward's more like me but moodier, whereas I'm all sweetness and light.' She beamed her slanting eyes.

'Absolutely,' said Ava, pulling up Tilly's pants.

'If you don't mind would you make a coffee, Ava, a double espresso?' said Vicky.

I do mind, thought Ava, but she knew her place in this pecking order.

'Please,' said Tilly, hand stroking her cigarette pack as she was lowered down on her chair. Vicky's eyebrows shot up.

'Of course, do excuse me.' Tilly gave the tiniest of smiles. 'Mummy's allowed a little brandy because we're celebrating Edward's girlfriend's September visit. She might be The One.' Vicky pressed her hands together. Tilly's eyes swivelled to the TV, which was off but she stared, regardless. Any mention of marriage in general left Tilly pulling a face like she wanted a sick bag. Ava made coffee but a bone china cup slipped off its tiny saucer and smashed on the tiles. Vicky's head poked around the door.

'Oh dear, that was one of an expensive set.' Ava's cheeks flamed as she brushed it all up.

'I'm sorry,' Ava said, taking another cup and carrying on. She was not going to offer to replace it.

'I'm vetoing more Press, given Mummy's age.'

'It's between you and your mother,' said Ava, knowing Vicky was clueless about the potential TV. She wasn't going to enlighten her. The clock sounded loud in the kitchen as did Round Hole and Vicky's breathing.

'Do you mind, while you're here, if I go out for a while?' asked Ava, handing over the espresso. She felt like she used to in physics, chemistry and maths lessons – that any second, she'd flee, screaming.

Vicky checked her watch. 'I'm taking Mummy to the Castle for a late lunch so we'll be back about 5pm. Edward's arriving then and we're going to a meeting at 6pm so if you can be here for handover promptly?'

'Of course,' repeated Ava, like the good servant she was,

thinking Tilly would be tired and she'd already eaten her fried egg-bread.

'Oh, and one more thing,' Vicky said, looking down at her nails. 'The optician is booked to check Mummy's eyes. It depends on what she says as Dr Singh is concerned about her vision, however, Edward and I feel that after her ninetieth we will carefully consider her future at Cliff View.' Ava collected her coat, got in her car and floored it along the gravel lane.

Chapter Thirty-Nine

Cliff View, 10th June 1944

After pounding dirty washing into submission in the Dolly Tub, Tilly fed dripping clothes and sheets through the mangle. Alex and Jamie half-helped, half-hindered her haul them into a sopping heap in the basket. Three times she repeated the Herculean task. The green crystals of Oxydol soap caught in her throat and eyes, stained her skin, turning her ruined hands red raw and flaking. When she married Jack, she would have a washing machine, weekly manicures and scarlet polish.

Finally, she stood straight and the softened ligaments of her lower back ached, and swollen breasts tingled. Tilly lightly touched her belly, eased back her shoulders. She was so slender that you couldn't tell in her loose dresses. Jack had been so good when she told him. She'd felt sick with fear but he'd held her and promised it would all be OK; that they'd be married and he'd kissed her stomach.

Now, the warm sun was on her skin, and soft wind brushing over her bare arms and legs: it was a perfect day to dry washing. A wave of nausea swept through her. She stilled until it receded. Martha had no idea. The white sheets, with a few stubborn stains, flapped on the line besides shirts, dresses, and trousers which appeared like a family of dancing ghosts. Alex ordered Jamie to chase him and they sped in and out of the damp clothes singing, *The*

Sun has got his Hat On, until Tilly enticed them onto a rug for a makeshift picnic of cold fried potato cakes, mashed with a teaspoon of tomato sauce.

The phone rang and Martha, resting on the sofa, answered.

'Tilly, Tilly,' her terrified voice rang out. Tilly ran, thinking something had happened to the Major and prised the phone from Martha's clenched fingers. She held the receiver to her ear, hand on Martha's shoulder, braced to be strong for her.

'Tilly?' The voice asked. American, nasal and instantly recognisable. Danny. It was as if the ground opened and she was falling, falling. Martha clutched the hem of Tilly's dress.

'Yes,' she whispered; heart racing, breath shallow and rapid.

'I'm sorry to inform you. Jack is dead. His plane crashed after a sortie over the beaches and he managed to bail but was too badly burned to survive.'

The phone fell out of her hands.

'Tilly?' came Danny's voice from the dangling cord.

She exhaled as if emptying and wondered where the screaming was coming from. Martha promised there and then she'd look after her. She put Tilly to bed and for days sat by her as much as she could, wiping her face after she frequently vomited. Tilly howled in nightmares and sobbed until there were no more tears. She couldn't even keep down Martha's home-made broth. On day four, Martha carried in a bowl of warm water, soap and flannel to her bedroom, insisting on giving her a bed bath. Washing Tilly's slender body, she saw the well-risen swell of belly, the faint line cleaving it and swollen breasts with darkened areola.

'Do you want to keep this baby?' asked Martha, tentatively,

plaiting her unwashed hair. Tilly nodded. 'Then you'll have to look after yourself. It's what Jack would have wanted.'

'I won't bring you scandal. I'll leave as soon as I can.' She went to sit up. Martha pushed her down.

'You aren't going anywhere. Eat now.' While Tilly slept, Martha wrote to the Major, explaining Tilly was pregnant and stating she was as necessary to her own future happiness as he was. His first reply was ten per cent sympathetic and ninety per cent condemnatory. How could Tilly be so stupid?

'Very easily,' Martha wrote back, reminding him she was pregnant when they married and that Alex was not premature as they'd told everyone but a bouncing full-term 9lb baby. His second letter was far more conciliatory, concerned about village gossip and the impact on Martha and their sons. A month later they'd abandoned Cliff View for their boarded-up Richmond property. Tilly barely spoke, often forgetting to fasten buttons, tie laces, brush her hair. Three months later, a quieter, calmer Tilly glowed with pregnancy, caressing the moving baby inside her which made her feel Jack was still with her. The boys attended school during the week and Martha found a post at a bank. She retrieved the boys' old crib, baby clothes, a pile of well-washed old nappies and together they transformed the attic into Tilly's private nursery. Neighbours were full of sympathy for Tilly's tragic story: the heartbroken widow with a solid 22ct gold wedding ring, which had belonged to Martha's mother.

In the early hours of a balmy 24th September 1944, Tilly gave birth to her 7lb daughter, with Martha by her side, wiping her brow and holding her hand. Any thoughts of adoption dissolved, seeing this briny, tiny-limbed creature with starfish fingers, Jack's dark eyes and her own sweet-biscuit scent. She could no more relinquish her than stop breathing. She liked the name Stella after the Cornish stars she was conceived under but the matter-of-fact midwife said that with victory so close, Victoria was the perfect choice, and so it proved to be. There were lots of women like her, with babies born out of wedlock who successfully covered their single tracks. She tried to contact Danny, so he could inform Jack's family of a new granddaughter. But he proved elusive, possibly dead. Tilly grew afraid someone might stake their claim on Vicky, so she let it be, eventually telling her daughter that her daddy was a very brave American reconnaissance pilot who died fighting the Nazis and never returned to his beloved Blue Ridge Mountains.

Martha wanted rid of Cliff View. For her it was a space brimming with past depression. It took no persuasion for Major Douglas to hand over the deeds to Tilly, when it was worth the princely sum of £200. As often as she could, Tilly took Vicky, Alex and Jamie there for holidays to see them run wild on the beach and for her to feel close to Jack.

Chapter Forty

Trevone Bay, August 2015

'Well, I'm very sorry,' Ava raged as she drove from Cliff View. 'And it won't be for much longer!' She cornered so fast she frightened herself into slowing. She deep-breathed through twisting lanes, joining a queue of vehicles laden with bikes, surfboards and kayaks. Walkers with maps around necks, and hiking poles in hands sauntered past. The open doors of the Golden Lion revealed sun-shy barflies glued to pints. After another slow mile, Ava parked the car at the edge of a wheat field. There was the sign she was looking for. She climbed over a style, walking alongside spongy ditches lined with peeling bulrushes whose distinct velvet buds swayed as if too heavy for stalks. A nearby field of wheat crackled in the heat. Ava's footsteps flushed out a couple of cackling ducks that sped away. In the distance, near a copse, stood the isolated red-brick forge with its navy slate roof. Parked outside was a battered green van which had seen far better days. Blue and grey smoke puffed from its chimney and a heap of coal spilt from the red wooden door. She heard whistling and rhythmical, ringing hammering. The hidden path allowed Ava to approach almost unseen. A black whippet peeped out of the door, lifted its pointed head and sniffed. It cocked a leg, peed, and bolted to her. Tail wagging, the dog shoved his nose forcibly up her dress and after that hello, trotted alongside. Ava smelt a drift of charcoal and metal.

Finn stood at the heart of the dark smithy with metal pincers in one hand, gripping a bar which glowed acid yellow, white and red. He struck it repeatedly on the anvil. The ringing noise reverberated, unsettling crows on the roof and field. Closer now, there was a tang of sulphur and beeswax. The metal which Finn held darkened as it cooled and was thinned, bent and twisted. Using pincers, he carried the bar near the door and plunged it into a barrel of water where it hissed and spat, sending up an enveloping cloud of steam. The whippet ran through it. As the air cleared Finn saw Ava, still twenty feet away. She folded her arms self consciously and he placed the bar into a trough. The forge's interior was lit by a furnace which glimmered black and red with licks of blue at its periphery. Finn wiped his blackened hands over his dirty torn leather apron.

'Bed,' he commanded, as Ava stepped into semi-darkness and for a second, she thought he was ordering her until the dog slunk to a tatty wicker basket in the corner. Finn rolled down the sleeves of his ragged blue shirt, spattered with soot marks and burns. A new, already grubby plaster was across the back of his left hand. Behind him, Ava spotted a cloth-covered ball, suspended from the ceiling by string, which swung wildly, as if of its own volition. Finn followed her gaze.

'Get off, you bugger,' he yelled, bashing the ball with his fist. A sooty mouse flew through the air, landed on the floor and scampered into a hole, fiercely, but fruitlessly, chased by the dog.

'Trapeze artist,' said Ava.

'After my damn lunch. It's one place I thought I could leave food. Walter, you're bloody useless.' Finn stroked the dog's ears as

243

he pulled down the muslin-wrapped bauble, revealing a huge pasty. He observed Ava in the fire-lit light where shadows danced on walls and ceiling. 'Cup of tea?' he offered. 'Kettle's on.' Ava was glad he didn't ask what brought her. It felt natural, easy, and her bad temper dissipated as easily as frost in May. A blackened kettle, hooked onto a triangular frame over the furnace began to steam, while at a tarnished sink Finn scrubbed his hands with carbolic soap and took a brush to his nails. He looked at her kindly, without smiling.

'You'll have a bit of dinner, untouched by mouse?' Ava nodded. Finn tipped a tea bag out a chipped china mug, dropped in a new one. He grabbed another metal cup, threw out what was left and cleaned the inside with a corner of his shirt. Ava liked the earthy scents, coal-blackened walls and general untidiness of the forge. Dust lay on every surface and motes floated in slanted bars of light from the smeared skylight. Next to her, stacked metal lay half-hidden under a stained oilcloth. Ava lifted one corner, revealing bundles of railings. Some had arrow-like heads and others were shaped into twisting vines embossed with flowers. She folded the cloth back further and saw three weather vanes: one with a hunting dog, its front leg bent, the second, a magnificently antlered stag in mid-leap and finally a male peacock, lacquered in gold, with each fanned-out tail glossed in turquoise, aquamarines and violets.

'Beautiful,' murmured Ava, tracing the intricate fretwork of feathers.

'Thank you. Tea's up,' said Finn, unscrewing a small plastic bottle of milk. He chucked a brown paper bag of sugar on the bench, with an encrusted spoon inside. 'The pasty's Greggs' finest.'

Moving closer, Ava picked up the stained metal mug and half

the flaky, buttery pasty smudged with his thumbprint.

'How are you?' he said, throwing a crust in the air, which Walter snapped and swallowed without a chew. Even near the furnace the skinny dog shivered. The silence between them filled with the crackling fire and crows resettling.

'Fine. How was London?' she said, not wishing to expand on what was happening at Cliff View.

'Busy, dirty, noisy but good for business. Glad to be back. Joe saw his mum on a flying visit.' The peculiar silence grew again but not like the prickly quiet between Vicky and Tilly. A partridge flew up outside, making a noise like a stalled engine. Finn drained his tea and padded his hand beneath the anvil. He brought out a delicate silver torque bangle; held it out to her. It was covered with intricate Celtic twists and Ava's name engraved on the inner surface. She slipped the cool metal over her wrist. It fitted perfectly. He turned her arm over to look at it and left a smudge on her skin.

'It's gorgeous,' Ava said and stepping forward, kissed him, tasting salty, metal lips, warm from tea and work. He was a good kisser. He pulled away and brushed a stray hair from Ava's cheek. 'Wait a minute,' and shooed Walter out to his old van. Returning, he latched the forge door shut. It was dark now but for the flickering fire and skylight. Unfolding an old rug on the floor (probably the dog's, thought Ava), Finn lay down.

'Come here,' he said. Ava didn't hesitate.

Chapter Forty-One

Trevone Bay, August 2015

They made love, quickly, urgently. Ava had never wanted a man like that. Finn was competent, assured. He did nothing Ava didn't enjoy. He'd brought condoms from his van, saying they'd been there for a while and that he wasn't ever-ready. Ava couldn't care less; here was careless rapture to be relished. The calloused hands that had saved her brought her back to life as he explored her and she him. Afterwards, Ava turned the bangle on her bare, tanned arm in the honey-coloured light. Rain pattered on the roof, the fire glowed and she felt cosy, safe and satiated. Vicky's deadline loomed but she was going to enjoy every moment she could with him. A memorable affair. For an hour they lay there until Finn had to pick Joe up from school. He told her to come back soon, invited her to dinner, to a film. She said yes to it all; to fleeting pleasure. To finally ridding herself of the pain Josh and Sadie had riven through her like a stake.

Ava drove to Padstow, wandering through gleaming cobbled streets, browsing shops crammed with art and pottery and the kind of clothes you wore by the sea and nowhere else. She bought a double chocolate ice-cream with a flake and was drawn to a crowd outside Peter Hogwood's estate agency. She, like other inquisitive onlookers, eyed the exorbitant prices.

'You couldn't buy a flipping kennel here, Dave,' one middle-aged woman said in awe, to her sunburned portly husband.

'Makes our pad look like the Ritz, love,' he answered, licking a mint-green cornet. 'Mind, we have a dual carriageway out front and Ikea at the rear.' Ava checked the sale tags. The smallest one-bed flat was nearly £300,000 and a two-bed terrace, a pound off £450,000. A three-bed family home, with garden and parking was £5 short of a million. Mr Hogwood sat at the far end of his office, dapper in navy; a little fish finning about in a very lucrative pool. No wonder land was a premium in Trevone. Ava sauntered to the harbour wall and sat, legs dangling, licking ice cream. Gulls swarmed on the lookout, attempting, sometimes successfully, to grab food out of hands. Fishermen unloaded still-moving crabs and lobsters from a small boat. Ava decided if she went to Spain, it was just a short break or she'd sign up to one of those agencies where you could look after empty homes and pets worldwide, which would be easier than looking after a person. She drove past the smithy on the way back and slowing, spotted Edward talking to Finn, him listening, arms folded with that serious look on his face which Ava found so endearing. Joe was throwing a ball for the whippet. She couldn't connect Edward, who seemed worldly and unscrupulous, with the man who gave her a silver bangle and made her laugh even as they made love. Instead, she concentrated on Tilly, who would be back from her fine dining experience at The Castle. She was sure Vicky's expectations of socially acceptable behaviour would be thinly stretched.

Vicky's car was there and she was in the kitchen, red-faced, frowning and knocking back wine. Ava saw the shed door open and a lot of rattling inside it, so went to have a look. There was Robbie, sweaty, smoking, sleeves rolled up, sorting through piles of tools.

The shed was warm and smelt rich with scents of cedar, oil, paint, wood preservatives combined with his less aromatic odour.

'Daughter and mother had a blistering row. Tilly's gone to bed,' he said. Midges hovered round Robbie. Ava hoped she sat far enough away so they wouldn't target her.

'Why are you here?' she asked, shaking her head when Robbie proffered a cigarette although she was glad he'd lit up as the insects flapped off. Another car pulled up and they spied Edward's arrival.

'Vicky asked me to clear out the shed, apart from the mower and a few bits.'

'Ahh,' said Ava, so Robbie was not likely to be needed at Cliff View soon either. Vicky let Edward in and barged back into the kitchen. Mr Finance stood near the window, arms limp by his side, wearing beige shorts and white polo shirt, (collar irritatingly up, noted Ava). Vicky looked at him pleadingly. They appeared totally unrelated.

The window was open enough to hear what was being said without being seen. Vicky filled the kettle so quickly water splashed her puffy face.

'I went to the bar, Edward,' Vicky snapped, 'and there were loads of free tables at The Castle. So, what did she do?' Vicky yanked open a cupboard, took out mugs, slammed it shut.

'Something badly behaved?' replied Edward neutrally. He handed Vicky the brandy he'd pulled from under the sink. Vicky took it, unscrewed the lid and taking a glug straight from the bottle, then added some to the mugs.

'She hauled herself on that damn frame to the only table with four men and plonked herself there. By the time I returned, with lemonade for myself and brandy for her, Mummy was on about winning the bloody war. I couldn't believe it.'

'It could have been worse.'

'They were German, Edward.'

'Oh,' he said, grimacing.

'Only Tilly,' whispered Robbie, stabbing his cigarette into the departing midge cloud.

'And you know what she said?' Vicky tried to put on Tilly's accent. 'I wish you handsome blond Germans had won. Far better looking than British men. Until the Americans arrived but even so I'd have welcomed you with open arms and more. Edward, I could have died. I placed our drinks on another table, apologised to them all and asked Mummy to move. She refused.'

'Serves Vicky right,' said Ava, she did not feel sorry for the woman about to sack her and force her mother into a nursing home.

'I had no choice but to sit with them,' spat Vicky. 'They kept laughing, Edward. Doesn't she realise it's at her? They probably thought she was on a dementia outing. I could hardly swallow my beef bourguignon. Mummy refused to eat her roast dinner. She said Ava was a better cook.' Robbie winked at Ava and she smiled. 'Mummy waffled on about celebrities and sex, so, I brought up Angela Merkel welcoming so many refugees. Mummy tapped my hand and said: *We did the same for the Jews.* That went down like a lead balloon. Then she had the gall to say to me, *Men aren't interested in intelligent women, Vicky. They're here to surf and have pleasure, something you haven't done ever.*'

'Ouch,' said Robbie.

Vicky slurped the coffee, leaving a frothy moustache on her

upper lip. Edward didn't point it out.

'I paid and told Mummy I'd be in the car park. She made me wait fifteen minutes before one of them escorted her out. She gave him her phone number for God's sake. He bowed and kissed her hand. I paid a hefty bill in that hotel, for what, to be utterly humiliated. Mark my words, Edward, we'll have the last laugh.'

'A nursing home would kill her, Mum,' said Edward.

'Exactly.'

'Does it matter if we wait six months? We're almost there.'

'I haven't got time to waste.'

Edward rubbed the back of his neck, poured a brandy and drank.

It seemed to Ava that the more money you had, the more you were determined to obtain. Her and Robbie, Evangeline, Becky, Charlie, Finn, most people she knew, scrabbled to pay bills, while the likes of Vicky and Edward, who were comfortably cushioned by cash, never felt they had enough and didn't care how they feathered their nests.

'What a pair,' Robbie whispered. 'Loaded and unhappy. If they knew what it was like for the rest of us.'

'Possibly that's why they behave like that. Do you think Tilly can hear?' Ava asked. Robbie shrugged.

'She's on her last legs, the doctor said so,' appealed Edward.

'She's a mentally ill narcissist and I'm sick of her. Her ninetieth is the deadline and we'll find Mummy somewhere suitable. If there is such a place. Frankly, I never thought Ava would last this long.'

'That's mean,' hissed Robbie. 'You've been very good.'

'If it wasn't for that woman,' said Vicky, tersely, 'Mummy

would have gone, and Cliff View with her.' Vicky checked her watch. 'And where's the perfect carer now?' Ava was in an awkward position whereby if she moved, she would be seen. She'd have to wait until they left the kitchen.

'I wouldn't mind, Edward but I thought a heartbroken, redundant copywriter wouldn't last the week. Pour me another.'

Ava smiled at that. At how far she had come from the desperate woman who couldn't imagine smiling again to one hiding in a shed in a Cornish village, caring for a seemingly impossible old woman she'd come to love. And finding a gorgeous man, even if it was temporary.

'Like you say, Mum,' said Edward, 'it's not long. Let Gran enjoy her ninetieth and meet Mackenzie.' They took their drinks and departed.

'Well,' murmured Robbie. 'Unpleasant that. At least with Tilly you get what you see.' He looked at Ava sympathetically and went back to sorting and packing. Ava crouched her way under the window to the front door and opened it with a great rattle of keys. Vicky glared as she entered. Her face was scarlet and her right hand twiddled with a string of pearls which Ava swore had been on Tilly's chest of drawers. Edward looked cool and collected. She didn't like the way his eyes flickered over her like a snake's tongue.

'Is Tilly up?' asked Ava, brightly.

'In bed, after lunch,' said Vicky, composing herself. 'She's tired. Edward and I are just on our way out. Oh, and SpecSorters is sending someone at 9.30am if you can be here.'

'I wasn't planning on being out,' Ava said, calmly.

'Good,' said Vicky smartly, and ushered her son out.

'Has she gone?' asked Tilly, lighting up a cigarette in bed. Ava nodded. 'Thank God. She tells me I've got to have my eyes tested tomorrow. Pointless. My back's buggered and legs are useless. It's not as if I'm going to have an operation. As long as I can see a decent-looking man on a big TV, it's fine.'

'How was lunch?'

'D.U.L.L.' Tilly breathed smoke out of both nostrils. 'I was having a bit of a laugh with four strapping Germans, built like Adonises, and Miss Misery Guts stormed off with a face like a bowel movement. I saw Robbie clearing out the shed. They can't wait to get shot of me. Can you ask him for the locked box – it's in the suitcase – before it gets thrown out? It doesn't feel like it's my home when Vicky's here.'

Robbie, wearing headphones, sang an unrecognisable tune in a flat, high voice at odds with his bulk. The shed was tidy now, apart from thick spiders' webs. Ava tapped his arm and he jumped.

'Tilly wants an old suitcase – do you know where it is?' Robbie padded his great hands on the timber roof frame. Spiders scuttled into dark recesses as he tugged.

'Got it,' said Robbie, his face glazed with sweat. There, covered in dust, rested a leather suitcase. Robbie lugged it down. A rusty key was taped on the outside. Ava took it in and unlocked the box on Tilly's bedroom floor. Inside, was an assortment of Kodapod canisters, cables, small, empty bottles, a broken thermometer and a timer. An internal compartment revealed another slim metal box. This was what Tilly wanted.

'Open it,' said Tilly, her eyes round as an owl's. Wrapped in cellophane and thick brown paper were three black and white photographs. There were faint water stains and mottling around the edges, like an old mirror. The first was of Tilly naked on a bed of rumpled white sheets, arms linked behind her head and tousled blonde hair loose over creamy shoulders. Her firm, long legs were crossed at the ankles and concave stomach highlighted the dark triangle of hair between slim thighs. The second featured Tilly lying on her stomach on a beach. The camera caught the pearling line of spine and rounded buttocks as the soft light turned Tilly's body into an oil painting. The third framed Tilly on her side, a dune as background and her smoking with half-closed eyes. She looked serene, feminine, feline. The curve of her waist and hips created a perfect guitar shape. Ava felt a flare of envy and admiration.

Tilly smiled, held out her hands and squinted lovingly at her younger self.

'I'm glad Jack took them. I was beautiful and so in love with him,' she exclaimed. 'The first time I met him, I was with Rose Sinclair at the Pier Head waiting for a ferry. Mum was right about Rose. A *Yes* woman. Rose married an accountant called Eric. We kept in touch, vaguely. I mostly lied to her about myself. Rose and Eric bought an executive house on the Wirral and spent weekends in a static caravan in North Wales. Pass me the smelling salts.' Ava laughed. 'And my magnifying glass. I want to look at my gorgeousness.' Tilly pored over the photographs tracing her body inch-by-inch with the illuminated lens that made her blue eyes balloon.

'Do you want to be alone?' asked Ava.

'Jesus wept, no! You're my witness. Every woman should have photographs like this to look back on, when their skin was fit to be seen and loved in. Like a Goddess coming out of the sea.'

'Botticelli's Venus.'

'Botty's Venus, I was. I've gone from God's gift to men to a blind bat that can't walk. I lived a life of Riley in that sumptuous body and don't regret a thing. How many people can say that? Now, hide those photographs in the bottom of the wardrobe before Vicky comes back. She'll think they're disgusting and destroy them. Maybe I'll send one to the paper to show the success of my diet?'

'No. We'll have every journalist in the UK here.'

'Really?' said Tilly, sounding pleased.

Chapter Forty-Two

Trevone Bay, August 2015

'I like that,' said Tilly, touching the bangle, turning it and tracing Ava's name. 'A love gift?'

'A gift,' said Ava, carefully. It felt like love, at least she'd always have this, if not Finn.

'Good, it's about time, and you look better than when you arrived. Your hair, nails, the way you hold yourself; all a vast improvement.'

'Thanks to you.' She twisted the bangle, loved how it glowed against her tanned wrist, the cool weight of it on her skin.

Tilly sighed. 'Vicky will soon be up to her eyeballs with the timetable for this girlfriend's visit. She will want everything to run like clockwork. Her main problem, of course, is me.' She smiled like a five-year-old.

'Tilly, she's your daughter,' said Ava, tapping her hand. Tilly shrugged.

'Vicky was a lovely little girl. I've not been the best mother by a long chalk. She met her husband, Martin, at university – in the first week – and married after they graduated. He departed five years later to New York for a florist he met at a conference, and Edward followed for work. I wish Jack could have seen him.'

'He'd be very proud – of them, and you.' She felt the tiniest bit sorry for Vicky.

Ava tucked Tilly in bed and retreated to her bedroom before Vicky returned. Later, she heard her trudge around, drop something, swear and go to bed. Eventually, Vicky's snoring matched her mother's.

At 7am Ava placed an empty bottle of upmarket Merlot in recycling. Tilly's daughter had the drinking capacity of her mother, but for fine wine. Ten minutes later, Vicky shuffled into the kitchen wearing pale-blue striped pyjamas. Without make-up her skin appeared waxy and sallow, her eyes puffy and bloodshot. Grey hair fluffed up on the right and flattened like straw on the left.

'I've got a very sore throat,' she said hoarsely, and halted before Ava. She opened her mouth for inspection and Ava saw the filled teeth, furry yellow tongue and flaming red throat. She stepped back instinctively.

'Painful,' Ava said, and satisfied, Vicky clamped her jaw shut and filled the kettle. The atmosphere tensed.

'I'm going for a quick run,' she said. 'Tilly won't wake for a while.' Vicky nodded, rooted in the medicine cabinet, popped out two painkillers and poured a glass of water. Ava ran fast; the gritty sand giving way under her bare feet. Cool soft rain fell, and clouds sagged as if they would spill and spread over the sea. There was the sound of gulls, her breathing, and waves shushing on stones. She was becoming a runner. Ava raced back and after a shower, found Vicky tucking into scrambled eggs, beans, sausages and bacon on hunks of thickly buttered white toast. Her sore throat didn't object.

'I woke Mummy,' she said, without looking up, 'and made her a light breakfast.' Ava looked in on Tilly who sat poking a soft-boiled egg with crustless, buttered bread.

'It's the crack of dawn,' she whispered. 'How do I get rid of this before she sees?' Ava did her the favour and ate it, gagging at the runny, yellow middle, hoping it would stay down. She liked eggs rock-hard.

Vicky barged in carrying her open laptop.

'Oh my God, you're all over the internet Mummy! Do you understand what this means? Thank God you can't Tweet or do YouTube. This stops right now!' Vicky shoved her computer in Tilly's face. Tilly's face screwed up so her eyes all but disappeared.

'Oh Vicky, stop exaggerating,' said Tilly.

'This is not on,' snarled Vicky, her lip curled, departing as Tilly lit up. Ava felt a rising dread.

At 9am the doorbell rang and Vicky, all instant charm, returned with the SpecSorters' representative. Yvonne Freeman flashed Tilly her ID which Tilly couldn't possibly read. The petite redhead had hundreds of freckles and pale blue eyes framed by square black glasses.

'Good morning, Mrs Barwise,' she blared in a bright, over-loud voice. 'I've come to see how your eyes are today.'

'I'm not deaf or senile.'

'No,' said Ms Freeman, quieter now. Vicky rolled her eyes and Ava tried not to laugh.

'My eyes are the same as every other day. Crap.' Ms Freeman visibly deflated although her smile remained fixed. Tilly stubbed out her cigarette. Vicky switched off the TV and removed her mother's cigarettes. Tilly raised the right side of her top lip as Ms Freeman unpacked her equipment. Ava stayed in the kitchen as the optician requested Tilly to read a line of the eye-test chart. Vicky hovered in the hall.

'B O R I N G,' Tilly spelt out gleefully.

'Err no,' Ms Freeman said, hesitantly. 'Let's try the line above, it might be easier.'

'S E X, C I G S and B R A N D Y.'

'For God's sake,' murmured Vicky outside the door.

'Ah, I see.' The penny dropped and so did Ms Freeman's voice which remained calm and professional. 'Well, if you don't want to do the test perhaps, I could look in your eyes?' There followed five minutes of questions Ava couldn't hear, only Tilly replying, 'Yes' or 'No' and finally, 'I can't be bloody bothered.' Vicky stormed in.

'What a waste. I'm sorry Ms Freeman.' The TV was switched back on and Vicky escorted the optician into the hallway.

'It's all part of my job,' said Ms Freeman politely, adding quietly. 'Mrs Barwise didn't complete the tests, so it's hard to give a definitive diagnosis. That needs hospital investigation but I'm fairly confident her issues are age-related *wet macula*. Simply put, this means blood vessels grow excessively behind the eye in a bid to fix her dwindling portal of vision. The rogue new supply spreads into the wrong places and results in swelling and bleeding. If left, these vessels will scar, causing rapid, irreversible sight loss. As it is, everything your mum sees must be as if through a gradually thickening veil.'

'Really. So, Mummy will go blind?' whispered Vicky, rather too brightly. Ava cringed. 'How soon?' she croaked.

'It's hard to say,' Ms Freeman said, gently. 'There's some damage limitation with AntiVEGF drugs. A consultant injects it into the eye's vitreous jelly. It will buy your mother time but there's no cure.'

'Ugh,' said Vicky. Ava touched her own eyes and thought of watching a needle piercing them.

'Mrs Barwise also has a cataract on her right eye which is removable,' Ms Freeman added.

'She won't have injections or an operation. Thank you Ms Freeman I'll contact her GP and get Mummy booked in with a specialist.'

'Have you seen how she signed the form?' Ms Freeman sounded amused.

'No,' Vicky said, warily.

'*Bullshit,*' read Vicky. 'How could she?'

Ava smiled.

'She did it with her eyes closed. I admire her spirit,' Ms Freeman said. 'She's the woman in the local paper and *Daily World,* isn't she? A few of my friends are trying her diet.'

'Thank you again,' said Vicky, bustling her out.

Ava stroked her bracelet. There wasn't a minute of pleasure to waste.

Chapter Forty-Three

Trevone Bay, September 2015

Ava returned to the forge as often as she could, leaving Vicky and Tilly to their circular, endless squabbles She wanted to ask Finn about Edward but instead, being naked, asked when he first liked her.

'I was drawn to your drunken dancing,' Finn said, as she lay next to him on the dog blanket, smelling of coal. Ava laughed. His fingers tasted of metal. Finn's lips brushed her belly. Ava thanked God there was less of it to grapple with. He pulled her to him; saying, 'Closer, closer,' and they made love again. She'd never cried out before.

'I take it as a compliment,' he said.

'Where did you learn to make love like that?'

'Not wide-ranging experience,' he whispered, 'but playing bass guitar helps, all that fretwork.' Ava kissed his cheek and lay her damp face on his chest like it was a huge open book, and felt his slowing heart. Finn stroked her hair. He took a sip of water from an old Nutella jar and offered it to her.

'Classy,' said Ava, tasting his salty shoulder; the one she'd bitten, that would have a rosy mark later. 'You smell of honey,' she said, inhaling the nape of his neck.

'Beeswax. Steel's got tiny pores and I rub in a thin layer so it won't rust. It seals the steel and makes it shine. Ava, if Tilly is going blind and into a home, what are your plans?'

She told him Vicky wanted her out and that her time was limited. Finn stayed quiet. To avoid further questions about her future she finally asked how he knew Edward.

'From school; he sounded me out about a development near Tilly's because of my engineering background. It's tricky because Cliff View partially blocks the site, so it would need to be flattened. I didn't help him. He doesn't care about this village.'

'Good. They're like vultures.'

'That's them, their lives. You needn't go Ava. Come live with me.'

She shook her head, without explaining. It was too soon. Finn had made it clear that Joe was going to be his only child and Ava very much wanted a baby one day.

'Closer,' he whispered but Ava felt herself move imperceptibly away.

Chapter Forty-Four

Cliff View, September 2015

At Cliff View, Ava found a note from Vicky. She was returning to London until the birthday. The atmosphere lifted and Tilly's home fell back to their routine.

'I'm not having injections in my eyes! Is it too early for a drink?'

'Yes,' said Ava, sympathetically, tucking Tilly's feet into cosy sheepskin slippers. Ava mused if it hadn't been for Josh and Sadie, she wouldn't be here at all or have found Finn. If it wasn't for Tilly, she wouldn't be so risk-taking and if it wasn't for Jack there'd be no love story or his daughter trying to get rid of her mother. Tilly lit a cigarette.

'Love doesn't happen often. Once is enough. If you're lucky twice, three, even four times is a luxury. I only loved Jack. I longed to live in West Virginia with a huge fridge, ice cubes, dishwasher, swimming pool and built-in wardrobe full of film-star clothes. I saw myself in a soft-top car and on horseback cantering through forests, even though I'd only ridden a donkey on Blackpool beach. I wanted that land of milk and honey and sun. I didn't think about Jack's family. I loved him body first and soul second. I was glad to be pregnant.' Tilly's eyes were dry and her face veiled by smoke. 'It's water under the bridge now. I was unusually lucky to marry Liam who understood.'

'You've never spoken about Liam.'

And Tilly began.

'Lovely Liam. I met him in The Blue Flame pub in Richmond on 1st July 1949. I'd persuaded Martha and her frowsy friend, Susan, of the mousey hair and fine down on her upper lip, to finally go out. They bought themselves two half beers and a rum with coke for me. While they ordered I sat directly opposite the bar. Martha and Susan would have preferred to tuck themselves away in the deserted lounge to babble about domestic trivia. I wasn't interested, then or now, in talking about cooking and children.' Ava smiled and nodded, as Tilly catapulted into her past.

'I remember what I wore. A low-cut, tight-fitting green dress, immaculately clean and ironed, pointed red shoes with kitten heels. Red and green should never be seen, my mother told me but I loved its elfishness. While they chatted, I surveyed the talent. There wasn't much and then, in he came, a man worth my time. Handsome, a little like Jack from the back. It took me fifteen seconds of staring at the rear of Liam's head for him to look around. It's a ninety-nine per cent reliable way to attract attention. He raised an eyebrow and mouthed: Would you like a drink? Well, I rose like a goddess with my show-stopping walk. The place came to a standstill.'

'I bet it did,' laughed Ava, thinking she'd practice her walk a lot more.

'Liam Carmichael was well-built, dark-haired and over six-foot. My kind of male. Expensive polished shoes, like my father's; ex-army but everyone was. He wore a smart navy suit, which showed off his firm bottom and broad shoulders. His face was rounder than Jack's. Pinocchio came to mind with a long nose, twinkly blue eyes and rosy cheeks. I thought it was down to the frothy beer but it turned out Liam felt heat like a polar bear in a desert.

'He bought me a drink; two in fact, despite Martha's warning glances and Susan looking appalled. Liam had money, not just the bundle of notes stuffed in his expensive leather wallet but in the cut of his cloth. I was a good talker and equally good listener when it came to stroking a man's ego. And any other part of his anatomy.'

'You're outrageous,' said Ava, smiling. She could imagine the scene.

'I asked Liam what he did and he said, Find people work, apart from brain surgery, then asked about me, Modelling, is that what you do? Or a wife of leisure?

'My husband died after D-Day,' I told him. This shut him up and I added, 'I have a four-year-old daughter.' That usually blew men out quicker than a match. But Liam Carmichael shrugged, said it must be hard. I told him I was looking for a brain surgeon to install some in me while I worked as a personal secretary. I said I could type with my eyes closed and do perfect Pitman's shorthand. Martha tapped me on the shoulder then and said they were leaving. Liam handed me a card stating, *Carmichael Recruitment Services, Oxford Street, London.*

'I went to see Liam, dressed in a cleavage-clinging white shirt, fitted grey skirt and matching heels. I was appointed his new secretary before I typed a word, with a cubbyhole attached to his office, and allowed home early to pick up Vicky from school. I greeted job-seekers and proved the perfect matchmaker for employers. Business poured in. Liam was funny, polite and charming to everyone but treated me no differently. It was like a force-field surrounded him. Six months later, Liam doubled my pay because profits had tripled. I put down a deposit on a maisonette in Notting Hill, as Martha and the Major were heading to a posting in Hong Kong. There was even enough money left over to pay for Vicky's childcare plus new clothes, handbags and make-up.'

'So how did you marry him?'

'I set out to woo him. I invited him for dinner. I sprayed polish so it smelt cleaner than it was and I'm no cook. I acquired two ropey chicken breasts which I battered to tenderness then doused in cheap wine and cream. Liam arrived with a dozen red roses and a nervous tic beneath his left eye. He smelt of gin, which wasn't like him and by the time I served dinner he was almost incoherent. He toyed with his food, perspired by the bucket and his face turned the colour of beetroot.

'I decided there was only one thing for it. I changed into a green silk dressing gown under which I wore a lace bra, matching French knickers and black stockings. When he saw me, Liam froze like a rabbit in headlights: his fork halfway to his open mouth. He pulled at the neck of his collar and gabbled something I couldn't hear. I'd never seen a man look stricken at the sight of me half-dressed.'

'I bet you hadn't,' Ava smiled.

'I asked if he was ill and he replied that a lot of people would say so and wrung his hands. He looked about to faint. He said I'd hate him. I had to beg him to tell me, in case it was contagious. Liam gave a half-cry and told me he was a homosexual. Well, I got up, knelt at his side and held his hand. I told him it didn't matter and that he was a very good friend to me.

'We tried to make love. He kept his eyes closed in bed, barely touched me, all very perfunctory. In the gloom, with his hairy body, he resembled a sweaty, furry bear.'

'Oh dear,' murmured Ava, thinking of how beautiful Finn was in bed and how different it had been compared to insipid Josh who took his own pleasure first.

'We came to an amicable arrangement. I would protect him by getting married, and he could look after me and Vicky financially while allowing each other our own freedom. As nobody was ever going to surpass Jack, I decided there were worse ways to approach marriage.'

Ava thought this perfectly reasonable.

'The wedding was a quiet affair. His mother had the measure of her beloved son and took an instant dislike to me for taking him away. We drank champagne and had a lovely, sexless, honeymoon in Edinburgh. When Liam disappeared for a night or two, I didn't ask. We slept in separate beds and shared a peaceful coexistence; one without jealousy or demands. Liam was a good stepfather and he turned a blind eye to my adventures.'

'Lucky you,' said Ava.

'I was, and I quickly learned the ropes of Carmichael Recruitment. We had a settled, peaceful coexistence in the leafy suburbs of Richmond with my own en-suite bedroom and exhilarating romantic life. I stuck to married men, as they had a lot more to lose if an affair came to light. They were kind, companionable and made me laugh in and out of bed. Liam died of a heart attack ten years later, aged fifty, and I missed him terribly.

But I rose to the challenge of running a business until Vicky took over. I kept a lot of lucrative shares which is how I pay for you.'

'That's amazing. I can see why you don't have regrets.'

Her red eyes focused. 'I knew Vicky wanted me out and that's why she employed you. She thought you'd be useless. You've simply been a stay of execution but I feel well enough to make my own decisions. Peter Hogwood, developers, Edward and Vicky. They're all circling. But they haven't reckoned on dealing with me.' A sly smile spread.

Chapter Forty-Five

Trevone Bay, September 2015

Days sweltered and broke early into full-blooded thunderstorms. Tilly's moods matched the weather. Her sight deteriorated but she point-blank refused treatment. Tourists left in droves, back to school, work, and shoreless, sand-free lives. Ava called her mother saying she'd be over soon but not giving a date. She saw Finn most days, trying to avoid his son. She didn't want to get close to Joe; it wouldn't be fair. Fan mail poured in and Ava loved responding to the letters, gentling Tilly's caustic advice with positive comments. Tilly granted no more Press interviews. She turned in on herself. On Saturday, Ava was meeting Finn for a drink and looking forward to a whole night together because Joe was staying at his grandmother's.

'I've run out of ciggies and I have to sort things out,' said Tilly, brushing her hair. Each stroke made the thin strands stand on end.

'May's bringing some over. What things?'

'Paperwork.' Ava found an emergency pack of cigarettes stuffed in the kitchen drawer. Others were in the bathroom cabinet and Tilly's wardrobe. 'Look at him dance,' said Tilly to the TV. 'He's got two left feet. The woman's professional but it's like a bear is dragging her across the floor.' The dancers were a spinning dazzle of sequins and feathers in skin-tight black costumes. Tilly's shoulders jutted to the Latin beat. She clapped as they finished and then scowled. Her moods swung in a heartbeat. May arrived with four more packs of cigarettes. She told Tilly the local newspaper editor wrote that sales had doubled with Tilly's campaign and they'd been shortlisted for an award. To celebrate May allowed Tilly an extra nip of brandy as they settled down to watch the *X-Factor*.

Ava parked near the Green Vine Wine Bar in Padstow. Balloon lights hung low over plum-coloured seats and scrubbed, long wooden tables. It was cosy, intimate and warm. She sat at the bar near a silent couple engrossed on their mobiles. The French bartender, with a glint in his dark eyes, asked what she'd like to drink in a halting accent Ava adored.

'A medium red,' she said, looking at bottles stocked from floor to ceiling. There was too much choice.

'Try one of our new autumn wines,' he said slowly. 'This rich full-bodied Merlot has your name on it. What's your name?' He smiled, kissed his fingers and opened them towards her.

'Ava.' Utter smarm but impeccable, irresistible Gallic execution, she decided.

'Like Gardner, you suit it,' he said, pouring. Nobody had ever said that before. 'This is fruity with a cherry and blackcurrant aftertaste.' Frankly, he could have sold her floor cleaner. Ava thanked him and sat by a window. Finn entered dead on time, wearing a black T-shirt, dark jeans and suede navy desert boots. *God, he's gorgeous*, Ava thought, and she couldn't wait to sleep with him a whole night.

The wine bar filled with a noisy hen party of about 20 women. The bride, dressed in a tiny pair of red sequinned shorts, wore a tight white T-shirt with list of dares printed across her generous chest.

Kiss a bald man

Act like a chicken laying an egg

Order a drink with a foreign accent

Call your ex and tell him you're getting married

She clucked like chicken, ordered a drink from the bald French barman, slurring his beautiful accent, and kissing him, then called her ex, elaborating on her successful fiancé: so nearly all boxes ticked in the first minute. A noisy group of office workers followed and took over the far corner. The couple at the bar glanced up from their phones to order wine and food.

Finn went outside to call his mum and check on Joe, who'd misplaced his favourite teddy. The barman placed a bowl of salty olives sprinkled with herbs on the table and winked at Ava. Jazz music played. The bride-to-be was now gently supported by women either side. Ava told Finn that Tilly knew all about Vicky and Edward's desire to demolish Cliff View to make way for the proposed new building plot.

'What will she do?' he said, holding her hand across the table. That was something Josh had never done, or looked in her eyes like Finn.

'Stitch them up like kippers, I hope, but not sure how,' said Ava. The bridesmaids helped the unsteady bride out, followed by her cheering party.

Wandering back, Finn bought a Margarita pizza which they shared along quiet cobbled streets glazed with rain. Stars glimmered over the ocean. Waves shushed.

'This was my Granddad's,' Finn said, stopping at a tiny terrace house. 'Two up, two down and a courtyard. We're lucky.'

'Do I take off my shoes?' Ava asked, as he opened the front

door.

'Err, no, you can take off your clothes, but heels are fine to keep on.' She laughed. His whitewashed home smelt of washing powder and a wood-burning stove. There were photographs of Joe everywhere. Toys were piled in boxes and spilt on the floor. One wall was crammed with books, CDs and records. Finn slid off her coat and kissed her.

'Thank God for a bed for a night,' he said, as the rest of her clothes followed quickly, including the heels.

Chapter Forty-Six

Trevone Bay, September 2015

On Saturday Finn brought Joe and insisted Ava spent the day with them. She hadn't explained why she was avoiding his son. A day felt as if she wasn't encroaching, running on sand and playing tag. The grazes on Joe's knees had healed into pale marks. He was an easy child to delight in, laughing and holding her hand naturally. It was one of those halcyon warm golden days. They bodyboarded near life guards and sunbathed away from the much-dwindled crowds. Later, they ate fish and chips, and drank lemonade. Ava returned to Cliff View, relaxed and energised enough to bake a banana cake which Tilly loved.

'During the war we swapped bananas for cooked parsnips because they were sweet,' she said, licking her lips. 'The first time I tasted a real one was 1945. We cut it lengthways and sliced it between me, Vicky, Martha, the boys, and the Major. Heaven. We'd learned to be grateful and unfussy in the war. We ate anything, even innards, especially tripe.' For Ava, the thought of swallowing soft, internal organs turned her stomach to mush. Her squeamish hypocrisy had never faced Tilly's challenges.

'Is Finn a good man?' asked Tilly, out of the blue, painting her nails aquamarine. There was rarely a connection between sentences. Whatever was in her head, from any time, popped out. She repeated herself more frequently, forgetting she'd just said the same thing.

Tilly expanded her views on ideal manliness.

'I prefer them clean, unperfumed and unkempt, with rumpled hair and a confident air. The way a man walks alerts you. I veto shufflers or marchers. He should be as coordinated on the pavement as the dancefloor and elsewhere,' she said with a wink. 'Shoes are a real giveaway. Nothing shiny, pointed or fussy. Remember, you should be the one checking yourself in the mirror, not him. No fussing with hair either. If he looks you in the eye, listens and makes you laugh, that's the man who's mostly likely to be good in bed. And out. And if he's free with his cash he's more likely to be generous elsewhere.'

'Really,' said Ava, smiling. In her head she had ticked off everything Tilly mentioned about Finn. Josh, on the other hand, had turned out to be a complete scrooge with a penchant for pointy shoes, and smiling at himself in the mirror while carefully brushing his thinning hair. The phone rang. It was Vicky, breathlessly announcing Mackenzie's flight into London.

*

Her arrival was the trigger for frenetic preparations for Tilly's ninetieth. Spreadsheets appeared. May was given a long list of Vicky's cleaning tasks without extra hours to fulfil them.

'Jeff's going ballistic with the amount I do here. Like a military operation this, Ava,' she said, dusting vigorously. 'A toothbrush to clean sink taps,' Vicky said, 'as if Edward's girlfriend's going to be checking taps. I ask you!' Her cheeks flushed. 'I'm surprised she's not detailed loo breaks.' She flicked a duster at a spider's web. 'I hope Mackenzie's not scared of spiders or daddy long-legs because they'll be out in force soon.' Ava made tea as May unpacked her sewing machine.

'Apparently,' said Ava, gently capturing a daddy long-legs and releasing it out the window, 'Mackenzie's spending a week in London being wined, dined and taken to the theatre, in preparation for being marooned here.' May unpacked yards of red and white fabric that would become bunting and table cloths to transform the Memorial Hall for Tilly's party. She told Tilly it was for the chip shop celebrating twenty years of opening and two decades of her life sweltering in it.

'It'll look like Liverpool Football Club,' said Tilly. Ava cut cloth to cardboard templates. 'I used to go out with one of their players.'

'Is there anyone you haven't gone out with?' asked May, talking around two pins held firmly in her lips.

'Chip shop owner,' Tilly smirked, and May spluttered as pins fell out. 'The footballer had a lovely body. I used to watch his team from the VIP box, before war stopped play. I didn't have a clue what was going on but liked seeing them running up and down, especially if it was against Everton. Every last man in the city was there. That left boring women, like my mother, at home or shopping. Is Mackenzie a football supporter?'

'Not sure,' said May. 'Anyway, it's baseball over there.'

'They're all padded up and bounce off each other,' said Tilly dismissively, switching to a TV programme in which three entrepreneurs made financial mincemeat out of desperate start-ups vying for cash. Tilly vetoed any participant she deemed unworthy, which was most of them. Ava loathed it, and gazed out of the window. The sun was swathed in a circle of brown-tinged cloud.

'You're quiet, Ava,' said Tilly. May looked up and gave a little smile.

'I have to concentrate on these templates,' she said but she was immersed in leaving a place that had come to make her so happy.

'Look who's coming,' Ava said, as Edward ambled up the path in ironed beige chinos and pointy shoes. Tilly's face lit up as he entered.

'Is Mackenzie with you?' she asked, smoothing her jogging bottoms and raking her terrible hair.

'At the Eden Project with Mum, who's given me a long list to go to the supermarket. I've got a lot of work, and wondering if either of you would go?' He glanced from May to Ava, eyebrows raised. He held Ava's eyes a little too long.

Servants, Ava thought, closely, followed by, not on your life.

'No,' said May quickly. 'I went this morning and haven't got a minute.' She sent the electric sewing machine into overdrive. 'Men hate shopping, don't they? Jeff does lists and wants me to walk up and down aisles methodically from one end to the other, ticking things off. I like to dart here and there because I've remembered something he's forgotten to add. He goes to pieces. I think he'd like one of those retractable dog leads to zap me back.'

'Ava?' Edward asked, proffering the list, anticipating she'd accept.

'No,' she said firmly, without explanation. She hadn't offered tea either.

His brow creased and face fell. 'Well, a man's got to do what a man hates doing.' He rose.

'Not often enough,' said May breezily, taking a pin from her mouth and pushing it sharply through a hem.

Chapter Forty-Seven

Trevone Bay, 18th September 2015

Bright bunting piled up in Cliff View's dining room, where nobody ever ate. The Golden Lion had become the nerve centre of *Operation Unmentionable Ninetieth*, and Sniffy Dave the linchpin. Ava and May coordinated several lists, without Vicky's spreadsheets, and a notebook was filled with who was sorting out food, drink and music. Favours came in from everyone who knew Tilly or had heard of her. Regional dance teachers accompanied the Glenn Miller tribute band and the Stray Surfboards warmed up for free. Women's Institute stalwarts, despite not being Tilly's favourite organisation, honoured one of the last local female war generation with a cake-making competition that brought out a furious floral-aproned battle. *The Cornish Mercury* wanted to send a photographer but Vicky vetoed it.

'Jeff will take some photographs and send them in,' said May. 'He's got this new-fangled camera. Mostly he takes photographs of birds. We've got albums of them. Humans don't get a look in, so it would make a change.'

Ava enjoyed herself and loved how villagers secretly slipped notes through the door or rang to whisper what they'd add to the feast. There was even a WhatsApp and Facebook group, not that Ava or May dealt with that. Tilly was oblivious.

'Here comes our lead coordinator,' May hissed as Vicky

276

marched up the path. 'Weather's coming in too.' May packed the sewing machine away as the first drops of rain pattered in, needle-sharp, against the window. Vicky had installed Mackenzie with Edward at The Castle Hotel and was directing Robbie, who'd teased the garden into floral perfection, to put up a welcoming string of bunting around the front door and an American flag. Vicky's face was tense and her fawn hair darkened in the rain. Ava couldn't help but admire her determination, so like her mother's but with zero focus on romance, cigarettes and brandy.

'Mummy's going to get a good party whether she likes it or not,' Vicky muttered to herself. The big send-off, thought Ava, before the care home. 'These windows should have been painted and cleaned,' Vicky fretted, entering Cliff View. 'But it's just a tiny holiday home.' Her waterproof coat crackled. 'Americans expect less.'

'Pity no American men are coming,' said Tilly. 'Their expectations are groin level.' Vicky ignored that. May and Ava could hardly keep a straight face.

'Mackenzie's caught a cold. Mummy,' she said, glumly. 'Don't smoke while she's here. She hates it, and please behave.'

'But,' Tilly said.

'No buts. Quiet,' Vicky commanded. 'For starters, no trash TV, like dating, auctions, and weddings. And I'm putting those dreadful magazines away,' she said crossly, scooping them up.

'Every woman likes a bit of trash in her life, apart from you,' Tilly retorted. 'But for the duration I'll restrict myself to luxury property developments. You know a lot about that don't you?'

'Suit yourself,' snapped Vicky.

'I'm not allowed to,' shot back Tilly. Vicky bustled to the kitchen. Ava heard the fridge open and the glug glug glug of wine. Smoke drifted from the living room as *Coronation Street* began. Ava folded bunting and popped them into a plastic bag. A car horn blared. Vicky yanked the dishwasher open, shoving her wine glass in. She was out of Cliff View in a flash and opening the passenger door of a sleek black BMW.

Tilly stubbed out her cigarette, turned off her favourite programme, slid her teeth in and blotted on lipstick.

'Welcome to Cornwall. I'm sorry about the rain,' Vicky announced loudly, as if the weather was in her power. 'So pleased you could come to Mummy's little holiday home.' Tilly heard that and a frown creased her whole face. Edward emerged, opened a black umbrella and passed it to his mother's outstretched hand. Mackenzie's legs swung out. Reed-thin, five foot two in high-heeled suede ankle boots, which promptly sank into gravelly mud. She sneezed, loudly.

'Well, what's she look like?' asked Tilly, brushing ash off her jogging pants.

'I can't see much yet. Petite, like a fairy,' whispered Ava. Tilly nodded approval. Mackenzie was enveloped in a padded, knee-length black coat with a voluminous fur-trimmed hood which concealed her face. A ripple of long blonde hair slipped out as Mackenzie leaned forward. The umbrella protected her cautious, dainty progress along the pool-sodden path. May joined Ava and Robbie at the door.

'This is Robbie. He does our groundwork,' said Vicky, imperiously. For a second Ava thought Robbie would bow.

Mackenzie extended her petite, pale left hand.

'How lovely, the yard's real beautiful,' said Mackenzie, smiling with perfect, white teeth. Her accent was delicious, soft and drawling.

'And this is May, who cleans,' said Vicky. May didn't look happy with that, shaking her hand briefly.

'And Ava, Mummy's carer.' Mackenzie's handshake was barely-there cool.

'Hi, pleased to meet you all,' Mackenzie said. Her porcelain-white skin appeared untouched by sun. She had hazel eyes and a red, sore-looking nose.

'Excuse me,' she said, extracting a paper handkerchief from her sleeve. 'I always get flu after flying.' She blew loudly for such a tiny woman and didn't have much idea of personal space while doing so.

'Would you like a drink?' Ava asked.

'Gee, yes, thank you. I don't drink caffeine or alcohol; warm water with a little lemon or ginger if you have any. Is it filtered?'

'No,' said Ava. She had lemon left over from May's tap cleaning and that would have to do. No ginger either. Mackenzie dipped her hand into her oversize black leather handbag and pulled out a flask.

'Just hot water is fine, this has an inbuilt filter,' she passed it to Ava and they trouped into Cliff View. Ava imagined no caffeine or alcohol, and filtered water would set a tricky precedent with Tilly as Mackenzie strolled into the old lioness's den.

Chapter Forty-Eight

Trevone Bay, 20th September 2015

In a few hours it would be Tilly's ninetieth birthday party. Villagers coordinated, decorated and delivered under May's able, secretive directions. Photographs of Tilly through the ages had been blown up and pinned across one wall. All were chosen for their beauty and only two with a man, one of Liam and Tilly on their wedding day, she looking gorgeous in calf-length lace, and Liam dapper. They weren't looking at each other. The other, of Edward at his graduation. In this, Ava saw a look of Jack about his eyes. Meanwhile, oblivious Tilly watched *Gone with the Wind*, imagining herself feisty, vampy Scarlett O'Hara with gorgeous Rhett Butler. Vicky drank wine and wrote a speech on the kitchen table.

At the Memorial Hall, Evangeline arrived and unfolded red and white covers over trestle tables. 'Well,' she said 'what's Mackenzie like and how was Tilly with her?' Ava glanced at May. May pursed her lips and strung up bunting.

'Mackenzie's got a cold,' said Ava. 'She was quiet and didn't like the smell of smoke. Vicky took her to a doctor for antibiotics but she was refused any. She's been at the hotel since.'

'You said Tilly didn't take to her,' May added, 'even though she's skinny and pretty. Probably because she's skinny and pretty. You also said that for ten minutes Tilly was pleasant enough but being polite for longer was impossible. Dinner got difficult didn't it,

Ava?'

'I was only in the kitchen,' she said. 'Serving.'

'You heard everything though.'

'Mmm…' murmured Ava. She didn't want to repeat it.

'Well,' May said, sweeping the floor, only too happy to repeat what Ava told her. 'Apparently, Tilly asked Mackenzie how she and Edward met. It was online. Tilly said that wasn't real dating because you can make any old thing up. Mackenzie went stone-cold silent. Apart from sneezing and blowing her nose.'

Ava hadn't mentioned how Tilly had extolled the virtues of American GIs and that Vicky had the very devil of a job to change the subject while Ava served up Marks & Spencer's finest coq au vin. Tilly had pushed the plate away after two bites saying it was too chewy for her and removed her teeth at the dinner table.

'And then Vicky,' May expanded, 'asked what an interior designer would do with Cliff View. Mackenzie said it was an interesting museum piece. Isn't that right Ava?'

'More or less. Tilly didn't like that.' She hadn't added that when Mackenzie went to the loo, Tilly stated she'd *Seen more colour in bleach*. When Mackenzie returned, she announced she felt poorly and left.

'Families,' said Evangeline, sighing. 'Glad mine all live far away. You've done brilliantly with the decor, May.' Evangeline sped up, laying cutlery until tables looked topped with silver scales.

'Jeff's moaning I'm never at the chippie,' said May. 'He's clueless about how much I do and I can't cope with the shop's heat. Look at this, Ava.' She peeled down the elasticated waist of her trousers, exposing a plaster on her right hip. 'Nicotine patches. If

Jeff sees one, I can say it's for the menopause and that'll be the end of that conversation.'

'Do patches work?' asked Ava, pinning bunting at every fourth loop so it looked perfectly even.

'Dunno, I only started an hour ago.'

Evangeline plucked loose straw fallen from the bale seats. 'Nicotine patches didn't work for me. I ate carrots. Now I can't bear them. Carrots or cigarettes.' Evangeline took over sweeping and May fanned herself with a serviette.

'The trouble is Jeff does online banking and sees where every penny goes. At £10 a packet it's impossible to hide, so I only buy them at petrol stations, merging the cost with fuel.'

'Kissing worked for Robbie,' added Evangeline, with a shy smile. 'Something good to do with his lips.' Ava didn't let on he was still smoking.

'I'm passing on that,' said May and they laughed. Ava was glad she had Finn to kiss for a while longer.

Onto each trestle table they placed a jam jar of fragrant white freesias and pastel sweet peas, tied with red ribbons. The hog roast machine was plugged in and a gingery carcass slowly revolved outside the marquee, and the aroma of pork circulated inside. Ava avoided the pig after glimpsing its closed, human-like eyes with long, strawberry-blond lashes. May sprayed polish on everything that wasn't moving and blasted passing flies with the aim of polishing them off. The stage was set for the fifteen-piece Glenn Miller tribute band.

'Tilly's clueless how big this is, isn't she?' said May, needlessly swiping trestle-table legs. 'She thinks it's the Golden Lion, chicken-in-the-basket and a Glenn Miller CD. You've hidden the booze at Cliff View, haven't you? I'd hate Tilly to find that!'

'Robbie locked it in the shed.'

'He's a love isn't he, Evangeline?' said May, smiling. 'He's changed for the better.'

'He's following Tilly's diet, but I like a man with a bit of weight on him,' said Evangeline. 'It's something to grapple with. Where do you want plates stacked, May?'

'Don't let Jeff hear anything about grappling. The plates go near the hog roast, so they pick meat and buns first, then the rest. Is Robbie moving in?'

'He's got to meet my kids yet. That's going to be make-or-break. I'm not sure about 24/7 because I like romance and my own space.'

'I'm so with you there,' sighed May, folding serviettes.

Ava balanced on a chair at the main door, pinning up a Happy Birthday sign without an age.

'Where do you want these?' asked Reg, sliding past her with two enormous silver platters. Each held sides of freshly cooked salmon on beds of watercress with wedges of lemon, plum tomatoes and cucumber.

'Reg, that looks delicious, where did you catch it?' asked May, pointing out a table for them.

'Tesco's, half-price,' he said. 'But don't let on. I hooked the mackerel. Jean's turned it into pâté, and there's fresh crab salad, plus brown shrimps. Jean's bought a biblical number of buns for pulled pork, along with salads, and made a sea of coleslaw.'

'Is it the one with raisins and cashew nuts?'

'No idea. If it hasn't got scales it's not my department.'

'That's the last lot of bunting hung, May, what do you think?' said Ava, stepping back to admire. May and Evangeline cooed.

'It's brilliant,' came Finn's mellow voice behind her. She turned and felt utterly happy. If she had a tail it would be wagging.

'Ooh look at you two lovebirds,' said May. 'I remember that in the dim and distant past.'

'How can I help?' said Finn, but was called away to lug out hay bales in zigzag herringbone fashion, at double height. It was a sweaty job. In the process, Finn became dishevelled with straw and dust. The women found it appealing to watch, especially when his son tried lifting bales.

'Oh, so easy on the eye and a lovely dad,' said May. Yep, thought Ava, to one child only. Joe swooped a toy Tyrannosaurus over hay bales and tables. He ran to Ava, smiling his sweet gap-toothed grin.

'I love this,' said Ava, bending down, and Joe flashed the dinosaur past her head.

'His teeth are bestest,' said Joe. 'I found a fossil one on the beach, look.' He uncurled his other hand to reveal a plastic four-inch tooth which Finn had planted. 'He could tear off your head with one bite.'

'Ouch! That's amazing,' said Ava. 'You're very clever finding something so precious. Imagine a whole mouthful like that? No wonder they didn't need big arms.' Joe raced to the hog roast, pretending to eat it through the glass.

'Careful Joe, that's getting hot,' warned Finn, heaving a bale into place.

'I will, Dad,' said Joe, babbling and flying his dinosaur in great loops.

'Finn, we're setting up,' said his bandmate, carrying a drum onto the smaller marquee stage next door.

'Better go. See you later, and all night because Joe's going to Mum's.' Finn stilled Ava's hand as she brushed straw from his shirt.

'I can't, I'm in charge of Tilly,' said Ava. He groaned.

'Come on, Joe.' His son ran into his arms, folding his little legs around his dad's waist.

'Gorgeous,' said May wistfully as they left. 'What are you wearing tonight then?'

'A pencil-skirt,' said Ava, 'and silk blouse from a charity shop.'

'I'd like to wiggle in a skirt like that. I've bought something at vast expense which Jeff will find out about online but not until after the event and I aim to get it back before he checks the account. I've also got an eighteen-hour corset and hope if I'm still standing at one minute past its deadline I don't explode. '

'Don't be uncomfortable,' said Evangeline, stacking plates. 'I'm wearing an elasticated skirt so I can dance, eat and breathe.'

The tables looked perfect and as the Glenn Miller tribute band tuned up Ava left to ensure Tilly was calm.

Chapter Forty-Nine

Cliff View, 20th September 2015

Tilly was in a foul mood.

'I don't care about my birthday,' she scowled. 'Who wants to celebrate getting this old and decrepit? I should be dead; it's stupid being alive this long.' There were two miniature bottles of brandy on the floor. Ava picked them up.

'I'm not a bloody child. If I choose to drink on my ninetieth, who are you to stop me?'

'Nobody. Trust me, you'll love tonight and you can have a sneaky drink there.'

'No. I'm going to bed. Vicky and Edward, and that mousey girlfriend of his, will sit around the pub table talking tripe and not mention chucking me out of my home.' Ava thought of all the preparations and panic rose.

'I'd feel just the same, Tilly. Anyway, I'm going to get dressed and could you help me with my make-up? Even if you don't want to go.' She had to be tactical.

'Whatever. There's good TV on,' said Tilly, lighting up and switching from rugby, which she declared watchable only for the muscular men, to a programme about sex and older people. Nobody, of course, had enjoyed sex like Tilly, nobody in the entire history of the universe, and she could tell them a thing or a million.

Ava zipped up the black pencil skirt – it fitted like a glove – and buttoned on the cream silk, sleeveless blouse. It made her arms look elegantly long and showed just enough cleavage, while maintaining a 40s elegance. She clipped on suspenders and stockings, loving the way they moved on her thighs and praying that's where they'd remain. She'd once worn hold-ups to a work Christmas party and one leg had dropped to an ankle on the dance floor. Josh and Sadie laughed as Ava hobbled off. They must have been seeing each other then, Ava realised with a sudden flare of old anger. She fixed in fake 50p pearl earrings and a matching £1 necklace. She was all set but for hair and make-up.

'Tilly, look,' said Ava. Tilly frowned. Her mouth dropped open. 'I know I'll never be as glamorous as you,' she added, hoping flattery would work its magic.

'No, you won't but you don't look bad at all.' She clapped her hands, a sure sign of pleasure.

'It's a 1940s theme at the pub. I found something for you too but if you aren't going please help me.'

'Is everyone dressing up?' she asked. 'Just for the pub?'

'Yes,' said Ava, holding up make-up, comb and pins.

'Come and sit on the pouf and let's see what I can do.'

Tilly's hands shook as she set to. Ava felt the thread-like beat of her wrist's pulse against her cheek as Tilly brushed, parted, pulled and pinned her hair.

'Ouch, that hurts,' said Ava several times, to which Tilly tutted and yanked.

'That's it, a perfect Victory roll. I used to be able to do it in seconds. Jack loved undoing it just as quickly. You're not to look until I've done your face.' Tilly gripped Ava's jaw with one unsteady hand as she applied foundation and powder, swearing every few seconds. Then she wiped one side off and restarted. Ava's skin stung. The lipstick proved trickiest.

'Press your lips together, Ava. Oh no, the Cupid's bow's smudged, I'll have to start-a-bloody-gain.' Ava's lips tingled. Finally, Tilly drew back. She spat on the mascara wand and looked shame-faced. 'Sorry, I got carried away – you don't need to do that these days.'

'Never mind, now the eyeliner.' It was peculiar having Tilly do something intimate for her. Her breath smelt faintly of sewage and even when Tilly wasn't speaking her lips moved to thoughts. 'Hold still, a little more rouge is required.' Ava felt like her cheeks were being exfoliated. Tilly beadily eyed her handiwork, applied another layer of scarlet lipstick.

'Stay still.' Ava pouted. 'Now, press your lips together. Sorry, I need to re-do your hair. Pass the brush.' Tilly attacked Ava's head, until her hair flew up. 'Good, it needs to be full of body.'

'That hurts, Tilly.' Tilly pinned her hair, scraping her scalp. She leaned back and narrowed her eyes.

'You look like I used to. Not as good but not bad. You'd get some glances – about half as much as mine.' They laughed. 'Now take a look.'

Ava stepped in front of the mirror. Her dark curls were slicked back into a face-framing roll. The pearl earrings glowed against pale, matt make-up and translucent, flawless skin. Tilly had tapered the eyeliner and the effect opened Ava's eyes, turning them sultry and feline. The painstakingly applied lipstick was arresting. Ava's full lips looked satiny and the creases, sensual. She wasn't sure how she was going to eat, let alone drink, but that was, as Tilly stated, irrelevant.

'Do you want to see what I've got for you?' said Ava.

'No, I can't go back in time. How can I dress up, sitting in that stupid chariot of a wheelchair?'

'I'm just going to let you have a peek at what I found.'

'The only change of scene that's going to happen to me is a coffin.'

'Oh, come on, you can't tell me to enjoy myself and be a misery. I'll let you drink but it's no smoking there,' said Ava, feeling desperate, wishing May was there to persuade.

'I'll smoke where I want.'

'Well, it's not like the police will make a show of you in court is it?'

'That'd be a good story.' Tilly laughed. 'Gut Buster queen gets busted.'

'You've already got more Press than you can handle. Is my walk OK?' Ava wiggled, shoulders back, head up, hips rolling, feet pointed at midnight.'

'Better but I'm not going,' said Tilly. A car beeped and door slammed. Vicky's shrill hello rattled through Cliff View as she stalked in. Tilly's mouth opened again. Vicky had poured herself into a ballooning blue uniform. A look of annoyance flashed across the daughter's face at the sight of Ava.

'Oh Ava, you're coming?' asked Vicky, her tone all surprised. 'I thought you'd like the night off?'

Ava, felt herself shrink.

'Of course she is but I'm not,' said Tilly. 'What are you dressed as?'

'WAAF Officer.' Vicky pressed her peach lips together. 'Mummy you have to come; it's all been done for you!'

'I never saw one like that.'

'That's because I don't fit your idea of what a woman should look like,' Vicky snapped. 'Ava, a chat in the kitchen, please.'

'Yes,' said Ava calmly. If she was getting the sack she'd still go and see her friends and Finn.

'There's been a family discussion and in appreciation of your work with Mummy we are giving you another month, if you can stay on? Please. And of course, you are welcome at the party.'

'Why stay on?'

'Arrangements are taking longer than expected.' Vicky looked up at the ceiling. 'Mummy's sight issues, on top of osteoporosis, drinking and smoking, means she needs a specialist care home to accommodate her needs. It may be out of Cornwall.'

'Does Tilly know?'

'Not yet.' Vicky laced her hands together and pressed them out.

'Right.' Ava felt sick. Vicky nodded and returned to her mother. The damn cheek, Ava fumed, telling me not to go to the party in one breath and asking me to collude with Tilly's rehoming far away. Tilly called for Ava.

'We'll just watch TV tonight,' Tilly addressed her daughter. 'Vicky you'd better get off. Enjoy yourself.'

'You must come, Mummy.' She held on to each side of the drill trousers, like a pleading child.

'No, I don't, not at ninety. I can do as I wish. Goodbye.'

'You've always been so bloody difficult,' said Vicky, as she slammed the front door.

'She's done it to show she's a dutiful daughter before I'm incarcerated and Cliff View demolished. I know I'm not easy but I'm honest.' Ava saw how badly Tilly's hands shook. Tears trickled down her cheeks and she wiped them angrily away. 'Damn it. I'll show her. What did you want me to wear?'

'So, we're going?'

'We shall go to the ball. I wasn't called Battle Maid for nothing.'

'Fantastic! May hired a lovely suit,' said Ava.

'Bugger that; get the herringbone one out of the trunk and put Glenn Miller on because I need a good kickstart. One more thing, if I go like this' – Tilly slow-winked at Ava – 'it means help me escape from whoever is talking to me.'

'Agreed.' They shook hands.

Chapter Fifty

Trevone Bay, 20th September 2015

'Look how good my figure still is!' crooned Tilly, smoothing the suit which had taken twenty minutes to gently ease on. Apart from a few snags and a section of unpicked hem – which Ava taped – it draped over Tilly's non-existent hips and flattened across her deflated breasts.

'What I'd give to have a new head, spine, arms, legs and tits. I can't have what I really want – to be young again – but as my eyes are rubbish, at least I'm spared looking at the wreckage.'

'You look amazing,' said Ava, handing Tilly her teeth. She wiggled her jaw and smiled like a crocodile as she liberally coated red lipstick and copiously sprayed Dior's heady, smoky Poison until they coughed.

'I can't really talk with these false teeth,' she hissed as if speaking with a mouthful of wet wipes. 'It's better for Vicky if I keep my gob shut. What a pity I didn't invite those Germans, they'd have been up for this. In their smart uniforms.'

'Vicky would faint and she'll be watching like a hawk for misdemeanours – particularly on the brandy front,' said Ava, as Tilly dabbed on another layer of lipstick.

'Good,' she said, peering at the hand mirror, 'My lips look like they've been in an accident. Let's hit the road.' Ava settled Tilly in the wheelchair, rearranging her skirt so the plastic bottle of ready-mixed brandy she'd made was invisible and accessible. 'Ready for action,' Tilly said, clasping a new packet of twenty cigarettes and lighter. Ava pushed Tilly down the path and could tell it hurt with every roll of the wheel.

'Ninety,' Tilly said, astounded, and sucked her teeth loudly. 'I hope these don't fly out of my mouth. I can tell you're walking with your feet at ten-to-two. Point them to midnight. That's better; I can feel the difference straight away.'

'So, can I,' said Ava. 'It's not easy in these shoes.'

'Doesn't matter so long as you don't walk like a duck. I thought we were heading for the Golden Lion; you're going the wrong way.'

'Surprise, surprise,' said Ava, pushing Tilly towards the Memorial Hall. It looked dark and empty with curtains closed. A head bobbed at a window and disappeared. Ava opened the double doors and rolled Tilly through. Lights blazed and a great cheer went up, like a goal had been scored. Ava thought there was more than two hundred people there, all in fancy dress. Clapping and cheering turned to *Hip Hip Hooray!* Tilly's age wasn't mentioned and Tilly, for once, was silenced and so open-mouthed Ava worried her teeth might fall out. May squeezed through to them, dressed in a vintage floral apron (one that had frequented Cliff View) over an orange dress held taut by her eighteen-hour girdle. She kissed Tilly, leaving an orange imprint which May tried to rub off but Tilly stopped her. Jeff bent and pecked Tilly on her forehead. He was a giant haystack of a farmer in tweedy plus-fours tied with string, checked shirt, and brown woollen waistcoat. His new camera was slung around his neck and he carried a potato sack over his shelf-like shoulders. It clinked and Ava suspected it held a bottle or two. He said May was his Land Girl which got him a dig in the ribs, then he started taking photographs until May told him he was not the bloody paparazzi and to belt up. Edward and Mackenzie glided over as Spencer Tracy and Betty Grable. Ava thought Mackenzie looked stunning, like a sparkly fairy queen on a Christmas tree, albeit with a red nose. She wouldn't kiss so she didn't spread germs. Edward embraced Tilly and kissed Ava on the lips. He tasted of whisky. She pulled away and caught Mackenzie's look of distaste. Reg strolled up, bowed and kissed Tilly's hand, which she loved. He'd come as *Dad's Army* TV spiv, Private Joe Walker. He'd shaved off his beard, leaving a pencil-thin moustache. Unfortunately, he'd forgotten that his chin hadn't seen sunlight for years and while his upper face was deeply-tanned and lined, the lower was startling white and smooth. Dr Singh appeared, in a green silk kurta and bowed to Tilly, then introduced his wife, Harjeet; a silver-haired woman in a gold salwar kameez. He informed his oldest patient that two-and-a-half million Indians took part in the war and showed his late father's Indian Distinguished Service Medal, who'd been decorated for his gallantry at Monte Cassino in May 1944. Tilly, in turn, told him her father had loved living in India and was so fond of gin and tonics that the habit lasted until the day he died.

'That doesn't surprise me,' replied Dr Singh.

'It's not my wake, you know,' Tilly announced, as Ava pushed her around to mingle with the great, the good, not-so-good, and badly-behaved of Trevone Bay and Padstow. Every charity and fancy-dress store far and wide must have been ransacked, thought Ava, given that particular musty-smell underneath lashings of perfume and deodorant. Tilly eyed up a strapping surfer dressed as a GI with tousled blond hair and flashy white smile. Girls in floral dresses milled around him.

'Like Pavlov's dogs for a uniform,' said May.

'No wonder,' sighed Tilly. 'May, can you actually breathe? You look like you might pass out.'

'Just about but it's worth it to get into this dress.'

'You look gorgeous,' Jeff said, pinching her rear. May beamed, even as she brushed his hand off.

'Who did all this?' asked Tilly, between handshakes, kisses and hellos.

'Everyone in the village chipped in,' May answered. 'And Vicky did a huge amount, of course.' Ava thought that was noble of her.

'Perhaps this could be my wake. Better to enjoy it while I have a pulse.' After ten minutes chatting to WI women, Tilly gave Ava the dramatic wink. Ava told the ensemble that Tilly needed her medication and pushed her to a long table set with vintage teacups and stands of artfully decorated pastel cakes.

'B O R I N G,' Tilly snapped, smiling and waving at the WI gaggle. 'Why are we at the tea and cakes?'

'So, Vicky doesn't suspect,' said Ava. 'Put your drink in that cup and it'll look like black tea with a slice of lemon.' She had been looking for Finn but couldn't see him, and her heart sank.

'You're getting more like me every day,' said Tilly, as Ava held the dainty cup and Tilly slid out her bottle from under her skirt and Ava poured. Vicky was nowhere to be seen, either. A couple, perfectly dressed in an evening suit and flowing dress, took to the floor – dance teachers who put twenty others through their jitterbug paces.

'Some look like they're wrestling not dancing,' said Tilly. 'I could knock spots off the lot of them.'

'Oh, Vicky alert,' said Ava, watching the daughter steam out of the kitchen, leading a team of women, in matching blue boiler suits and transporting plates of food. She spotted Tilly with a big smile and was all dramatic kisses for Mummy and delighted greetings for Ava. The performance turned Ava's stomach.

'We'll bring Mummy home later, Ava. Let's hope she makes it for Glenn Miller.'

'You bet I will, and Ava will take me home,' snapped Tilly. 'I might tell everyone why this is being laid on for me. My last outing. Your plans for me. And Cliff View.'

'But Mummy,' said Vicky, 'it's your eyes.'

'Eyes, my arse. I see clear as day what you want and won't get – even over my dead body.'

'Are you drinking?' she asked, peering at the tea. Tilly shook the cup and the liquid fizzed.

'Dead right.'

'I see,' snapped Vicky. 'I can't talk to you then.' She stormed to the other end of the bar and collared Edward.

'She'll get over it,' Tilly said, sipping. 'Look at them.' She pointed to the dance experts. 'They're nearly like me and Jack!' Ava scanned for Finn and felt keen disappointment. Perhaps Joe was ill. She emulated the dance teachers' steps holding onto Tilly's wheelchair. A couple, the man dressed as a British soldier and the woman in a tight red tea dress, attempted moves that would have challenged Olympic gymnasts. She slipped on the floor, he nearly landed on top of her and they struggled up to applause.

'Go and get yourself a drink, Ava.' She tried to give her £20.

'I'm not taking a penny.'

'Then at least do the walk. Part that crowd like the Red Sea.'

Ava straightened her back, pulled in her no longer-existent stomach and stepped out like a catwalk model towards the cider-end of the bar. Nobody noticed, being far too intent in the tussle to buy a pint. There was going to be quite a wait. Finally, she saw Finn beckon her at the busy far side and about to be served. He'd been watching and couldn't lose his place; even for her. He wore a 1940s-style dinner suit and looked like he was going to be married. Ava felt her stomach flutter for the first time since, forever. She wiggled to him through the crowds.

'Sensational. I don't say that often. Maybe when England win a trophy, or even a match. I'd ask you to dance but I'm embarrassing, until I've drunk enough not to care. Cider?'

'God no. White wine, please, and Tilly could do with ice for her secret stash of brandy,' said Ava. 'You look good too.' He kissed her in front of everyone. There were whistles and calls to, *Get a room.*

Ava laughed and then caught Vicky's eye. She looked as if she was about to throw up.

'There's a bottle of fizz on the table.'

'Thank you.' She squeezed his hand, ignored Vicky. 'Have you played yet?'

'Warmed up the crowd before you came.' The Miller tribute band struck up *Chattanooga Choo Choo* and Ava saw Tilly's face light up as the young surfer swayed to the music by her side.

Finn held Ava's hand and wound his way to his friends; ones she'd not met. They introduced themselves, were really friendly, teasing Finn about punching above his weight. Ava sipped her drink and spying Tilly alone, brought her over.

'They asked me where I found you,' whispered Finn when she returned, 'I told them you made a grab for me swimming.' She pinched his arm.

'Careful, Tilly,' said Ava, as she poured more brandy in her cup, 'anyone would think it's your twenty-first.'

'It feels like it.' May appeared with Jeff, him nursing his pint like an anchor and her itching to dance.

'Hogwood's a good mover, isn't he? Fancy a jitterbug?' May said, nudging Jeff. He shook his head; not even ten pints would make him take to the dance floor.

'He's also a good mover at buying and selling homes,' Jeff said.

'Jealous. I'm asking him to dance.'

'Best of luck,' said Jeff. May shot across the floor and into the arms of Padstow's most successful estate agent. He was impeccably dressed as a British officer with false handlebar moustache that accentuated his beady eyes. The trousers had been badly-hemmed to shorten them. He was four inches smaller and half the size of May.

'Hogwood can handle her better than I can,' mused Jeff. Tilly nodded. Hogwood held May in a firm pose as if they were about to run and then foxtrotted quickly across the floor. He was light on his feet and kept May on her toes.

'Jeff?' asked Tilly, 'if I buy you cider will you lift me up and dance me, so my feet don't have to touch the floor?'

'Just for you and because it's your birthday, I'd make an

exception,' Jeff said, as the band launched in to *Pennsylvania 6-5000* but off he strolled. Finn kept glancing at Ava, a look that was a bond between them even as they spoke to others. A few yards away, Vicky gabbled to Edward and tucked into a sausage roll. Mackenzie stood beside them like a bored ice queen. Gobbets of pastry stuck to Vicky's mouth and lapels of her suit. Edward listened; eyes glazed. Drunk, she thought. Vicky turned her attention to Mackenzie; whose delicate features froze as Vicky's mouth opened and closed like a fish.

Mackenzie seized her chance to escape with the next dance, pulling Edward onto the floor. He looked like a dog being dragged to see a vet. They both tried to follow moves but gave up and stayed awkwardly together. They didn't look into each other's eyes or speak. Vicky reloaded her plate. Finn joined the food queue now the frenzy had melted away.

'How did I give birth to her?' asked Tilly, watching her daughter refuel with a pulled pork bun, quiche, coleslaw, and crisps.

'Vicky probably wonders the same about you,' replied Ava. 'Sorry.'

'You're right,' laughed Tilly. 'But I'm more fun. Go on, admit it, you'd rather spend a day with me than half an hour with Her Highness?'

'I couldn't possibly say. Your daughter chose me for you, so she did well, didn't she?'

'Yes, but only because she thought you'd fail.'

Finn returned with two plates and Joe carried another for Tilly. Joe wore corduroy trousers with black braces, a white collarless shirt and peaked cap. His name was written on a piece of cardboard strung around his neck. He clasped a teddy and his blond hair was parted on the left and plastered down. Finn whispered to Joe, who handed Tilly a plate of crustless sandwiches and showed Ava his name tag and one-eyed toy.

'He's lovely but where's your dinosaur?' said Ava.

'At Granny's. He's waiting for me there. She gave me her old teddy. His name is Willy, which is very, very rude,' said Joe, delighted.

'He's been in the wars, with his poorly eye,' said Ava. 'It's a good job he's being looked after by you.' Joe looked at Tilly curiously, making his teddy do somersaults.

'Are you very old?' Joe asked Tilly.

'Ancient but only on the outside. Sometimes I feel as young as you.'

'Were you in World War II, because that's our school project?'
'I was.'

'Is that why you can't walk? Did the Germans shoot you?' Joe sidled nearer, and Finn winced.

'Joe, come on now, Granny's waiting for you,' he said.

'I wasn't hurt in the war,' said Tilly. 'I was an evacuee though and sent to a horrible family who made us stay out all day with hardly any food.'

'Did they have yellow teeth and scary beards? Were they called *The Twits*?' asked Joe, his eyes rounding.

'Yes, how clever of you. They had beards, even the woman, and they were twits.'

'Daddy read me their story,' said Joe, sitting his teddy on Tilly's lap. Finn smiled. 'Daddy, I want to jitter the bug now.' Joe grabbed Finn's hand and pulled.

'I don't jitter bugs but we'll have a go,' he said. Joe insisted teddy danced too. Ava watched and thought Finn did remarkably for a sober Englishman.

'He's hot,' said Tilly.

'He's the best hot I've had.' And she thought sadly, not for much longer.

'Beautiful eyes,' Tilly smiled. 'Good body and that voice. You could listen to him repeat the alphabet, let alone saying lovely things. Lucky you.' She pulled her brandy out, added more.

'Who supplies it, and where's it hidden?'

'Not saying. Anyway, this cache is almost gone. But that doesn't matter now. When I was able to get about in the village, I bought my cigs tax-free from a pub; the kind frequented by men and avoided by women. A bloke came in carrying a big bag and people kept giving him a nod and wink and he'd sit at each table. He placed the bag on the floor and brought out ciggies; careful, not flashy. Well, I put my hand up like I was at school. He looks up, gives me a wink and bingo, I had my dealer. Once, I had to pick up a prescription and would have missed him, so I gave the barmaid £50 for my 200 cigs. She did the deal and popped them in my shopping trolley later. That's customer service. Then he was arrested and I'm back to paying a bloody fortune.'

'Cornwall's still a smugglers' haven isn't it?' said Ava, as the dance ended. Mr Hogwood's finale saw him dramatically tip May back but he couldn't quite hold her and she slid slowly on the floor. It took him and Jeff to get her upright.

'May needs to lose weight,' Tilly said and sipped. 'I need a ciggie now because the WI lot are heading over for cakes and tea, so emergency exit please. I might find another dealer.'

'Illegal contraband's going to get you in trouble.'

'I'll plead dementia in court and I'm already a prisoner. Get me out of here.'

Outside, a dozen smokers gathered around an old Fiesta. They'd brought out their drinks and transformed the car roof into a bristling mini-bar, like a glass hedgehog.

'Alright, Tilly,' said a man in the darkness, 'joining us rebels? We've got the heater on.' Ava rolled Tilly to them and settled her by the open passenger's door. It was cosy. Tilly rubbed her hands.

'This is where the gossip is,' she said. 'Tell me, who's doing who, and where can I get cheap cigs?' Numerous answers were forthcoming.

'Can someone get me when Tilly wants to come in?' said Ava, shivering at the edge. She returned to the warmth and light, skirting the room to avoid Vicky and Edward. Finn talked to an elegant older woman in a cream and red dress. Her blonde hair was cut in a sharp bob. She handed Joe crisps whenever his little hand reached out from under the food table.

The band struck up *Moonlight Serenade* and all lights dimmed as the disco ball turned blue. It was like they were underwater. Finn put his arm out for her and said something to the woman who smiled at Ava.

'This is mum. Beth, meet Ava.' He brought her close.

Beth kissed her. 'Lovely to meet you,' she said. 'I've heard lots.' She dropped another crisp into her grandson's hand. Ava thought about the risk her son had taken to save a stranger. His mum must not have been happy. It was thankfully too loud to talk.

'Come and dance,' said Finn and led Ava away. 'You're beautiful as a 1940s woman. And any other era. You smell gorgeous too.'

'Poison.' He frowned. 'Tilly's perfume.' They began the waltz awkwardly, stepping on each other's feet and laughing. After a few minutes they got their bearings, barring Finn's apologies and Ava's ouches.

'Bye Daddy, see you tomorrow. Bye Ava,' shouted Joe as he left holding Beth's hand and waving his teddy. Finn blew him a kiss.

'He's a happy, lovely boy,' said Ava.

'Got a lot of love around him and that's all that counts,' said Finn, pressing the small of her back. 'Can I come by later?'

'I have to get Tilly to bed and Vicky might be around.'

'Damn and blast.'

Vicky bumped into them, weaving, as she carried a bottle of red across the dance floor.

'Oops, a few too many,' said Finn, stroking Ava's back. 'She might not be up much longer by the look of her, and I'll depart at dawn.'

The music stopped and there was a roll of drums. The white-suited bald bandleader stepped to a microphone and cleared his throat.

'Has Tilly Barwise graced us with her presence?' he asked, in a pronounced Welsh accent of which there was no trace when he sang.

'She's disgracing herself outside having a fag,' someone shouted. Ava ran to get her. The room erupted with chants of *Tilly,*

Tilly. Ava rolled her in and Tilly waived regally, wafting her cigarette, trailing a nicotine cloud. Vicky removed it as she sailed by. Tilly pulled a face that made the crowd roar. Edward trundled in a huge cake with the picture of Tilly in her red costume. There was no 90 on it, just *Happy Birthday Beautiful.*

'Gorgeous, wasn't I? exclaimed Tilly, hissing into the microphone which the bandleader held, and waved at her photographs on the wall. Her teeth were still in but looked loose. 'Let this be a lesson to all of you who don't look after your figures.' Ava noted there was no mention of dental work. 'I'm sure you've seen my story in *The Cornish Mercury* and the *Daily World.* There's life in the old bitch yet.' A bearded, older photographer in faded black T-shirt and jeans appeared out of nowhere. He lined up a reluctant Vicky, Edward, and Mackenzie behind Tilly. Their smiles appeared pasted on. Jeff stood at the side of the snapper, thinking of himself as the designated photographer. Ava didn't have a chance to ask where the man was from because, like all photographers she knew, he disappeared straight after. Who cares now, she thought.

'Fame, darlings,' Tilly announced. 'I still weigh the same as when this photograph was taken, although everything has slid south or, in the case of my teeth, disappeared completely.' Tilly pushed her false teeth slightly out, much to the delight of children and horror of adults. Ava foresaw a rush for dental check-ups.

'Three cheers for Tilly,' hiccupped May, stepping forward. She held up a card emblazoned, *21 Again.* 'To the least boring woman in the world! Hip Hip Hooray!' And three times the crowd cheered and toasted. Beneath Tilly's smile, Ava thought she looked drained. 'And of course,' added May, as she raised her glass, yet again, 'let's not forget Vicky, born seventy years ago.' Vicky blanched; it seemed she, like her mother, hated age mentioned. 'And raise your glasses to Edward and Mackenzie, showing cross-Atlantic relationships continue to be a family tradition.' You could hear stifled giggles. Tilly clapped but Vicky's face filled with fury at the public airing of her mother's affair. The band struck up *Have Ya Got Any Gum, Chum?* Everyone joined hands and danced around Tilly, while Vicky stood stolidly, sourly outside the circle. She crumpled the speech in her hand.

'Excuse me,' Vicky slurred to Ava, when the song ended. 'Edward will take Mummy home now, as you obviously have somewhere better to go.' Vicky's glass tipped to one side and half-spilt.

'For God's sake someone sober needs to put me to bed,' snapped Tilly. 'Ava, I'd rather you took me please. My back's killing.'

'Mum you're coming to The Castle,' said Edward to Vicky. Mackenzie looked at her Apple watch. It had zero signal. Her face was pained, lips tight, a full frown.

'The taxi's outside now,' Mackenzie said, shrugging on a cream trench coat. She yawned, without covering her mouth. Red lipstick stained her top front teeth. Vicky went to say something but faltered, or had forgotten. Edward removed her glass and steered her unsteadily out.

'Oh dear,' said Tilly, brightly. 'Well, now we can have fun. My back suddenly feels better.'

An hour later, Ava was home with Tilly, who was medicated, smiling and asleep in minutes. Ava showered and picked up a sample of organic body lotion from Padstow. *Goat's Milk Mousse with notes of Nettle and Moss*, she read. She didn't think Finn would appreciate a mouthful and put it down. She brushed her teeth, swilled with minty mouthwash. Ready, she thought, slipping on her short dressing gown. There was a crunch of feet on gravel and a tentative knock.

'Finn?' Ava whispered.

'No, Father bloody Christmas,' he said. She slid off the chain and into his arms.

Chapter Fifty-One

Trevone, 20th September 2015

Ava ached for Tilly, lying alone with her crooked, broken and untouched body, while she curled against the warmth of Finn. To feel his skin, his muscular arms about her and lovely face so close, was bliss.

'Next month, I'm heading to Spain when Tilly's put in a home,' she said quietly, in the dawn's grey light. Finn stroked her cheek but didn't ask her to stay. He left before 6am and Ava's thoughts bristled with the idea of leaving Trevone. She had, without realising, or even wanting to, become anchored there.

Tilly refused breakfast but allowed Ava to bathe her. She no longer found Tilly's body repulsive; its folds and lines, the way flesh hung off her hips like vellum. Ava unclipped the hoist and Tilly settled in the deep warm water scented with lavender salts.

'It was a great night last night, apart from my daughter's performance. I loved every minute. I hope you had a good time with Finn.' Ava wasn't sure if she knew he'd stayed over.

'I loved it too, especially your entrance for the cake. I think there's a lot of people who'd never have a ninetieth like that.' They were quiet for a little while. A blackbird trilled outside.

'If I'm forced into a home,' considered Tilly, 'I'd like you to stay on here for a while.'

'There's no point Tilly, I'm going to Spain.'

'I loved Spain in the 80s. All sun, Sangria, sea and attractive Spaniards. What about Finn?'

Ava bit her lip: 'It's early days and he has his son to think of. He doesn't want more children.'

'He'd come around, men do and if they don't, well I coped alone and look how she turned out!' Tilly laughed, her feet swishing, so ripples of light flowed across her body.

'I need a proper job.'

'You can't get more proper than looking after me! But I might find you one.' Ava liked how the freckles on her shoulders trickled and thickened down her arms and back.

'Will you go to the WI market for me today?' Tilly asked, as Ava poured bergamot gel on a flannel. She delicately washed Tilly's back, tracing the bent shoulders, brittle nodules of spine and slender fan of ribs. 'I'd like their dark chutney, fruit cake, and orange marmalade. It's a pity I can't stand the jam and Jerusalem WI. I prefer the Men's Institute.'

'Is there one?' asked Ava, picking up warm towels and placing fresh clothes on the radiator.

'Thousands. Pubs, of course,' laughed Tilly, soaping her face, rinsing and blinking.

'Of course,' laughed Ava. Dressing was painful and protracted. Ava administered morphine. 'You'll feel better soon.'

Ava put together a fish pie with cod, salmon, shrimps, creamy leeks and Tilly's favourite mashed potatoes with spring onions. May arrived clutching a new *Hello* magazine.

'That was a brilliant night, apart from me mentioning cross-Atlantic romances,' she said. 'My mega-mouth. Everyone loved

Tilly, well, maybe not some of the WI women when she nearly put her teeth out. One nearly choked on her Earl Grey. And I'm never wearing a girdle again. I've damaged my blood supply.' She handed the magazine over. 'There's a singer in this who was nearly arrested for licking a doughnut in a bakery.'

'Why's that a crime?' asked Tilly.

'She hadn't paid, and she criticised America. But then she apologised and paid. Not exactly *Sex, Drugs and Rock and Roll* is it?' said May. 'And there's a transgender Olympian athlete who used to be called Bruce with six kids. He doesn't look in his mid-sixties mind. But men age better even if they become women.'

'Why a man would choose to be a woman beggars belief,' said Tilly, wafting her cigarette. 'I'm coming back as a man in my next life.'

Ava put the fish pie in the oven, and chopped carrots. Outside, the air had that crisp feel of early autumn. Mist settled and lingered in the dips and hollows of Trevone. She remembered the scent and feel of September from the start of the school year. It had filled her with novelty, until she'd endured a week of maths, physics and chemistry. Walking to the WI she watched starlings and swallows swoop and gather on telegraph pole lines, preening and chattering. The urge to move rose in Ava too, her life was changing again but she was not afraid like she had been when she arrived in Trevone.

The Memorial Hall was transformed back to its functional self; gone were the balloons, banners and bunting. Surging through its entrance were throngs of chattering, middle-aged and older women. They appeared dressed in uniform pastel or beige tops, sensible skirts, dark slacks and flat, laced shoes. They entered with empty shopping bags and exited laden. Standing guard at the front door appeared a well-built matron in brogues, navy kilt, matching cardigan and helmet of startling white hair set in a style royalty would admire. She offered Ava the briefest of smiles: like it was an honour to enter and spend.

'I haven't seen you before,' she said, brusquely. 'I'm Mrs Reaper, the WI's membership officer.' Ava gulped. Mrs Reaper ploughed on as regular visitors circled them. 'If you're interested in joining let me know. We have a few young ones in our ranks and some very interesting talks to get us through the winter months. Do you know how this works?' Ava shook her head. 'Well, we don't pay individual members for their produce but use a tried and trusted system. You choose what you want and the stall holder gives you a pink ticket with a price on. OK?' Ava nodded, feeling five years old. 'Then you present the tickets to Mrs Soames, here.' The scrawny woman, stationed at a desk beside her, mouthed, *Hello*. Her hollow-cheeked face was heavily dusted with beige powder, which Ava imagined could leave a vapour trail in a fair wind. 'It's cash only and there's tea and cakes to purchase in the back room, all made by us and needing to be bought today.' Mrs Reaper added with finality.

'Right, thank you,' said Ava, understanding why Tilly never darkened these doors. Last night's trestle tables were laden with cakes, chutneys, jams, flowers, seeds, and plants, as well as clothes, books. and honey (jars, candles, and creams). Sales were controlled by formidable women who sat on foldable chairs, gossiping to each other but not to browsers. A shapely customer near Ava examined a hand-knitted blue cardigan. The seller (herself no slimster) looked up and placed a mottled, bejewelled hand on the item.

'That won't fit you dear. It's too small,' and seamlessly returned to her conversation, leaving the potential buyer shamed and speechless. Sellers neither seemed to appreciate interruptions or anyone departing without buying. Ava picked up what Tilly requested, plus a bunch of pastel-coloured sweet peas and jar of home-made raspberry jam which, now Tilly was toothless, wouldn't irritate with its tiny seeds. The bill was £20. She thought some London markets were less pricey but with additional smiles and flattery. Tilly didn't want her back until 11am so Ava joined the counter-scrum for strong WI tea and coffee cake. She just managed to squeeze a place at tables crowded with women saving friends' seats, the odd silent man and a collection of bags, sticks, walking frames, and wheelchairs. The conversations were their children, the weather, grandchildren, and who they were hoping to land on for Christmas. Mrs Reaper curtly nodded approval at Ava's bulging bag as she left. Ava wondered how so many women settled happily with teamwork, while the likes of Tilly only settled for their own pleasures.

At Cliff View's door Ava heard the deep timbre of a male whose upmarket voice pronounced and elongated each vowel. 'Reeeaaally Tiiiilly, I'm veeeryyyy proud of myself to achieeeeeve this and you must be reeeelieved. It is raaaaather out of the ooordinaaaary though.'

Ava slipped into the kitchen and unpacked. May was sprawled outside on a lounger drinking tea and stuck into *Hello*. She sipped and waved at Ava.

'I'm done my dear, goodbye,' the man said, coming into the hall, adding, 'I'm not sure how good I am with this but it's a brave new world, Tilly!'

'Not so brave as mine was,' Tilly responded. The man acknowledged Ava. He was in his late fifties with a creased, kindly face. He wore an expensively-tailored navy suit, round steel-framed glasses and his wispy white hair was neatly side-combed. City man, Ava guessed, and rather a fish out-of-water here.

'How do you do,' he said formally with those elongated vowels, shaking her hand firmly. 'You must be Ms Westmorland.' Ava nodded. 'I'm glad to say Tilly's so much better under your care, given her track record, you must be very special. Well done.' He carried a black briefcase.

'Thank you, Mr Forbes,' said Tilly. 'My track record is good with you, and I appreciate your time, as always. I won't get up, Ava come here. Please.'

'Don't move a muscle darling. I'm off to test-drive superlative French wines on the cross-Channel ferry,' and Mr Forbes departed, face turned to the sun.

'Tell May she can go,' said Tilly, 'and I'm hungry now.' Ava noticed Tilly's teeth on the table, a trace of lipstick smeared them. She'd also combed her hair. May sauntered away smoking, her nicotine patch abandoned in Tilly's ashtray. Ava buttered thin toast and smothered it in ruby-red jam.

Tilly mouthed it. 'Mmm. Lovely. Was the WI its usual denizen of morality?'

'Saintly, with a sea of pastel cardigans, icy stares and a handful of tame men.'

'Never been any different. Was the Grim Reaper there?

'She certainly was, and scary,' Ava laughed.

'Glad she's still captain of that ship. Are you happy here Ava?'

'Yes,' Ava said firmly. She picked at the skin around her thumb. 'At first I wasn't and was frightened of you.' Tilly smiled. 'But I've come to care about you deeply.'

'Foolish girl,' laughed Tilly. 'I'd like you to do me a big favour.'

'As long as it's not brandy,' answered Ava and wished she hadn't because Tilly's face flinched.

'Tomorrow morning, I'd need you to send a letter to Vicky.' She rooted through her handbag and shifted on her haunches. Pain flashed across her face. 'It's important she gets something in black and white after what she's plotting. You'll do this for me won't you, it's very important?' Ava nodded as Tilly pulled out the large envelope, securely sealed with sticky tape. 'Send it Recorded Delivery. It needs to get there for 9am the following day. I'd like you to do this from Padstow, not Trevone because post takes for bloody ever. I've asked May to come over. While you're there, I want orange lilies from the flower shop in the square. It's the best one, along with a scented candle. And please take the rest of the day off. Be back no earlier than 4pm. Is that clear?' Ava nodded. 'I have a friend visiting. A man of course.'

'Of course,' said Ava, thrilled at a mid-week day off. She'd call Finn and arrange to meet for lunch.

'And this is for you to buy a treat while you're out.' She handed Ava £50.

'I don't want that. I'll get a sandwich.'

'No, I want you to treat yourself. Note that I haven't said this before because you were a little overweight. Now you have leeway.'

Ava laughed, pocketed the money. 'I'll bring the change.'

'I don't want it. If you could take this by hand as well?' She handed Ava a large, hard-backed envelope, addressed to the editor of *The Cornish Mercury*. It too was well stuck down and across the front stated, *Not to be opened until Friday*. 'It's a surprise,' said Tilly, sweetly. Give me your hand Ava.' Ava took hold and Tilly kissed her knuckles.

'Always be strong. Now, put Nat's *Unforgettable* on for me. Please.' Ava left her with his soothing, gorgeous tones and Tilly crooned croakily along.

Chapter Fifty-Two

Trevone Bay, 22nd September 2015

Ava very reluctantly left Tilly following her insistence that May was going to be there any minute and she absolutely must have her letters posted by 9am. From Padstow. Tilly promised to stay in bed with her tea and toast until May arrived and to call Ava if needed.

'Now go. Please. You only have twenty minutes. I'm counting on you, Ava.'

With her mission accomplished, Ava rang Tilly who brightly told her May was outside hanging out washing. Relieved, Ava had a wander, and a black coffee in a harbour cafe, trying to memorise the view and scents for when she was gone. She met up with Finn at his cottage and there followed two blissful hours in bed. At one point, a thunderstorm flashed overhead and lightning illuminated their curtained room. Rain briefly belted down, then swept on inland. Ava loved how cosy they were; the way Finn scratched his stubble, the nicks and wounds on his hard-working hands, his two pairs of glasses on the bedside table, the shredded ends of his blacksmithing trousers, patched, holed and patterned with stains and soot which were cast on the floor. Perfect but for the fact he didn't want more children. At 3pm, Finn went to fetch Joe and she popped into the Co-op, buying a buttery croissant, *Grazia* and *Cosmo* magazines for Tilly. Driving back, a mist softened the lush, verdant landscape. The green sea was calm, and pink-tinged clouds floated across pale sky.

She would miss this beautiful ever-changing coast, miss Tilly, miss Finn.

'Tilly,' called Ava, brightly, arms laden with gifts. Silence. No blaring TV. Ava checked the front room. Empty. 'May.' No answer either. The bathroom door was open. Tilly's was firmly shut. Taped on it was a letter addressed to her. Ave froze, her heart thudded and stomach turned. She dropped all she held. May appeared, like a wraith at her side, tore down the note and flung open the door.

Tilly lay curled in a foetal position, open-eyed, slack-jawed and marble-white. A sweet odour tainted the air. Outside, a crow flapped off the window ledge, cawing.

'Oh God, no. Please no,' howled Ava. 'She made me go, May. It's my fault. How could you, Tilly?' She doubled over, tasting bile in her mouth.

'Dear God,' said May, picking up a floppy wrist, padding for a pulse and placing an ear by Tilly's mouth. Shook her head. Tilly's pitch-black pupils had ballooned so only a filament of blue was left. May stroked Tilly's cheek and kissed her forehead. She picked through some of the empty bottles and packets strewn around. Ava knelt on the floor, sobbing.

'Where the hell did she get this lot?' May examined the plastic box where Vicky's childhood cards and treasured photographs were kept. May had once opened the lid, seen nothing to concern her and left it. 'They must have been tucked underneath.'

'No, no, no!' cried Ava. May helped her to a chair, murmuring 'There, there.' She rifled through the neatly stacked envelopes on the bedside drawer.

'She's been very thorough but it's going to be hell for us,' May said. She smoothed Tilly's hair. 'You always said you'd choose when to go. Ava, please don't blame yourself; this has been meticulously planned. She looks so peaceful.'

'We have to tell Vicky,' Ava said, putting her head in her hands. 'And Edward and the police. What about an ambulance and doctor?'

'Edward's best,' decided May, checking her watch. 'Calmer than Vicky.' Edward's number was taped to the wall, scrawled in large handwriting. May used the landline, her voice deadly serious: 'Edward, it's May. Please call, it's urgent.' He'd know in a second.

'I'm to blame,' repeated Ava. She saw herself in court, prosecuted for dereliction of duty. The headlines. She was thinking of herself even with Tilly's body stretched before her. 'She told me you were here and forced me to go to Padstow early.'

'You aren't to blame,' said May. 'Vicky wanted to frog-march her mother into a home. Tilly wouldn't put up with that. She was very specific today. She told me to come just before 4pm. I just left a hypnotist because Jeff caught me smoking at Tilly's party and you'd have thought I'd had an affair with Mr Silk Cut. Tilly was determined to be alone.' Silence stretched like a tightrope. 'You better read her letter to you before anyone else,' warned May.

'I can't,' said Ava. 'Please, can you?'

May opened it and read silently.

'Well?' Ava clasping her hands over her eyes. She could not look at lifeless Tilly, arms out, eyes open.

'Her bloody writing's so bad, it's taking me ages to decipher. She really couldn't see,' May said. 'OK here goes.'

Dearest Ava,

I'm sorry about this. Please don't be upset or angry, well, I'd rather you were the latter. I sent you away and lied May was looking after me. She will help you. I want you both to attend Crispin Forbes' reading of the will. The letter I sent to Vicky explains this too. The letter to The Cornish Mercury *contained two of my special photographs. I aim to go out in a blaze of glory.*

Ava, I didn't want you with me at all but I have grown to love you. I've chosen the time to die and stay in my home. If there is a heaven, I'm going to be happy with Jack, free cigarettes, brandy and dancing.

May took a deep breath and wiped her eyes. She held Ava's hand.

I'm not frightened of dying. I'm more fearful of being buried alive with the living dead. I've had 90 pleasurable years and it's more than many. All necessary arrangements are included in the other envelopes.

Most importantly, Ava, embrace life and love.

Love, Tilly xxx

Ava wept and May hugged her.

'It'll be OK.' May crossed Tilly's arms across her chest and after tenderly closing her eyes, placed a pound coin on each one. She carefully folded a towel under Tilly's slack jaw, closing her mouth. Finally, May opened the bedroom window. Crows lifted and cawed, their wings balanced against buffeting wind. 'Off you go now, Tilly. Look at those light rays on the sea. I couldn't see you watching *Songs of Praise* in a nursing home. Ava, love, you're white as a sheet. I'll call Dr Singh and make some sweet tea with brandy for us.'

They drank in silence for a while and May lit the geranium-scented candle Ava had bought.

'I shouldn't have left her,' Ava said, biting her nails.

'Tilly lied to get you out. Nobody would blame you.'

'Vicky?' Ava chewed skin around her thumbnail.

'Vicky has a self-righteous mind, which is why Tilly has written all these letters. My mum got dementia and spent four years bed-bound in a home. She didn't know who I was. If Tom Jones had walked in singing *Sex Bomb* she would have been unmoved. It was a living death. Tilly's chosen and it's what I'd do, too. I'll try Edward and Vicky now. Drink your tea. I'll take the phone outside. I could do with a smoke.'

Ava pointed to a packet. May hesitated and took one.

'The hypnotist would understand it's an emergency. Giving up is going to have to wait.' Ava half-expected Tilly to sit up, fling off the coins, chuck the towel on the floor and demand a drink. The quietness was all-encompassing.

'Poor Vicky,' said May, coming in. 'She loathes Tilly but I've left her bawling.'

Chapter Fifty-Three

Trevone Bay, 30th September 2015

Vicky walked down the path at Cliff View. She wore a black tent of a dress teamed with a white silk scarf. Edward, sombrely-dressed went silently beside her. The funeral hearse idled in the bay, beneath trees that rustled and rattled in the wind. Tilly lay, as desired, in a wicker coffin, surrounded by white lilies. The photograph of her in the scarlet swimming costume balanced in the middle of the blooms. A half-empty bottle of brandy was to one side. Vicky cried when she saw them, her cheeks and neck splotched red.

'Always about her isn't it?' Vicky muttered. 'Who else would go to their funeral with brandy and in a bloody swimming costume?' Edward put his arm around her. Vicky yanked the limousine door open and struggled into the back seat.

Finn, holding Ava's hand tightly, was behind the hearse in May and Jeff's chip shop Volvo.

'I bet Mackenzie's pleased to be back in the US and free of Edward and Vicky, seems the romance is off.' May said: 'He doesn't seem too unhappy.' The cortège made its slow journey to St Enodoc's Church in Trebetherick. The twelfth-century sanctuary nestled in sand dunes near Brea Hill on the River Camel, had sweeping views across the Atlantic which was wild and grey with crashing white-tipped waves. They drove through mizzle that turned to pelting rain. The gorse, roads, and slate-roofed homes gleamed. More cars joined them. A handful of bedraggled passers-by caught in the downpour halted, bowed their heads under umbrellas and some made the sign of the cross. Jeff's estate had been specially cleaned and a pine air freshener strung up but nothing masked the underlying aroma of vegetable oil and fish. Jeff, with a captive audience, cleared his throat.

'The church is known as Sinkininny or Sinking Neddy,' he began. 'After the hermit who lived there once until the church became entombed in dunes for three hundred years. For a long time, the only way in was through the roof and once a year, to keep receiving parish tithes, a vicar was lowered through to conduct a service to nobody. John Betjeman's buried there and it's my favourite church in the world.'

'Here endeth the lesson,' said May, briskly. 'And what is the other reason, dearest?'

'Why sweetness, we married there.'

'Yes, we tied the knot shortly after the hermit died in the ninth century. Oh look, what's happened?' May pointed up the road. The cortège had ground to a halt. Smoke rose from the hearse's engine.

'Oh dear,' May said, 'it's serious if men are piling out of cars in the rain.' Six impeccably-dressed undertakers inspected the car. They looked troubled, poked around and then appeared resigned. Edward got out and listened. Suits were soaked, mobiles wafted about for signals. Edward walked to Jeff's car. His hair was plastered and his black overcoat looked like a wet towel.

'Major electrical problem and there's no back-up.'

'What are they going to do?' asked Jeff, looking around the Volvo. 'I might squeeze her in with the back seat down.'

'We're a quarter of a mile away so they're putting the casket on a gurney and pushing. One of them has run ahead to tell the vicar and he's coming to meet us.'

'How can we help?' asked Finn, buttoning his coat and opening the door.

'Pass the message on and tell them to go slow behind the gurney,' said Edward, returning to his mother.

'I bet Vicky's threatening all sorts of legal action. Oh my God, look,' said May. The undertakers steadied the steel gurney on the road, lifted and lowered Tilly's casket upon it. They lay the photograph face-down on top and shielded everything with huge black brollies. One held the brandy. The vicar strode towards them holding a bronze cross upright, like a shield, while the wind whipped what was left of his hair into froth. Finn got back in the car and they set off at a snail's pace.

'Trust Tilly to be late for her own funeral,' said May.

'That's dreadful,' said Jeff. 'But she'd love it.'

'If Tilly's having the last laugh, I'm walking with her,' said Ava, unbuckling her seat belt.

'Count me in,' said May, and Finn came too. Edward and Vicky remained in their car. The soggy procession went up a steep incline. Vicky's fractious pale face pressed to the car window, aghast. The rain stopped as quickly as it had begun. The wind eased and flitting birds took up their singing. Vehicles on the other side of the road braked when confronted by walking vicar, coffin and cortège. A lorry driver scraped his vehicle into the hedge to let them pass.

St Enodoc's stone walls came into view. Snug against the

hillside, its wet slate roof and tapering octagonal broach spire was a relief to see. Around it waited scores of women. Many held up damp posters of Tilly in her red bathing costume, inscribed with, *Thank you* and, *My Ration Heroine* and, *Tilly: Our World War II Queen.* The Press was there.

'Look,' said May, grabbing Ava's arm. 'Tilly would have loved that. She'll be revolving in her coffin missing this. Even Vicky's bucked up; she's waving like royalty!'

Finn squeezed Ava's hand. 'She was loved,' he said, 'and chose to go.' Ava's face clenched.

'Thank God,' said May, dabbing mud-spattered black tights as they reached the church door. 'OK Tilly,' she whispered, as the coffin rested in the shelter of the porch and waited for mourners to join them. Fluffy clouds streamed across the estuary, blowing remnants of rain into the blue distance. The church's fridge-like interior was perfumed with lilies and frankincense. The two small electric heaters had zero effect on bone chill.

Somerway staff were already seated. All were noticeably lighter, thought Ava, than when she'd last seen them. Sister Lynch's hair had blonde highlights, her breasts trussed to half their size and gone was the monobrow and moustache. Evangeline sat, straight backed and curvaceous, in a 50s-style black dress, complete with stiff turquoise petticoat. Robbie was shoehorned into a grey suit with a new white shirt. It was too tight around the neck and a bulge of flesh oozed over the collar, making him, thought Ava, the most likely candidate to pass out. Captain Birds Eye, in a wheelchair, attended with a woman who must have been his daughter, she looked so like him, minus the beard. Dr Singh sat by Mr Hogwood, chatting amiably. Next to them, Becky and Charlie smiled at Ava. Squeezed in the rest of the pews were villagers, shop owners, post office manager, post woman and Sniffy Dave of The Golden Lion. At the back, on his own, was a squat man in his thirties. He wore a damp trench coat and had distinct blue eyes and blond hair.

'Who's he?' said May, who knew everyone.

'Well, if you don't know, he's a mystery,' whispered Jeff. Ava wondered if he was a tourist caught by the rain.

Everyone gradually settled; their warm breaths in the tiny church condensed against the brightly-stained glass windows. A granite font with intricate cable moulding around its base was the perfect container for a bouquet of white lilies.

There was coughing, throat clearing and a bout of loud sneezing. At the raised pulpit Reverend Draycott turned the music system on with an ear-splitting hiss. He waited calmly as Queen's song, *Another One Bites the Dust* blasted out.

'Christ, what a choice!' hissed Vicky. 'Who allowed this?' She glared at Ava and May behind. Finn stared Vicky down.

'Gran's request,' whispered Edward, as Tilly's coffin rolled through the aisle, flanked by damp undertakers. An L-plate decorated with shamrocks was hung off the front and the photograph was reinstated on the coffin lid. Vicky wailed.

'You go, Tilly,' May whispered, dabbing her eyes. Jeff curled his hand over hers. 'I can't believe she's in there.' May blew her nose on a soggy tissue that left white scraps of paper on her face. Jeff brushed them off.

Reverend Draycott coughed for attention and all eyes fell upon his tall, wiry frame. His large head looked out of balance on narrow bony shoulders, long thin arms, and gangly legs. Like a spider, thought Ava. He wore round steel-rimmed glasses and his grey hair was now flattened down but rain and wind had played havoc with it, so hairs stuck up and waved in the shadowed light. Some scent must have smelt attractive given the number of midges gathering over his head. They flitted in beams of sunlight like a revolving, translucent halo. Every few seconds Reverend Draycott flapped a hand to disperse them. They came straight back.

'Welcome everyone on this sad day for family and friends of Tilly Barwise,' he began. 'I'm most sorry about her journey here but I'm sure it would be part of her inimitable style.' He patted his hair and wafted midges. 'I met Tilly Barwise,' he addressed the coffin now, as if Tilly was listening, 'twice. Not much you may think but enough that both times are imprinted, or should I say branded on my mind.' Reverend Draycott adjusted his glasses up his nose, from where they again gradually slipped down.

'The first time she told me I needed to change my aftershave because it smelt of urine.' There was an intake of breath, laughter and a strangled gasp from Vicky. 'And you know she was right because I asked around. Everyone had been far too polite to tell me that I'd trailed that unpleasant aroma for years. Thanks to Tilly, whose signature scent was cigarettes and brandy, I bought something recommended to me by a lovely woman in Boots the Chemist. She became my wife. It's called Amber Smoke, which sounds rather like church incense and about which I've only ever received compliments. Although I'm concerned about the preference these flies are showing.' He wafted them.

'When I saw Tilly again, prepared with my new aftershave, she told me I, *Smelt wealthy, which must be a disappointment to women when you're so obviously not.* She asked about my love life and what I should do to change the loveless ox-bow lake I was marooned in. I never revealed how my aftershave purchase had found me romance because it was a little too new then. Now I wish I had.' May sighed, Jeff rolled his eyes. Ava thought it was beautiful.

'I think everyone who came across Tilly,' the Vicar carried on, pushing up his glasses fruitlessly, 'will agree she changed lives. Even if the trigger for that transformation was like being catapulted from a cannon without a safety net. Now, it seems all of Cornwall is marching to her dietary World War II tune. The region was indeed her oyster, although Tilly never liked that particular dish. She told me it was like eating a bad cold. Tilly was a woman with an unusually spacious heart. One that could be cruel to be kind and never tempered her words.'

'She certainly didn't,' hissed Vicky, who had rarely felt the gentle side of her mother's tongue. Now it was her turn to speak. Ava expected eloquence and possibly the temptation to twist the knife in. Vicky mounted the pulpit like she was climbing a mountain. She wiped her brow and dabbed her eyes. Putty-coloured foundation stained the tissue.

'Mummy loved music, dancing, and men. Preferably at the same time. The latter were most important. I know she loved me; well, tried her best to, and while we've lived very different lives, I'm glad she was my Mummy.' Vicky bowed her head and her shoulders heaved. She blew her nose loudly. 'I was also relieved to live in London and make what I thought were adequate arrangements to look after her.'

'Adequate,' whispered Ava, bridling. Finn wrapped his arm around her.

May tapped the order of service on her hand and hissed, 'It's the first time Vicky's been able to speak without Tilly interrupting. Take no notice.'

Vicky's speech incorporated the war (with no mention of her conception), her mother's business and her own life at boarding school – from the age of eight. Ava saw the troubled, unwanted daughter packed off as a little girl. Her tone was regal but the pews grew increasingly restless as Vicky droned on about her own achievements.

'No wonder Tilly interrupted,' murmured May. Reverend Draycott, sensing a mood change, laid a hand gently on Vicky's shoulder and began the traditional prayer. Vicky froze.

'Lord our God,' he began, 'you are the source of life. In you we live and move and have our being. Keep us in life and death in your love, and, by your grace, lead us to your kingdom. Through your son, Jesus Christ, our Lord.'

The congregation answered: 'Amen.'

The next record began as Vicky edged down the steps: AC/DC's, *Highway to Hell.*

'Great song. Pity he died six months later,' said Finn, tapping the rhythm on the pew. Edward went to speak. He talked about his grandmother being the life and soul of any party, even if she was the only one there. He described how Tilly sought the Achilles heel of everyone she met, kicked it hard, and he wouldn't have swapped her for the world. Evangeline climbed next.

'At her birthday party I told Tilly that Robbie had asked me to marry him,' she began, 'and how happy I was – because she'd got us together. I'm sure you've also heard she was a one-woman regional gastric band. Not only have Somerway staff raised more than £1,000 for charity but Tilly received letters worldwide from people saying she'd changed their lives. She certainly changed mine for the better.'

Reverend Draycott asked people to pray. Those who wanted bowed their heads. The funeral directors paired at each side of the coffin. Ava wondered about transport to the crematorium. Tilly was rolled out to The Doors song: *Come on Baby Light My Fire.*

'Gutsy woman,' said Finn. Ava cried. A sparkling limousine had turned up to transport Tilly's coffin to the crematorium with Vicky and Edward. Rain swept in again over the turbulent grey sea and people raced to cars and The Golden Lion. Tilly had put £1,000 behind the bar. Sniffy Dave had drafted five extra staff in.

The pub's fires were lit and candles flickered, even though it was daylight. Finn's whippet lay on a tartan blanket in front of one, panting but refusing to budge. A huge pan of *Scouse* was brought out and placed near crusty bread, bowls of buttery red cabbage and sliced carrots. There were glamorous photographs of Tilly crammed along one wall. People drank and reminisced about Tilly's misdemeanours, legendary drinking and smoking and how the village had lost its greatest character. There were uneasy mutterings about the future of Cliff View.

'She's on her last journey now,' said May, sipping a large gin and tonic, tinkling with ice. 'And we're escaping to Lanzarote in November. But first there's the will. I'm sure she's got a trick or two to play.'

Ava picked the cuticle of her nail; she couldn't drink her fizz.

Dr Singh touched her arm and said Tilly had often told him she would never go into a home. Everyone was trying to comfort her but the guilt was overwhelming. She watched Finn chat with Becky and Charlie and the way people gravitated to his calm demeanour and how he listened with his head slightly to one side. He caught Ava's eye and a minute later sat by her. May gossiped to Robbie and Evangeline, who were wrapped up in each other's arms as she showed off her glinting engagement ring. Food was served and there was the usual rush to queue. Ava remained where she was.

'Free food and booze bring out the maniac in people,' May sighed as she joined them.

'I'll get you a plate,' Finn said. 'Are you OK? If it wasn't for the fact, you'd be missed I'd take you back home right now.' He leant forward and kissed her in the empty inglenook.

'That's rich,' said Vicky. Mascara smudged her face and white tracks showed between make-up and skin. 'If that's what you were doing the day my mother took her own life, it's downright appalling you showed up.' Edward shamefaced, tried to pull her away.

'That's enough,' Finn said, standing. The queue had a perfect vantage point for the exchange.

'I left you in charge and you weren't there,' said Vicky, loudly.

'Vicky, you left Tilly alone for years,' said Reg, spooning in a large mouthful of stew. 'Christ that's hot.' He blew out his cheeks. Others nodded.

'Ava was brilliant to your mother,' said May. 'She didn't leave her. Tilly sent her away. On purpose, because she didn't want you to put her in a home. Or sell Cliff View and clear off because you don't care how we live here. It's all about money.'

There were muted, 'Hear, hears.'

'Your Mum had a new lease of life with Ava,' said Charlie, wading in. 'Everyone knows what you were up to and nobody around here wants it, or the likes of you.'

'Mum, I think we should go,' said Edward, tugging her sleeve, pushing her towards the door. Vicky shook him off.

'Don't come to the will reading. You aren't wanted.'

Ava finally stood. 'You employed me because you wanted me to fail. I came to love and admire your mother. I feel sorry for the way she treated you. I know she wanted me out that day and I will always feel terrible. But you wanted to lock her up permanently.'

'Bravo,' someone said and there was clapping. Finn put his arm around Ava, and Vicky stomped out of the door followed by Edward. After a few seconds' silence, people gathered, congratulating Ava and saying how happy Tilly would have been.

'I want to go now,' Ava whispered to May.

'No, Ava, stay. You've done nothing wrong,' insisted May patting her arm. 'And we're going to the solicitor's because it's a legal requirement.'

'I looked after Tilly for eight weeks with a whole team in Clover House,' added Evangeline. 'I thought she'd never find anyone willing to care for her for eight minutes. You've been amazing.'

'And I was with her for ten years,' added Robbie. 'Mind you, only in the garden. I don't think I could have managed inside four walls. Although, it does show what a saint of a man I am with tricky women.' Evangeline elbowed him. That broke the tension and more stories flowed, of Tilly dancing on tables, flirting for England and paying the bill for an old woman at a supermarket who'd run out of money.

Finn held Ava's hand firmly. 'I'd never be consigned to a nursing home for strangers to deal with me. I wouldn't burden Joe or give money away that should go to him.'

'I'll never forget her face on that bed,' Ava said, as the blond man who'd been in church walked from the back of the bar and out the door. He'd witnessed everything.

'Who's that?' Ava asked.

'No idea,' said Finn. 'Slipped in for free food and drink. It's a hobby for some, sponging at funerals.' Reg turned on the Karaoke machine. For a man who could hardly look anyone in the eye, Reg transformed into a confident singer, belting out Frank Sinatra's *My Way*. It was a perfect song for Tilly.

An hour and several ciders later, Robbie stood on a chair and sang *You're the One that I Want*, like he was John Travolta and Evangeline was Olivia Newton John. He followed it up with The Troggs *Wild Thing*. His tie was pulled askew and white shirt, undone at the neck, stained with blobs of tomato sauce. Unstoppable, he launched into Louis Armstrong's *It's a Wonderful World*, crooning into an empty beer bottle like it was a microphone. Everyone held hands and joined in.

Chapter Fifty-Four

Padstow, 15th October 2015

Ava and May stood before Crispin Forbes' ochre-coloured, eighteenth-century home. The three-storey townhouse was tucked high above Padstow's High Street with panoramic harbour views. In the distance, autumn trees appeared like an impressionist painting in yellow, gold, and scarlet against an azure sky. Leaves piled up in gutters, stuck to shoes, were kicked by little children in wellies. May lifted the polished lion's head knocker on the shiny navy door, dropped it loudly twice. A copper plaque on the wall stated: *Mr Crispin Forbes.*

'This place cost a packet,' May said, dabbing her upper lip. The sun was meltingly warm for October. Ava wore her usual navy dress and black, kitten-heel shoes.

'My stomach's in knots,' she said. Her mouth felt watery.

'You'll be fine, mark my words, and this fleece is off,' May sighed, tearing open a packet of baby wipes and swishing one over her face. She wore a loose white T-shirt underneath with, *Cod Above the Rest.*

A well-groomed, late-middle-aged woman with short, silver hair opened the door, wearing a crisp white shirt and knee-length black skirt.

'Good afternoon, I'm Ms Maple, please follow me to the drawing room.'

'OK Ruth,' said May, stepping into the hall. The woman looked displeased. They walked through a high-ceilinged hall; their footsteps echoing over black and white tiles. It smelt of beeswax. There were gilt-framed oil portraits and landscapes hanging upon crimson walls. A grandfather clock ticked outside the door Ruth turned the handle on.

'Mr Forbes will attend when the others arrive. You're a little early,' she said curtly. 'Do please sit, and if you don't mind, I'll wait to make refreshments.'

'Thank you,' said Ava, 'and sorry.' Ruth gave a barely perceptible nod and left. 'Sorry, May, I'm always early in case I get lost.' May scanned the spacious room.

'Stop saying sorry. Don't worry about Ms Airs and Graces. I knew where Mr Forbes lived and wanted a bit of a nose before the others came because chances are I won't again. Who says drawing room now? The rest of us have a living room and if we're lucky a lounge. Not that I ever bloody lounge.'

May edged around a huge, gleaming mahogany table. A gilt-edged mirror hung over the expansive marble fireplace, china figurines and sculptures sat on shelves. The walls were papered with a delicate bird and butterfly print with silk-like sheen. One held hundreds of books from floor to ceiling. A pile of *National Geographic* and *Private Eye* magazines were haphazardly stacked on a shaded window seat.

'Too much work this place; bit stuffy, like a museum,' May said. 'Ava, I've decided to go for HRT. I can't stand the sleeplessness and boiling-up like a volcano. I'm thinking of swapping Lanzarote for an iceberg cruise to Anchorage. I'll be a baked-Alaskan if I don't do something.' Footsteps could be heard in the room above.

'I'm so nervous,' said Ava.

'You look white as a sheet, get a drink of water,' said May, wiping the back of her hand across her forehead. 'So, the worst is we get left Tilly's false teeth?' she mused. 'I've never been to a will reading and I'm treating it as an experience. Jeff's fantasising I come back with a million, and he can hang up his apron.'

Ava drank. The door knocker echoed. They both tensed, senses sharpened. Ruth's quick steps were followed by formal greetings. Vicky and Edward entered the drawing room. Vicky was dressed in the same outfit as for the funeral. She acknowledged Ava and May with a curt nod. May slid her foot to Ava's, gave it a friendly tap and said hello for both of them. The pair sat some distance away and nobody spoke. Edward cleared his throat loudly. The icy silence was accompanied by the ticking clock.

'Well, well,' said Mr Forbes, breezily as he strode in wearing a perfect pin-striped suit. 'Here we are then.' He shook hands with everyone, saying their name and how pleased he was to see them.

As May had rightly guessed, Mr Forbes chose the ornately carved chair and, clasping his hands, keeping forefingers extended, he moved them up and down as he spoke slowly and clearly.

'Please do call me Crispin.' He tapped a sheaf of papers. 'We have to wait for one other person.'

'Who?' demanded Vicky, perplexed, frowning, affronted. Crispin leant his head forward, kept his counsel. The solicitor made small talk about changeable weather and Rick Stein's new gourmet pub. The door knocker banged again and now, behind Ruth, came the mysterious man seen at the funeral and wake.

'Ah, Mr Chester Pierce,' said Crispin, rising and shaking his hand firmly. 'Welcome and so glad you could join us. We'll begin now, shall we? Let me introduce everyone to you.'

Ava tried not to study the stranger. May, a woman who prided herself on knowing everyone in a twenty-mile radius, had no such hang-ups. Edward turned off his mobile while Vicky looked blank. The newcomer smiled at each of them. He reminded Ava of an English bull terrier; all meat and muscle with narrow eyes whose whites were tinged red, and felt-like hair on his beefy head.

'We are here to read Tilly's will,' stated Crispin in his cut-glass accent, 'but she insisted on making a DVD instead. How very Tilly... I've also written the content down as back-up and apologise now because I didn't realise how shaky my hands were.'

'Oh God no!' said Vicky. 'Please can you just read it out?' She twisted a paper hanky until it shredded.

'I'm afraid not. Your mother stipulated,' said Crispin. 'Now where's the remote control? I put it somewhere safe.' He pulled at the drawer under the table until it came out completely in his hands. 'Ah, here we go.' He waved it in the direction of the TV like he was conducting an orchestra. 'Apologies, I don't watch much TV.' The screen flickered into life. An advert for tampons flashed on before Crispin switched to the DVD channel. A wobbling view of Tilly's room came into view. The camera focused, unfocused and flashed about without Tilly appearing.

'I do apologise,' said Mr Forbes. Eventually, the camera alighted, like a fly, on the expectant face of Tilly. She had her teeth in and lipstick on for eternal posterity. 'It gets better now, and let's turn up the volume.' He pressed the control to ear-splitting, then down.

'Hello,' croaked Tilly. She looked pleased. Ava remembered the pink-stained tissue and teeth on the table after Mr Forbes' visit. May sat up straight. 'This is my last Will and Testament and I have to start like this because it makes it legal, doesn't it, Mr Forbes?' There was a little cough from Mr Forbes.

'Oh yes, I have to pretend you aren't here, don't I? Well here goes. As nicotine and alcohol haven't killed me, I thought I might have to throw myself under a bus. Preferably, it would have been under a man but there's none lining up. Don't worry Mr Forbes, I don't do posh.' Mr Forbes coughed again. Tilly laughed, took a breather, sucked in her teeth and looked at the camera. She'd painted her nails purple and crayoned on matching eyebrows.

'Vicky,' said Tilly. Her daughter sat bolt upright. 'If you desire to get your hands on some of my money, I prescribe a two-week holiday first. A yoga break in an Indian Ashram. Colonic irrigation is optional.' Vicky spluttered and put her head in her hands. Edward raised an eyebrow. 'On your return, you'll get £200,000 in stocks and shares which will be useful given your rapidly advancing age but you leave my home and land alone.' Vicky stopped crying. She'll go, thought Ava.

'Darling Edward,' said Tilly, giving a little wave. 'I bequeath to you (that's the one and only time I'll utter that word) another £200,000 of stocks and shares, again, only if you leave my land alone. Otherwise, the money will go to the dogs' home.' Edward frowned and clenched his hands together. 'Oh, I'm enjoying this. Mr Forbes, sorry, and I know you hate smoking but I'll be in hell soon enough, so you'll have to endure it.' She lit up and Mr Forbes could be heard to sigh.

'May,' Tilly said, with a warm smile. Ava's throat constricted and May held on to her arm. 'I give you £10,000 plus my silver watch and pearl necklace – which by the way, is real and worth as you say, a bob or two. I'd like you to stay on at Cliff View for a time and there's money set aside for this. Double what you're paid now to make it worthwhile and the reason will become apparent.'

'Thank you,' replied May, as if Tilly was really there and Tilly, as if she knew May would say that, responded.

'You're welcome.'

May smiled but nobody else did. Vicky's mouth drooped as she fingered the fine pearl necklace around her throat that would have to be handed over.

'Ava,' began Tilly. Ava's pounding heart felt it was going to burst out of her chest. 'When I met you, I could see how striking you were but terribly unhappy. Thanks to me you have become arresting. You are also beautiful inside and I doubt you'll be a doormat again. But you will have to be vigilant.' Ava held her breath. 'When I die, Cliff View is to be sold.' Vicky perked up. 'To a charitable housing association.' Vicky's mouth fell open. 'Cliff View is long past its sell-by-date and I've asked Crispin to employ an architect to design plans for ten affordable homes. They are for local young people who earn less than £25,000 a year.' Vicky looked incandescent. 'Don't be selfish, Vicky. I was given a leg-up on the housing ladder by the kindness of former employers. Ava, one of these homes is yours if you want, and you can help choose the other occupants. In fact, given your capability in looking after me I would like you to be in charge of what goes on. You will be paid a proportion of the rent to ensure everything is done correctly. You said you wanted a proper job, so here it is. That's all I have to say. I bet you're relieved? I only hope when you see this, I am in the right kind of heaven for a woman like me. Have a long, happy and healthy life all of you! Cheers.' She raised her glass.

The DVD froze, with Tilly caught in a final mischievous, toothy, lipstick grin, cigarette and drink in hand. Vicky started sniffing and crying, Mr Forbes held his palms up. It was then Mr Pierce stood, splaying his hands on the table. They had forgotten he was there. Ava surmised he was a man used to public speaking; confident and waiting for silence. Vicky stopped blubbing.

'I apologise about my somewhat impersonal presence,' he said, in an easy-going southern American accent. Vicky leant forward. 'I see how distressing this is and what a remarkable woman Tilly was. I only wish I'd known her. My Grandpa, Danny Pierce, was Jack Turner's best friend from childhood. I have to inform you that both men survived the war.' Astonished eyes turned on him. Even Tilly appeared mesmerised on screen.

'Survived?' said Vicky, her mouth hanging.

'It is because of what my Grandpa did that I'm here today. My Grandpa told a lie to Tilly for the sake of Jack's family. Jack's younger brother, Joey, was killed two days after D-Day, less than a month since he'd joined the war. His family was devastated. His Mom had a heart attack because Jack was initially reported missing in action and she was an invalid for the last five years of her life.

Jack was found near death from burns and contracted double pneumonia. He was shipped unconscious to the US and took six months to begin to recover. My Grandpa phoned Tilly, telling her

Jack had been killed. He thought he was doing right to help Jack's family. Jess, his cousin, was Jack's former fiancée and he went on to marry her.' My Grandpa's lie and Joey's death trapped Jack. He never spoke to my Grandpa again. I only found out this summer when Grandpa showed me a letter from Jack, written in 2007, a month before he died of cancer.

Vicky stared at Tilly on screen. Poor Vicky, thought Ava, her father apparently killed before she was born, only to have him resurrected and die seconds later.

'I'm sorry, Vicky and Edward,' said Chester, rubbing a hand over his face. 'It's a raw deal but I hope to ease your pain. Grandpa was a difficult man with a short fuse.' Chester picked up a creased and folded envelope. 'I brought the letter Jack mailed to Grandpa.'

May's eyes were like saucers. She was in the midst of the best gossip of the decade. Ava barely breathed. Vicky's nose leaked and she didn't wipe it. Mr Forbes pulled a linen hanky from his top pocket and passed it to her. Chester began:

Dear Danny,

It's nearly sixty years since I've seen you. I hear you're in good health, given we're such old guys. Congratulations on four children and last time I heard, nine grandchildren? You're blessed. There isn't a day goes by when I don't think about what you did, out of kindness to my family and love for your cousin. I forgive you Danny. I'm writing because I'm dying and while you can't remove sorrow from a heart you can help heal it with forgiveness.

I never told Jess about Tilly's baby. It was bad enough she knew about Tilly. I stayed because it felt down to me to hold what was left of our family together. Pa never was the same man again. But you know, don't you? I didn't write to Tilly; how could I come back from the dead? I felt it was my punishment that Jess and I never had children of our own. For years she cried when friends had babies. It was a hungry longing that never eased. I found my daughter on the internet ten years ago but didn't get in touch. How could I intrude on their lives after I'd abandoned them? She's called Victoria and is a twin of Mom by the look of her.

May's face was a picture of satisfaction, she knew it.

A real clever girl, I expect, like Mom. I've a grandson too, Edward, and he looks the spit of Joey.

Chester coughed, shook his head and read on:

Jess and I moved wherever oil exploration took us and not being still was a good distraction. I came to love Jess. With Tilly there was no arriving, love was there the moment I saw her. Jess and I returned to Woodburn six months ago when I was diagnosed with lung cancer. It's strange how time collapses in on itself. Like the last 70 years is nothing. Remember those days when we were kids swinging over the river? Days which felt like they'd last forever. Now life seems like it's been the blink of an eye.'

May, Mr Forbes and Vicky looked as if they knew exactly what he meant.

The nightmares I used to have about Tilly are less now. I haven't got long to carry the corrosive lie that's dripped through my life like poison. I'm not scared of death – not after all we saw in the war. I've lived long and when I think of those young guys who didn't make it, well, it still breaks my heart. I want to ask you one last thing because there's no one else I trust, and please don't tell Jess. It's your final secret. I've enclosed a letter and after Jess dies, (my lawyer has been instructed to tell you) would you send it to Cliff View? If Tilly's dead then it's for Victoria or Edward. If you die first, the lawyer is instructed to contact a family member of your choice, so you may have to tell someone.

It's my apology to Tilly, my daughter and grandson. I've put money away for them in a trust fund.

Vicky's head jolted up.

If you don't want to do this, let me know real soon. It's too late to do the right thing by the past but not the future. One lie leads to another until it snarls up your life. I still have my diaries and letters and I'd like you to give them to Tilly's family. I know you tried to do the right thing, Danny. And you'll do it now. You're a good man.
Yours,
Jack

Vicky, May and Ava cried. Mr Forbes took out three more ironed linen handkerchiefs from his drawer. Edward looked resolute.

'Grandpa died in July and Jess, a month ago,' Chester said

carefully. 'Vicky and Edward have $3 million between them. We hope, in the future, you'll come visit and get to know more about your family in the Blue Ridge Mountains.'

May looked slowly around. She needed to get out to gossip like a geyser. Ava stared at the ever-flickering smile of Tilly on TV.

Chapter Fifty-Five

Trevone Bay, 19th October 2015

May arrived at Cliff View, fully-armed for a final deep clean, wearing Tilly's pearl necklace, to find tearful Ava staring out of the kitchen window and a battered old suitcase of Tilly's at her feet.

'What's up luvvie? she asked, scanning Ava's face. 'You look terribly upset.'

'I'm going to Spain. The taxi's on its way.' Ava desperately wanted a Valium she didn't have; her chest felt tight, she was sweating and preflight tremors rippled from ankles to spine. There was a watery, metallic taste in her mouth.

'Why?' May asked. 'Does Finn know?'

'I have to go.' Her hands shook as she lifted the suitcase and handbag.

'Ava, I've no idea why you're running away when everything is here for you.'

Ava shook her head. A horn beeped outside and Reg, the man Ava swore would never drive her from Cornwall, waited. She hugged May who held her close. Ava pulled away and didn't look back, even as May called out to her.

Reg lifted Ava's case into the boot, his smile vanished when he saw her white face and red eyes. Without a beard to chew he nibbled his stubble and they drove in silence. At the airport he shook her hand and, as usual, was unable to look her in the eye. Ava leant in and kissed his rough cheek.

'We're gonna miss you, Ava. Are you coming back?'

'I'll miss you too. All of you.'

Ava turned and hurried into the airport, her breath catching. The flight desk wasn't yet open. She felt shivery and cold, as if she was going down with flu. Her stomach lurched. All around people chatted and laughed, hugged and kissed. It was as if a plate glass wall had once more slid between herself and the world. She found a chair tucked away from the crowd and sat, staring ahead.

Memories of her time at Trevone crowded her mind, memories she could not easily push away. Her escape to Cornwall, her near drowning and first fateful meeting with Tilly. The trials and tribulations of living with that difficult, maddening, yet charismatic old woman. The bet that she wouldn't stay, and admiration of locals when she did. The friendships she made with May, Evangeline, and Robbie. And, of course, Finn.

She swallowed hard, twisting the bangle he'd made. What they'd had was... what? Special? Of course. Healing? Yes. The blacksmith with the gentle smile had banished all the creeping nightmares about Josh and Sadie, and their backstairs deception. Finn had been loving, kind, attentive, funny. In short, perfect. But she had to get away.

Ava sipped water and wandered aimlessly around the small shops. There was nothing she desired. Her flight was called and she joined the queue behind a group of joshing, jostling lads, obviously on their first holiday abroad. As she rooted in her bag for passport and boarding card, she felt their exuberance tipping over into her personal space. As one gawky youth bumped into her yet again, mumbling 'Sorry, love,' she wanted to scream, *Be careful!* They carried on like a tight pack of young bulls about to be freed from their pen.

The queue shuffled forward towards the gate. *I'm heading to a new life'* Ava coached herself. In all senses. Why then did she feel so utterly downhearted and desolate?

'Could passenger Ava Westmorland, heading for Flight ESO276 to Alicante please return to the check-in desk. Passenger Ava Westmorland to the check-in desk please.' The tannoy announced.

Her stomach turned as she looked around, almost expecting another Ava to step out of line and head to the exit. Blushing furiously, she shoved her passport into her bag and scuttled out of the queue; all eyes on her. She felt like some idiot who'd accidentally packed something dodgy into her hold bag. She walked towards check-in, only looking up when she felt a breath of sea breeze swirling into the airport via its sliding doors.

And there he was. Finn Blake, flushed, seemingly panicky, his right hand gripping his shirt. He rushed at her.

'Shit, Ava! I thought you'd gone! I thought I'd missed you. I was behind a bloody tractor for two miles and was in such a state.'

'I'm not good at goodbyes.' She felt her body light as air, as if she could blow away.

'So, if it's goodbye, what's this?' He thrust out a crushed box concealed in his left hand. 'May found it.' *PregnaQuest... for immediate, accurate results*, it stated. 'Ava, forgive me for swearing, but what the fuck? Were you going to tell me?'

'Why would I?' she replied flatly. 'You don't want another

child. You told me that the first time and plenty since. I don't want to force you to become a father again. You've got your life sorted and I'll be OK. My time here has taught me that.'

'Oh, for God's sake, I didn't realise what I was saying. Please. I'm sorry. Come here.' Finn pressed her head to his chest, kissing her hair. Ava's body relaxed and she wept, oblivious of the many eyes on them. 'I know what I said, but I hardly knew you. It was bollocks. Don't go. Please. Not now. I love you. This is Joe's sibling.' He dabbed her eyes and nose with his torn shirtsleeve.

Ava brushed his hand away and looked at her watch. 'I've probably missed my flight now and I'm in no state to run for it. There's another this afternoon. I'll get that instead. It'll be fine. I'll be fine.'

'Then if it isn't a bit too *Brief Encounter*, maybe we could have a talk first with a farewell cup of tea?' Finn said.

*

Two weeks later the Press reported on the long life of a World War II beauty, with her romantic, transatlantic back story, who'd become the driving force of a twenty-first-century weight loss campaign. Her naked photographs were tastefully used. To her daughter's absolute mortification, Tilly languished in global newspapers and magazines. Vicky lost a stone at the Ashram and decided it was time to get in touch with her feelings, her clothes stylist, and new figure. She refused interviews about her mother but not the generous, all-expenses paid invite to West Virginia where she and Edward were feted as one of their own come home.

The publicity saw regional council backing for Tilly's social housing plans rubber-stamped in record time. Ava was interviewed in the Press as the new project manager and Gillian Jones praised Tilly for, *Her generosity and care to those whose needs were greatest in an area sorely lacking in social housing.* With a new affordable home on the horizon, May's son returned to Trevone with a pregnant Australian, sending May into orbit with joy and finally swapping cigarettes for knitting needles.

Ava visited Cliff View one last time before it was demolished. Empty now, the front room had paler yellow gaps on walls where the war photographs had been removed. They'd been given to the local historical society and copies sent to Woodburn. Nothing would rid the bricks and mortar of the decades-long taint of nicotine. Without the ever-present TV blaring, it was eerie. Round Hole, gulls, crows and the sound of waves echoed in shadowed rooms. Dust sifted through sunlight and a strand of Tilly's hair floated across the floor. A glittery purple half-moon of fingernail was stuck in a crevice by the fire.

Ava wrapped up warmly and walked down to Trevone Bay with a backpack containing Jack's diaries brought over by Chester. Ava already had Jack's letters to Tilly. The cold, clear sky was a cerulean blue and fluffy clouds glided over surfers, riding in on perfect evening swells. A man pulled up in a council van and emptied overflowing bins, followed by screeching gulls. There was Finn, skipping flat stones across the ocean. Joe jumped waves with his tyrannosaurus.

'Hello,' said Ava. Finn turned and his eyes darkened as he gathered her to him.

'That's sooooooo yuck!' said Joe as they kissed, briefly, for decorum's sake. There was all the time in the world for more sensual pleasures. The three held hands and sauntered along the shoreline to a sheltered sand dune.

'I love you,' Finn said, kissing her forehead, cheeks and lips. They found the perfect place to relax – a dip in the dune surrounded by whispering grass. Moths fluttered and green-black beetles scuttled away as Finn spread out the blanket, and poured hot chocolate from a flask.

'Beautiful,' said Ava, looking out from their private hollow over the rolling Atlantic. Joe collected shells and stones for a dinosaur nest. Ava watched and allowed herself to be content.

'The light's perfect,' said Finn, his fingers skimming her shoulder. He took photographs of her, natural, smiling, and of Joe jumping down dunes, dinosaur flying. Joe took snaps of them cuddling, and gulls wheeling overhead. They ate Jaffa cakes, with a dusting of sand grains, and flicked through the digital shots. None would ever see the light of social media.

'Ava Westmorland,' said Finn, looking out to sea, 'is going to be a brilliant surfer.'

'I'm only paddling until our baby is born,' said Ava, leaning back on him. She undid the backpack and slid out a heavy envelope. Here they were, Jack's pocket-sized black diaries from 1943 and 1944, and thick wad of letters. Jack's microscopic writing and doodles crammed pages. Ava carefully took out a letter with S.W.A.L.K across the front and read it to Finn while Joe buried his dinosaur.

The Blue Hour

US Fighter Command
St Eval Airbase
Cornwall
June 2nd, 1944

Darling Tilly,

The sight of us all going left a kind of tingling in my blood as we drive slowly to the harbour. The men are all cheerful and cracking jokes because the days to come are going to put an end to the long suspense.

I want you to know how much I love you. You mean everything to me and this gives me the courage to continue. When, if, I return we'll be married and head home to West Virginia with our baby.

My dreams for our future even outnumber yours and your plans are made of so many dreams! I think of every minor detail a hundred times. The money enclosed is for emergencies. I pray I live to make you happy my darling.

For always,
Jack

Chapter Fifty-Six

Trevone Bay, 22nd September 2015

Tilly's mind is crystal-clear despite the searing, burning pain along her spine that grinds like broken glass through hips. She plays Nat King Cole's *Unforgettable*.

Outside, thunder rolls and a flash of lightning rents clouds. The noise reminds her of bombing. Even now, her decrepit body wants to automatically take cover but there's no shifting. She places badly handwritten letters to Doctor Singh, Edward, and May on the bedside table. Ava's is taped on the door. All Jack's correspondence is in an envelope with Ava's name on.

'The last effing effort,' Tilly sighs.

She takes the phone off the hook, eases into bed and opens a plastic box. The top of it is filled with Vicky's hand-drawn birthday, Christmas and Mother's Day cards, which Tilly can no longer read. She touches them and thinks of Vicky when she was small and resolute and loved her. Her school reports were all straight As. Tilly is proud of that and Jack would have been. Underneath is what she seeks; an old tin, sealed with surgical tape. Tilly unpicks it and empties out secreted sleeping tablets, anti-emetics, morphine and Co-codamol. She eases back and drinks some of the last hidden brandy.

Tilly hesitates. 'There's still time,' she murmurs, 'but for what?' She never wanted to leave this home. Tilly empties the tablets and her heart races. She feels exhilarated and deadly calm, like when she stepped on the train from Liverpool to Newquay to leave everything behind, when she found she was pregnant, when she held infant Vicky in her arms. Tilly swallows a dozen tablets with sips of brandy.

She lights another cigarette and inhales as if from the soles of her feet. Outside, two planes leave vapour trails in the shape of a cross through turbulent, grey sky.

'How appropriate,' she smiles, as they dissipate. 'I've had an interesting life, Jack first, then money and pleasure.' Round Hole screeches. 'I won't miss that bloody noise,' she mutters. Rain dances down and sideways across the window. Leaves shimmer with the faintest blush of russet at their edges and clouds tear apart and re-form, allowing sunbeams to radiate on sea and headland.

'Crepuscular rays! I haven't forgotten what you said, Jack, about God's fingers.' She swallows more tablets and shakily lifts the glass, drinking, drinking. The carpet rumples, walls soften and blur and the photograph of her young self in the red costume doubles. Tilly presses a finger to her right eye and she's singular again.

'The most important thing is; nobody can say I was boring or lived a dull, uneventful life. Nobody.'

Her dead father appears, leaning against a wall. William looks, not unsurprisingly, Tilly considers, pale and tired. He plays, *Oh Danny Boy* on a harmonica wearing his full Colour Sergeant uniform. A half-smoked cigarette is tucked behind his left ear and his hair has a grey, seam-like parting.

'You never played an instrument in your damn life,' Tilly mocks. He carries on and Tilly hums a few bars. 'Do you remember when we got back from church and you were in bed with Aunty Vi, and mum went mad?' Tilly laughs. Her father fades. Sunlight pools and spreads over her bed as thunder rolls out to sea.

'They'll be here later', says Tilly, imagining Vicky and Edward, striding up the path; mother and grandson with confident smiles and loud voices full of plans about her going forward into care. Like she was senile and blind. But they'd be too late.

Tilly's mother drifts by the mirror; an apparition rubbing moisturiser into her hands. She pulls on a pair of grey gloves and fastens pearly buttons up each wrist.

'Matilda,' says Elizabeth, in that harsh familiar tone, with icicle eyes, 'you were always difficult. Now look at you. If you'd kept with the Church, you'd be happy with your family.'

'Doubt it, given what they've planned for me.' Tilly finishes the brandy and stubs the cigarette out in the glass. The room swims as she slides down the bed, curling in on herself. Her voice echoes. 'At least Dad didn't go on and on. It's all you ever did.' Implacable, Christian, Elizabeth stands like a sombre bookend in her black, ankle-length dress with pale, freckled arms folded, no make-up and lank grey hair, pinned severely back. Tilly remembered her voluminous pink flannelette nightdress and matching curlers. 'A winning contraceptive combination,' murmurs Tilly.

'Always restless,' Elizabeth hisses. 'Nothing ever good enough. Married but always dallying, like my sister.'

'Liam preferred men, Mum.' Tilly smiles. Her mother sighs and melts away. 'Always right and always bloody miserable,' Tilly says, putting up two fingers. She thinks of her parents' marriage as a thousand shepherd's pies and meaty casseroles, grunting at the dinner table, dirty socks in buckets, smells in the bathroom, penny-pinching and zero romance. At least with Liam there was fun, a comfortable home, lovely holidays. He accommodated her waywardness as much as she did his.

She rests her eyes and feels someone sit on the bed. She knows that scent. Jack. Tilly stares up; he's older now, bald but still handsome in that soft-fleshed American way. Flight Lieutenant Jack Turner squeezes her thigh, just like he used to. He sings *Unforgettable* slowly, in gravelly southern tones.

'We were in love, weren't we?' she says. 'Really in love. But I had others, just so you know I didn't spend the rest of my life pining. Always a Battle Maid!' Jack picks up his camera, floats through the window, beckons her. She imagines dancing with him, light as a feather, a perfect team again.

'*Unforgettable*,' she begins, as words elude her, Tilly hums, softer and softer, then falls silent.

Her breath slows, stops, for seconds; a minute. She is like the bow of a ship, rising and falling deeper. The pattern changes to a congested gurgle as her breath shallows and quietens to a long, drawn-out emptying. There are soft, audible sighs as air passes over relaxed, vibrating vocal cords.

At this moment, Ava is making love with Finn. The condom breaks and there will be a baby girl whose middle name will be Matilda. Vicky is at SpecSorters having an eye test with patient Ms Freeman and selecting one pair of glasses, with another half-price. Edward is checking his latest financial investments. May is not in the least bit hypnotised but pretends to be while she daydreams about seeing her beloved son. Charlie will ask Becky to marry her when she gets home and plan the eventual opening of their own little seafood cafe.

Tilly's room has an acetone-reek. Her eyes flutter and lower jaw moves. She is wordless now, for such a word-filled woman. As vital organs close, blood pools in bruise-like patches at the base of her marbled, ruined spine. Her long, drawn-out breath stutters, stops. On the window ledge, a bedraggled crow preens and caws.

The End

M J Greenwood is a journalist and editor for regional and national press. *The Blue Hour* is her debut novel begun while studying an MA in Creative Writing at Bath Spa University. Born in Liverpool, the mother-of-four lives in North Somerset. As well as writing and reading, she loves gardening and exploring the beautiful Mendips.

Acknowledgements

Thank you to so many who have helped on this long and often fraught journey; first as a journalist, stumbling upon a story about a WW2 love affair and its lifelong shadow, to holding the *The Blue Hour* in my hand. I've learned such a lot; especially how patient friends and family are.

I took a year off work to study for an MA in Creative Writing at Bath Spa University. I'm grateful to the guidance of lecturers, particularly Philip Hensher and Lucy English, to help me complete the first draft.

Thank you to Lucy Morris at Curtis Brown. She was unfailingly generous, patient, diplomatic, and supportive. She gently steered me in the right direction and helped develop my literary voice. The Blue Hour would not have existed without her expertise.

Thank you to generous friends Jeanette Read and Gill Fowkes for lending me their lovely spaces, accompanied by my beloved whippet. Free time to write and long windswept walks were vital.

Thank you to novelist Louise Douglas, one of the first readers and to whom I owe so, so much. To my cousin, Caroline Rigby, who knows Tilly like the back of her hand. And other careful readers: Hazel Douglas, Marie Stubbs, Kate Davies, Debbie Hinnigan and Kirsten Lass. Your comments were invaluable.

To fellow writers, journalists and hot tub besties: Lesley Turney, Carol Deacon and Heather Pickstock. The fizz is on me. To my brother Clive; we've gone through lots. To fun, fine wine and dining, with Scott Arrowsmith and Michael Berkley for being who you are.

Thank you to my eldest daughter, Laura, who backed me all the way, reading The Blue Hour many times and pushing me on. Thank you to my youngest daughter, Rowan, and sons James and Adam for your absolute backing. To Jody, for her amazing technical knowledge with my website and Emma, for her kindness and belief. To my ex-husband, Steve, who helped along the way and love to the little ones: Jago, Jowan, Ashton, Ruby, Juniper and Wren.

Thank you to my publisher, Iain Parke, who believed in the story the instant he read the manuscript and to Pat, for her careful proof reading. I really appreciate you being at my side.

Finally, thank you to my husband, Tom Henry, who has endured this process and challenged me in all the right ways. As a writer you know exactly how I feel 24/7.

I undertook a huge amount of research about reconnaissance pilots in WW2 and watched numerous films and documentaries. The following books were invaluable: Cornwall at War 1939–1945 by Peter Hancock, and What Soldiers Do – Sex and the American GI in World War II France by Mary Louise Roberts.

If you've been affected by any of the issues raised in this book, The Samaritans is a registered charity aimed at providing emotional support to anyone in emotional distress, struggling to cope, or at risk of suicide throughout the United Kingdom and Ireland:

www.samaritans.org

or call for free:

116 123

Just when you thought it was safe
to go back in the bookstore...
www.badpress.ink

BAD PRESS iNK,
publishers of niche, alternative and cult fiction

Visit

www.BADPRESS.iNK

for details of all our books, and sign up to
be notified of future releases and offers

YOUR INDEPENDENT BOOKSHOP NEEDS YOU!

Help us support local independent bookshops, visit:

www.BADPRESS.iNK/bookshops

to find your local bookshop

WHILE NOBODY IS WATCHING

MICHELLE DUNNE

Another riveting read from a debut novelist
and BAD PRESS iNK